MW01134991

HUNT for
THE LOST
TREASURE of
San Jose

PAUL CAETANO

authorHOUSE

AuthorHouse™
1663 Liberty Drive
Bloomington, IN 47403
www.authorhouse.com
Phone: 833-262-8899

Published by AuthorHouse   06/21/2022

ISBN: 978-1-6655-6235-5 (sc)
ISBN: 978-1-6655-6234-8 (e)

Print information available on the last page.

Any people depicted in stock imagery provided by Getty Images are models,
and such images are being used for illustrative purposes only.
Certain stock imagery © Getty Images.

Credits
Cover – Adriano Patriani
Author's photo: Mabille Caselatto
Text Review: Thalyta Rizzo

This book is printed on acid-free paper.

Because of the dynamic nature of the Internet, any web addresses or links contained in
this book may have changed since publication and may no longer be valid. The views
expressed in this work are solely those of the author and do not necessarily reflect the
views of the publisher, and the publisher hereby disclaims any responsibility for them.

*I thank God for all that He has given me,
especially for the family and
the gift of creativity.*

CONTENTS

CHAPTER I
THE BATTLE OF BARÚ BAY

NAVAL SCHOOL OF THE UNIVERSITY OF CÁDIZ, PUERTO REAL CAMPUS, SPAIN - YEAR 2021

The lights go out and the projection of some well-illustrated slides begins, changing along with the narrative:

"The arrival of Christopher Columbus, in 1492, to what is now the island of the Bahamas began Spanish colonization in what they called the New World. Dozens of Spanish conquerors braved seas, forests, and mountains, facing dangers and challenges that cost the lives of hundreds of soldiers, servants, and settlers.

From the 15th to the 16th century, explorers, under the service of the Spanish Crown, descended the Western slopes of the South American territory, founding several cities in a region extending to what nowadays goes from Panama to Uruguay, respecting the Treaty of Tordesillas which was concluded on June 7, 1494 between the Kingdom of Portugal and the Crown of Castile, which divided the American continent into two hemispheres: the Eastern one would belong to Portugal - Brazil - and the Western one, to Spain.

In addition to the natural challenges, the conquerors – keeping an eye, of course, on the riches and spices – faced the indigenous peoples who occupied such lands, especially three very well developed great empires: that of the Aztecs, who occupied Central America in the Region of Mexico; that of the Mayans, also in Central America in the region where Guatemala and Honduras are nowadays; and that of the Incas, in the Midwest of the continent, a region that today comprises Peru, Bolivia and Ecuador.

Such civilizations had for centuries been powerful and very, very rich: the exploration of gold, silver, and precious stones – such as the famous Potosi silver mine, now in Bolivian territory – filled pagan temples, ornamented palaces, found idols and brought prosperity to build cities of more than one hundred thousand inhabitants. Advanced engineering techniques for that time were employed in the constructions, plantations, and irrigation systems in mountainous and desert regions, remaining to this day a mystery that our history cannot unravel.

Unfortunately, such empires, already weakened by internal divisions, were extinguished by the ambition of the explorers. In 1519, Hernan Cortés imprisoned Montezuma, the last Emperor of the Aztecs in Mexico; in 1697, Martin of Ursúa conquered Tayasal, the last city of the Mayans; and in 1532, Francisco Pizarro imprisoned and executed Atahualpa, emperor of the Incas, weakened by war with his brother Huáscar."

Professor Perez stops the presentation and asks for the lights to be turned on. This reveals several students napping on top of their tables.

He clears his throat:

- Any questions, so far?

Half disguising, students straighten in their chair, in silence. Perez pretends it's going well:

- May I continue with the second part of the class?

Isabel, who is super awake, answers with double meaning:

- Of course, Master, it's very interesting, I can't wait to hear the end of it.

Without moving her head and with a slight smile on her lip, she moves her eyes from side to side to see the reaction of her colleagues, not good. The teacher chooses to interpret her answer in a positive way:

- Just you wait, then, Isabel! For now we get to the most interesting part of today's theme!

He asks for the lights to be turned off and continues the projection of his PowerPoint presentation. A picture of an old men in long white curly wig, sitting comes up.

"We arrive at the turn from the seventeenth to the eighteenth century. He is Philip de Bourbon, Duke of Anjour, French and grandson of Louis XIV, kind of France, In 1700, after the death of Charles II, king of Spain and last descendant of the Habsburg dynasty without leaving an heir-successor. he changed his name to Philip V and he was chosen to become the next monarch of Spain, beginning the dynasty of the House of Bourbons in the Iberian country.

France and Spain, now allied, were a major threat to the other dynasties that prevailed in European absolutist kingdoms, where wealthy families sought to perpetuate themselves in power struggle which lasted for generations and generations, such as had been with the House of Habsburg.

Concerned about the possibility of Louis XV, grandson of Louis XIV, becoming king of both France and Spain, Austria, England, Holland, Sweden, and Denmark signed, in 1701, the Treaty of The Hague to close the so-called Grand Alliance. These countries' war against France and Spain would begin the following year.

There have been several battles, both on land and on sea. England, which at the time had the best navy, had secured victories in Cadiz and Gibraltar in the 1680s. Such wars extended to the colonies and there were frequent persecutions and fighting in the Caribbean and

Pacific seas, which were in themselves already very dangerous due to the presence of the famous pirates from all nationalities who attacked vessels and increased the smuggling of goods between the Old and the New World.

Meanwhile, in the Americas, prosperity ran in fullspeed in the Spanish colonies: trade, both legal and illegal, enriched those who ventured to live there and explore the local riches, especially silver.

In the 18th century, two great viceroyalties were outlined by the Spanish crown: that of Mexico, known then as The New Spain, whose capital was Vera Cruz; and that of Peru, whose capital was Lima. The territory of the viceroyalty of Peru was not like the country we know today: it comprised the region of today's Venezuela extending all the way down to the south of Argentina. It was divided into administrative units called Royal Audiences. The Real Audiencias of Lima, Panama, Portobello, Santa Fe Bogotá, Santiago de Chile and Charkas, whose capital was Buenos Aires, were very active.

Lima was the most prosperous colonized city of all and its inhabitants' boasted luxury, gastronomy and development that carried the image of wealth and prosperity amongst Europeans. Between the years 1500-1600, the class of merchant traders became very strengthened, influential and was the one who supported the local viceroy, in addition to generating thousands of pesos in tax collection to the Spanish crown.

To manage nearly five and a half million inhabitants during Peru's reign, Spain appointed a viceroy, who was the legal representative of the crown. To get an idea, Melchor de Navarra y Rocafull, Duke of La Palata and viceroy of Peru from 1681 to 1689, was greeted in Lima with a two-blocks-long street paved with silver bricks which led to his official residence.

When he died, he was succeeded by another Melchor, Portocarrero, Count of the Monclova, who reigned in Peru from 1689 to 1705, after having been viceroy of Mexico (New Spain) between 1686 and 1688, dead by 1705."

Perez does not hear a single noise in the room and decides to stop the presentation again. He turns on the lights and, surprised, sees that half of the students have left and the other half are sliding their fingers through their phones' screens.

- Where is everybody?

Isabel, always helpful, tries to explain:

- Well, professor, they were leaving gradually... I think they went to the bathroom.

- So young and already having kidney problems? – mocks Perez.

- It's just that... - the girl is defensive, raising her shoulders.

Lorenzo, sitting next to her, tries to help:

- ... we're going to have a test in the next class, and I think they went to study, dear master.

Professor Perez pretends to believe:

- Oh, I know... study... yes, of course, I think that's what your colleagues are doing there on their phones, right?

Everyone tries swiftly to turn off their smartphone. Paloma, from the back, asks:

- Professor, this is all very well, but... Where are we going with that? I believe History shouldn't be just facts and dates, that it serves to put in context processes of change that carry lessons that apply the present moment and experiences to avoid its repetition in the future.

Perez walks towards her, to the back of the room, half threatening. The girl gets defensive, but lets her guard down when he opens a smile and explains:

- Paloma Rodriguez! Very well! That's exactly it. History is no longer made up of facts and dates to be known by heart. It should be understood as a sequence of evolutions and revolutions that have altered the course of humanity. And that has an impact on the actions of the present. Is everyone listening?

Everyone turns to the back of the room. He continues:

- And it is in this direction that I am leading you... – he walks back towards the laptop at the teacher's desk – first, I present a contextualization of the problem, so you understand the current theme that I want to present.

He takes the slides out of presentation mode and, with his finger, presses the arrow key to advance to several other slides ahead, until it stops in the photo of a battle of caravels at sea:

- The sinking of the Galleon San José – he strategically pauses for suspense – with a fortune now estimated in... twenty billion dollars!

It is as if an icy water balloon exploded on top of the class. Everybody wakes up, whistles, grumbles, claps.

- Wow!

- What?!

- How Much?

- Dope!

- Now that's something!

- Shut up, man!

Satisfied that the reaction was the one he wanted to achieve, Perez asks:

- So, guys? Can I go on?

They answer all together:

- Let's go, teach!

One of the students sends a message through the class's WhatsApp group chat and, gradually, the students who had left begin to re-enter the room.

Perez returns to the slide at which he had left, opens in presentation mode, showing an engraving of an ancient city in black-and-white. He takes back his narrative.

"This is an old engraving of the city of Portobello, in Northeastern Panama. Until the 18th century, it was an important exporting goods hub, especially silver, from the Mexican and South American colonies. Its strategic position, at the Northern tip of Panama, ensured that the Caribbean Sea was accessible both for the arrival of Old-World ships, and for the departure of goods coming by land from Panama City, since at that time the channel which allows direct navigation from the Pacific Ocean to the Caribbean Sea did not exist.

From time to time, the famous Portobello Fair was held, where millions of pesos were exchanged between traders from all regions, who brought silver, gold or precious stones to exchange for clothes, perfumes, fabrics and other products from the European continent and the Indies as well as to export their pieces of silver and gold cast at Peruvian workshops.

In May 1708 there was one of the most striking fairs in Portobello, because it took place in a very troubled political context. King Philip V of Spain needed money to pay for the expenses of the Succession War and demanded that the viceroyalty sent all the proceeds they could. The Viceroy of Peru, Don Manuel de Oms y Sentmenat, Marquis of Castelldosrius, recently sworn in Lima in 1707, owed thousands of pesos to creditors in Spain and was accused of being corrupt and of embezzling funds: he was suspected of taking a portion of the tax collection for himself as well as part of the illegal trade he pretended to fight off, in order to pay for his extraordinary expenses with the entourage he had brought with him from France. Piracy and the smuggling of goods increased in the Pacific coast and in the Caribbean Sea, which left Lima's traders increasingly disgruntled. The French, now allies, had access to the colonized cities, especially Cartagena de Indias, the largest and most important port city of that time, at the Northern tip of today's Colombia. In contrast, English and Dutch ships, enemies, also sailed the Caribbean Sea, settling a base in the island of Jamaica.

Castelldosrius managed to convince the Lima traders to take place in the Portobello fair and, on December 19, 1707, a large contingent of them departed from the port of Callao, Lima, bringing about seven million pesos and goods for their operations. But the most valuable cargo was the 1,379,310 pesos that the Government of Lima had collected for years on end in taxes and was sending to the King of Spain"

A student raises his hand and Perez interrupts his explanation, stopping at the slide that showed the figure of wooden chests crammed with gold and silver coins.

- Master, How much would that amount be worth nowadays?

- Let's make the conversion of these amounts later? There's more treasure.

- Cool!

The next slide shows two old wooden sail ships, which change as the teacher explains the themes:

"These two ships were the Galleon San José and the Galleon San Joaquin. They were built at the same time at the Shipyard of Guipuzcoa, Biscay, between 1697 and 1698. Each of them weighed 2,645 pounds and measured about 1575 inches from stem to stern. They were the pride of the Spanish armed fleet at the time. They were made of cedar and oak, had three masts and that typical silhouette of the large old ships: the bow – with that sword-like tip, with a carved sculpture of the saint that named each ship – was a little lower than the stern, which was the back, straight, with windows and all carved decoratively. Speaking of decoration, notice this detail: every cannon, cast in bronze, had to have handles to be loaded. It was customary to shape these handles with the figure of some animal, such as lions, bulls, fish and even mermaids. The sixty-four cannons of the San José had their handles in the shape of dolphins.

In 1706, after participating in several fights, especially for the defense of the port of Cadiz, they set sail to Cartagena de Indias and, from there, in May 1708, to Portobello to ensure the safety of the fair and of the traders who would participate in it, especially the Peruvians arriving from the port of Lima. The black plague, brought from Europe, decimated thousands of lives due to poor hygiene conditions and lack of public health care.

Composed of sixteen ships, the fleet was called Tierra Firme. The leading ship –the captaincy – was the Galleon San José, commanded by Don José Fernandez de Santillán, the Count of Casa Alegre. The second ship in the fleet was the Galleon San Joaquín –the admiral – was commanded by Don Miguel Augustin de Villanueva, an honorable member of the Order of Santiago. Both were experienced navigators and warriors, often commended by the Spanish Crown for their warlike or exploratory missions.

Despite the plague, the Portobello fair was a success: thousands of gold coins, silver ingots and precious stones were exchanged for European dresses, furniture, tobacco, spices, indigenous crafts, mirrors and other goods with demands much higher than their supply at the turn of the 18th century".

The teacher is interrupted by Paloma when the figure of a tax collector sitting at the table, writing something with a feather, with a row of men holding small bags of dirty burlap in front of him shows up in the screen.

- Taxes, taxes, taxes… thought it was only now that we supported expensive, inefficient, and corrupt government – disputes the girl.

Everyone turns to the redhead girl, thin, short hair with a mixture of approving and recriminatory look. The teacher intervenes:

- Dear and sweet child! Taxes have always accompanied the evolution of civilization, from ancient Egypt to the Roman Empire, which perfected it.

- I don't think it's fair to pay that much tax on everything you earn and consume. The government, even…

Lorenzo tries to interrupt:

- ... to fund public universities, like this one we're in.

She blasts him with her eyes but keeps quiet. The teacher resumes:

- Well, let's talk about this later, okay? Continuing...

He projects a slide with the figure of two old galleons sailing from a port.

"The galleons had to return to Spain as soon as possible, but news arrived in Portobello that an English fleet was surrounding the coast of Cartagena, awaiting their return to pillage them. In fear, Santillán and Villanueva met with nobles, military, politicians, and influential traders at the end of May 1708 at the home of Don José Antônio de la Rocha y Carranza, the president of the Panama Royal Audience. They discussed several possibilities, and it was the meeting's consensus that it would be very risky for the fleet to leave at that moment that they should wait longer. To this date it is not known the reasons which led the two fleet commanders not to adhere to that decision and to start preparations for departure, even knowing the risks of being intercepted by the English. Overconfidence? Arrogance and superiority? Financial pressure from Spain? Strong recommendation from the indebted viceroy of Peru, who had to please the king of Spain? We don't know. *La mar era ancha, diversos sus rumbos',* supposedly said Captain Santillán to end the meeting. What is known is that, in the Hispanic population of the city, there were English spies who were very well-informed and who rushed to warn Captain Charles Wager, who with his four ships, was keeping surveillance on the hills of Cartagena."

Perez stops the narration and casts a suspicious glance at Thomas, the foreign student who is part of the class.

- Right, Mr. Dowell?

The blond very white boy, widens his blue-water eyes on his 28th, and defends himself with a strong British accent:

- Well... All right, Professor... Why do you ask me?

All thirty-two students in the room look at him with a suspicious look, leaving him more intimidated. The boy begins to shrink in his chair, until Perez smiles:

- Because since ancient times the English have been well-informed, that's all!

The gang laughs. Thomas smiles too.

The teacher continues with the photo an old maritime map, with the dotted line indicating the path of a trip:

"On May 28, 1708, the Tierra Firme Fleet departs from the port of Portobello, Panama, bound for Cartagena de Indias. It is not known exactly how much they carried, but historians have found that The San José carried between five and seven million pesos and the San Joaquín, between four and six million pesos, in values of that time. The account list prepared by the tax charger alone was seven-pages-long, showing a total of 1,551,609 pesos, not accounting for the undeclared wealth, since tax evasion was also present in those times. There were gold bars, gold coins, silver ingots, emeralds, gold nuggets and goods made in Peru cramming the holds of the two vessels.

Sixteen heavily armed ships set sail that day, captained by Fernandez de Santillán: his Galleon San José, equipped with 64 cannons and 600 passengers, of which 113 were soldiers; the Galleon San Joaquín, carrying with 64 cannons and 500 passengers under Admiral Villanueva; the Santa Cruz, an infantry frigate, also called Gobierno, with 50 cannons and 300 soldiers under the command of Captain Don Nicolás de la Rosa y Suárez, the Count of Vega Florida; the Nuestra Señora de la Concepción, a hulk equipped with 34 cannons and carrying 140 passengers, owned by Don Francisco Nieto; the French frigate Sancti Spiritus, which had 32 cannons and 150 men that were part of the French escort sent by Louis XIV as a sign of allegiance; and other smaller ships, each with its function and positioning in the formation of the armada, carrying all civil merchants, travelers and military sailors.

They were all wind-powered and depended on it for speed. The smaller boats dictated the course of the journey, since they had lower performance. Therefore, the galleons sometimes arrived first in one place and had to wait for the others who stayed behind. Such a misstep was fatal to be surprised by the English a few days later. On May 31, bordering the Colombian coast, they arrived in Punta de San Bass and remained there for two days. Following the cabotage of the Panamanian continent, they passed through Cape Tiburón and headed North to the Islands of San Fernando, already on the Colombian coast, arriving there on June 7, 1708, and waiting overnight for the stragglers.

Contrary to all who recommended staying there longer as a precaution, because the news of the English presence was stronger, Captain Conde de Casa Alegre decides to raise anchors and set sail towards the open sea, straight to the port of Havana where, after fueling, they would leave straight for Europe".

To break the monologue and bring a little more action to the class, the teacher opens a YouTube video, authored by Francisco Hernando Muñoz Atuesta, which continues to narrate the action of the ships. The students gets even more connected.

"On the morning of June 8, 1708, the weather was rainy, and the wind was blowing Northwest. The Spanish fleet resumes its path. They go Northwest of The Island of Barú and sail in search of Boca Chica, near the Rosario Islands, already part of the archipelago near Cartagena de Indias. The British fleet is in front of Cartagena, patrolling the area with four warships: the Expedition – commanded by Commodore Charles Wager – the Kingston, the Portland, and the Vulture. The latter is the first to see the Tierra Firme Fleet approaching and notifies the others at around 9:00 a.m. The English are willing to intercept them when the wind ceases for both fleets. At around 3:00 p.m., a wind coming from Northeast of the continent allows navigation. The British – who are further North of the archipelago – know that they must reach the Spanish fleet – which is further Southeast – before nightfall. The English are sailing South while the Spanish are moving North, passing through the Rosario Islands, both to a convergent point: Treasure Island.

Upon sighting the English squad coming to meet them at around 4:30 p.m., the Spanish try to get around the right side of Treasure Island to begin to enter the bay of the Barú Peninsula, towards the city of Cartagena, but the winds again do not cooperate. So, they are forced to turn left, towards the open sea and face the enemy.

The alignment for the battle of the Spanish fleet was positioned as follows: at the center of the vanguard was the Galleon San José, the French frigate Sancti Spiritus, downwind, and the hulk of Nieto, in front of it. Behind the San José come the French frigate and, a little further behind, on the left diagonal, the San Joaquin. Santa Cruz, the main navy in charge of the fleet's infantry, was late, but soon overtakes everyone and positions itself ahead of the San José. The English fleet, in turn, makes a strategic siege: while the, Expedition, Portland and Kingston, larger ships, stand parallel to the galleons, the Vulture sits in the rear, creating an obstacle on the way back to Cartagena.

At five hours and forty-five minutes, the fight begins, five leagues northwest of Treasure Island. Kingston stands next to Admiral San Joaquín and, upon reaching half cannon fire, initiates the English ship first shots, which knocks down its main mast and it loses speed. With the first cannon fire, the merchant ships of the Spanish fleet, which were further behind, take the southeast direction and lean against the two French schooners, followed by the hulk Nuestra Señora, which received, before withdrawing, a burst of cannon fire because it was very close to the San José. The Santa Cruz infantry frigate, followed by the galleon San José, the patache Biscain and the damaged Galleon San Joaquín remain in the battle line.

When the attack began, the San José Galleon turned Northwest of the Expedition, as it, with all its force and cannonball bombardment, caused the Spanish ships to stray from it to avoid a collision. The Count of Casa Alegre prepares his artillery to give a warm greeting to the daring Englishmen, who, intrepidly, swarm up with the wind in their favor, leaving behind a thick cloud of smoke from the cannon fire. At 328 yards, the Count fires his first burst of fire, with no major effects on the enemy's ship. In its stead, it reaches a mere 219 yards before responding. Its fire is directed to damage the integrity of the galleon's hull, causing serious damage and death to the crew. The two ships part: the San José follows the North-Northwest course, turning to the coast; the Expedition returns South-Southwest to go in its pursuit, despite the other ships fire.

Around 7:30 pm, Galleon San José and Expedition meet alone. The darkness is total, the visibility is even worse by the smoke of battle. They are about 164 yards apart when the San José makes new shots against the Expedition, again doing little damage to the hull of Charles Wager's ship. The English are able approach to a distance of just 65 yards and prepare to board the Spanish ship. Their men are on deck, armed and prepared for the approach. On the Spanish ship, the passengers, hidden in the lower parts, pray that God have mercy on them. Fernandez de Santillán, who is over seventy years old, is willing to do anything to repel the approach. His soldiers, on deck, fire the harquebuses. The English soldiers, with guns, ropes, pistols, and swords on hands, shouting threats, await orders to begin the boarding. In the galleon, the shipowners load the cannons for further firing. When they suddenly hear a terrible explosion, making San Jose stop and roll over itself. The darkness is broken by the splendor of the explosion and burning pieces of wood fly over the English ship. A large wave, caused by the explosion, hits the compartment of cannons. In an instant, the ship disappears from the surface of the sea. Only a few burned pieces float like inert witnesses. Of the 600 passengers and crew, only eleven were able to survive."

The video ends. Silence takes over the room. Everyone is sad and thoughtful with the grief of the great loss.

After a few minutes, Isabel raises her hand and asks:

- I don't get it, Professor. Was it an Expedition shot that blew up the ship?

Perez, who was facing the blackboard, turns to answer:

- This is still an unsolved mystery, Isabel. It is unclear what caused such an explosion. It must not have been a shot of the English ship, because the naval technique of approach recommends that you do not shoot to avoid shrapnel.

- A cannon of the galleon itself could have exploded? – asks Lorenzo

- Intelligent question, Lorenzo, this is one of the hypotheses defended by some historians – comments Perez, looking at him and reconnecting the projector.

A reproduction of the famous oil on canvas "The Action of Charles Wager in Cartagena", by the English painter Samuel Scott, appears on the big screen.

"The report of some witnesses during the ensuing inquest in Cartagena after the incident did not come to a firm conclusion. Some claimed to have heard no explosion, only a strange click; others said they saw large flames coming out of the ship's deck. The English, of course, said the ship exploded in the air.

Research by historians lists the most plausible hypotheses: a cannonball from another ship hit the gunpowder compartment of the San José; one or more cannons of the galleon itself exploded and the fire struck such a compartment; the swing of the rough sea may have caused friction between the ammunition, and some even say that to prevent such great fortune from falling into the hands of the enemy, Captain Fernandez de Santillán himself would have shot the gunpowder barrels and..."

This is interrupted by the surprise of the students:

- Crazy!

- Dead!

- What?!

- Too bad!

- Coward! – it is heard with an English accent.

Everyone looks again at Thomas, who tries to fix what he's let slip out of his mouth:

- Well, well, I'm sorry... well.... I meant.... It must have been an accident anyway...

- Anyway – continued Perez – the galleon broke in half and sank in a few minutes, one of the great tragedies of Spanish naval history.

- And then what? - Paloma asks - The battle ceased?

- Important question. Let's see what happened?

He turns to the laptop that is still connected to the data show and continues the lesson, also showing the naval battle painted on the board.

"On the morning of the following day, Saturday, June 9, 1708, Commodore Wager planned to attack the San Joaquín, the other galleon full of money. That's when, to everyone's surprise, he realized that both Admiral Villanueva and the hulk Santa Cruz, taking advantage of the fighting, smoke and darkness of the night, fled to the coast of Cartagena with the other ships, leaving behind only the infantry frigate Santa Cruz, the Gobierno, from Captain Vega Florida.

Fulfilling his role as head of fleet defense, Vega Florida fought bravely, but it was one against four. "Lower your sails to Queen Anne," they shouted from Kingston before they started to fire. The bombardment was heavy; The Santa Cruz was virtually obliterated by cannon fire, three hundred soldiers lost their lives before Florida had to surrender. His ship was towed by the British squadron as a prisoner and, in respect of the international treaties of that time, abandoned on one of the inhabited islands of the region.

Meanwhile, the hulk Nuestra Señora de Concepción, the freighter full of goods and other valuables, had beached on one of Cartagena beaches. As it was also very damaged by cannon fire, and, afraid of the English coming to loot its valuable cargo, its commander, Francisco Nieto, had it set on fire."

Iago Perez, 60, Naval History professor, renowned Spanish researcher, finishes his presentation and asks them to turn the lights of the room back on. His red-haired well-trimmed moustache and beard, harmonize very well with his light brown eyes and grey hair down to his nape.

- And so ends our story about one of the most famous sea excursions to the Spanish colonies in South America between the 17th and 18th centuries.

Lorenzo Garcia, 27, green eyes, short golden hair, Millennial heartthrob style, raises his hand:

- But... and then... no one's ever gone after it again?

- Three hundred years later, today the fortune sunk with it is estimated to be between seventeen and twenty billion dollars. It's called the Holy Grail of Shipwrecks.

- So, tell us who's been after that? – asks Isabel.

Perez looks at the wall clock and determines:

- After the break, in the second class, we keep going, OK?

He leaves the room, followed by several students. Lorenzo speaks to Isabel:

- Hey, what's up?

- I found this story of the galleon fantastic - says the beautiful 25 years-old girl in jeans, pink t-shirt dug, medium corn-cob-colored hair, blue eyes, typical of the modern Spanish generation.

- I wasn't asking about the galleon, I meant about you. What you thought of my proposal yesterday?

- That we go out to some bar on date?

The boy pulls his chair a little closer and uses a gallant tone:

- Not to "some bar", but to a cool, tasty, lively, place where we can enjoy the fresh sea breeze. Huh?

She signals in agreement:

- I love the sea!

- One more thing we have in common.

- One more thing? Is there anymore?

He brings his face a little closer:

- Several...

- Tell me a few more!

He begins to count on the fingers of his right hand:

- We're young, beautiful, healthy, we like naval engineering, the sea and to enjoy life!

- Dude – she mocks – you've filled a whole hand already!

- So, we're going todate and find out what else we like, huh?

His face is very close to hers. She looks very seriously into his eyes, smiles and whispers in his ear:

- First fill the other hand with more things we have in common, okay? Bragger!

After the burn, the boy realigns his chair in the row where he was and slides his finger over the phone screen to disguise his discomfort. A few more minutes after, Professor Perez returns and reconnects the data show to his laptop. Gradually, students come in and take their places.

Perez asks as if he didn't know:

- All right, where did we stop?

- You were going to talk about looking for San José – Paloma recalls.

- Oh, yes, of course, thank you. Come on, let's go!

He speaks while showing images on slides or movies:

"For hundreds of years, the San José has been submerged and abandoned by divers because no one knew its exact location. Several expeditions were organized, but none were successful, as the depth at which the boat was likely to be did not allow for human diving with normal equipment.

Then, in the early 1980s, the Colombian government, through its Maritime Research Department, hired Glocca Mora Company, a U.S. company specializing in maritime research, to scour the Colombian coast for the San José. In 1981, GMC divers found traces of the wreck. They agreed with the Colombian Department that they would be entitled to 35% of all recovered treasure, but when they were about to sign such an agreement, the Colombian government pulled back and, in 1984, issued a law saying that every treasure found in Colombian waters belonged to the government and that the explorer would be entitled only to a 5.0% commission, which would also be taxed as income tax at a 45% rate, which would come close to $302.5 million! It prohibited the U.S. company from continuing its search, which caused it in 1989 to sue the Colombian government for contract break. This litigation continues to run in international courts up today, even with the 50% division edited by the Colombian government a few years ahead."

Perez pauses briefly and looks at Paloma, who seems disgusted by the confiscation of governments, making an all-governments-are-the-same face, but without commenting on the issue. The Professor continues to project the slide of a small submerged yellow submarine:

"As an archaeological interest, a joint action between the Colombian Navy, the Colombian Institute of Anthropology and History and the Woods Hole Oceanographic Institution - again, American - launched the REMUS 6000 probe into the sea in 2015, which specializes in searches for shipwrecks and air accidents fallen into the sea. After months of searching, the small submarine, through sound waves, in November 2015, took pictures of what was later confirmed as traces of the San José, about 300 meters deep".

- Anybody wants to guess what confirmed the ship id? – asks Perez

After a few minutes of silence, Lorenzo risks:

- Chests full of coins?

- No...

- a mast? - risks Isabel

- No...

- The sculpture of St. Joseph at the tip of the bow?

- Not that either... nothing made of wood could survive 300 years underwater, gentlemen – says the teacher.

When the moods are high, the classroom buzzing with curiosity and he is about to reveal the answer, there comes the British statement from the back of the room:

- The dolphins of the cannon handles!

Everybody looks at Thomas. Perez congratulates him:

- All right, British boy! How did you kill it?

- You asked us to notice the details at the beginning of the class... and I also already read something on the subject... – replies the boy, shyly.

Perez projects black-and-white photos of cannons lying on the bottom of the sea, one crossed over the other.

"That's right. The dolphins carved into the bronze cannons confirmed that it was really the galleon, although other ships could also use the same small decoration. But as it was in the vicinity of where the sinking must have happened, the Colombian government, in the figure of President Juan Manuel Santos, announced its official discovery and celebrated for the whole world to see that, finally, the treasure was all for Colombia.

But what he did not reveal was the exact location of the found traces, not only to keep the information secret from pirates or other maritime rescue entrepreneurs, but also because the REMUS 6000, as an area search probe, could just delimit in which area it is situated. Only a high-capacity compression underwater robot could accurately locate where the remains of the St. José are.

To make things more complicated, Spain –the owner of the ship and of the fortune it was carrying when it wrecked – filed a request with UNESCO to consider the findings as a world heritage site and, therefore, not owner by only one party."

Isabel tries to summarize the dispute:

- So... there are many people wanting to own the ship: Colombia for it has sunk in their waters; Spain for being the owner of the galleon and the United States for the first discovery of the wreckage...

- ... England, for having almost approached and stolen the treasure and, perhaps, Peru, because, in the end, most of the gold and silver they took was made up by the taxes accumulated by the Viceroy of Lima – concludes Lorenzo.

He holds all the fingers of his right hand and one from the left up to Isabel, symbolizing one more thing in common: intelligence. She pretends not to get it.

- Well, it is, as we have seen, a beautiful international dispute, as if that war of the eighteenth century continued today – adds Perez.

Isabel is thoughtful. After a few moments, she speaks, thinking out loud:

- Oh, if we could go back to the past...

- Why, Isabel? – asks Professor Perez, curious.

- I would try to prevent this Count of Casa Alegre from going on a trip in those days... – she replies, looking away.

Perez, with a discreet smile on his lips and sparkle in his eyes, replies:

- Who knows, Miss Lopez... how knows!

The bell rang signaling the end of the class. Everyone leaves the room, except for Lorenzo, Isabel, Paloma, and Thomas. Interested in the continuation of the subject, they surround the teacher, who is packing his laptop into his briefcase on the front table.

Lorenzo takes the initiative:

- Hey, master. Does the story end like this?

Perez is thoughtful, looking at all four. He decides to tell them something else:

- There's one more version of the facts, but that could be legend.

- Tell us, please! - encourages Isabel

- You swear to keep it a secret?

The four raise their right hands as Boy Scouts making an oath.

- All right, sit down.

He turns the Data show back on, picks another file in the laptop directory and restarts his presentation, now only for the four young people in the room.

"Legend has it that one of the eleven survivors of the sinking was Don Alejandro Cesar de Sabogal, the first captain, who is second in command of the ship, just below Fernandez de Santillán. He did not present himself on the list of rescued people afraid of being punished by the Spanish Crown.

He swam to Treasure Island, which was the closest. There, he would have drawn a map with the exact coordinates of where the galleon sank. And after many years, he died on the same island, old and forgotten by the world."

They, surprised, do not know what to say. Paloma reacts:

- Shut up!

- I don't know, but it's possible - Perez replies

- Where did he hide the map? – asks Thomas

- Nobody knows if it even exists.

- Has somebody tried looking for it? – asks Isabel

Perez looks around to make sure there's no one else around.

- I have followed some expeditions that have traveled the entire archipelago of Barú, but all of them were fruitless...

- Again, it's like I said - concludes Isabel - if we could go back to the past...

The teacher again casts that bright look on her:

- Would you go, Miss Lopez?

- I? Of course! If it's for the good of history...

The four of them look at her, like they don't believe their ears.

- Come on! - doubts Thomas.

- The good of history... Yeah, right! - mocks Paloma

Perez comes to her rescue:

- Tomorrow at 2:00 p.m. in my office. If you won't miss any classes, of course!

Leaving the suspense in the air, he takes hisstuffs and leaves the room.

In the hallway that leads to the cafeteria, the four young students walk side by side, among other students, and spend their break time talking excitedly in pairs.

Paloma breaks the silence:

- Did you, like me, feel there's some mystery there?

- I felt it – confirms Lorenzo.

- He seems to know a lot more than he told us – suggests Isabel.

- Like what? –Thomas asks interestedly.

- Stories of lost treasure are always full of mystery – says Lorenzo

- The way he told the story, it seemed so close to us – Isabel comments.

- Close... to him - disagrees Paloma.

Thomas, as usual facing some difficulty in understanding the words in Spanish, asks:

- What do you mean, you don't know?

- He knows something more than what is in the books - determines Paloma.

The four arrive at the food court of the campus central building, which is very busy by snack time. The steel and glass structure provides great lighting to the internal garden, where it is difficult to find a place to sit. Some students leave a table next to them, at which they try to sit down quickly. Instinctively, Isabel, Thomas and Lorenzo get their smartphones out and start sliding their fingers through the screen. Paloma just stares. After about ten minutes sitting there, without any conversation, she mocks:

- Heloooo! The conversation is very lively!

All three are still concentrated on their phones. She gets up, goes to the diner, and comes back with her snack on a tray. No one notices her presence.

- Hey guys, isn't anybody hungry?

No one answers. She picks up her own smartphone, opens the WhatsApp group chat and says "Hi, all right?"

Lorenzo sends a message back: "Hi, beauty, what's up?"

Paloma says, "I'm okay, have you seen Isabel today?".

Isabel replies in the group chat: "Hi, I'm here! What do you want?"

"I want to talk to Thomas; do you know where he is?"

Thomas typing...

"Hello! Speak, bae."

Paloma typing...

"I'M HERE BY YOUR SIDE, LOOK AT ME!"

The three of them stop typing and look at her.

- Gosh! At last!

- What's the big deal? – asks Lorenzo.

- Tech addiction much? - she replies.

- Tech... what?

She takes a bite of her snack:

- You're addicted to your phones, for God's sake!

- We need to keep connected, that's all – Isabel defends herself.

- Connected? Like every young people of our generation, you're addicted to swiping your finger across your cell phone screen. You don't even notice what you're seeing, so much information that's enough!

- I am normal! – justifies Thomas.

- You're part of the system.

- Here she comes again with radicalization against the system... – mumbles Lorenzo - okay, let's get something to eat and...

The bell rings indicating it is time to return to the classrooms. The students get up and start leaving the food court. The three of them set of in their way. Paloma gets up, grabs her snack and holds it out:

- Do you want a piece?

CHAPTER II
THE EXPEDITION

The next day, at two in the afternoon, Isabel, Lorenzo, Paloma, and Thomas knock on the wooden door to which the small sign "Dr. Iago Perez" is nailed.

After a few minutes, the door opens on its own. They stare into the room, not understanding. Suddenly, a female voice coming from below breaks the silence:

- You must be the four Apocalypse horsemen?

They look down. A woman in her 35s, short-haired, redhead, light brown eyes and a little more than one meter tall is looking at them:

- Come in, Iago is waiting for you!

Surprised and suspicious, they begin to enter the room looking everywhere, Isabel hugging her notebooks, Lorenzo holding his tablet, Paloma and Thomas with their backpacks hanging from their shoulders. They are impressed by what they see: a very large room, with walls lined with antique wooden bookshelves full of books. In the center of the room, a round table of solid wood, with a colorful mock-up of an archipelago, covered by a large glass dome. Further down, in front of a high bay-window, a rectangular wooden and iron table, the top of which was hidden by a big mess of objects upon it. In fact, things were messy all over the room: spread throughout the floor were hundreds of maps, papers, small objects, replicas of caravels, trestles with bezels and other items covering the floor and making it difficult to get near the wall full of shellss. From the ceiling a small crystal chandelier was hanging, completing the magical, kind of scary, atmosphere of the environment.

The little woman closes the door behind them. Between the rectangular table and the window, a reddish leather armchair is turned with its back to them, allowing them to see only something that looked like a bird feather coming out from behind it. Lorenzo casts Isabel a weird look, she responds by looking equally uneasy.

The armchair slowly begins to spin and finally they get to see who is sitting in it: Professor Perez, dressed as an 18th-century Spanish officer, stares at the astonished guests. Black soft velvet pants ending inside white socks up to the knees; ivory shirt with large lace ruffles on the chest and on the tips of the sleeves, cobalt blue velvet overcoat, with golden buttons and with yellow trimmings. To complete the look, a large three-pointed dark blue hat trimmed in yellow, in which was the blue feather they had seen.

With his legs crossed, Iago opens his arms and smiles:

- Punctuality is one of the brave's virtues!

They don't know what to answer.

- Don't you recognize me?

They look at the little woman, whose smile, once friendly, has something cynical.

- Now, let me introduce you: Luna Gonzalez, my research and development assistant, specialist in geography and computational engineering.

- Hello! – Luna nods.

They're still kind of dumbfounded. Lorenzo is the first to speak:

- Pleasure... It's just that we didn't expect such a surprise...

- Life is no fun without surprises – comments Perez the armchair and going to meet them.

- It's just about us. We'll get used to it – says Isabe

- Cool! – likes Thomas.

- Yes, cool – agrees Paloma, more natural.

- That's it, Thomas, cool! – smiles Perez and continues – in fact, my dear young people, I am dressed like this for two reasons: first to see your reaction – normal – and second, to set the tone of the story and adventure that I will show you..

- He's wearing a Spanish naval fleet captain's uniform from the 1700s, somewhat restored, of course – explains Luna.

- Like Captain Santillan's? – asks Isabel.

- You got it, Isabel! – Perez replies.

- I like it - agrees Lorenzo. - Is there one my size?

The Professor gets all mysterious again:

- We'll see that soon, Captain Lorenzo, we'll see...

Perez leads everyone to the round table with the glass dome which is in the center of the room, gesturing a lot while explaining:

- This is a replica of The Bay of Barú, off the coast of Cartagena de Indias, in Colombia. This port city, founded by the Spanish in 1533, has almost one million inhabitants nowadays.

- Why does it have that name? – asks Isabel.

- Because when the Spanish arrived, they still thought they were on the Way to the India, such a coveted trade route, and thought the maritime bay was very similar to that of Carthage on the Mediterranean coast.

He pauses and looks very serious to the young people. After a few minutes of hesitation, he asks:

- What I'll show you is extremely confidential... Can I trust you?

They look at each other. Paloma replies, jokingly:

- Of course, Professor, we take secrets to our graves!

- Careful, child... this can happen...

Perez widens his smile, framed by the grey moustache and beard, making the mood a little bolder. He turns to Luna and exclaims, half theatrical:

- Luna... The show has just begun!

Thomas finds the phrase peculiar when spoken with a Spanish accent. Luna presses a button below the edge of the round table and the window curtains begin to close, darkening the room. The edge of the table lights up with a fluorescent white ring, illuminating part of the body of those present around it. Luna presses another button and a medium-sized panel, with keys of various illuminated colors, slides from under the edge where she is. She takes another look at the teacher, who nods his head. She begins to push some buttons and laser rays beams come out of small designs within the dome, forming 3D holograms of blue, orange and green color.

Luna begins the narration and images emerge as if suspended in the air inside the dome, to the amazement of the young people present:

- Cartagena is situated on the Northern tip of Colombia, in South America continent, bathed entirely by the Caribbean Sea. With entirely crystalline waters due to large amounts of corals, it has several points of tourist and commercial interest, but I will highlight the geographically important ones for our plan...

- "Our plan"? - Lorenzo thinks.

A satellite image of a C-shaped seacoast with an irregularly shaped island in the middle protrudes into the air inside the dome.

- The so-called Cartagena Bay is shaped like a inverted C and bounded to the North by a rocky isthmus that protrudes from the continent towards the sea. That's where the Castillo Grande is built. The South of the bay is bordered by the so-called Peninsula of Barú, of greater extension.

The projection zooms on the satellite image of the island showing the middle of the sea.

- Isla Tierra Bomba is located between the open sea and the Cartagena Bay. Due to its size, divides the access for those who come from the sea in two entrances, almost closing the bay as if it were a lake. At the North entrance, between the island and the Castillo Grande, the entrance is wider and, therefore, called Boca Grande...

Images of the access channel, photos of the castle, cargo ships passing through the entrance and other real images appear in focus.

- ... while, between the South side of the island and the Peninsula of Barú, the entrance is narrower and as such, called Boca Chica. At the best-known end of the island, there is the Fuerte de San Fernando de Boca Chica.

A photo of the fort rotates in the air inside the dome, which soon changes into the satellite image of a peninsula with several islands at its tip.

- The Barú peninsula is a large stretch of land that is narrows as it advances towards the sea. Stretches of it are so narrow that you can see all the way from one end to the other, especially where it crosses the Corals del Rosario Natural Park. At the tip of the peninsula, in the region called Barú, we find the Rosario Archipelago, composed of ten islands...

Laser-ray images project islands of various shapes and sizes, highlighting the coconut-tree-filled tropical vegetation.

- Isla Grande, Isla Marina, Isla Pajarales, Isla Arena, Isla del Rosário and Isla del Tesoro, among others.

- Whoa! Treasury? I'm in! – Lorenzo jokes.

- Wasn't that where San Jose went down? – recalls Isabel

- Now, a good student is something else. - comments Prof. Perez.

Zooming in Rosario Islands region, Luna continues the projections. This time, a small caravel sails in the air between the islands, leaving a dotted line through which it passes, all in 3D.

- San José came from Panama in the South, bordering the Colombian mainland. After a few stops, it had to turn left to get around Punta Barú, which is at the end of the peninsula, passing between it and the Rosario islands...

Black dots show on a satellite map, as if seen from above.

- ... and evidence shows that it was right after making the right turn that they meet the English stakeout...

- Stake... what? – asks Thomas

General laugh.

- Ambush, trap - explains Paloma in solidarity.

- Oh, thanks!

- Well... –the little scientist continues – with no way out ahead, when it had to bypass Isla del Tesoro (now called Pirate Island) to enter the Cartagena bay, the galleon had to turn left again, trying to escape to open sea, when everyone already knows what happened.

Scenes from the battle of the caravels appear projected within the dome. The San José Galleon explodes and sinks. Brief silence among all.

- We had more, let's say, private access – Perez points out – to research data done by both the American team in 1986 and the Oceanographic Institute in 2015, and we conclude that the sinking of the ship is circumscribed in this region.

With a laser pointer in hand, he makes a red holographic circle in the projection of the maritime map that now floats inside the dome. The image shows a ship sinking toward the seabed, in a virtual blue sea with drawings of fish, algae and waves. Upon reaching the bottom, it lifts a cloud of sand that spreads throughout the dome. Perez continues:

- By the weight it carried, it is estimated that the ship sank about 656 yards straight from sea level, in no more than ten minutes. Upon reaching the seabed, the impact was very large, it got severely dismantled and today, after more than three hundred years, is covered by a layer of sand that should be about one hundred and sixty four yards thick.

- Buried one-hundred-and-sixty-four yards-deep? – asks Lorenzo.

- But what about the cannons that were seen? – remembers Thomas.

The light blue cannon photos taken by the underwater robot appear on the dome.

- You see that only they appear on the sand bed; you cannot see any other part of the wood of the ship – continues Perez, taking off his hat.

The hologram simulates a ship being covered by layers of sand on the seabed. Luna handles the rotation of the ship's computerized 3D image.

- Years passed and layers of sand and marine slime were covering the hull of the ship and everything in it, cargo and passengers. By the Physycal laws, due to the immobility of the seabed, the remains – however broken – are supposed to be intact. As for the treasure, we know that gold, silver, and precious stones do not deteriorate, even submerged for long years.

- Other shipwrecks, not as old as this one, were rescued and had their metal cargo taken advantage – complements Isabel – I've researched.

Lorenzo admires his colleague's initiative:

- That's right, Isabel, but... Will we be able to rescue the buried treasure?

Luna responds, handling the images of what the galleon would be like:

- First, it would have to confirm the exact maritime coordinates of the site, because it has not been fully confirmed, at least by the Colombian government. Then, only a piloted underwater robot, which can take high sea pressures, would have to get very close to the estimated location. Through sonar waves, the robot would measure the length and positioning of the hull, as well as the exact depth at which it is buried. Then, a long-range resistant drill rig would need to be lowered, one more powerful than those used in underwater oil drilling at offshore oil platforms. When it reached something solid strong enough to be drilled, underwater backhoes would have to be sent down to "scrape" the sand, like digging a tunnel through the middle of the seabed. Once they reached the solid point found by the driller (where other perforations would have to have been made), a long giant floating platform would descend double lifting cables called lifts. Then those cables would pierce what was left of the ship's hull, now without the sand on top of it, and would be clasped to the strongest and deepest part of the hull. They would look like a suspension bridge supported by steel cables of very high strength. Employing over-the-front pneumatic force, they would begin to lift the entire hull, distributing its proportionally longitudinal force in its length.

- But the wooden hoof, all rotten, wouldn't it come undone when it was hoisted? – asks Lorenzo.

- Yes, elementary, my dear Watson – continues Luna, projecting the film inside the dome – that is why, before lifting, they would have to pass an iron beam underneath its entire length so that it does not break, making a kind of lifting box. As it goes up – and this could take days – the water pressure decreases and, theoretically, you could hoist the boat entirely.

The film of a submarine being hoisted appears in the dome. Luna continues:

- This process was used to rescue the Russian submarine Kursk, sunk off the coast of Norway in 2000 and rescued by Putin in 2001.

- Damn it! – exclaims Paloma – Is there no other option?

Luna illustrates, via computerized panel, the descent of a large collapsible tube to the seabed and jets of things are shot into a tank-like ship, like a large fishing boat.

- Difficult? Almost impossible! And millionaire costy! Another option would be not to rescue the entire ship in full, as the Colombian government wished for the its historic purposes. If interested only in the twenty-billion-dollars-cargo, it would be possible to dig a tunnel directly into the cargo bay and its removal through very high-powered suction pumps. Maybe it was possible to suck the load, but tons of mud would come together.

The four young people look at one another, suffocated by the difficulty of it. Lorenzo reflects:

- Both options appear to me impossible. How much would that cost? Millions of dollars? How long would it take? Months, years? How many lives endangered? Is it worth it?

- We came to the point, my dear young man – Perez amends. He pauses to bring more suspense to what he will say – we have been researching this for dozens of years, funded by the Spanish government, and we have come up with another plan.

Everyone looks at him, who takes turns looking fixedly at each student. He completes:

- We don't let the San José sink!

No one understands.

- What?

- I didn't hear right.

- Nuts!

Isabel looks at Perez, then to Luna, both so serious they look like they are at a funeral. Isabel asks:

- Professor Perez, I'm sorry, but you invited us for a serious purpose, which was to learn a little more about naval history, but... You're kidding, aren't you?

As Perez remains serious, Lorenzo reinforces:

- Did you say... "we don't let the San José sink"?

- Yes, that's what I said.

- But... how? – asks Paloma, laughing – Only if we go back to the past in a time machine!

Perez and Luna look at her seriously, which makes her stop laughing. After a few minutes, everyone looking at each other in silence, Perez goes to his desk, takes out an envelope and delivers it to Lorenzo.

- Be at this address in three days, Saturday, 2:00 p.m. sharp. Men in suits, girls in skirts and tailleur, all navy blue. Now you can go.

Perez shows them the exit. Without understanding yet, the four take a few steps towards it, when they stop, listening to Perez say behind them:

- This is extremely confidential. Don't tell anyone.

They come out of the room, closing the door behind them. Lorenzo opens the envelope, where he finds four air tickets to Madrid and a business card, which has a symbol of the government of Spain, Ministry of Defense - National Intelligence Center - NIC - and, under the name of Iago Perez, the position of Head of the Department of Scientific Research.

Lorenzo, Thomas, Paloma, and Isabel are sitting at the same table in the college food court, looking at what is at its the center: the NIC card. The noise of other students' movement does not bother them. After some minutes, Lorenzo decides to ask:

- What's up, guys?

- I am completely confused – Isabel replies.

- Who's not? It was all so fast, so unexpected – Paloma continues.

Lorenzo begins to reason:

- It was a simple history class, now it looks like we're in a... a.... I don't know what to say.

- ... secret mission? - risks Isabel.

The three of them look at her. She had said what they didn't want to face.

- But is it true? – asks Thomas

Suddenly, the sound of an SMS message reaches the cell phones of the four at the same second. They look at the notification and don't believe what they read. Thomas, as always, doesn't understand:

- "NIC wants to track your location. Allow?"

- Oh my God! –Isabel exclaims.

- I became a secret agent? – asks Lorenzo.

- Or... a spy? – asks Paloma.

They keep quiet again for some minutes. Paloma asks:

- This is getting really serious, guys, better give up.

- Is it dangerous? – asks Thomas.

- Let's revise: the San José story was true. After class, the teacher calls us to a corner and tells us that extended version of it. Then he invites us to his office. We entered without knowing what he was going to tell us, he is dressed as an old Spanish admiral and his mysterious dwarf makes a virtual reality presentation. Then came the "we don't let the ship sink" thing.

- Going back to the past is not real – sentences Paloma.

- I think the teacher meant something else – defends Isabel.

- I don't know, he seemed very serious at this point – Lorenzo points out.

- But... What's up? What's to be done? – instigates Thomas.

- By the way: are we in or are we out? – asks Paloma.

After a thoughtful few minute, Lorenzo shows the cell phone screen to them and, with his finger, clicks "Allow". Look at Isabel, who, encouraged, clicks "Allow" too. Thomas's turn, without hesitation, he agrees to be tracked. The three of them look at Paloma, still undecided. She pulls the phone away from her face, closes one eye, stretches the other arm, and clicks the "Allow" option as well. She takes the card from the center of the table and asks:

- They already know my cell phone.

- Surely, they already know that you like vanilla milk-shake and run every morning – completes Lorenzo.

- What I'm asking is... Why us? - thinks Paloma.

- It was like Lorenzo said, I think the teacher saw something different that aroused his confidence on us – explains Isabel.

- But we are simple students - comments Thomas.

- Hum... I don't know if we are so "simple".- Isabel ponders - we always underestimate ourselves.

- And tend to look only at our small, negative side – agrees Paloma. Lorenzo asks Thomas:

- Look at Isabel, for example, isn't she beautiful?

The other two get the tension. Thomas hits back:

- I think Paloma is more beautiful than her.

Paloma looks at him, surprised. The other two get this new tension. Isabel tries to change the subject:

- Well, beauty is no requirement for any mission success. Shall we play talking good things about us?

- Speak well of us? This is not normal! – comments Lorenzo.

- Yes, I know, in general people only look at their defects, so let's look at our virtues?

- Sheesh... you look like those high-spirited motivational coaches. But let's do it. You start, Paloma – says Thomas.

- I haveenvironmental engineering degree, I participate in environmental advocacy groups, I live alone, I work at night in a cafeteria to pay for my studies, I consider myself smart... a little above average. Oh, I also like vanilla milk-shake – explains Paloma and looks at Isabel

- Well... I... Let me see... I have a degree in Archaeology, specializing in American ancient civilizations, working in a museum during weekends... uh, I'm very curious...

- Don't say that! – interrupts Lorenzo.

- ... I like music, dancing, I live with my parents, and I fight jiu-jitsu – she completes, casting a challenging look at Lorenzo who was pouting with a look of "all this"?

It's Lorenzo's turn:

- I'm studying naval engineering to complete my military course in Oceanography, with specialization in tropical marine life... – pauses to see the admiration of the girls, which does not come - ... I was commander of an army battalion on a mission on Mallorca Island during a small rebellion that occurred...

- Have you ever killed people? – asks Isabel, worried.

- No, it didn't come to that, but there were many missions on land and sea, heavy artillery training. I live with my mom and I fix everything she's got at home, from a car to a broken roof. I enjoy a lot of family, I like to do gym, I consider myself charming ... – once again pauses to receive the agreement of the girls, who remain serious - ... and I've won two marathons in the city where I live! Ready!

All three look at Thomas:

- Well, I'm sorry ... I do not like to talk about me...

- Oh, come on – encourages Isabel -... Just say good stuff.

- OK, I... work with all kinds of technology. I have a lot of knowledge in communication, radio, computing, and all forms of computer science. In England, I used to be a hacker...

All three arch their eyebrows.

- ... good hacker, the service of software companies who pay for this type of specialist to see if there is no hole – hole, is this how you talk here? OK, hole in your security systems. I like to read many books and do application development and communication. I've participated in endurance competitions, endurance in difficult places like islands, mountains, and deserts. I don't think I'm pretty, but I really like helping people.

- You are not ugly – adds Paloma, kidding.

- Hey, guys, did you catch up? – Lorenzo asks – does our profile have qualities that fit some kind of mission that involves: science, history, sea, extreme conditions and physical endurance?

- Dope! - agrees Isabel after thinking a little – did you see how good it is to speak well of yourself from time to time?

At this point they receive another notification on their phones. Looking at the screen, it is a link for confirmation of the check-in for the flight in two days time. They look to one another, again looking for moral support about the team decision. Lorenzo stretches out his arm and puts his hand on top of the card in the center of the table. He looks at Isabel, who puts her hand on his. She looks at Thomas who, smiling, also puts his hand on top of both of theirs. The three of them look at Paloma, still undecided. She ends up putting her hand on top of the others'.

Lorenzo pulls the tribe choir:

- Ooh! Ooh! Ooh! Ooh! Ooh!

Everyone enters the choir and, at the end, raises their hands in the air. They start filling in the data on the airline's website and therefore do not realize when the NIC card flies from the table and falls at the feet of a guy with a moustache with curved tips who is sitting next to them.

The guy takes tit and looks at them. Lorenzo turns his face and sees that he is looking. Lorenzo makes waves briefly, which the guy does not reciprocate. The man gets up and leaves.

GC HEADQUARTERS - CHELTENHAM, UNITED KINGDOM - YEAR: 2021

The flying-saucer-shaped building of the Government Communication Headquarter – GCHQ looked sad on that cold drizzly morning in Cheltenham, Northern United Kingdom.

A beautiful young black woman in British military uniform walks down the curved corridor lined on both sides by doors of work or meeting rooms, passing through other military, walking in pairs, talking to each other, going on the opposite direction. She carries a tablet in her left hand.

In front of a door with a sign that read "DSRC - Department of Scientific Research and Counterintelligence", she runs her badge through the electronic lock, which lights a green light and unlocks the door. She crosses a large glass room, full of people working at tables with small partitions, but what draws attention is a large blue LED panel with the world map on it, full of lit dots with light blue lines connecting several of them.

She walks through the long open hall until she reaches a room closed by a translucent glass partition, knocks on the door and another young military black man opens it. Recognizing that she is an authorized person, he makes a signal for her to enter and close the door. In the middle of the mid-sized room, some white-haired military men chat around a U-shaped table with other gentlemen in suits. The monochrome tone of the room is broken by the presence of the flags of the United Kingdom and a picture of the Queen. After few steps, the young woman stops and awaits permission to proceed.

A gentleman with gray military-cut hair, gray eyes, looking to be in his sixties, his chest full of merit badges, signals for her to approach. She stops in front of him and stands at attention.

- Good afternoon, Sergeant Jones. Make yourself at home.

- Good afternoon, General Walsh, thank you.

- I received your request for a hearing. What do you have to tell us?

Realizing the presence of strange civilians in the room, including a woman, she hesitates a little to continue. General Walsh understands and makes the proper presentations:

- Gentlemen and madam, this is Miss Birdie Jones, a brilliant career soldier, currently in the rank of sergeant in Her Majesty's Fifth Infantry Battalion. She's working on the SJG project.

The general points at a very well-dressed man, in a suit and vest, black hair and eyes, looking forty-four years old, athletic type. He scans the girl from the bottom up and smiles letting his very well-tended white teeth show, surrounded by a black moustache and beard.

- This is Mr. River Smith and Ms. Emmett O' Sullivan, owners of Floyds Bank and one of the sponsors to this project.

A woman dressed in a black tailleur ensemble with red collar, blonde hair pined with a small red bow, brown eyes, and very white skin, simulates a smile so small that it can only be noticed by the movement of the red lipstick on her thin lips.

- Delighted, Miss Jones - River replies.

She nods in a brief respectful way.

- So, Sergeant, do you have any news?

She turns on the tablet.

- I received an important message today from our informant in Spain. They called a team of students to be at the NIC in Madrid on Saturday.

- Students?

- Yes, sir.

- Amateurs? – River questions.

- I can't judge, sir. I processed their data in our database, and these are them, here.

She begins to show pictures of Isabel, Lorenzo, Thomas and Paloma, while describing each one of their profiles. After finishing, River comments:

- They are just kids to me.

- General Walsh, you know how much we are investing in this project – Emmett recalls, in a tone of slight arrogance – and therefore we cannot take any chances with strangers.

- They are not absolutely unknown, ma'am – argues Birdie.

- I asked to the General, darling.

More out of interest than to defend her, River asks:

- Why do you think that, Sergeant?

- In my brief evaluation, every one of them has some quality necessary for the development of this project, such as knowledge in archaeology, engineering, oceanography, and other exploratory resources.

- All right, Sergeant - Walsh reinforces – but is this information sound?

- My informant is well on top of what's going on, Sir.

- And who is he, may I ask? – questions Emmett.

- This is a project monitored by the top of the British intelligence service, ma'am, so we can't divulge anything – Walsh explains.

- Well... – River says, raising his hands – what's the next step?

The general looks at Sergeant Jones, who replies:

- We will monitor the meeting in Madrid, where we will also be on the inside.

- Then what?

- Then we must meet with the members of our work team and continue to follow the outlined plan.

- Oh! – Emmett looks interested – Do you already have a team formed?

- Yes, milady - replies Walsh.

River mocks:

- And are they... of the same "more-or-less-skilled-profile" as the Spanish?

Birdie looks at the young soldier who opened the door, who gets serious. Walsh responds with a half-smile:

- Nothing equals the quality of those who serve Her Majesty the Queen, Mr. Smith. Not in this century, not in the past.

He waves to the young guard at the door and asks:

- Major Brown, please turn on the presentation devices.

The guard activates a remote control, making steel curtains close the circular windows, while a wall opens revealing a large LED screen.

The image appears to be recorded from some flying device, a drone perhaps, filming a terrestrial area covered by a fog. As it approaches the ground, it shows a small town further away and strays into the image of a campus surrounded by wire fences and several dark brown brick buildings with gray roofs, some interconnected by covered corridors, others isolated, constructed in a 1960s style.

The flying camera, approaches a sign that is affixed to an entrance door, guarded by sentry boxes with armed soldiers. On the board, an acronym: DSTL.

A female narrator's voice begins to come out of the footage as the images advance in high resolution:

"Welcome to the Defense Science and Technology Laboratory campus in Port Down, Wiltshire. We are the executive agency of the Ministry of Defense, whose main purpose is to maximize the impact of science and technology on UK's defense and security."

- Is not that where they tortured animals in experiments? - whispers Emmett to Walsh.

- Slander from activists who have nothing better to do – defends the general, frowning.

The camera continues its low flight through the paved streets surrounded by trees and a slight mist, approaching the main building of dark brown bricks and windows with white frames. The narrator continues her description:

"Our expertise is scientific defense research on all kinds of weapons, such as chemical, nuclear, biological and any other that human beings can imagine."

The image passes through several corridors, enters rooms occupied by people dressed in military uniform, others all covered by white overalls, protective masks, and hoods with visors, handling test tubes, pipettes, microscopes, ovens and other equipment of research laboratories.

"The laboratory has two major fronts of research and work:

Chemistry and Physics. Since 2001, our renowned scientists have invented weapons for various types of attack and..."

River yawns loudly:

- General, this I have seen in several government advertisements or documentaries.

- But this you haven't seen yet – points out the general.

The flying image enters through some corridors, passes through several doors that open after a manual entry of security password, sliding doors, down some stairs, through more maximum-security doors, until stopping in front of an elevator guarded by four heavily armed soldiers.

"This is the access to the Quantum Physics Laboratory. Because it is of maximum security, it is built a hundred and thirty four yards below ground, protected against any nuclear attack."

The stainless-steel elevator doors open, and the image enters a spacious brushed steel elevator, which begins its descent at high speed. When the doors open, the image reveals a hall so large that it is not possible to see its end, almost like a tunnel. When leaving the elevator, it is noticeable that we are on a higher platform, with iron staircase lined by handrails, which ends two floors lower. There are several elevated walkways crossing the hall, with intense movement of people that cross from one side to another, carrying briefcases, cases of equipment, weapons, and other paraphernalia. The lighting brings a grayish-blue tone to the environment. But what calls the major attention is a cylinder about 33 yards in diameter that is installed on the floor of the hall the end of which cannot be seen either. It is all metal, a mix of copper and stainless steel, surrounded by rings in the form of gears, scale-shaped plates, giant screws that complete the spiral tube recall. Around it, hundreds of men and women in white aprons or mechanics uniform work on its fuselage, like ants around a giant insect.

"This is TRON, the most advanced linear particle accelerator in the world. It enables the concentration of large volume of energy generated by electrons in rectilinear form through a powerful electromagnetic effect field in the radio frequency region. After more than ten years of research and investment of around £100 million..."

River interrupts the narrative with a half-voice comment:

- I am finally seeing where my money has been used for!

The flying camera advances rapidly and "enters" the tubular machine, letting see circular walls filled with metal plates of various colors, wires, multicolored lights, beams of light and people working inside it. It is closed by a lid of shiny steel plates at both ends, making the compartment look like a cylindrical room.

Suddenly, the actual image of the machine turns into computerized drawing of a tube in the form of green light beams, yellow parallel discs and red particles floating randomly.

"... the modern structure of a linear accelerator is cut into several parallel titanium discs, with a hole in the center. Uranium electron particles, dispersed along the entire tube, are being directed to an invisible central axis, driven by radio frequency walker waves..."

The third-dimensional design begins to produce a pink line that represents a radio frequency wave that goes from the tube ceiling to its bottom, forming a curved zigzag, which moves as if pushing the red dots to the center of the image, causing them to be aligned and move from left to right. A dotted axis points to the right side of the image, forming a walking row of grouped red molecules.

"The wave increases in speed as it advances along the machine, causing such a large acceleration that in a few seconds they reach the light speed. This happens at both ends of the accelerator, i.e., from the right end to the center and from the left end to the center, concentrating both in the center of the accelerator, where the concentration and formation cabin of the wormhole is located."

The image of two large, thick red beams, coming against each other, appear in the computerized drawing, forming a carousel of lights that rotates very fast. Suddenly, the lid of an overpass opens and the beam of red light let slip, which, spiraling out, forms a cylindrical tunnel upwards, with a great bright force.

- Hole of what? – River questions.

Jones interrupts the presentation and repeats:

- Wormhole, sir. The passage from the present to another point in time and space.

She continues the presentation, which, in a few minutes, continues to show the ray of light rising in spiral form as drilling the sky. However, after a few minutes, it ceases, goes out and everything turns dark.

- What happened? – questions Emmett.

The virtual narrator, as if listening to her question, answers:

"But such a wormhole tunnel has not lasted more than ten seconds, because we still could not find the answer to a quantum physics equation, the key to making such a passage last for a more permanent time, without closing and endangering the entire operation."

The video ends. The lights in the room come on. Everyone looks at each other to watch their reaction.

River is the first to speak:

- Just ten seconds? This is nothing!

- According to the Relativity General Theory, at the light speed, it would be the equivalent of seventy-five days on Earth and enough to travel a distance of 18.6 million miles, sir –Birdie clarifies.

After recomposing his face, he insists:

- Anyway, the project is not finished yet.

- Not quite, Mr. Sullivan. – the general replies – We need to get the answer to a variable of the formula that our physicists haven't been able to solve for many years, despite all the tests and sacrifices that have been made.

Emmett, very serious, orders:

- Try to work this out soon! You know we can't wait any longer after all the investment my bank has made. I don't have how to explain anything else to the investors.

General Walsh looks at her seriously, then at River, and then, wondering if he could divulge such information, says:

- Spanish physicists working on similar projects have already discovered the solution.

River sends another harassing look at the girl and smiles, as if he had finally understood:

- Keep your informant satisfied, Sergeant Jones.

- We'll keep him with lots of professional information, Sir. – cuts the girl.

NATIONAL INTELLIGENCE CENTRE - MADRID, YEAR 2021

Isabel is taking a selfie with her cell phone next to the iron-pipes cube sculpture in the small circular square is in front of the three-pointed star-shaped building of the National Intelligence Center in the Valderín district in the Northwestern region of Madrid.

From the central gatehouse entrance, Lorenzo yells at her:

- Come on, Isabel, we're already late!

She shoots three more photos from different angles and runs to where he is, accompanied by Paloma and Thomas. The two boys in slim cut black suit and the girls in tailleurs with straight skirts, also black, form a harmonious uniformed quartet. Thomas says:

- We're looking like the MIB.

- We're missing the sunglasses - corrects Paloma.

- Let's go in, ten minutes to 2 p.m. – commands Lorenzo.

Passing through the glass doors, they enter the reception hall, with high ceilings and surrounded by cameras and armed soldiers on both sides accompanying them with surveillance. They head to the window where a lady in a brown uniform and cap answers through a circular intercom attached to the thick protective glass. Lorenzo approaches and speaks:

- Good afternoon, how are you doing?

- Speak! – she says, shortly and rudely

- We have a meeting with Professor Perez.

- There's no professor here!

- Oh, yes... I meant Mr. Iago, Iago Perez – corrects Lorenzo.

The receptionist seems increasingly irritated:

- Which department?

- Don't you know him? – asks Isabel.

- Young lady, there are more than 2000 people working here, how am I going to memorize the names of all of them?

- Well... it is just that you seem to work here for so long that... – says Thomas.

Paloma interrupts Thomas' out:

- He meant that you seem to have a lot of experience!

- I have been working at this post for 30 years!

- Lorenzo, show her the teacher's card. – Paloma continues.

The boy searches his pockets, nothing. He takes the wallet out of his pocket, opens it, look for the card, it's not there. He looks in the pockets of his jacket, then in the pants' ones again, the woman behind the glass frowning ever harder.

- Don't tell me you didn't bring the card? – asks Isabel.

- It was with me.

- You, always messes up!

- So... shall you tell what sector? – grumbles the receptionist.

- It was that of... –try to remember Lorenzo - ... Laboratory...

- There is a lot of labs in here!

The receptionist makes a signal for the security to approach.

- Take this gang out to refresh their memory!

Two soldiers begin escorting the four towards the exit.

- Hey, hey, hold on! – Thomas warns.

- This is a maximum-security area, you can't stay!

The security guards open the glass door and, when they are about to push the four out, a voice is heard coming from behind:

- They came see me!

They all looked at each other and then inside the central lobby, there was Professor Perez, in a blue shirt, red tie and white coat.

- Professor! –all four shouts at the same time.

- Go back to the counter to get entry badges, please.

The soldiers free them and they go back to the scowling woman's counter. Thomas speaks:

- That's Professor Perez, see?

Frowning even more, the receptionist asks some regular questions for registering visitors, takes photos with a webcam installed in the glass and delivers electronic badges through the metal drawer in the glass below the intercom. They put on the badges with the NIC logo and head to the entrance with X-ray device where Perez is waiting. Isabel turns around and waves to the woman, who remains serious and looking at nothing.

- Bye, thank you!

They place their backpacks and briefcases on the conveyor belt of the X-ray machine as they pass through the metal detector gate. Then they walk through a human body safety scanner. They pick their things up at the end of the conveyor and accompany the teacher towards the central lobby. Paloma jokes:

- Was the reception the most difficult test on this mission?

- Absolutely! – Perez takes the joke – but where is the card I gave you?

Everyone looks at Lorenzo:

- Well, it was with me, but I've lost it.

- No! Really? – mocks Isabel.

- All right, all right, we're already inside – explains Lorenzo – and now, Professor, it's 2:00 in the afternoon, where are we going?

- Nothing you see from here on should be commented with anybody, understood?

They run their hands over their lips, as if zipping them. Following Perez, they climb the staircase that leads up to the top floor and walk through one of the three of the postmodernist building's wings, full of rooms on both sides of the corridor from which, from time to time, some people emerge in their lab coats and cross them in the passages. At the end of the hall, Perez stops and opens a door, signaling them to enter first.

The glass-framed room overlooking the beautiful back garden has bookshelves covering all the walls, full of books and academic-style décor objects. In the middle of the room, a round table with blue leather high-backed swivel chairs. Sitting on one of them there is a completely bald gentleman, in his 70s, thin, brown eyes, in a tie and lab coat, who turns around as they enter. Sitting next to him, an attractive woman who appears to be about thirty-eight years old, her red hair stretched back in a ponytail, with blue eyes and a very thin face with some freckles on it, looks at everyone seriously. Next to her there is another man, in a black suit, well-groomed gray beard, forty years old, well-defined body and fair skin, green eyes. He looks at each one as if analyzing their profile.

Lorenzo whispers to Isabel:

- Why does every science room have a round table?

She whispers back:

- I think it is 'cause it has no beginning or end.

Perez rushes to introduce them all:

- Boys, this is Doctor Jimenez, Ph.D. in Quantum Physics, one of the oeldest and most renowned scientists in Spain.

- Now, dear Iago – he replies – you could have dispensed with the old thing.

- Most experienced – says Paloma.

- Good start, young lady – completes the friendly elder.

- This is Paloma Rodriguez, one of the best students in the environmental area.

Paloma smiles and nods her head in thanks. Perez continues

- Dr. Inez Suarez is sitting next to him, one of the most...

- Are you going to say I am old too?

- ... No... one of the most semi-young biomedical professional of our research center, post doctorate student in Human Molecular Biometrics.

- Did he say semi-young? – asks Dr. Inez to Dr. Jimenez, revealing an accent from the Northern regions of Spain.

- It's better than old - he tries to comfort her

- ... and this is Mr. Martinez, PhD in financial sciences – concludes Perez.

Isabel seems to recognize him:

- I think I have seen you in a television interview... aren't you CEO of The Martinez Financial Group, the largest private bank in the country?

- Pablo - he says in a cordial tone.

- Pablo Martinez! The richest man in Spain! – Lorenzo comments in a tone of admiration.

- Less rich than Scrooge McDuck.

Everyone laughs, what ends up breaking the ice between the newly met. Perez continues:

- All right, now, the introductions are done, let's get to the point. Please choose an armchair and sit down.

The four of them head to the high-backed armchairs, realizing that they are equipped with cushioned arms and a shoulder and abdomen seat belt. They find it weird, but they sit down. Perez waits a few minutes, staring seriously at the four youngsters, which makes them a little uncomfortable. Thomas decides to break the silence.

- Doctor Perez, one question: why us?

- Very well, my young Englishman, you read my thoughts! That is exactly what I was going to say. Listen carefully once again to what my warning and think once again which way you wish to go, because from now on there will be no turning back. There's the exit door, you can leave without looking back and forget you were ever here.

Lorenzo looks at Isabel who looks at Paloma who looks at Thomas. All four of them nod affirmatively. Perez looks at Dr. Inez, who looks at Dr. Jimenez, who looks at Pablo Martinez, and they too nod. Iago Perez continues:

- Although you do not present all the necessary conditions, you have several qualifications for this project. You are young, stand out in your studies, have already had first-rate training in areas of useful knowledge, such as... he looks at Lorenzo – oceanography, militaries, athletics, general maintenance –, looking at Thomas – information technology, media, cryptography, radical outdoor activities –, turning to Isabel – archaeology, South American history, cartography, martial arts –, staring at Paloma – environmental engineering, politics, human rights, meteorology, navigation, and commitment.

All four are speechless. Still looking at Paloma, Perez ends:

- Not to mention the vanilla milk-shake.

Half awkward, she looks at Pablo, who gives her the thumbs-up:

- It's my favorite too!

Turning her eyes from side to side, Isabel concludes by shrugging her shoulders, her arms in a V with her palms up:

- This really is intelligence. Since you all know us, what's next?

- Fasten your seat belts, please –asks Dr. Jimenez, buckling his

Everyone fastens their three-point belt. Dr. Jimenez presses a red button under the table and begins counting down:

- Five... four... three... two... one... Hold on!

Suddenly, the floor that holds the table opens and both the table and the armchairs plummet at high speed. After a few seconds falling through an illuminated elevator tunnel, the fall speed decreases and the set of oval table and eight chairs opens at one of the ends, turning from an oval shape into u-shape table. Just like in an amusement park cart, there's a ninety-degrees rotation on the axis and it heads toward one of the tunnel's walls, which is closed by a round iron door. As the cart approaches it, a presence sensor emits green digital web-shaped rays and scans everyone's face. When it identifies Dr. Jimenez's face, a green light appears on the sensor and the automatic middle door open, sliding sideways.

The cart rides along the rails into a round tunnel, illuminated on each side by bundles of bluish green, fluorescent lights. The temperature decreases a little and, after the cart advances a few yards, it turns ninety degrees so that everyone is facing the wall on the right side of the tunnel. After riding a few more meters, the projection of a high-digital resolution film in starts on the wall of the tunnel. The image of little Luna Gonzalez comes on, she's wearing a scientist's lab coat.

- Welcome to The Tempor Experimental Station! It is the largest nuclear research project in human history. After dozens of years of research and billions of euros invested, we've reached the production phase of the main project: space-time travel.

The U-shaped cart, now idling, enters an area of the tunnel whose walls are made of transparent polycarbonate sheets. On both sides, as if on a train platform, emerges an immense laboratory with counters, appliances of all shapes and sizes, conveyor belts up high, and people, lots of people in coats, working at the stands, computers, and other equipment of this scientific research environment. Armed uniformed guards, wearing masks, stand sentinel.

The scenery and intense hustle enthrall the youngsters, who look back and forth, not wanting to miss a thing. The cart turns around one hundred and eighty degrees and passes nearby a platform where several robots are being built and repaired by scientists. Luna's voice comes out of microphones installed on the armchairs, at the seaters ears' height:

"This is the Robotics Center, one of the most advanced in the world. Here we develop artificial cyber intelligence, with software installed to train robots that will be the future guardians of national security. Several prototypes have been developed and we have reached the top standing version in terms of intelligence, motor coordination, speed and fidelity to the national defense program."

The set of table, armchairs and rails passes through a section in which armed robots are marching, fighting with swords, lifting weights, undergoing military training and performing other activities much more perfectly than humans could do. The cart enters a rounded room and stops. Suddenly, it starts spinning slowly and a 360°-film is projected while Luna's narrative continues and her image shows up in a window on part of the screen.

The first image to appear is one of ancient caravels in a naval cannon- war in high-seas.

"More than three hundred years ago, Galleon San José was sunk by the English fleet on the Cartagena coast, in Colombia. Along with it, about six hundred souls and a treasure valued today at more than twenty billion dollars were sunk."

The film features images of the seabed, where ancient cannons are partially visible in the computer-taken photos.

"In 2015, an expedition commissioned by the Colombian government found what appears to be traces of the wreckage and a major international dispute has begun since then, arousing the interests of the United States, Colombia and Spain. Since then, no other measure has been attempted to pinpoint the true site of the shipwreck, which remains uncertain and kept as a national secret."

The film now shows an 18th-century cartographic map of Northern South America, as well as an updated map of the same region. The figure of an old man, in a white wig, wearing the uniform of a Spanish commander, appears on the screen, overlapping the two maps, projected along the walls of the 360° screen. He is sitting at an old table and holds a writing feather, by the light of a candlestick.

"There are indications that Don Alejandro Cesar de Sabogal, the second commander of the shipwrecked galleon, survived and drew a map where he identified the exact sinking location. This map has never been found and it is the main objective of the FSJ Mission".

The walls now show the outer space. The solar system, planets, stars, galaxies, and comets pass by in seconds before everyone, like they were on a journey inside a spaceship. The universe opens up before everyone. Figures of cavemen, Einstein, ancient rockets, physics formulas, molecules, and other figures are shown, flying from side to side.

"Travels both to the past and the future have always been the motives of science fiction books and films and hardly proven. However, since Einstein's disclosure of the Theory General of the Relativity in 1915, it has become clear that time is not something absolute, but relative. And that it passes faster to an observer who is still than to another one who is in motion.

This is called time dilation, theoretically proven by physicist Hendrick Lorentz in the early 20th century, who realized the temporal difference of events, which, with the weightings of Newton's gravitational forces observed by Einstein, set the foundation for the whole theory of relativity".

The cart turns to the other side of the tunnel and the projection begins to show a drawing of a rocket flying through space, with a person standing inside it and the planet Earth, also in drawing, to one side.

"In a simple figuration, we have an astronaut inside a spaceship who releases a ping-pong ball from the height of his arm to the floor of the ship. As the ship is in horizontal motion, the trajectory of the ball is a straight line, from the arm of the astronaut to the floor of the ship. However, for an observer who is standing still on Earth, the trajectory of the ball will appear to be a diagonal line, because the horizontal displacement is added to the vertical fall, forming a triangle-rectangle which formed the basis for Lorentz to create his famous time dilation formula:

$$\Delta t = t_2 - t_1 = \frac{\Delta t'}{\sqrt{1 - v^2/c^2}}$$

Therefore, for the observer who is standing still on Earth, the ball took longer to complete its trajectory than for the astronaut who is in movement inside the ship.

In the scientific field, another great German physicist and astronomer, Karl Schwarzschild proposed, in the years 1910-1915, that the distances between parallel universes in time and space could be quickly and directly transposed through a tunnel connecting its extremities. Because of its appearance, this tunnel was called a wormhole."

The black and white photos of Einstein, Schwarzschild and John Wheeler also appear in the background, hovering. A worm going through an apple appears next.

"In 1957, John Wheeler, an American physicist, published the theory of space-time interconnection, considering the possibility of travels both to the future and the past. A worm could move from one end of an apple to the other by two paths: either walking on its surface (which would take more time and effort) or crossing through the middle of it, through a tunnel. Similarly, this could happen between two parallel universes, joining their extremities by an electromagnetic, gravitational channel and using quantum energy at the speed of light."

The cart moves a little further forward, in the tunnel, entering a domed-ceiling room. Dr. Inez distributes 3D glasses among those present, which are passed along by one another.

The projection of a Science Every Day YouTube video, made by the Brazilian physicist and Professor Pedro Loos, is now also projected on the ceiling, producing an effect similar to the universe. The kids are increasingly dazzled.

"Einstein's Relativity General Theory describes how matter behaves within the four dimensions of our Universe: three space dimensions (width, height, and depth) and one time dimension. The presence of matter in space distorts and bends it at the same time, causing notable effects, such as gravity which, in turn, affects the movement of matter. Matter tells the space how to bend and space bend, in turn, tells matter how to move.

And this relationship is described by a very famous equation, known as Einstein's Field equation.

$$G_{uv} = R_{uv} - 1\, Rg_{uv,}$$

The term represented by the letter G describes how matter is distributed in space, and the R terms describe how space is bent.

It was by studying this equation that two of the most famous results of the theory of relativity were found: the first of these was the prediction of the existence of black holes, made by Schwarzschild in 1916, and which had their existence definitively proven in the 90s. And the second, are wormholes that, in theory, can connect two points in space-time on through an extremely short path. For example, if you wanted to leave Planet Earth and move to the Andromeda Galaxy, this trip would take at least three million years, if you could move at the speed of light, which is impossible. Now, if you would find a wormhole in the way, you could reduce the duration of this trip to a few years or, who knows, even to a single day.

The classic explanation of how this super-fast passage through the universe works is to imagine that you are the inhabitant of a sheet of paper. You exist in the two dimensions of the sheet, and you can move through it at your will. And if you want to go from one end of the sheet to the other, you have to go through its the entire length of the sheet. This trip would take a few inches. But imagine that your sheet is not straight but folded. And in addition to being folded, there is a path that connects the two ends, without having to go through the entire sheet. So instead of you going through the whole sheet surface, you can go through this short connection which is like a wormhole.

Using Einstein's Field Equation, which disciplines the curvature of space with the distribution of matter through said space, it would be possible to create a wormhole, which relates the curvature of space to the distribution of matter through it."

Several beams of yellow laser intersect, forming a flat, transverse web. As the narrative progresses, the flat web folds over itself, in horseshoe-shape, and a cylinder begins to rise from its lower end to the upper end.

"In terms of the wormhole, we know how the curvature of space should behave. We want two distant regions in space to be connected by a short path, like a handle, which is basically the definition of a wormhole. Adding our requirements to Einstein's Field Equation, the result is that wormholes seem possible. But quite unlikely."

The animated drawing of a ship crossing the tunnel dissolves with it at a point.

"One of the problems we have to solve is that wormholes are not stable, they collapse instantly. Let's say you are going through a wormhole in your way to Andromeda and that, halfway through, it dissolves, tearing you apart along with space-time. So, we need to add another component to the equation, which is stability."

The animation showing the tube of laser beams starts to shrink and expand in its midst.

"Solutions for stable wormholes are not static. This means that the inside of a wormhole does not stand still, it keeps opening and closing, again and again, very quickly, making it impossible to cross it. So, we have to add yet one more variable to the equation, which is static."

The figure of a ship crossing the laser tube facing a sort of turbulence appears through the walls and ceiling. In the middle of the journey, the ship disintegrates.

"A stable static wormhole is possible, however, the gravitational forces would be so large that they would destroy any ship that tried to cross it. In fact, some of these solutions bring a combination of black hole-like events, just so you can get an idea of what the gravitational forces involved in this event are like. Therefore, we need to find a solution to create a stable, static wormhole that does not destroy ships and does not turn into a black hole.

The good news is that it would be possible to build a wormhole like this; the bad news is that it would take an almost infinite time to go through it. That is, you would enter a wormhole and only get out of it at the end of the universe. Adding this fifth variable, there is a solution in Einstein's Field Equation. Finally, a perfect solution. It's just that... there is a problem.

We know what kind of wormhole we want: we use Einstein's equation to know how matter has to be distributed to form this wormhole and what properties this matter should have. And here is the problem."

Images of various materials in their three possible states – solid, liquid, or gas – float all over the room. A bubble in the shape of a human cell starts to grow amongst them.

"The solution to the equation requires a material with properties that are literally impossible in any type of matter that we know. To produce it, you need something called exotic matter. Exotic matter is literally a completely new type of matter and has basically magical properties. It would have to be a material with more resistance to stress than there is energy in its atoms or particles, better yet, than whatever this exotic matter is made of. And here we are just considering the energy that in this matter requires simply to exist, according to the $E = mc^2$ equation".

The glowing mushroom shape of an atomic explosion swallows the environment.

"Which means, in a way, that this material should be able to withstand a nuclear explosion on its surface. And this is not the most extreme property this exotic matter would need to have. An alternative way to achieve this would be using a matter with negative energy density. In other words, it is like asking this matter to have a negative mass, which seems to be completely absurd, inconceivable within the Theory of General Relativity. But not in another theory of physics."

The film stops and the U-shaped armchairs move further forward, in an fast way. They stop in another room with a single projection screen this time. Images of magnets with multiple poles emit electromagnetic waves in the form of multicolored laser beams, entering and leaving each of the poles.

"There is one thing known to modern physics that is capable of generating negative energy in very specific conditions: quantum fields. Quantum fields are what modern quantum mechanics uses to explain fundamental particles of the Universe. Some of these fields, under very specific situations, can generate negative energy. But there's a problem here. Currently quantum fields theory is incompatible with Einstein's General Relativity Theory. Putting the two together is probably the most difficult problem in physics.

So finally, the answer to the question: is it possible to create wormholes? We don't know. We need to know how to solve the most difficult problem of physics before, which is to unite general relativity with quantum fields theory.

However, very hypothetically speaking, an ultra-futuristic civilization, capable of fine controlling quantum effects might be able to create something very similar to wormholes."

The video is interrupted before its end and several lights come on, overshadowing the staff who had been watching to everything in the dark. They remove their 3D goggles and, after a lot of blinking and eye rubbing, Perez asks the youngsters:

- So, what did you think?

After looking at each other, Thomas risks:

- It reminded me a lot of a Disneyland attraction!

The three doctors look at him seriously.

- Sorry, I was kidding...

Paloma, as usual, comes to his rescue:

- He meant he thought this was all fantastic and unbelievable!

- And it really is - agrees Dr. Jimenez.

Isabel raises her hand, as if she were in class:

- Isabel? – Perez allows

- I found all this fascinating too, but... at one point, there is mention of a FSJ Mission. What would that be, in short?

Dr. Jimenez explains:

- A journey to the past to "**Find the San José**".

- Through a wormhole? – asks Lorenzo.

- Yes – explains Dr. Inez.

- But... – Lorenzo continues – from what we have seen and heard, not all variables are resolved yet...

- ... there is no solution known to modern physics – completes Paloma.

Dr. Jimenez smiles:

- After decades of research...

- ...financed by my bank... – interrupts Pablo.

- ... *gracias!* – continues Jimenez – We were able to equate the Relativity General Theory, the dilation of time and Einstein's other past geniuses' Field Equation, formulating – he begins to count on the fingers of the hand – a static, stable earthworm hole with controlled gravitational force, whose crossing would last a finite and short period of time and whose transportation ship would not be destroyed.

He turns to Dr. Inez and asks:

- Time for the highlight of the show!

Dr. Inez takes something that looks like a remote-control and pushes a button. The four iron walls that encircle the room begin to lift, letting them see that behind them there are transparent polycarbonate fiber walls. As soon as the ceiling becomes transparent, they all marvel at what they find out: they are inside a glass cube in the middle of a large, tall factory shed, full of people working on a gigantic, round, cookie-shaped machine whose walls are made out of shiny and reflective metal, circling all sides of the cube. Several colorful panels, wires, conductive ducts coming out of the ceiling of the round metal tunnel, lights, stairs, and platforms suspended on the shed's walls complete the extraordinary scenery of a time machine.

Dr. Inez starts explaining:

- This is MÍNION, the cyclic particle accelerator developed in conjunction with CERN's LHC project. It enables the concentration of a large volume of energy generated by beams of electrically charged subatomic particles.

- Is it a cyclotron or a synchrotron? – asks Thomas.

His three colleagues cast him an inquisitive look, as if asking "how do you know this?". The scientists are equally amazed, but Dr. Inez continues her explanation:

- It's a synchrotron that accelerates silicon protons at speeds over 1,000 Giga electron-volt, enough energy for a round trip to Neptune in 10 hours.

- Wow! – says Thomas, amazed

Dr. Inez continues:

- All matter is made of atoms, which in turn are composed of particles such as protons, electrons and neutrons. A particle accelerator, simply speaking, forces the two particles of different chemical elements to collide against each other so that they release kinetic energy. The temperature at this time can reach over a million times the heat of the sun and the particles reach 99.9% the light speed. Using such potential, we believe it will propel a capsule into a wormhole and cause the crew to travel through time.

- But... – remembers Thomas – ... what about the ship disintegration issue? Did you find the exotic material that would be resistant to the pressure and energy involved?

Dr. Jimenez intervenes:

- After many years of research in our testing laboratories with various materials, both organic and inorganic, we have discovered, almost unintentionally, that silica is said magical material that will resist time travel.

- Silica is made of silicon and oxygen – defines Lorenzo.

- That is correct, showing that nature provides solutions for everything in this scientific life – Perez continues.

At that moment, the fiberglass cube's walls slide down into the floor, releasing the armchairs into space in the middle of the factory lobby, whose ceiling is so high that they can hardly see it.

Perez invites:

- You can unbuckle your belts and come with me, I have something to show you.

- I was getting suffocated inside this glass cube already – comments Pablo, loosening tie a little.

- Me too – says Thomas, releasing his collar button and putting a pen in his shirt pocket.

Everyone goes down the step and stands at ground level. They are fascinated, looking all over at once. They are right-smack in the core of the aluminum ring-shaped particle accelerator.

Following the scientists who are a few steps ahead, they head to one of the walls of this tunnel, stopping in front of a door. The height of the tunnel is almost four times that of their own. Dr. Jimenez approaches the retina reader, and the door opens on its own.

The inside resembles a circular-tunneled subway station in. They look to the right and to left and the view is lost due to the curvature. The floor is made of raw cement, painted with blue electrostatic paint with white bands very close to the walls signaling the circulation of people. Long LED lamps fixed to the ceiling compose the lighting of the place, lining besides gas and electrical wiring ducts. In the middle of the tunnel, a metal tube about one meter in diameter, fully closed, extends itself to the right and to left farther than the eye can see. Emergency lights, fire extinguishers, railings and other protective materials complete the setting of an installation reminiscent of a large circular blue iron sewer duct in an underground gallery.

Isabel asks:

- What's the extension of this tube?

- About one and a half mile, rather smaller than the Swiss LHC seventeen miles..

They walk to the right following the central tube. Some technicians and engineers pass through them, some walking, others biking. The group arrives at a kind of special compartment, separated by a thick transparent acrylic wall. They walk through the open door that divides the space and are amazed by what they envision.

The cyclic accelerator tube continues to run through the middle of the compartment, but other pipes of smaller diameter and length, like cannons come out from various parts of it, and point to the top of the room. Panels flashlights of all colors intermittently. Computer screens show waves of various frequencies and speeds. On the walls, screens and monitors show graphs, numbers, temperatures, and formulas being developed and data being recorded. Emergency lights rotate inside the spots, like those of ambulances, completing the scene of fascinating technology.

However, what catches the young people's attention the most is at the top of this special room: above the pipes and the cannons pointed at it, a silvery oval sphere, with bright gray pigments, floats in the air.

- What? – asks Pablo

- It is... floating? – admires Lorenzo

- Young men and women – says Professor Perez – welcome to *Columbus,* the time and space travel capsule

- Why that name? – asks Paloma

- In honor of Cristobal Colombo, our hero explorer – explains Perez

- What's holding it up? – asks Thomas, advancing further underneath it and examining every possible detail

- Accelerated particle rays of silicon and lead, the result of the quantum formula we've developed – explains Dr. Jimenez – at this moment, as you see, in infinitely reduced force. Shall we go up?

Perez leads the group a few steps ahead, revealing that, at the other end, there is an identical super-resistant acrylic wall, enclosing the about third-yards-long compartment. In the middle of the right wall, there is a large rectangular window that shows a control room, where some scientists are sitting in front of several panels. Lorenzo recognizes one of them.

- Hey, isn't that Luna?

- Dr. Luna Gonzalez, head of the capsule development team.

Perez signals to her, and she pushes a button on a panel in front of her. A trapdoor-type ladder, with structure and steps made out of transparent and luminous acrylic descends in a left upper corner of the compartment. The eight people enter the egg-shaped ship, which rocks a little as they walk.

- Here you'll need your balance a little bit – warns Dr. Inez

Inside, eight white leather and high-backed armchairs are attached to the circular walls, facing one another. Spacesuits with breathing helmets are placed on them, tied by seat belts. On the oval silicon walls, more colorful panels and computer monitors complete the science fiction scenery. From the center of the ceiling, a digital panel shows today's date and time and a rotating world globe in its left corner.

Doctors observe the reaction of the youngsters, who all around. Lorenzo asks:

- Have you already... tested all this?

- With mice in a miniature prototype, yes, everything worked out fine – confirms Dr. Jimenez

- But not yet with humans on this of real greatness scale – deduces Paloma

Their silence confirms it. Dr. Inez rushes to explain:

- This capsule can only be used for a round trip, after which it will be virtually destroyed. But don't worry, honey, the chances of fatal failure are statistically null, less than 0.000000001%

- The hard part is if we are in the statistics – jokes Isabel seriously

- Well... anyway, what will be our mission? – asks Pablo, walking and examining the place

Perez explains once again:

- Your mission will be to go back to the year 1708 and find out where Captain Sabogal hid the location map of the San José and bring it to us.

Isabel has an idea:

- What if, instead, we stopped the ship from going sinking? We can try to make the fleet not get ambushed by the English.

- We cannot change the past, miss, at the risk of having catastrophic effects here in the present – Dr. Jimenez's explains

- How long are you going to keep the wormhole portal open? – asks Thomas

- Wonderful question, boy – dr. Perez jokes – that was a problem until last week, when we couldn't keep the portal open for more than ten seconds. After several quantum analyses, we solved the last component of the equation, and now the portal will be open for twenty-four hours in Earth's time.

- Are we going to have only one day to find the ship's location? – asks Lorenzo

- This will correspond to ten days in the past – adds Perez

Thomas shoots:

- If energy is equal to the mass times gravity squared and the time delta over the square root of a smaller gravitational field squared minus velocity squared, what was the solution? Extract the neperian exponent from the quantum field of silicon?

Astonished by the boy's reasoning, Perez takes the tablet from Dr. Inez's hand and, after searching through menus and schematics, he shows him the screen:

- We took Lorentz formula with the quantified variables, extracted the square root from it and used the result as an exponent of the R variable in the Einstein Field Equation formula. When we combine all this with silica molecules, we were able to prolong the sustention period of the distribution of matter through the black hole for a longer time.

Thomas looks closely at the screen, making a face like he didn't understand, but he's okay with it. Perez finally asks:

- So, what's up? In or out?

- Super in - says Pablo – when are we leaving?

- "We"? – asks Lorenzo – is he going too?

- I paid for a business class ticket, of course I am going!

Lorenzo looks at the scientists, who agree:

- The team will be made up of the four of you, Mr. Martinez, Dr. Luna and two of our best and most prepared Marines.

Isabel looks at Lorenzo and asks:

- One last question, Professor... After all, is there a life-threatening risk for the team?

Perez thinks a little before answering and, staring into the girl's eyes, says:

- I am not going to say no, child; there is some, yes, under control; but the benefit this will bring to your lives and to the history of our country will be immeasurable. If I was a little younger, I'd go with you.

Lorenzo, Paloma, Isabel and Thomas gather together to talk privately, like football players, with their arms on each other's shoulders. After a few minutes, they look the others and Lorenzo speaks on their behalf:

- You can count on us!

- All right, I knew it! – says Perez happily – Then let's start training so that in four weeks you are ready for the adventure!

Dr. Inez completes:

- The training program includes physical preparation, ship controlling, event planning, gravitational simulation, and other attributes you'll need for the mission's success.

- When do we start? – asks Pablo, enthusiastic.

As they walk down the corridor almost at the building's exit, Lorenzo walks past a man with a moustache with curved tips, in a lab coat, who comes in the opposite direction. He figures he's seen him before, but he can't remember where.

DSTL HEADQUARTERS - CHELTENHAM, UNITED KINGDOM - YEAR: 2021

Sergeant Jones, standing in front of the table at which General Walsh is sitting, delivers a sheet of paper to him:

- The solution to the formula that was missing, sir.

The General takes the sheet, reads it, looks at it and smiles.

CHAPTER III
RACE AGAINST TIME

NATIONAL INTELLIGENCE CENTRE - MADRID, YEAR 2021

The Tempor Experimental Station is busy as never before. People, electric carts, cranes, physicians, scientists, maintenance operators, in short, all kinds of professionals are there in order to, after thirty days of training, send the rescue team to the past. Many flashing lights, siren sounds and a small mist enveloping the large metal ring compose the emergency and hectic scenario of the ship's pre-launch.

At 1:30 p.m., everyone stops and stands in front of a round stainless-steel gate that separates the lobby from other room next door. After a few minutes, the gate opens showing, standing next to one another, dressed in travel clothes and holding helmets under their arm, like astronauts, the crew members, lined up from left to right in descending order of height: two Marines, Lorenzo, Pablo, Isabel, Thomas, Paloma and Luna.

A simplified version of the Spanish national anthem starts playing and everyone stands in a respectful position. After its completion, under applause, the team advances towards the tunnel where the Columbus capsule is located. They walk through the tunnel, accompanied by security guards, to the launch bay. The tubular accelerator is emitting a stronger buzz than it was when they'd been there previously, as if warming up. The vertical tubes coming out the accelerator pointing to the capsule are emitting continuous colored rings, which go up through them and make the capsule to float with more oscillations. They come to stop in front of the control room window, where, inside, are several scientists and navy officers. Dr. Perez, Dr. Inez and Dr. Jimenez are standing behind various panel operators, counters, and video monitors.

The climate is one of great expectation. Lorenzo looks at Isabel, as if asking for final approval. She nods her head. In silence, they all climb the ladder and enter the capsule, now more illuminated and agitated, whit optical fibers of various colors emit light around the ceiling and walls full of appliances. The floor is oscillating more than before, requiring more balance when walking. The eight travelers sit in their respective seats and fasten their seat belts. They put their helmets on their lap and exchange anxious glances.

At this point, Professor Perez's voice rings through the capsule's internal speaker, lowering the anxiety level slightly:

- Do I have to ask how you're feeling?

Lorenzo replies:

- Hearing your voice just now reminded me of that airplane stewardesses always say something when the plane is taking off and that makes us feel less afraid.

Perez laughs:

- And to think it all this started with a History class!

- If it weren't for Isabel's questions, however... – Lorenzo looks at her, who gets a little angry

- Oh, yeah? Now it's my fault?

- No, no, no, no. Would I be crazy if I created trouble now?

The general laugh does not disguise the nervousness. Paloma asks:

- How long before launching?

- Fifteen minutes - says an operator

He types some commands and, on the dial of the digital clock at the ceiling of the capsule, it shows "Isla Grande, Bay of Barú, 06-June-1708". Perez, through the microphone, continues:

- Let's do a quick recap of the plans. The capsule will land at Isla Grande in Barú Bay, which is the closest point to where the Tierra Firme Fleet was ambushed by the English, two days before it happens. Somehow, you will have to, at night and clandestinely, embark on Galleon San Joaquin, which did not sink. You'll blend in with the crew – there are time-appropriate clothes in the closet – and follow the trajectory for another day. As soon as The San José sinks – beware of danger – you escape in a lifeboat and rescue the survivors. The second captain should be among them. Then you'll follow him and see where he hid the map with the exact location of the wreckage, then go back to Isla Grande and embark back to the present. You'll have ten days to do this, the maximum time we can keep the wormhole open, because the wave cannon emitter will run out of power.

Dr. Inez continues:

- You will be monitored all the time through this belt you are wearing. It provides tracking and communication with the control base and among yourselves. You will carry weapons and ammunition to defend yourselves against any threat. Remember, you'll be going over three hundred years back, and you're certainly not going to find anything like we know it today. There may be different geography, people, customs, and unknown dangers.

Dr. Jimenez completes:

- Lorenzo Garcia. You are in charge of this expedition. Two of our most capable Marines in the Spanish Navy are with you: Diego Sanchez – everyone looks at the strong blue-eyed African-descendant with a military hair-cut, who looks around and nods – and Soledad Flores – they all look at her, who is a strong woman around 28 years old, with almond complexion, black eyes, her hair stuck in a ponytail, which makes a brief salute with her hand.

- It is an honor, Professor – Lorenzo replies – but I will do nothing without everybody's help.

- Only by combining everyone's skills this will work – comments Luna

- If you need to negotiate a loan, count on me – jokes Pablo

- The countdown will begin in five minutes. We will increase the power of the accelerator – warns the operator. He increases synchrotron load.

The buzzing sound increases, making the capsule vibrate. A medium-sized panel with black background shows green bar that goes up, showing 200 Giga-electrons.

Lorenzo starts stating the commands.

- Crew, prepare for departure.

The crew put on their astronaut helmets. They open the covers on the armrests of their seats on each side and start pushing a few buttons. Lorenzo continues:

- Check power source.

- Clear – answers Thomas, after checking a small panel

- Check enablement of landing mattress.

- OK – answers Isabel

- Check route computation.

- OK – Paloma says, pressing a few buttons on the arm of her chair

- Check ship structure resistance.

- Stable – answers Marine Soledad, looking at the pointers on the panels

The bar on the panel rises a little further, turning yellow and showing 600 Giga electrons. The entire lobby of the scientific base begins to shudder.

- Check route and destination.

- All in order – says Pablo, checking some panels and adjusting some keys

- Check oxygen.

- OK – answers Diego

"One minute to launch" is heard on the helmet's internal communication devices. The vibration of the capsule increases even more, the dial reaches 900 Giga electrons and becomes orange.

- Check safety equipment and escape route.

- OK – answers Thomas

The entire metal ring of the particle accelerator shudders, emitting a sound like an engine at extremely high speed. The scientists inside the control room look at each other worried. The ceiling of the launch room opens slowly in the middle, showing the full moon illuminating the starry sky.

- Ten... nine... eight... seven...

A silver laser beam begins to rotate as a centrifuge in the center of the ship. The rings rising around the accelerator's ray ducts increase in speed to the point that they turn into single orange, red, and blue lights. The vibration increases and so does the noise. It seems that everything is spinning in an invisible axis.

- Six... five... four...

The light beams of widen, reaching the walls of the capsule and the people sitting there. They feel the pressure increasing in their heads, causing a lot of discomfort and shortness of breath.

Suddenly, the silver-ray beam goes up over itself, overtaking the capsule's ceiling. The power dial shows a flashing red bar, indicating 995... 996... 997. The operator's voice is hardly heard inside the ship. The beam of silver-bluish lights bursts up to the sky, forming a tube about six yards in diameter, spinning like a cyclone whose core can be seen from underneath. The image of the eight crew members slowly disappears.

- Three... two... one!

The dial reaches 1000 GeV. The accelerator is at its maximum power, which had never been used. Protons and electrons are crashing at such a high speed that they generate a force equivalent to ten atomic bombs beneath the ship. The time tunnel opens to infinity, making it impossible to see its the end.

- Hold on tight! – shouts Lorenzo.

There's barely time for him to look at his wristwatch, which shows 11:25:30 a.m. A large flash and the sound of an explosion fill the launch bay, causing scientists inside the control room to turn their faces, shielding them with their hand. In fractions of seconds, the capsule disappears, flung into space leaving a trail of small bright spiral-shaped sparkles.

DEFENSE, SCIENCE AND TECHNOLOGY LABORATORY - PORT DOWN, UK - YEAR: 2021

Projected on a big screen, a chorus of uniformed men and women sing the Anthem of England as an orchestra plays its majestic melody. Nine people dressed in 18th-century English squadron soldiers' uniforms or in old English ship workers' clothes are standing side-by-side, some of them military-saluting, with their backs to TRON.

Next to them, a little further back, is General Walsh in a military gala suit. A United Kingdom flag is being hoisted on a mast near them, causing the general to salute as a sign of respect for the symbols of that great nation.

As soon as the anthem ends and the flag is raised, everything is silent, or almost silent, as the time machine is activated and emitting a sound of metal beating.

General Walsh goes to the far left and inspects the nine crew members of the time travel ship. A large group of scientists and soldiers is stationed a little further away, watching in silence. Light white smoke is rising from the linear particle accelerators, forming a fascinating rocket launch scenario.

Walsh moves to a small acrylic pulpit, the flags of Britain and the United Kingdom Navy on each side of it. *Eternal Father, Strong to Save*, the British naval anthem, starts playing in the background. Walsh, thrilled, begins his speech:

- How should I address you? Ladies and gentlemen? Soldiers? Explorers? Any way I chose, I couldn't express the fantastic adventure, the venerable honor, and the eternal feat you are about to accomplish. Three hundred years ago, a great battle was the apex of a dispute between two great nations with identical purposes: to prevent the concentration of power, to fight injustice and to prevent individual interest from overcoming the collective one. Kingdoms split and others united around an alliance that would bring serious problems to world peace. Unfortunately, we were not successful, neither party won.

He takes a strategic pause, and soon continues, looking into the eyes of each one of the crew members:

- Young warriors, today you are making a great commitment to humanity: the rescue of a legacy that belonged not only to the English nation, but to all of those who defend equal human rights, the fairness of treatment and the justice of the commission. You will enter an innovative experience, going back in time and space, an unimaginable journey to our modern world. Be strong, be brave, be true to your beliefs. This team was selected and trained among the best, strongest and most skilled servants of our nation. However, the greatest quality we saw in you was – pauses to create suspense – bravery. Use it to guide your decisions. We sincerely hope that you will have God's protection in face of all the dangers that will come your way and that you will return safe and sound. Even so, should anything happen, remember the milestone you will leave to the History of our country. I started this speech by referring to you as ladies and gentlemen; I end it up by saying you're heroes!

Walsh raises his right arm and shouts:

- God Save the Queen!

Everyone raises their right arm and shouts:

- God Save the Queen!

Confetti cannons shoot a rain of blue, white and red bits of paper over everyone. The nine crew members begin to enter into the launch room, which is between the ends of the two gigantic cylindrical tunnels which come out from the right and from the left and extend farther than it is possible to see, closed by gear-shaped iron rings.

The room also has cylindrical shape with stainless steel walls attached to each other by large silver screws. All the walls are filled with flashing lights and some panels show sine waves moving from side to side. The smell resembles burnt plastic and the temperature is around 86 degrees Fahrenheit. A yellow laser beam comes out of one end and ends at the other, at about one yard above the ground. Separated by this beam, in the middle of the room, nine totems are arranged in a circle, they are wide and carved in the shape of a human body. There are LED flashing lights around these shapes, from the back of which oxygenation ducts and other wires with sensors at the tips show.

The crew quietly heads to each of these totems and, with their backs to them, fasten their safety belts around the ankles, waist and chest. They attach the sensors to their hearts and wrists and connect the oxygen tubes to the inlets on their helmets, which they proceed to put on. They're all standing and respectfully awaiting instructions.

Suddenly, in the center of the circle, the bright blue hologram of a man dressed in a white apron is projected and rotates while talking to them:

- Good night, everyone, how are you?

Emmett O' Sullivan, with her usual pleasantness, replies:

- Like canned sardines, which is better than your mother!

The hologram man turns to her trying to restrain himself:

- Well, Miss Sullivan, there's still time to give up, especially you, since you weren't supposed to be on the team.

- If you want something done right, do it yourself!

- Or ask your banker – confirms River, another crew member tied to his totem.

The scientist's hologram turns to a tall, strong thirty-five years old man, with blond hair and moustache, blue eyes, the scar on his forehead half hidden by the helmet visor.

- Captain James O'Connor, sir, you who is leading this mission, would you agree with the gentleman and the lady?

He casts a half-reprehensible, half-supportive look at both:

- We're poor, but we're a team.

The hologram continues rotating to speak to everyone:

- Last recap before the launch countdown. Your mission is not to let San José sink. For this reason, you will be transported to the 7th of June, 1708 directly into the expedition ship of Captain Charles Wager. You are already disguised as that period's marines or as the sailors working on the vessels then. Try to talk like them, try to blend in as much as possible. Try to influence both the captain and his second men in command. Be careful not to be discovered and arrested, or killed. Once the San Jose is sighted, prevent the English fleet from starting firing on it. We believe that without a war, the docking of the ship and the overtaking of the San José crew will be more successful. At the end of the rendition, you must trigger your electromagnetic belt and make your teleporter return to its normal size. Put on your helmets and set the date for ten days from now. But remember, the return will only be activated here at the HQ if we receive at least five belts' signals in all. Less than five, you won't be able to come back.

A woman with very white skin, short red hair and freckles on her face, looking about thirty-four years old, raises her arm in a question sign:

- Yes, Miss White?

- What if... we fail with this mission and the ship actually sinks?

The hologram answer is interrupted by the beginning of the thickening of the yellow beam of laser beam passing through the middle of the room, accompanied by the intermittent sound resembling the beating of a hammer on a nail:

- If so, Kendall – replies the hologram – you will have to find the supposed map made by Captain Sabogal with the site of the galleon's sinking, which will be more difficult for everyone. Our spy warned us that the Spanish team has already left, so we don't have time to waste.

- Let's not fail, dear – Emmett says in a sarcastic tone.

- We have to work with all the options – ponders Kendall

The yellow beam, which was straight up till then, begins to ripple in a zigzag. The hologram gradually goes out:

- Silicon and lead particles are starting to shock more intensely. God bless you all and come back safe and sound!

The scientist disappears. The panel on one of the walls shows a date: 07-June-1708 and another shows a digital dial counting down from 60. The hammering noise starts to increase in volume and intensity while the lights in the launch room turn off. The wall panel lights flash faster. The yellow beam wave in the center of the room, going up and down in S-shape, increases the frequency, going from one end to another. The room starts shaking, making everyone very nervous.

Sergeant Birdie Jones looks at her neighbor, that African-descendent military man who stood next to her in the meeting room, who gives her a reassuring look. The room trembles more and more, the sound of hammering becomes unbearable. The time display shows ten seconds... nine... eight... A blue and red light starts to form in the middle of the room, surrounded by the sine wave in S shape, which is more intense and faster than before. Small sparkles of various colors start to appear in the air.... Seven... six... five...

The accelerator is at its maximum capacity. Tons of energy come from one end of the tunnel on the right and collide with the energy coming from the tunnel on the left, concentrating in the room where the nine crew members are standing, agonizing with shortness of breath due to the pressure they feel in their chest. River shouts:

- Help! Get me out of here! The pain is unbearable!

The reddish-blue flash takes over the entire room. The steel ceiling starts to open from side to side, revealing the typical cloudy night sky of the British Island. Four... three... two... one...

- Arrrrgggghh! – screams River – my head will explode!

The flash mixes with the high-frequency wave and explodes into a ball of light, forming an energy cyclone. The crew's bodies start disintegrating. One... zero! The spiral energy maelstrom is brutally thrown upwards, forming a vertical spiral-shaped beam. It pierces the sky and, in a matter of milliseconds, surpasses the gravitational layer of planet Earth set to outer space, leaving a trail of reddish blue sparkles in its wake.

From a nearby armored room, General Walsh accompanies everything through a monitor that shows the interior of TRON launch room.

- May God save the Queen... and save all of you too!

ISLA GRANDE, ROSARIO ARCHIPELAGO, COLOMBIA - YEAR: 1708

The darkness of the new moon night is broken by a spiral of orange-blue laser beams that descends from the sky, leaving a tunnel-shaped illuminated trail. Upon reaching the ground, it explodes into a ball of light that radiates from the center to the sides, in circles. The Columbus capsule appears, pushing away all the coconut-filled rainforest around it with a wind wave. Some maritacas fly away scared, making noise.

Within the capsule, the circulation of laser beams gradually decreases, letting the shape of its crew members reappear. They are all dizzy motion-sick, with headaches, and gradually become aware of where they are and what has happened.

Lorenzo looks at his wristwatch: 11:25:31 a.m.

- I think my watch stopped: only a tenth of a second has gone by?

Luna explains, beginning to unbuckle her seat belts:

- It actually took a long time for travelling at the speed of light.

The other crew members also begin to unbuckle their belts and remove their helmets. The internal lighting is stabilized, the propulsion sound has ceased. Paloma tries to get up from her chair, but sits back down, dizzy. Thomas takes her hand and helps her, getting a smile in thanks. Pablo gets up and runs to a corner to throw up in a sickness bag. Everyone's a little off, not knowing what to do, so Lorenzo goes to the ship door and starts opening it from the inside. The door opens and he jumps on the floor of the island, about half a yard down. After a quick look around, he helps the others get out in one by one. When the eight of them are on the ground, they start checking where they are. Although the moonlight is weak, the lack of pollution makes the sky all starry, showing even white clouds of nebulae and galaxies. The tunnel formed by orange-blue laser beams continues to rotate, in a spiral, coming from the infinite sky to the top of the parked ship, forming a space cybernetic show.

Diego goes back inside and brings out a flashlight, and starts to sweep the surroundings. Tropical palm trees, ferns, flowers buds, the sound of the sea nearby. The others follow him a few steps and, when they turn to illuminate behind the oval ship, they realize it has landed on some rocks on the edge of a large mountain. They look up and discover its top emits orange-red light and releases a roll of gray smoke.

- Is that what I think it is? – asks Isabel

Luna quickly takes off a tablet she carries in her uniform pocket. She opens a map on the screen and everyone gathers around it. Diego and Soledad continue looking around them from time to time.

- This map of Isla Grande here shows no volcano.

- Did we end up in the wrong island? – asks Isabel

- No, the navigator doesn't err.

- So, could it be that, geography in these times is different from that we know in the present?

- Yes, Isabel – replies Thomas – it is possible, because the data were recorded by sailors, pirates, old cartographers, who did not always portray reality due to scarce technology resources.

- Well... then... – adds Pablo, walking a little behind – we have yet one more reason not to take too long. This baby here looks like he's waking up.

The volcano emits a low loud roaring sound. Soledad asks Lorenzo, as he is the expedition leader:

- Our next orders, sir?

- Luna, checks the map, how do we get to the fleet's interception point?

She checks the tablet once more, swiping the screen with her finger and says:

- On the other side of the island is the Orika village, there we must rent a boat that'll take us to where the ship is anchored.

- Rent? Do they accept euros? – asks Pablo, taking some out of his pocket.

- I do not believe you brought euros in your pocket – Paloma comments.

- A banker without money is like a fisherman without a rod on a fishing boat.

- This century's currency is *real, pesos, pesetas,* and *ducados,* there's some in the luggage – explains Luna.

- Are there people living here? – asks Paloma

- It is a small settlement made by African slaves who escaped from Cartagena's slavery.

- Let's! – she starts, pulling Pablo along.

- Wait! We have to change clothes not to draw attention - Lorenzo reminds them

- True, to the ship. Ladies first!

The four women go inside, open a box at the end of the ship and get 18th-century Spanish military uniforms: white long- and puff-sleeved shirt, tight beige pants and vest, and blue long-tailed jacket. Not to mention the blue hat, beige-trimmed edges folded up. High boots into where the pants or white socks are tucked complete the look. They find it impossible not to laugh at one another. Soon after, they go out and it is the turn of the men, who, in addition to the uniforms, wear ordinary people and servile sailors clothing. Luna fills a backpack with basic survival and exploration equipment, and concentrated food. Pablo hides a grenade in his coat pocket without anyone else realizing it.

As they all left dressed, Luna, with her pack on her back, reminds them:

- We have to behave like crew 18th-century crew members ships. There were defined positions and hierarchy to obey: captain, ship's master, attendants, cannon handlers, cook, pilot as well as other civilian employees, not to mention military positions. Also do not forget that the language of this century has different words than our time's, so try to speak as little as possible.

- In addition, - Lorenzo reminds them – the women have to pretend to be men.

Paloma mimics "packing her balls" and walks away like a man. Thomas criticizes:

- You look more like a monkey than a man.

- Orangutans and men walk very alike – defends Isabel.

- Guys, it's good you're in a good mood – Lorenzo recalls – but we have a very dangerous mission ahead of us. And we must be back here in four days at most. Let's go?

Pablo walks out in front. Luna calls him back:

- It's this way, Pablo.

In the darkness of the night, they begin the march through the woods, in a line. Diego, armed with a musket, goes ahead, guided by Luna and her tablet. Covering the rear, Soledad, attentive and armed with a rifle, looks all around. The forest is dense, full of vines, fallen branches and stones on the way.

Paloma, fascinated by the vegetation, enjoys everything around. After about twenty minutes walking, a small light catches her eye to the right. Overtaken by curiosity, she does not realize that she leaves the line to move towards the light, which gets stronger as she approaches. Making way through some intertwined foliage, she is met by a stunning sight: a lake emits phosphorescent light. She crouches and runs her hand thought the water surface, producing a phosphorescent trail towards the middle of the lake. She plunges her hand into the water again, making waves of lemon-yellow plankton.

Suddenly, a large snake appears from the bottom and lunges towards her. She barely has time to scream when she feels a hand on her shoulder, pulling her back just microseconds away from being bitten by the large open mouth and sharp teeth. Soledad fires a sharp shot into the anaconda's head, which falls dead back into the pond and disappears.

- Don't walk away from the group! – Soledad says harshly.

- But... it was so... fascinating... – says Paloma, almost breathless.

Attracted by the shot, the other companions approach the pond.

- This must be the Enchanted Lagoon - explains Luna.

- Enchanted and dangerous – Soledad amends.

- In our time, it's seen by so many tourists, there are no longer so many wild animals on the island, but today, beware – Luna continues.

They all go back to the woods and, before long, find a machete-open trail. Even at night the heat is very strong. They walk very carefully, until they arrive at a small village, with dry-straw-ceilinged wooden huts, along a street that gives access to a wooden platform which extends over the sea, like a pier. There are few lit torches, transpiring that, due the advanced hour, there seems to be no one awake. They walk in silence, towards the pier, to which some boats and canoes are tied with ropes.

Isabel whispers to Lorenzo:

- We're not going to be able to rent anything at this hour.

- I hear you... So let's steal one.

- Steal?

- We don't have time to waste.

- I've never stolen anything in my life.

- Neither have I, but there's no other way. Let's go.

He signals to the others to start walking on to the wooden platform. All of a sudden, out of nowhere, dozens of very dark-skinned men appear, wearing few clothes, and wielding wooden clubs and sharp metal machetes. The moonlight intensifies, and they can see anger in their eyes. The group is not sure what to do. The marines point the muskets at them. Lorenzo tries to regain command:

- We... friends.

No one answers. Lorenzo points at himself again to one of the men who is at the head of the group, and is probably the leader:

- I... friend.

The black man replies:

- *Ungubani*?

- What? – asks Pablo, taking a step forward.

The man shows him the machete, making him stop.

- *Wama*!

- What language are they speaking? – asks Lorenzo

- Ancient Zulu – Luna replies, reading on her tablet

- Can you translate it?

- I'll try, the battery is running low – she touches some commands and asks Lorenzo to talk near the microphone.

- I... friend - he repeats, indicating himself.

"*Mina mngani*" says the tablet.

The natives are frightened to hear a voice coming out of the strange device in her hand. They point the machete more aggressively yet.

- Mina mngani - repeats Lorenzo

- *Cha mngani* – says the leading man, showing the soldier's clothing that Lorenzo is wearing.

"You not friend" - comes out of the tablet.

- I'm not a soldier – he speaks into the microphone.

- "*Angisona isosha*" translates the device.

- *Kungani ugkoke kanjalo*? – asks the leader.

"Why are you dressed like this?" – repeats the device.

Pablo loses his temper:

- Oh, this guy's dumb, let's not waste time explaining, let's go!

"*Uisymungulu*" translates the tablet.

The man glares at him. They all lift the clubs and machetes.

- Ihhh... We're fucked! - says Pablo.

"*Ihhh... ujijile*" - repeats the tablet.

- Turn that shit off!

"*Ugunkcola*" releases the tablet.

Thinking he was cursing them, the natives get even angrier, going up to Pablo, who, terrified, hides behind Diego who is still pointing his gun. Isabel tries to fix it. She takes some coins out of the coat and show the group:

- We... Want... A boat, please.

"*Sifuna... Isikhebe... ngiyacela*" - says the translator-tablet.

The leader, club still raised ready to strike, stares at her hand. She repeats herself:

- *Sifuna isikhebe ngiyacela.*

The man takes the coins and clears the way for them to pass. One of them signals with his head for them to follow him. In silence, tension still in the air, the eight of them follow the man to the top of the platform. There they see a medium-sized boat with six oars. Thomas is the first to jump in, helping the others get on the boat. They take the oars and paddle away from the pier, the African former-slaves still looking suspiciously after them. The darkness of the night begins to lessen, a sign that the sun is about to rise.

- Quick, we need to get to the ship before the light betrays us – warns Lorenzo.

- If we hadn't wasted time with that bunch of... – Pablo looks at the tablet, now off – ... thugs.

- They are not thugs – Paloma corrects – but men who have been deceived on their homeland, brought to this place as slaves, mistreated and killed by the ambition of white men.

Diego, Lorenzo, Thomas and Soledad paddle very hardly, making the boat glide over the sea swiftly. The island gets further away, and the volcano lets out a strong roar, releasing a thicker cloud of smoke. The daylight intensifies, but after about ten minutes, they spot several caravels anchored in the middle of the sea. Two of them larger than the others.

Isabel exclaims:

- Look, a galleon!

- Is that San Joaquin? – asks Pablo.

- I don't know, they're totally alike – Luna replies.

- The professor told us to go aboard the San Joaquin, remember?

- I don't see any other ship – Lorenzo says – and it is dawning already... let's board this one.

They paddle even harder, Lorenzo taking over for Pablo. Gradually, the great galleon shows its majestic size. About 40 meters long and 10 meters high, with the wooden stern all carved in symmetrical images of small railings, and with panoramic glass windows. The statue of a saint stands out from the other three human figures, among flags of imperial Spain. Three masts hold three cloth sails, each: the latch mast, in front, the tallest main mast, in the middle, and the mizzen mast at the rear of the ship, which is higher than the front of the ship, giving the impression that the deck is tilted forward. The galleon is still, with the anchor stuck to the bottom of the sea.

They paddle more quietly, towards the front of the ship, a little lower than the rear, until they reach a rope ladder that leads from the rail on the left side to near the water, a ladder used for maintenance and repairs. Hoping no one on board sees them, Lorenzo is the first to climb the ladder. Close to the rail he takes a look to see if there is anyone on deck which, luckily, is empty, even though the sailors' routine on board begins at sunrise. He signals the others to come up and, one by one, they board on the front deck. As soon as everyone is aboard, they run to an entrance that gives access to the lower levels of the ship, where both the passengers' and the infantry officers' accommodations are located. Since they've been trained, they already know how to disguise themselves amongst the on-board jobs. They pass along the passengers' dormitories and, tired, look for a place to lie down. The hiding place they can find is near the gunpowder compartment, the only one where there was no one.

It is June 7, 1708, the day before the battle.

The dormitory is full of English infantry soldiers. Coats, hats, boots and other pieces men's clothing are hanging everywhere among the dozens of hammocks. The place is damp, dirty and, despite being only dawn, the heat is already stifling. Some soldiers are by the door of the basement on the second floor, finishing the night watch. The Expedition is anchored in a cove near Rosario Island along with its three companions: the Kingston, the Portland and the Vulture, all of which are high-speed ships of the strongest and most modern naval squadron of the 1700s-1800s.

Suddenly, in the Expedition basement, at a free-space corner, a small swirl of reddish blue light begins to form in the air, increasing its diameter, rotating at a faster speed, until it takes almost the entire compartment. Rats, scared, run into another room.

From the middle of the light swirl, human figures begin to take form, in a circle, standing, facing each other. A soldier, near the scene, wakes up in a start and watches as suddenly the light swirl expands and disappears, leaving behind nine people who have appeared out of nowhere. Terrified, thinking they were ghosts, the soldier flees to the deck.

Captain O'Connor is the first to regain consciousness:

- Guys... guys... are you all alright?

A few moans here, and grumbling there, little by little everyone wakes up. O'Connor follows military procedure and starts calling out the names:

- Sergeant Jones?

- Here! – she replies, raising her head, a little dizzy

- Alfie Taylor, the geologist?

A fat, short, brown-eyed guy, around 235 years old, answers:

- Here!

- Emmett Sullivan, support?

- I am much more than "support", dear – she replies, looking at herself in a small pocket mirror

- Laureen Montgomery, the archeologist?

A short, white-haired lady in her 60s, with gray eyes, answers:

- You remind me of my high school teacher, young man!

- Jackson Lee, the jungle survival expert?

A young Asian looking 35 years old, with his black hair almost shaved around the head, built like a jiu-jitsu fighter answers with a Chinese accent:

- Here!

- Marine Winston Brown?

- Here, sir! – says the 26 years old, strong, blue-eyed, dark skinned young man who attended the project recognition meeting, his hair cut military style.

- Kendall White, physician?

- I got here the same way you did, baby!

- Mmmmm... – River lets out with a hint of malice

- River Smith, support...

- ... financial support, specifically. Ouch, what a headache!

O'Connor unbuckles the belts that fasten him to the totem and presses a button on the side of the panel.

- Unbuckle belts and shrink the teleporter.

Everyone does what's asked, and by pressing the button, the human-shaped capsule shrinks and enters the electronic belt that each of them is wearing, disguised among the uniforms of English soldiers.

- Come on, quick, before someone finds us. Women, attach the fake moustaches, don't forget we're in the middle of a bunch of men who've been at high seas for months.

He addresses Birdie and Winston:

- I'm sorry, but you must put on those white-skinned masks you brought. We've come to a period years before the abolition of slavery in England and they cannot see people with dark skin color walking on deck. You too, Jack, there's no way an Asian is enlisted in Her Majesty's artillery this century.

Birdie, Winston and Jack take very adherent plastic masks and put them on, they're so perfect they look natural. Birdie says:

- You don't have to apologize, sir. We feel that the abolition is not fully respected by people even in the 21st century.

O'Connor warns:

- Today is the day before the fight with the Spanish fleet. Our mission is to make sure this doesn't happen.

- And how are we going to do this? – asks Emmett.

- I don't know yet, I count on a little bit of luck - replies the captain.

That soldier, who had fled scared when the light swirl exploded, reappears on the stairs, still in his sleeping underclothes, accompanied by two other ensigns wielding swords. He gets confused when he sees the seemingly normal people. O´Connor, in silence, makes a signal slightly for the others to follow him and begins to climb the stairs. It's a dramatic test for their disguises. He passes the three soldiers, who stare at them trying to remember if they have seen him before. In the end, they all climb to the top floor of the ship, where the cannons are and, yet up another flight of stairs, where the higher-ranked commanders' quarters are located and finally reach the deck, completely illuminated by the beautiful daylight.

Even at that time of the morning the deck is already hectic, with crew members and soldiers running from side to side, all very busy. The team members quickly seek to blend in, pulling ropes, hoisting sails, washing the floor, cleaning weapons and performing other activities preparing to lift anchor and set sail.

The Expedition is a long and agile frigate, fit for combat, measuring about 150 feet and carrying seventy cannons. At around 9:00 a.m., a soldier plays a trumpet, and everyone stops their tasks. At the rear (stern) of the ship, where the deck is higher, there is a wooden door with checkered windows, its frame ornamented with naval symbols. This door opens from the inside and out come two soldiers. After them, wearing a higher-ranking uniform, comes out a man in his thirties, with thin face, his long blond hair tied in a ponytail-style with a ribbon. He stops near the door's entrance, takes a look at how the day is and, exiting, stands next to the door, as if to guard the next man who comes out of it: a tall Englishman, with a potbelly, temperate countenance, white-skinned, but with rosy cheeks, wearing a red coat fastened with yellow trimmings on blue pants and white lacy ruffled shirt.

All other crew members around there stand respectfully, some holding the barrel of guns propped upright. The two soldiers climb the ladder overlooking the upper deck and receive a spyglass from an ensign there.

Everyone goes back to their activities. O'Connor, who is cleaning the floor with a mop, addresses a young soldier who is doing the same by his side:

- Hey, buddy.

The young man does not understand:

- Pardon, sir? – asks the boy, with a very strong English accent.

O'Connor repeats:

- Hey, buddy, how are you?

- What is "buddy"?

- Buddy? It means... friend, brother, partner.

The boy looks at him as if he had spoken in another language:

- Excuse me, your lordship an English gentleman, sir?

This time O'Connor doesn't understand:

- My... what?

- Could you kindly explain what is it you want to know, sir?

O'Connor recalls that the English language of the time is the Anglo-Saxon.

- Would your lordship do the kindness of informing me who are those noble lords who ascended to the upper deck?

The young man looks at who he is indicating and explains:

- The younger gentleman, with his hair tied, is Henry Every, captain-of-the-sea and the other gentleman is the great Commodore Sir Charles Wager, this fleet commander. All noble servants of Queen Anne of Great Britain.

- Henry Every? You said that's Captain Henry Every?

- Yes, that was what I said, sir.

- He was one of the greatest pirates in the Caribbean!

The word pirate startles some soldiers passing by. It scares the boy:

- Excuse me?

- No... I mean... gentlemen heroes...

- If I may, sir, I will continue my laboral activities.

The boy starts moping the floor again and walks away, suspicious. O'Connor tries to figure out how to get close to those officers. Meanwhile, there's chat on the high deck, Captain Henry still with the spyglass to his eye, looking for something. Sir Charles asks:

- Squad in sight?

- Nothing yet, your excellency.

- Will they come?

- They surely will, last night a local punt passed along, informing that *Tierra Firme* was anchored near Isla Grande.

- This network of information of yours is admirable, Sir Every!

- It does not cost cheap to the Queen's coffers, sir.

- Cost versus benefit, it is all about this.

- Wise words, Lord. Can we lift anchors and move on?

- What is the itinerary?

- With winds in our favor, we will sail towards the channel between Treasure Island and the mainland, where space is tighter for escape. We will lie in wait there.

The two of them approach the edge of the wooden deck guard. Charles stares into Captain Henry's eyes. After a few seconds, he asks:

- How do you feel, Captain?

- What do you mean, "how do I feel," sir?

- I have noticed your behavior these last few days, Captain, and I feel you have been a little disgruntled.

- Your Excellency is mistaken – Henry replies, looking away from him – I feel normal.

- I also have my information network, Captain Henry.

Henry thinks a little before answering:

- Well, sir, since you have noticed, yes, I have been a little worried.

- And... about what, specifically?

- About... the fact that... – he hesitates, not knowing if he can trust the Commodore.

- You can trust me like you trust your father.

- My father abandoned me when I was five, sir.

- Well... Then... like you trust your dear mother.

- Soon after that she left me in an orphanage to run asway with a sailor.

Charles pauses thinking how to approach:

- Childhood traumas revolve themselves by transferring the lack of affection to older fellow travelers, young man.

The chief officer of the ship appears and asks:

- Ready to go, Captain!

- Permission granted, officer! Send the signal to the other nautical ships.

- Yes, sir!

The chief officer descends the stairs and shouts:

- Raise sails!

The assistants that are up on the masts, including Jack, repeat in choir:

- Raise sails!

The thick ivory-colored canvases unfurl almost at the same time, making the boat swing a lot. The ship is splendid, at its full wind power. The chief officer shouts:

- Hoist anchors!

An attendant shouts to the operators on the lower deck:

- Hoist anchors!

The operators, including Lieutenant Wilson, whose white mask is starting to peel off due to the hellish heat, begin turning the large wooden pulley to pull the iron chain that holds the anchor. The boat begins to swing even more, as normal at the beginning of the journey.

However, when the second anchor is out of the water, a strong gust of wind inflates the sails with such momentum that this makes the Expedition start forward much faster than normal. On the deck, Commodore Charles loses his balance, is brutally thrown back and stumbles onto the stern wall, falling from a height of fifteen feet directly into the water. Captain Henry, unable to hold him, shouts:

- Man overboard! Man overboard!

Frightened, all the sailors are trying to see where the man is. Sir Charles knows how to swim but he cannot compete against the waves caused by the passage of the large ship and begins to drown. Floating, he passes along the right edge of the Expedition, under the sight of several soldiers who stare, not knowing what to do.

Driven by impulse, O'Connor takes off his coat and, without hesitation, jumps overboard. He swims along the side of the ship, through a lot of waves and foam, to where the Commodore is and holds him from behind, leaving his head out of the water. With a lot of effort, paddling with only one arm due to Charles' weight, he manages to approach the hull of the ship that is still sailing quickly forward.

Sergeant Jones, seeing the situation, throws a rope ladder into the water. O'Connor barely has time to hold it with his free hand, still trying to keep Charles with his head above water. With a lot of effort, he clings to the rope, when Birdie shouts to the other soldiers nearby:

- Come on! Pull!

A little clumsily, waiting for an order, eight strong men begin to pull the rope, hoisting O'Connor and the commodore upwards. When they reach the ship's guard, Birdie and the group pull them both into the deck. O'Connor, panting, crawls for a little distance. Kendall arrives, making way among the crowd gathered together to see the unconscious Commodore on the ground. Captain Henry arrives and watches. Kendall quickly begins a cardiac massage on the chest of the Commodore. Nothing. She alternates from mouth-to-mouth breathing to chest massaging, leaving everyone baffled by the procedure they had never seen.

After a few minutes and much effort from Kendall, commodore Charles coughs, spits a lot of seawater and regains consciousness. Captain Henry helps him get up. Still half-dizzy, with the uniform heavy with the water, Charles asks:

- Who jumped in the water?

Everyone makes way and lets O'Connor be seen, standing, panting and still dripping water. Charles approaches him:

- What is your name, good sir?

- O'Connor, sir. James O'Connor.

- I do not remember you well, sir. What is your rank?

He thinks a little, looks at Kendall and says what first comes to his mind:

- Second naval captain, sir!

- Very well, Mr. O'Connor, we have a hero here then!

- I have only done my duty, sir. But I would not have succeeded if she... I mean, if he had not provided first aid.

Commodore Wager looks at Kendall:

- And your lordship... I also do not remember you being in my previous squad... what is your name and rank?

Kendall makes her voice as low as she can:

- Hum... Hum... My name is White, aspiring maritime medicine officer, serving Her Majesty in Bristol, sir!

- Well, well... we have a physician on board, and we did not know! – he says, looking at Henry, who finds it strange to see that people on his ship.

As the journey had begun very hectically, Charles goes towards his cabin, but first turns to the two of them and says:

- In gratitude for what you have done for me, I invite your excellencies to dinner in my cabin tonight.

- I am very honored, sir – replies O'Connor, bowing.

- Nevertheless, milord - says Henry, a little jealous – we had our plans review scheduled for tonight, remember?

Charles stops, looks him in the eye and replies:

- He jumped in the water, Captain Every... You did not.

And goes to commodore room. O'Connor winks at Kendall and they both do back to their tasks, followed by Henry's jealous look. He goes to the helmsman to give instructions.

A bucket of water is thrown over Lorenzo, who sleeps heavily next to the others. Soon after, other buckets of water are thrown into the faces of the other seven companions, who are also sleeping on each other. Thomas gets up, not really remembering where he is:

- What the fuck...?

When he realizes that everyone is looking at him, he tries to disguise:

- *¡Mucha mierda!*

After a few seconds, there's general laughter. A gunner shouts:

- It's past waking time! Get to work!

Not really knowing where to go, they go towards the ladder that leads to the crew's dining room, which it is full of soldiers, gunners, handlers, assistants and other members of the hundred and three combatants who were on the ship, all under the command of Artillery Captain Diego Gil Delgado, in addition to the two hundred sailors and operational cabin boys.

When they enter the dining hall, the noise of the conversations gradually diminishes, because everyone is staring at them, not only because they look new onboard, but because their uniforms are dirty and different from what they should be wearing at that morning time. Luna, obviously, is the one attracting the most attention.

They pass by the table where breakfast is being served and the kitchen servants, half serious, half suspicious, put the ration of the day in dirty wooden dishes with signs of rats' gnawing. In silence, they sit at an empty table in the corner of the room and start eating, avoiding looking around.

After a little while, Captain Delgado appears in front of the table: black hair and moustache, dark brown eyes, smooth skin despite his forty-five years of sea work. Lorenzo looks at him and they stare at each other for a few minutes. Delgado breaks the silence, with a strong accent from Northern Spain:

- What be your nameth, soldier?

- Nameth?

- Your name – whispers Isabel.

- Lorenzo Garcia, at your command!

- What about your patent?

He looks again at Isabel, who translates softly:

- What's your rank in the naval infantry?

- Oh, yes... I am... First Sergeant, sir.

- Which armada?

- Cádiz.

- Where did you board the San José?

Lorenzo looks at Isabel, who looks at Paloma who looks at Luna. Lorenzo asks, suprised:

- Are we not in San Joaquin?

Isabel pokes him under the table, so he doesn't give them away. The situation gets more tense. He thinks for a while and replies:

- We boarded in Portobello, sir, along with the other passengers and crew.

The captain calls a young man in light clothes and a white cap, a cabin boy.

- Corporal, ask Mr. Diego Obregón, royal clerk and ship notary, to come here with his registered passengers 'book.

The young man leaves. Delgado looks at the other companions and asks:

- What about those, your comrades?

They get even more uncomfortable; Lorenzo is getting angry:

- Yes, my companions, why?

- I do not remember their enlistment in the infantry either. Especially the little one there – he points to Luna, who lowers her face not to be recognized.

- Maybe because it is too many people for you to keep in your memory.

- My memory does not fail, Sergeant... sergeant what, again?

Lorenzo gets up and faces the captain:

- Garcia, do I need to repeat?

At this moment the notary arrives, he is short, bald, wears thick-lensed glasses, and is carrying a large hardcover book.

- Did you call, sir?

Captain Delgado asks him, looking ironically at Lorenzo:

- Don Diego, check if there's any Lorenzo Garcia, first sergeant from Cádiz, on board. My memory works, does it not?

The notary goes through several pages, following the list with his finger from top to bottom, face glued to the book due to myopia. After a few minutes, he finds nothing:

- No, sir, there's no one by that name in my book.

Paloma tries to come to her friend's aid:

- There may have been a failure in the registry...

This makes things worse, because she catches the attention of the captain, who approaches her (him):

- And this thin, delicate face... I would not forget! Are you not on the list either?

The captain raises his hand to touch her face, when Lorenzo, on impulse, picks up the trebuchet that is in the captain's holster, sets the trigger and points it at his face. Everyone's amazed by the gesture. Things get heavier.

- It's not our fault if your notary doesn't write down everything he should – Lorenzo says, seriously.

Five soldiers, who were at their posts, point muskets at Lorenzo in a sign of retaliation. If he shoots the captain, he gets shot. Diego and Soledad also raise their weapons toward them.

- Threatening a senior officer means death at the gallows – Delgado reminds him

- We are all mercenaries; we are not afraid of death – says Lorenzo

- Oh... I knew it! Mercenaries! And who recruited you?

At this point, the ship starts swinging, because upstairs, they hoist the sails, lift anchors, and start the departure towards the high-sea. Isabel looks around, distressed, looking for a solution to the situation that is getting out of control. She sees the tablet in Luna's purse and she has an idea. She shouts:

- Everybody stop!

She pulls the tablet out of Luna's purse, turns on and shows the screen, with pictures and text. They are amazed by the light-emitting device, without fire. She slides her finger through the app windows until she finds what she is looking for. She raises her arm and shows the famous painting of the Battle of San José painted by Samuel Scott. Half serious, half angry, she prophesies:

- Tomorrow, at this hour, you will all be dead!

Her female voice undoes her disguise. Lorenzo, desperate, asks:

- What're you doing?

One of the soldiers who stands near the stair's shouts:

- A witch! There's a witch on board!

And that's when the confusion gets out of hand. Everyone runs to the exit staircase. Dishes fly, pots drop to the ground, there's a lot of shouting and astonishment. Only the eight crew members of the capsule and Captain Delgado remain in the hall, he says, in a sarcastic tone:

- I see the party is going to grow: gallows and a fire pit.

Isabel rips off her false moustache, her hat and loosens her beautiful blonde hair. She is still holding the tablet in her hand:

- I'm not a witch!

- I see, by your beauty, that you bewitch men - Delgado flirts

Lorenzo presses the pistol barrel harder against his head:

- Watch what you say, Captain!

Thomas tries to help:

- Lorenzo, the situation is not going as planned, let's go?

His Spanish speak full of British accent betrays him, too.

- What? – Delgado widens his eyes – is there an Englishman on board?

In that moment, a group of armed soldiers begins to descend the stairs coming from the deck. In front of them, a fat, white-haired gentleman with hair receding on the side of his forehead, wearing uniform, but with a red liturgical band with golden Christian inscriptions around his neck, and falling over his chest, holds a golden cross on his hand. He stands at the foot of the stairs and looks frightened, without really understanding what he should do. Captain Delgado welcomes him:

- You're just in time, Don...

- ... Joseph Belmori, the chaplain-major – completes Isabel, looking at the tablet screen

The chaplain is even more frightened. Delgado tells her:

- Another divination, beautiful witch?

Lorenzo positions himself behind the captain, taking him hostage to protect himself from the attacks that may begin. Isabel replies:

- No... I'm looking at the passenger list that's here.

Paloma takes off her fake hat, mustache, and beard, revealing her real identity. She addresses Delgado, trying to find a way out of the situation:

- Sir, we need to speak urgently to Captain José Fernandez de Santillán.

Captain Delgado laughs ironically:

- Ha, ha, you want to talk to the Count of Casa Alegre? He only talks, at best, with top-ranking officers, not to mercenaries, even strangers like you – he shouts – guards, arrest these men... and women!

The guards advance, causing Lorenzo to bluff again:

- One more step and he dies!

The soldiers are undecided. Then, Melendo Suarez de Miranda, captain of the sea and third in the command on the ship, wearing uniform full of medals, short, wearing a brown wavy wig, around fifty years old, with tanned skin, appears at the foot of the stairs:

- You can go ahead, this boy will not do anything!

- Captain Melendo! - exclaims Delgado.

The guards slowly advance towards Lorenzo who, with some hesitation, gradually lowers the gun from the captain's face. He is grabbed by the soldiers, his hands held behind his back.

- What is happening here? – asks Don Melendo.

Captain Delgado answers, while arranging his vest and returning his pistol in the holster:

- I do not know it either, sir. These stowaways just came out of nowhere. There are two women...

Luna and Soledad reveal their identities as well.

- ... I mean, four women: this man claiming to be first sergeant in Cádiz and presenting the other as mercenaries. And worst of all: an Englishman among them – he points at Thomas, who doesn't know where to hide.

- "That is all"? – asks ironically, Melendo, walking and facing each of the eight young people – someone went up there on deck saying that someone down here showed a magic mirror and said we will all die tomorrow – he pauses and faces everyone again – who said that?

The soldiers point to Isabel, who, awkwardly, looks at everyone there judging her. She begins to feel sorry for them and, with her eyes full of tears, she stares at Captain Melendo and says:

- I did, sir, I let it slip away, I did not mean to.

Captain Melendo gives her a fatherly look:

- You remind me a lot of my daughter, young lady. But on what basis do you let slip such terrible affirmation?

- It is... that... well... – she looks at the other colleagues, looking for support in what she will say

- Is it by any chance you who will kill us all?

- No... I would never do that... it is that... we... - she has a nervous breakdown, crying a lot.

- We come from the future – declares Pablo.

Captain Melendo goes to him, staring him in the eye:

- What did you say, sir...?

Pablo reaches out to greet the old commander, a little taller than him:

- Pablo. Pablo Martinez, owner of Martinez Financial Bank.

The commander did not return the greeting, but asks:

- Are you from the family of Diogo Martinez, who received the coat of arms of the Queen of Spain in 1560?

- It could be... I was not born yet – he tries to joke.

- And how do you expect me to believe that you came from the future?

The room starts swinging more strongly due to the waves at high sea. They look at each other, thinking about how they could convince the others of something unthinkable in those years. Captain Melendo orders one of the soldiers:

- Guards! Escort this young woman and that young man – he points to Lorenzo – to the command room. The rest of them... – he takes pauses – take them to the ship's dungeon.

- No! – Pablo tries to escape.

The guards advance on the young group, who try to disentangle themselves. Diego and Soledad, better trained in combat, throw a few punches and take some soldiers out of the fight, but, as they are outnumbered by much, soon they are surrendered and all taken, by force, to the lower floor. Pablo, in the confusion, manages to escape without being noticed.

With their hands tied in their backs, Isabel and Lorenzo are led up the stairs until they reach the deck. The sun is shining on a beautiful cloudless day and the wind is blowing very hard, causing all the sails to inflate. They are at high-sea and, next to them, sail three other boats: the Galleon San Joaquín, the combat ship Santa Cruz (el Gobierno) and the hulk Santa Cruz de la Concepción, as well as four other smaller ships.

Despite the situation, Isabel is dazzled by everything she sees. Escorted by the two captains and the five soldiers, they are followed by the curious and frightened looks from the sailors, soldiers, and passengers who, stopping what they were doing, want to understand what is happening.

It is possible to see in the distance a little stretch of land with vegetation, since they are passing along the Rosario Peninsula, where the beautiful colored corals can be seen at the bottom of the crystal-clear waters that the boat cuts through, leaving behind a beautiful line of white foam.

The group arrives at the rear of the galleon, which has the highest walls, and which can be accessed by a high cedar staircase carved with marine sculptures. Instead of climbing to the second floor, the escort directs Isabel and Lorenzo into the cabin below this deck. They go down a flight of stairs and they are outside the captain's cabin. Captain Delgado knocks on the door and a servant, after few minutes, opens it from the inside.

- We ask permission to speak to His Lordship the Count of Casa Alegre.

The pageboy closes the door and, after few minutes, reopens it and signals them to enter. The interior room is richly decorated, looking more like a castle room than a cabin at high-sea. A large window in the background, overlooking the sea, is framed by red velvet curtains, tied with yellow strings in various parts. In front of this window, a large rectangular mahogany table all carved with plants, ivy, and fairies motifs. Several golden ornaments are on the table, drawing attention to a peacock tail writing feather.

Several golden-footed and -armed armchairs and patterned upholstery are scattered throughout the room, with a divin in the corner. A globe shows the ancient style world map, not portraying all countries and with the compass rose indicating the eight cardinal points which completes the baroque air of the environment. The flag of imperial Spain is stuck in a bracket next to the back window, the ceiling is decorated with a classic painting of cherubim in a garden, bordered by golden wooden support moldings. A crystal chandelier with lit candles hangs from the ceiling, which swings a lot due to the movement of the ship.

Isabel cannot hold her enchantment, speaking softly to Lorenzo:

- Wow! Just like the pirate movies we watch!

- The problem is that, this is not a movie...– laments Lorenzo

A hoarse voice comes from behind a bamboo screen illustrated with a bullfight:

- What's a... "movie"?

They look to where the voice comes from. From behind the screen comes a man of striking appearance: forty-seven years old, square face, glass-colored eyes, thin nose, thin lips and short golden hair, tied-up in a ponytail. He wears a green velvet robe with gold embroidery over the old-period undergarments. He looks coldly, directly, and bluntly to the two of them, who stay without reaction for some seconds. He is José Fernandez de Santillán, the Count of Casa Alegre.

Sitting in a high-backed mustard velvet armchair, a little further ahead, is another man with curly long dark brown hair, light brown eyes, with a somewhat big belly, pointy nose and hoarse voice, who, with a sharp look, observes the explanation. He is the first captain Don Alejandro César de Sabogal.

Lorenzo tries to explain:

- It's .... well... like... – he sees a candlestick with a solitary candle on the counter next to it, picks it up and makes movements with his fingers, projecting shadows of birds, butterfly, and other animals onto the side wall of the cabin – this! This is like a movie!

The insightful and direct José Fernandes de Santillán replies:

- Moving images projected on the wall?

- Exact!

- Is this the witchcraft you told me about?

- No, it's pure Optical Physics.

- I don't know that word, is it magic?

- Science.

Santillán approaches Lorenzo, always looking deeply into his eye:

- Science and magic are very close. Where are you from?

- From Cádiz, sir.

- What about you, lady?

- I am also from there, milord – says Isabel, looking away.

The disgusting Alejandro rises from his armchair, crosses the room, and, with a finger of his hand, lifts her chin. She takes her chin off his fingers, looking defiant.

- You don't look like a witch, but you have the audacity of one.

- This is harassment, sir – she says.

- Harass... what?

- Ha-rass-ment – repeats Isabel.

- Are you going to explain to me that it's also an image projection?

- No – Lorenzo interrupts – it's when a man touches a woman without her allowance

- I have lived in Cádiz and things are not like that there. Women ask to be touched.

- Times have changed, sir – says Lorenzo.

Sabogal gets a little more nervous:

- You realize that he can touch your bodies as much as he wants? To the point of having your cut your heads off?

They realize they have to back off. Lorenzo explains:

- We have done nothing against this fleet, Captain, we serve the same king.

Santillán returns to his desk and sits in the high-backed red velvet armchair with golden edges. Behind him, sunlight shines over the transparent waters of the Caribbean. The ship seems to be slowing down. He puts both feet on the table, revealing long navy-blue leather boots.

- Serious accusations have been made against you. You are stowaways. You have threatened us all with death. You have showed a mirror of witchcraft. And even worse – he pauses – there's an Englishman, our enemy, with you. And now you say you serve Philip V? – one more pause and he asks – What is your purpose here?

Lorenzo looks at Isabel, who nods as a sign that the time for revelation has come. He says:

- Look, everything we are going to say, you are surely not going to believe it.

- You can try...

- We came from the future.

Santillán, Captain Sabogal and the others exchange looks. Sabogal asks in a kind of ironic tone:

- Indeed? And from what year are you?

- 2021

- Will the world go this far?

- We hope it will go further, sir.

The ironic tone increases a little more:

- And why have you chosen precisely our ship to visit after three hundred and thirteen years?

Isabel takes courage and says:

- To avoid a tragedy, sir.

The two secondary captains look at each other, worried. Isabel continues:

- The English squadron is waiting for you to attack the entire Tierra Firme fleet tomorrow and this galleon will sink. Only eleven people will survive.

The discomfort increases among the captains, but Santillán remains indifferent, holding the writing feather:

- Will I be among these eleven?

Isabel hesitates to speak. Lorenzo takes the lead:

- No, sir, I'm sorry. All the books, records and annals of the Hispanic navy history show tomorrow as being the date of your death.

They hear a knock at the door. Captain Delgado opens and the helmsman appears:

- Excellence! We're going to have to lower anchors again.

- Again? Why is that? – Delgado asks

- Because El Gobierno Santa Cruz and the merchant Rey David were left behind.

- Vega Florida, instead of hanging out with us to protect us, is falling behind. Where are we now?

- Near the Islas de San Bernardo, sir.

- When we get close, lower anchors. We will stay there overnight to wait for the smaller ships to catch up with us.

- Yes, Captain!

The officer goes out and closes the door.

- This delay will be fatal, Captain... – warns Lorenzo.

- For it will give time for the English to mount the ambush – completes Isabel.

- You should swerve and sail to Cartagena to protect yourselves.

Sabogal takes the dagger-shaped letter opener and asks:

- I like enigmas… how can you prove that?

- With this.

Isabel takes the tablet, but its battery is over. She doesn't know what to do.

- Well... it is unloaded...

- It seems that your magical mirror is over – Sabogal makes fun of her.

- You wouldn't understand.

Angry, Sabogal flings the letter opener toward her, which hits the tablet, causing her to drop it. The little dagger sticks into the cabin wall, right behind where she is. Isabel gets really scared. Sabogal gets up, takes a sword and goes towards them. Lorenzo puts himself in front of Isabel to defend her. Sabogal puts the tip of the sword against Lorenzo's chest and says:

- Villanueva did warn me not to listen to traitorous spies. You have come to spread fear and to delay our mission, as have many other cowards! You do not understand we are in a hurry. Spain is running out of money to keep our war to which privateers like you have revolted against the succession of Don Felipe. My promotion depends on it! But I'm not afraid! Let the English, Roman, French come, I have the courage and the ability to face them! Or mislead them!

Santillán confirms Sabogal, saying:

- ¡La mar era ancha, diversos sus rumbos!

Sabogal lowers his sword and orders the captains:

- Throw them in the dungeon along with the other traitors! And tomorrow, throw them in the sea.

Isabel has time to duck and pick up the tablet while the guards push them out. When they go out to the deck, there is a large group of people who, listening to the conversation from within, began to shout and raise their hands with guns and swords:

- Death to traitors!
- Witch!
- Spies from hell!
- Throw them overboard!

Escorted by the soldiers, with a lot of pushing about, they cross through the mob of angry people. During their walk, they can see the vegetation of two nearby islands, while the San Joaquín, which is where they were supposed to be, sails nearby. The afternoon is about to end and the sun is down, close to the horizon line, reflecting its last orange rays.

Pushed and cursed, they go down three flights of stairs, until they find the prison cage in the basement, a suffocating, dirty place with little light, rats walking everywhere amid an unbreathable smell. They pass through several cells, where some dirty, bearded men are thrown in the middle of scraps of food. They arrive at the last cell, with dark iron bars, of larger size, where are Luna, Diego, Paloma, Thomas, and Soledad. The soldiers open the doors and push the two of them inside, then locking it with a big rusty padlock.

Paloma and Isabel embrace each other, crying:

- I thought I'd never see you again!

- I thought I would never meet you again either!

Thomas complains:

- Nothing went as planned!

- What's next? – asks Thomas – what are we going to do?

- Locked here, we will die along with everyone – concludes Soledad

Isabel notices someone's missing:

- Where's Pablo?

- We don't know, in that mess he managed to escape – Luna replies.

After a short silence, everyone looks at Lorenzo demanding a position. He says:

- We'll find a way out. But as Professor Perez warned us... we can't change the past.

Sneaking, looking all around, Pablo goes down a staircase that leads to the ship's third lower deck. Coming from above, voices of drunken sailors, music and noise of furniture being dragged are heard as a backdrop. He holds a candle in his hands due to low lighting in that part of the ship.

He arrives at the floor of the third deck and sees that there is a very large, empty space, no cannons, no people. Only wooden columns supporting the ceiling, amid combat material such as swords, shotguns, and muskets. Looking at the walls, he sees that there are some lanterns hanging and lights them with the flame of the candle he holds. When the lighting increases in the room, he opens a wide smile of fascination with what he sees at the bottom of that compartment.

From floor to ceiling, at the back of the room, hundreds of wooden chests are piled on top of each other, some open and revealing that they are crammed with coins. Pablo approaches them and sees that they are silver and gold pesos, some coined with the figure of Spanish kings and others, with the figure of Castelldosrius, the Peru viceroy. He dips his hand in that coin pool, take one of them and bites it, proving it is pure gold.

He looks back to see if there's anyone there, and with a small knife that's nearby, he opens another chest, which isn't locked. Stunning vision: it is packed with shiny emerald stones, of all sizes and shapes, some in raw state. It picks up an emerald about fifteen centimeters in diameter, whose reflection of the candle flame emits light green rays throughout the room, like a crystal spectrum. Pablo is fascinated.

He kneels over to another chest and, opening it, loses his breath: it is so crammed, white and black pearls fall and roll across the floor, leaving some necklaces hanging from its edge. He quickly picks them all up and puts them back, closing the lid of the chest. When opening another, more silver and gold coins, mixed with necklaces of pearls, rubies, emeralds, and sapphires.

Illuminating the back of the room, between the chests, he notices small sculptures of pure gold in the shape of gods, birds, suns, indigenous people and other handicrafts typical of Inca and Mayan culture.

When Pablo thinks he's seen it all, he turns to leave, but on the other side of the deck, further down, another pile of objects catches his eye. He walks to the two lanterns near the sides and lights them.

- Holy shet!

From one side of the ship to the other and piled up to the ceiling, gold bars, on top of each other, rest there, asking to be touched. Many, many gold bars the size of a building brick, so many that he could not count. Pablo approaches that pile, the back of which cannot be measured by local lighting. He takes a bar and feels the weight: "it must weigh about 45 pounds," he thinks.

In fact, there are two piles of bars, one leaning against the right wall and the other against the left one, separated by a small corridor where only one person fit. Pablo enters this corridor, trying to balance himself due to the swing of the moving ship and feels inside a gold catacomb. After walking about ten steps, he sees that he has not yet reached the back, he looks up and sees the pile of gold bars up to the wooden ceiling upstairs; he looks behind himself, another pile, this time of silver bars, also pile up to the ceiling. "Potosi silver," he recalls the explanation at the Technical Center. He tries to illuminate the end of that narrow corridor, but the light doesn't let him see how far it goes, it seems endless.

Astonished, he runs his hand on the pile of cold bars and speaks softly to himself

- It's worth more than twenty billion... I must find a way to get all this to my bank... but how?

At this point, he hears voices of people who must be close to the descent from the upper floor. Very quickly, he comes out of the ingots corridor, puts out the lanterns from that part of the room, runs to the other side and puts out the lanterns on the side of the room. Three soldiers are walking down the stairs, chatting excitedly to each other. Seeing that there is nowhere to hide on the treasure deck, Pablo goes down the stairs leading to the galleon's fourth deck, quietly. The guards come to the treasure deck and feel there was something strange there, but, doing a little inspection, they find nothing.

In the fourth deck, which is completely empty, damp, and dark, Pablo hides behind a furniture that is next to the stairs, crouched. He waits for the voices of the soldiers in the compartment above to decrease, which does not occur in a short time. Tired, discouraged and hungry, he considers sleeping right there for the night, despite the strong heat, muffling and the smell of sulfur. He gropes his pants pockets looking for matches to light the stump of the candle he still has, to see if there's a more comfortable place to take shelter. He lights the wick of the candle stump and sees where it is: in the galleon's ammunition storage!

Tons of gunpowder are stowed into hundreds of wooden barrels, arranged side by side in piles that go up to the wooden ceiling. Cannonballs, bomb fuses, pistol and musket ammunition, paper and hay to fill the cannons and other war artifacts fill the entire compartment, with almost no room left for anything else. Scared, Pablo looks at the "furniture" against which he is leaning and sees a symbol of a skull and crossed bones. He illuminates up to its top and realizes that it is a large wooden barrel with capacity for 1.100 pounds of gunpowder, with a tap valve for the loading of smaller barrels, reminiscent of a wine barrel.

Desperate, he puts out the candle and tries to stay as quiet as possible, sweating tons and trying to get rid of the rats that, from time to time, pass over his legs.

Fear begins to take over his soul.

The night descends serenely over the Caribbean Sea, calm and indifferent on the eve of the battle. A gentle breeze hits the sails of the Expedition, but its anchors keep it stationary. Its silhouette and those of the other three ships can be seen by the faint lights of the few lit lanterns, in preparation for the ambush of the Spanish.

The English team is gathered near the front mast, talking in low tones not to draw the attention of the other crewmen.

O'Connor is the first to speak:

- How was your day?

Emmett shows her left hand and complains:

- I broke three nails washing the filthy floor.

- I prepared the fish and sauce for lunch – says Jack

- But I was the one who caught the fish – explains Laureen

- I spent the day cleaning guns – comments Birdie

- And, I, cannons – completes Winston

- I cleaned the toilets... Ewww! – explains Alfie

All that's left is for River to explain what he's been up to all day. Everybody looks at him.

- Well... I... I tested the resistance of the dorm cots.

- And what's the result? – asks Kendall

- Very, very resistant. I'd buy one.

- Shame on you, River... – Emmett reproaches him.

Everyone thinks she's reproaching River for killing time, but she adds...

- ... for not calling me to test them along with you. You left me here in this maid's life. Ugh!

Birdie addresses O'Connor:

- What's the plan, Captain?

He checks that there's no one around and speaks lower:

- Here it goes: Kendall and I are having dinner tonight at Captain Wager's cabin. We'll try to dissuade him from attacking the San José tomorrow. We'll try to convince him to just board the ship without firing the cannons.

- What if he doesn't go for it? – asks Alfie.

- Then we try plan B: during battle, should it happen, we will escape in a boat that is tied to the end of the ship. We flee to Cartagena and wait to see if Captain Sabogal really survives, we follow him and see where he will hide the map of the wreckage.

- I understand peanuts about sea survival – declares Emmett

- Here are the instructions for what each one should do during the battle tomorrow – proceeds O'Connor, turning to each in turn as he speaks – Emmett and River, you stand guard at the stern of the ship, and be careful that no one notices or takes our boat.

Emmett and River look at each other, an imperceptible smile forming on their thin lips.

- Alfie, you climb the main mast and stand watch for the approaching of the Spanish galleons. You, Birdie and Winston, go to the cannon floor and surreptitiously delay the reloading of their ammo. You, Kendall and Laureen, stay prompt to rescue the wounded in combat. Lee, I'm counting on you to defend the civilians here in case of a sword fight breaks.

A strong sense of fear and anxiety in the face of danger takes hold of everyone. O'Connor tries to inject some confidence:

- Comrades, tomorrow will be a day of great danger for all of us. Cannon wars aren't an easy feat. A single projectile destroys a large piece of a ship. Protect yourselves as better as you can; I'm counting on the other soldiers being distracted by the battle, focused on attacking the enemy, to not notice anything we're doing. If we can convince the captain tonight, so much the better.

Laureen recalls History:

- According to History, there will be a small exchange of bullets between the Expedition and the San José. In the late afternoon, the Expedition will try to approach the galleon and pillage it. The more violent battle will take place on the next day, because El Gobierno, the guarding warship of the fleet, is the one who will open fire against the Expedition, although it will be defeated and towed to England.

- So we have to get out of this hell right after whatever happens to the San José – concludes Birdie.

- Exactly – agrees O'Connor – which means running away in the boat early in the night, without anyone noticing. However, if the San José does not sink, it will mean that the English ship has won the battle and will probably return home with the fortune to the coffers of England.

- Now you said a friendly word: "fortune" – remembers River.

They disguise their conversation a little, while guards are passing by them towards the dormitories. O´Connor gives them a last guidance:

- Anyways, in case of extreme need – he points at the time-travel's transmission belt under his uniform – do not hesitate to press the panic button for immediate return to the laboratory.

A disheveled cabin boy appears behind the group as if looking for someone and, identifying O'Connor, comes to announce:

- Are you Captain O'Connor?

- Yes.

- The illustrious Captain Wager is calling you for dinner, sir. Please, come with me.

He looks at Kendall, and gets a "good luck" look from the others. They all head to the dirty, stuffy basement where the crew's bunk beds are, while Kendall and O'Connor follow the young man through the deck full of ropes, cloths, buckets, and other objects typical of that time's ships.

They arrive at the entrance to the captain's cabin, at the bow of the frigate, where a soldier awaits them, holding an iron bowl and a jar full of water. O'Connor doesn't understand the scene, and looks at Kendall, who extends her hands over the bowl. The soldier pours water for her to wash them and she is soon followed by the captain. The same soldier sprays flower-scented water on them to disguise the strong smell of the galleys.

Another soldier leads them down a short staircase, leading to the compartment where the upper-ranking office and dormitory is. He opens a heavy wooden door with sandblasted glass fittings and, taking the lead of them, announces their arrival with pomp and circumstance, which sounds ill-suited to such an environment:

- Second Captain O'Connor and Dr. White!

They enter a not very luxurious but comfortable environment: from the not too high ceiling, a crystal chandelier with lit candles hangs over a rectangular table where there are various dishes with roasted birds, fruits, corn flour and other spices. The British Empire flag is next to a picture depicting Queen Anne, while rustic wooden shelves show miniature ships, crosses, marine animals and other ornament objects. On one of the shelves, golden-covered books are in a pile.

A worktable with an ancient globe is further to the right, sided by the sculptures of two seated setter dogs. To complete the decoration, further along in the room, there is a double bed with columns at its four corners, which support a yellowish tulle mosquito net.

Sitting at one end of the food table, illuminated with silver candlesticks, is Captain Wager and, on his right, is Captain Henry. The servants are standing, awaiting instructions to serve dinner.

The night is cool, and the ship swings a little, making the wine wobble in the glasses that are already filled. O'Connor and Kendall are a little hesitant to move forward when Captain Wager invites them:

- A little late for British, gentlemen.

- Beg your pardon, sir, without any clocks, we lost track of time – explains O'Connor

- You do not own a clock?

- No, milord.

- Come closer, young man, and show me your hand.

They approach the chair where he is sitting. Commodore Wager takes a gold watch out of his pocket, which is fastened by a gold chain. He releases the chain clip, puts the watch in O'Connor's hand and closes it:

- A little retribution for what you have done today, young man!

O'Connor opens his hand and sees that it is a gold watch, rich in engravings, with rubies as hour markers, another ruby ornamenting its wind-up pin. On the back of the lid, in a beautiful calligraphy, the initials CW are engraved.

- Sir, I cannot accept this... I have but fulfilled my obligation and...

- ... I know, I know, however keep it as a souvenir of our journey!

O'Connor, felling awkward, puts the watch in his pocket. Henry can't disguise the jealousy on his face. Kendall deepens her voice to disguise it:

- We are honored by your invitation, your lordship.

- I am the one who is honored to be able to eat with such brave people! Do sit down, dinner shall be served. Would you please accept wine?

- I thank you, sir, but we do not drink while on duty – O'Connor automatically justifies.

- Now, Captain – Henry mocks – we do not have to be fanatics!

- But we do need to be prudent, sir – defends O'Connor.

- Prudence is a virtue we no longer see in young officers – Wager laments, while filling a glass with wine – they are intrepid, distracted, and easy prey for the enemy.

Kendall takes his cue:

- Speaking of the enemy... Do you believe the Spanish will show up tomorrow, sir?

At that point, somebody knocks on the door. A servant opens it and a soldier appears, enters reverently and places himself in front of the table, addressing Captain Henry:

- You may talk, Lieutenant Cooper.

- Message from Captain Bridges, sir!

He delivers a closed note to Captain Henry, who opens it and reads it aloud:

- "A small punt docked today in Kingston to report that the Tierra Firme Fleet is anchored near the Isla de San Bernardo on the Coral Peninsula. They plan to continue their journey towards Havana tomorrow morning. We await instructions to prepare for combat. Sincerely, Captain Bridges."

- Thank you very much, Lieutenant, you can retire.

The soldier bows in reverence and leaves. Henry addresses Kendall:

- Has this answered your question?

- All information can be flawed.

- The information comes from those colonized by Spain - continues Henry

- Why would they be against their own Crown?

Wager intervenes:

- That is the point, Officer White. The colonies can no longer stand the exploratory model adopted by the Iberians. They only take away their wealth, with very low returns for the local population. Especially now, Philip V being French, what interest does he have in advancing the Spanish colonies? The Bourbons only play political interests for the purpose of enriching their family and sustaining the luxury and *ostentatius* of Versailles.

- Is there, indeed, a public management model which is not exploratory? – asks Kendall

- I don't know that word... "management"?

- Command, organization, coordination, are synonymous.

- You talk a little progressively for our times, officer – Henry says suspicious.

- Very well – Wager continues – look at the ambience of this last fair in Portobello: the Spanish crown wanted the return of the Portobello fair to collect taxes; consumers wanted the return of legitimate products no more smuggling; kingdom officials wanted their salaries back to have purchasing power and, finally, the traders of Lima wanted to make a profit again, but were afraid for the security of the fair due to English piracy throughout the Pacific, in addition to illegally traded goods. Within a troubled international scenario, because the Viceroy of

Peru had authorized support to the French fleet, which is now an ally, forgetting that, not long ago, it was an enemy and had caused various damages in the Caribbean; in the midst of Dutch pirates.

- And English pirates, army deserters – O'Connor adds, looking at Captain Henry, who feels a little uneasy, looking away.

O'Connor continues:

- Even so, is it worth it to attack and sink the entire Tierra Firme Fleet? Would it not be... prudent to try and imprison it without recurring to heavy artillery?

Henry feels like they're getting up in his space:

- You cannot conquer a galleon without bombarding it, we are at war – answers Henry

- Winning a battle does not mean you won the war. It all depends on the combating strategy.

- We have already planned all of the strategies, sir, we do not need any other opinion – Henry cuts in

But Wager is interested:

- Tell me more about your idea, Captain.

The servants start to serve the roasts and vegetables on the porcelain plates. O'Connor launches his attempt to dissuade them from bombing the San José:

- I am also a hunter in the woods. Whenever I want to hunt a big live deer, I first set up a bait that interests it. As it approaches, I position myself behind it, setting up a large net. Then, while it takes the bait, my hunting companion shoots a tree that is in front of it. Frightened, logically, the deer runs in the opposite direction to where the shot happened and falls into the net that I had set up behind it.

The commodore's attention is fixed on what he's hearing. Henry, increasingly jealous, tries to cut in:

- Ships are not animals, sir, they are equipped with cannons and protective frigates.

- I know that, but look – O'Connor takes a ream of paper that's on the next table and an writing pen filled with ink and starts drawing boats on the paper, next to his plate – here we have the Expedition, the Kingston, the Vulture and the Portland. And here, on the other side, the Spanish squadron with seven ships. This is the San José, and this is the San Joaquin. If you attack these two big boys directly, in addition to putting the valuable cargo at risk, they will flee because they want to protect the riches.

Commodore Wager stands up on the other end of the table and go to stand next to O'Connor's drawing, paying close attention:

- So, in my opinion, the Vulture and the Portland aim at another ship, the Santa Cruz hulk, for example, and start bombing it. This will draw the attention of the other ships in the fleet, who will try to defend it, mind you, it also carries interesting goods. The Kingston goes after the San Joaquin. While they are distracted, the Expedition maneuvers, comes behind the San José, not paralleling it, to avoid the confrontation of the 35 cannons that are along its side. As the Portland continues bombarding the hulk, the Kingston fires towards the tip of the San José, just to get its attention. It will attempt to fire back at the Kingston, without realizing that the Expedition is approaching at port. When they realize, it will be too late: we have rammed into its side and jumped inside engaging in hand-to-hand combat. That way, we do not damage its riches and will be guaranteed a clean victory, because our men are much more combative than those of the Count of Casa Alegre.

O'Connor is so focused in his drawing that when he looks up at the three of them, they are looking at him completely astonished and surprised. Charles Wager smiles and goes back to his armchair, restarting his dinner:

- I see you, sir, are not only good at swimming, but also at naval strategy.

O'Connor a bit embarrassed bites a piece of the bird on his plate:

- Thank you, Sir, this is a little bit of what I have studied at the royal academy.

- Hum... I do not know if it is a good strategy – poisons Henry Wager, who is already captive to O'Connor's talent, cuts in:

- While he is a deer hunter, I see that you are a duck hunter, Captain Henry.

- What do you mean, ducks, sir?

- In duck hunting, when they all take flight, you soon shoot one of them, so that they do not reach altitude, correct?

- Yes, correct, but what does that have to do with our conversation, milord?

- There are those who will kill ideas as they kill ducks: as soon as someone poses a good idea, someone else appears and shoots, kills the idea before one can even try it. Morrow we will employ this captain's strategy. Send these guidelines to Bridges, Windsor, and Brooks. They shall be enforced.

Kendall tries to hold a laugh. Henry, humiliated, faces O'Connor and, after a few seconds, predicts:

- I believe we are still going to meet somewhere in the future, Captain O'Connor.

O'Connor raises a glass of wine and proposes a toast:

- To the future, Captain Every!

Everyone raises their glasses:

- To the future!

O'Connor looks at Kendall. She reciprocates with a smile and a mixed look of congratulations, pride, and something else. They continue to dine talking about other lively subjects.

Later, as they leave the cabin, they walk slowly to the edge of the ship. The new moon night is not one of the brightest, but the cloudless sky brings magical luminosity to the calm waveless waters. A light breeze blows bringing with it the freshness of tropical winter nights.

There are not many people walking on the deck at that advanced hour. Kendall breaks the silence:

- You did very well in there!

- What a struggle! That Henry can't stand me.

- He really seems angry about everything, but to be fair that boss of his cuts him at the root, poor thing!

- Yes, it's a problem. Do you think they were convinced?

- I'm sure of it. Your plan was very clear and good. I'm so proud of you!

She stops and leans over the bow rails, looking at the reflection of the moonlight on the water. He leans next to her. The very starry sky adds up to a certain romantic atmosphere. She, livelier, he, shyer.

- I never thought I'd be in this place this way – comments O'Connor

- Neither have I.... but any place is a good one when you have the right person by your side.

- Yes, it must be - he masks it.

- Why "must be"? Don't you have anyone special?

- Yes, I do...

She is disappointed, but he completes:

- ... my dear mother.

- Oh, you know what I'm talking about... love life.

- Yes, I used to have someone, but it's been a long time since she left. She wasn't ready to compete with my military life.

- So wasn't my partner, with my life dedicated to medicine.

She takes his hand, but he looks back and let's go of it.

- If they see two soldiers here holding hands, they're going to shoot us.

- You think?

- They've found it strange enough to see you doing mouth-to-mouth resuscitation on the commodore, they did not understand what you were doing, if they see us both holding hands now, we're screwed.

She turns and stares at him with a passionate look:

- Were you jealous?

- Jealous? Who, me? – he tries to dismiss it

She advances and quickly steals a kiss on his mouth. She has to stay on her toes due to his height.

- See? You don't have to drown to get a kiss from me!

He doesn't disguise that he liked it, but he looks around worried. He sees two guards making the rounds and getting close to where they are.

- We'd better get in; things are going to be pretty hectic tomorrow.

- At your orders, captain! – she says, saluting him

They both head downstairs, joining the others who, at that time, were already sleeping in the messy bunk beds.

On that morning of June 8, 1708, the day dawns to a rainy weather and the wind blows softly from Northwest. The Spanish fleet resumes its path, they are to the Southwest of the Isla de Barú and sailing in search of Boca Chica, which is a narrow passage between Isla Grande and the mainland, and which gives access to the Cartagena Bay.

The passengers are very tense due to the growing rumors of the impending encounter with the British fleet. They don't know that would be their last sunrise.

In the basement, after a terrible sleepless night, the travelers from the future do not know how to make their escape. Lorenzo goes to the cast iron railing and tries to shake them, but they don't move from the place. He asks the help of Diego and Soledad who, even though are in good physical shape, also fail at their attempt.

Isabel starts to cry:

- I didn't expect to die like this.

Paloma tries to comfort her:

- Who says we're going to die?

- Let's come up with an escape plan – encourages Thomas

- If my tablet's battery weren't dead... – comments Luna, looking at the dark device's screen.

- What would you do? – asks Lorenzo

- This is a multi-function device. One of the functionalities in it is a high-power laser torch.

This information cheers people up. Lorenzo continues:

- And how is it reloaded?

- With solar energy.

They look through the cracks of the roof and wall of the ship, but not a single ray of sunshine shines through them.

- Today of all days it is cloudy out there – moans Soledad

They hear a hoarse voice coming from the other cell:

- We are all going to die!

A thin man with decayed teeth, long white beard, wearing only torn shorts, comes closer and holds the bars of his cell in front of theirs, with a macabre smile and repeats:

- They are going to leave us in this cell until we die from starvation and from the cold!

- Who are you, sir? – asks Lorenzo

- Me? I am Captain Sanchez... I am a poor soul convicted by that crazy Sabogal...

- And why are you in jail? – asks Lorenzo

The man seems to deliberate, remembering the past:

- Because I stood up to him in Portobello, so he would not make this trip... I warned him about the ambush of the English, but arrogant, full of pride, he did not listen to me.... he preferred to listen to Alcázar, that ambitious privateer... and threw me in this cell... I have not eaten in ten days...

- Listened to whom? – asks Isabel

- Alcázar... Don Juan Santín de Alcázar, the second admiral of the San Joaquin, Villanueva's right-hand man.

They're saddened by the man's situation. Isabel takes a piece of bread left over from yesterday's breakfast and throws it into his cell. The man eats it like a hungry dog.

- And how were you so sure there would be an attack by the English, sir? – asks Thomas

- Because... because... – the man hesitates to tell them, but, looking at their situation, he decides to reveal it – ... I was a spy hired by them to monitor and pass information on their plans.

Thomas is very, very embarrassed. Paloma, beside him, notices his discomfort and asks:

- Is there a problem, Thomas?

- No... nothing... I'm fine...

Lorenzo is intrigued. He stands in front of him and asks, looking him in the eyes:

- Are you hiding something, Thomas?

He can't face him. All of them surround him. Lorenzo holds him by the shoulders and firmly repeats the question:

- Tell me what's going on, Thomas!

Seeing that he had been discovered, he decides to tell it all:

- I also passed on information from our project to the British government.

- You did what? – Paloma is disappointed.

- I'm sorry, it was my duty. We had been following the evolution of Prof. Perez's study on time travel for many years. We copied all the calculations and improved the space travel device and built our own wormhole ship. The British government also wanted to know where the sunken ship is so...

- ... so what? – asks Lorenzo, very angry.

He looks at Paloma, who has a tear coming down her face. He takes courage and reveals:

- ... they also sent a rescue team to the past.

They can't believe their ears. Isabel tries to confirm:

- You meant there's another team of scientists who came from the future and are after this ship?

- Yes...

- And they know we are here?

- Yes...

- And... where should they be now?

Thomas pauses and looks away, like a vision:

- At this moment, inside the English ship that's going to bomb this one...

It's 9:00 in the morning. The Vulture frigate is the first to spot the Spanish fleet in the distance and returns to warn the other English ships, which are sailing near the Barú Bay, Southwest of their positions. The wind is strong and it drives the fleet forward to begin its ambush formation. They position themselves near the Isla del Tesoro, where the passage into Cartagena Bay is narrow making it is easier to surround their prey.

Lorenzo tries to organize his thoughts:

- Hold on. Everything was already messed up, it's gotten even worse. You mean we have an English competing team, coming from the same year we have, looking for the map of the San José's wreckage location?

Thomas nods affirmatively. Paloma comes closer and, crying, slaps him across the face. He stares at her, saddened, without reaction.

- How can you betray us like that?

- I´m so sorry...

- "Sorry", huh? Is that all you can talk say? "Sorry"?

- I was recruited for this, it was my job in the British Navy...

Some sunshine rays begin to seep through the cracks on the boat. Luna quickly puts the tablet on the ground to be illuminated by them, but they are very weak.

- How long will it take to recharge? – asks Soledad

- With such weak light... about six hours – Luna estimates

- What time is it now? – asks Isabel

Lorenzo looks at his wrist brace given by Prof. Perez when they embarked:

- Around noon.

- And what time did the war even start?

- Around 4 p.m. – Luna reminds her

- Oh, my God!... – moans Paloma – there will be no time!

They are all at a corner of the cell, they turn when they hear a metallic voice coming from behind:

- No time for what?

It's Captain Sabogal, in his official uniform, accompanied by captains Melendo and Delgado. Lorenzo, nervous, advances and holds the cell bars. He orders almost without moving his lips:

- You have to get us out of here!

- Give me just one reason, sailor.

- We are the only ones who can stop a tragedy.

- Are you going to talk again about your magical predictions? – he asks with disdain.

- They are not imagination; they are part of the History of Spain!

- The History of Spain has always shown our supremacy!

- Arrogance has caused many kingdoms to fall.

Sabogal comes even closer to the prison grates and turns to look around:

- Arrogant? Me? You do not understand. We have goals to meet. We are under heavy pressure from the Crown. The kingdom is at stake, and we have to get there as soon as possible.

He feels something sting his leg, which makes him jump back. He looks down and sees nothing, except for Luna, who's next to the grates, facing the other side of the cell.

- What is this hideous creature doing?

Lorenzo tries to get his attention back:

- Do you risk your own life in the name of power?

- Look around you. Tierra Firme has more than two hundred cannons.

- This does not guarantee victory – Isabel comes to join the grates.

- Well, well... does the witch also understands war strategy?

- In a few minutes we will hear the announcement of the encounter with the English fleet – prophesies her

At that moment, a cry is heard from the top of the deck: "Enemy in sight! English fleet at port! Attention! Enemy in sight!" Captain Melendo, surprised and concerned, explains:

- That is the main mast watchman, sir.

Captain Sanchez, from his cell, starts shouting non-stop:

- They are here! We are all going to die!

Sabogal looks at Isabel, who looks back with "What-did-I-tell-you?" look. Captain Delgado asks:

- Should we divert our route to Cartagena, sir?

- Sabogal is a crazy man – shouts Sanchez – We are all going to die!

- Think about how many lives are at stake! – asks Lorenzo.

- So, Captain, what are we going to do? – Delgado asks again.

- God have mercy on our souls! – cries Sanchez, desperate.

Sabogal takes out his pistol, raises his right arm and, still looking at Isabel, shoots at the prisoner, who is thrown to the bottom of the cell, dead. Isabel screams, frightened, putting her hands on her head.

Sabogal, without any expression on his face, replaces the pistol in the holster and says, coldly:

- Prepare the artillery, Captain Delgado. Tell Admiral Villanueva and Captain Nieto to begin battle formation. Spain will never be defeated!

He turns around and leaves, hearing Isabel shouting from behind:

- Assassin! Crazy! How many lives will be lost!

Lorenzo covers her mouth, so she doesn't take a shot like the other prisoner.

- It's useless, he's blind and deaf by greed.

Isabel collapses. Paloma comes to help her sit down.

- We've got to get out of here! – Diego says, trying once again to force the bars.

Luna looks at battery charge indicator: 20%

The English are seven leagues far and turn to the direction of the Spanish squadron, announced by the watchman who is at the mast's post. However, the wind that was in his favor before ceases completely.

Captain Wager is on the higher stern deck, looking through the spyglass. Next to him are Captain Henry and O'Connor, talking about the simulated attack plan.

The other team members are carrying out the tasks set to them, in special Emmett and River are preparing a lifeboat, on the right side of the bow.

Around three o'clock in the afternoon, a gentle breeze starts again from Northeast, propelling the sails of the four vessels to the side where the Spanish were at standstill, also waiting for wind.

Instead of fleeing, the Spanish fleet, in battle formation, begins its path to meet them. The deck of the San José looks like an anthill: passengers and soldiers run everywhere, arming ropes, hoisting sails, supplying the cannons with projectiles and ammunition, distributing swords, knives, and pistols. The atmosphere of anxiety increases with each passing minute, as the survival instinct causes a surge of adrenaline in their bloodstream. Some say prayers, others cry, others hide, others train with their sword, revealing the fragility and deepest feelings of the human being at the death brink.

At 4:30 p.m., the Captaincy San José, which is by the low bank of the Isla del Tesoro, swerves towards the high seas at Northwest. The Count of Casa Alegre looks through the spyglass and sees the proximity of the four English ships. Based on their position, he instructs his commanding parties:

- Send messengers for our bodyguards to position themselves in battle formation IV: have them surround the San José and the San Joaquín in an oval formation. The French frigate Spiritu Sanctis and the hulk Nieto shall stay in front of us; the French frigate La Mieta and the ship Nuestra Señora de Carmen, behind us. When Gobierno Santa Cruz reaches us, tell them to scout ahead of us.

The messengers descend in small boats and, paddling, go to the respective ships to pass the battle instructions given by the captain. As this was the communication way at the time, there was a common transit of boats and larger ships, exchanging information, food, and weapons among the navy.

Commodore Wager, who also looked through the spyglass, watches the movement of the Spanish fleet and orders Captain Henry:

- We are going position ourselves according to the military-diamond-position: the Expedition goes ahead, put the Portland to our right, a little further back, and the Kingston, to the left, parallel to it, at a distance of a quarter of a league. Leave the Vulture frigate, more agile, behind and blocking the narrow channel between Isla del Tesoro and the continent, so that they do not try to escape. Send the Kingston to attack the San Joaquin, we will attack the San Jose, but we want the ships in one piece. We will approach them both and take them by mooring. Send messengers with these instructions and let us march on them at leeward.

Messengers descend on boats and paddle towards the other ships. O'Connor, however, notes that a dinghy boat is moving away from the Expedition towards the Spanish fleet. He finds this very strange and asks Captain Wager for the spyglass. Looking through it, he sees that the lonely sailor, almost breathless with the effort to paddle, is River.

O'Connor runs to the place where he is supposed to be and can't find him, nor Emmett, nor the reserve boat. He starts to panic and goes looking for her but has difficulty walking due to the turbulence on deck, with all the soldiers taking a combat position, the chaplain performing an impromptu mass and other members of the artillery preparing the ships for the terrible battle that would soon begin.

At 5:45 p.m., the two enemy fleets met at five leagues Northwest of Isla del Tesoro. Following the outlined strategies, the Kingston is positioned close to the San Joaquin and, at half-cannon fire of distance, fires its first cannon blast. One of the projectiles knocks down the galleon's main mast, causing it to lose speed and others cause several holes on its walls.

The Expedition chases the San José, but when the first shooting is made, the hulk Nieto, whis passed in front of it, takes the shots, receiving several damages to its hull.

Inside the San José, panic begins to prevail, making soldiers realize they are more vulnerable than they thought. The sea, turbulent due to the waves caused by passing ships from all sides, makes the large galleon swing about everywhere, making it difficult to target the attackers.

The Spanish ships gather further South, along with the French frigates. The San Joaquin, with serious damage to its structure, retreats to the Southeast, bound for Cartagena, cowardly abandoning its comrades. On the front line of the battle remain the Galleon San José and the Gobierno Santa Cruz, of the brave commander Vega Florida, whose mission is to protect the others.

In the basement where Lorenzo and his team are imprisoned, the panic is even greater, because they cannot see what is going on, they can only hear the cannon fires and feel the swing of the rough sea. Thomas shouts:

- We have to get away from this ship!
- Luna, how's the charger? – shouts Lorenzo
- Still at fifty percent charge – Luna shouts
- So activate it as it is!
- The device won't hold!

A cannonball enters with full force next to where they are, causing a large hole in the hull, spreading smoke and wood chips everywhere. The women scream, Lorenzo orders:

- You have to try!

Luna turns on the tablet and an orange light comes on.

- When it gets red, it means I can turn on the laser torch – she explains
- Quick!

The Count of Casa Alegre, on the upper deck, shouts:
- Fire!

The thirty-five cannons on one side of the ship fire at once, but they do little damage to the Expedition, which moves with full force towards it, leaving a cloud of smoke from heavy artillery. At a distance of 28 yards, the Expedition shoots over the San José, careful not to destroy the ship but to paralyze it.

On deck, amid the smoke of heavy artillery, people run and shout everywhere. Passengers bump into soldiers; masts fall on the deck; canvas sails are knocked down and the gunners reload the cannons incessantly. Pieces of human bodies are scattered across the deck, pain, panic, and destruction.

In that mess, no one notices a boat approaching the bow and a man climbing the rope ladder over the South wall.

- Red!

- Cut it!

Luna pushes a button, and a bunch of concentrated red laser beams start coming out from the tablet and cutting the prison iron bars. Sparks come out of them, amid the smoke from the bombing.

Another shot hits a compartment further ahead, wood chips hit them, who protect themselves with their hands, completely vulnerable.

- Fast! – shouts Lorenzo, who comes over to help Luna hold the tablet-cannon.

Hidden in the deck that holds the treasure of the San José, Pablo is terrified, crying in fear of all that noise and smoke that invades the treasure room. Suddenly, he sees someone coming down the stairs, sneakily, in a blue military uniform, unlike the Spanish ones. The unknown man, holding a lamp that swings with the ship, approaches the chests full of coins and emeralds. He opens one of them, dips his hand and lets out a scream that sounds more like a wolf howl.

Pablo takes courage and shouts:

- *Quien es usted?*

The man turns around and replies, in English:

- What?

- Thomas! Is that you?

Pablo comes out of the middle of the gold ingots and lets himself be seen by the light of the lanterns. But he realizes it wasn't who he thought it was:

- What do you want here?

River replies:

- I've come to take what's mine!

Pablo understands that he is not friendly and starts to get angry:

- This is all mine! Are you crazy! Go!

River pulls a dagger out of his belt, fills his other hand with pearls and shouts, menacingly:

- Well, come and get it!

A life and death fight begins between Pablo and River.

The two enemy ships part ways. The San José heads North-Northeast, turning to the coast, towards where the San Joaquin had already disappeared, fleeing. The Expedition, turns South-Southwest, making a turn to remain in search of the galleon, not minding the open fire from the other Spanish ships, in an attempt to protect the largest vessel.

The battle is intense, the Vulture bombards the Gobierno, breaking several parts of its hull; some smaller Spanish ships still shoot the Portland, while the Kingston goes after the San Joaquin, still intent on capturing it.

It's seven o'clock and the night is already descending over the bloody Caribbean Sea. On the expedition's first deck, O'Connor meets with his other team members:

- Is everyone okay?

A burst of bullets from San José, which was already at shotgun distance, sweeps the wooden walls, causing everyone to duck.

- We're all going to die here! – shouts Emmett

They all begin to run, among the cannon gunners, who shoot non-stop, making a deafening noise. The smell of gunpowder makes it hard for them to breathe.

- Where's River? – shouts O'Connor

- He went to kidnap the galleon – cries Emmett

- He... what? – asks Kendall

A cannon explodes as it expels its projectile, burning the boy who was charging it. He runs with his body on fire, but no one helps him.

- How are we going to not get shot? – asks Alfie

O'Connor thinks hard, but Jack has an idea:

- History says that Captain Wager was unharmed from the battle. So, let's stay close to him!

- Great idea, come on!

They all climb to the main deck, where the scenery is also chaotic: pieces of wood on fire on all sides, one of the sails was hit and is fallen and on fire also, soldiers try to throw water to put it out, when they hear an order from Captain Henry, repeated by supervisors along the deck:

- Prepare to board!

Hundreds of soldiers run and set themselves by the ship's left wall, armed with machetes, ropes, muskets, swords, hooks, and clubs, shouting words of hate.

- Look! – shouts Laureen, pointing at something that is behind this wall of soldiers.

Gradually, amid the smoke of the bombing, the silhouette of the San José begins to appear at twilight...

The tablet battery runs out and the laser beam stops to be emitted. But the grates are enough cut. Diego, Lorenzo, Soledad and Thomas push hard to detach them from the ground and ceiling. Diego commands:

- On three, we're going to throw ourselves against it hard!

They move away and stay in running position:

- One... two... three!

The four of them throw themselves against the bars, knocking them to the ground. Free, they run through the damaged ship corridors, some of them with water already gushing through the walls. They're heading for the stairs that access the upper decks. Luna asks Lorenzo:

- What time is it?

He looks on the wristwatch:

- Seven twenty. Why?

- The ship will explode at 7:30!

- We have to find a lifeboat! Run!

Running for dear life, they stumble up the stairs, passing amongst fire, mutilated bodies, passengers kneeling in prayer, desperate soldiers, the sound of cannon fire and a lot of smoke.

As they reach the deck, at the bow, they look and see Fernandez de Santillán, standing proudly, wielding a sword and shouting:

- Death to the English! Prepare for their approach!

On the right wall of the San José, hundreds of soldiers line up next to each other, shooting archebuses. In the background, the silhouette of the Expedition can already be seen. Only 218 yards between life and death.

Lorenzo, Paloma, Thomas, Isabel, Diego, Luna, and Soledad run to the other side of the ship, which is almost empty, passing over debris from parts of the San José. They find a boat hung by ropes, just below the wall and start jumping into it. The wind blows very strong, the waves are angry, the darkness of the night is partially broken by the new moon, and with all these difficulties, they easy down the ropes of the boat when Isabel asks:

- What about Pablo? Where's Pablo?

- I don't know – Lorenzo speaks aloud

- We can't leave him!

Lorenzo must make a decision. Either they come back and everyone dies, or they leave a man behind. He looks at the clock: seven twenty-five! He looks up: no one appears over the wall. He shouts:

- Cut the ropes!

The boat falls brutally on the water, almost turning over.

The fight in the treasure's room is fierce. Pablo and River are overcome with anger. The madness of ambition makes them blind. River attacks with a dagger, Pablo dodges and holds River's arm. He spins around himself and free his arm, punching Pablo in the stomach. He wields the knife and swings his arm around to cut Pablo's throat, but he bends back and suffers a scratch on his neck. He holds River's arm again and twist it, forcing him drop the knife.

- This treasure is all mine! – shouts, threateningly, River.

- Never! It's mine alone, you miserable gringo – replies Pablo.

River frees himself and punches Pablo in the face, making him fall to the ground. River jumps on top of him and they roll towards the staircase that leads to the lower floor. Pablo is on top and he begins to strangle River, who, with both hands, pushes the opponent up. The strength is great, the blood from Pablo's cut drips over the enemy's face. It was as if the hatred between the English and the Spanish, fighting outside, was all concentrated on them, inside.

River, suffocating, takes a last chance: he folds his legs, puts his feet on Pablo's pelvic region and throws him up. Pablo loses his balance and falls to the side. His pocket is torn and the grenade, he was keeping there, falls, rolling down the stairs...

River jumps on Pablo again, but an instinctive noise catches their attention: lying on top of each other, they look and see the grenade jumping from step to step downstairs, on the penultimate step its trigger is released and it falls, rolling, right under the ship's gigantic gunpowder barrel, which was on the deck below... there's nothing left to do.

The grenade detonates, causing the gunpowder barrel to explode into a gigantic cloud of fire, which hits the other ammunition barrels, and, in a matter of seconds, the entire ship explodes.

The Expedition is about one hundred ninety-six feet from the Galleon San José and it is possible to hear the screams of the Spanish, whose archebuses shots hit and kill some English soldiers who are by the wall.

When, suddenly, a large explosion happens in the ship's stern hold, causing it to turn over itself. The explosion is so strong that it knocks down the soldiers who are on the Expedition, burning pieces of wood fly over them and a great flash of light illuminates the entire sea around them. A large wave hits the hull of the English ship, causing it to swing very strongly. Starboard, the wave advances and hits the escaping boat hard, causing it to turn and throw the guys and girls to the water. With a lot of effort, they all come back swimming, manage to roll the boat, and climbing into it, flee paddling desperately.

In minutes, the San José Galleon breaks in half and sinks, taking with it 600 passengers and crewmen, including the bankers Pablo Martinez and River Smith. There are burning pieces of wood floating on the sea surface.

Eleven survivors, floating on the waters, are rescued by the very same English ship that had attacked them.

CHAPTER IV
TREASURE MAP HUNT

HQGC HEADQUARTERS - CHELTENHAM, UNITED KINGDOM -
YEAR: 2021

General Walsh puts a report he has just read on his office desk. Worried, he looks at the sergeant in front of him and asks:

- So, we lose his signal…

- Yes, sir, I'm sorry.

- And what do the scientists think happened?

- They raised a few hypotheses. The belt is connected to various of the travelers' functions and these can be monitored by control panels. When a signal is lost, it could mean the belt was lost, there was an interruption of the wormhole or...

- Or...

- The carrier has died, sir.

The general closes the report folder:

- Call a meeting with the scientists immediately.

- Yes, sir!

The sergeant leaves, closing the door behind him. General Walsh looks out the window, very worried.

NATIONAL INTELLIGENCE CENTRE - MADRID, YEAR 2021

Professor Perez, Dr. Inez and Dr. Jimenez are around the oval table in the meeting room above the lab. Three other officers and two men in dark suits are also seated at the table. Dr. Jimenez comments:

- So, you're from the Ministry of Justice?

- Yes – answers one of them, with short hair, light brown mustache, green eyes, appearing to be thirty-one years old – the Spanish Government learned of your experiences with the time machine.

- It was an operation authorized by the President in person, is legal – Perez immediately justifies himself.

- Yes, we know – continues the man with the mustache – but we have information that you may not know.

- Scientists are so confined in laboratories that they are always the last to know – kidds Dr. Inez.

The other man in a suit, who is bald, with black eyes and beard, looking about forty-eight years old, cuts the informal tone:

- The United States' lawsuit against Colombia took a new turn: the International Court of Justice recognized their right to re-explore the area where they found the remains of the ship wreckage in 1986, in that case held against Colombia for breach of contract.

- Additionally – continues the mustached government agent– we learned that England has also sent a team back to the past, to look for the said "map of the ship's location".

The three scientists look very frightened, but the news is not over yet:

- And the Government of Colombia resumed searches in the area, based on the research conducted by the REMUS 6000 in 2015.

- So – concludes Perez – it seems that we have an international turmoil on hands?

- The Spanish government is very concerned about this expedition conducted by the NIC, sir – comments the mustached agent– we need it to be completed quickly, and successfully.

- According to the decision, if the United States finds the treasure first, they will own its full content – conjectures the bald agent

The third officer, of Latin American appearance, with dark skin, white mustache, gray hair, wearing a military cap, who until that moment had been quiet, asks a direct and harsh question:

- How's the expedition so far?

The doctors look at each other deciding who's going to answer. Dr. Jimenez says:

- We believe it's going all right, sir.

- "We believe"?

- We have no means of communicating with them, sir – explains Dr. Inez.

- And how do you know they're okay?

- The wormhole is open, stable and can be kept for another week. If they had a problem, they'd be back by now.

The mustached man delivers a card to Prof. Perez:

- In two days, come to Parliament, we will have a meeting with the President to draw up an emergency action plan. We don't have time to waste.

- Time – comments Perez – is the thing against which we have been racing for many years in our research, sir.

The Latin American officer cuts in again:

- We're in a war amongst four countries, ladies and gentlemen. And in war – he takes off his cap revealing a deep scar on his forehead – time may cost lives.

CARTAGENA DE INDIAS - COLOMBIA, YEAR 1708

Cartagena de Indias was one of the most bustling cities on the Northern coast of South America, at the time called the Viceroyalty of Peru. Founded in 1533 by the Spanish explorer Pedro de Heredía, guided by the indigene Catalina, of the Calamarí tribe, it was all influenced by Spanish-Caribbean culture.

Narrow streets with cobblestone pavement separate colorful two-stored townhouses, with wooden balconies covered with small roofs suspended and supported by wood posts, with colorful wooden fences that reminded the cheerful of Barcelona's air.

The population of almost eighteen thousand inhabitants is a mixture of indigenous peoples, Spanish, and French, who came to the Caribbean coast looking for wealth. And wealth was not lacking, because Cartagena is the main port for exporting gold and silver from Peru and emeralds and other precious gems produced in Colombia, which, loaded on to Spanish galleons, went through Havana, in Cuba, and then headed to Europe.

For this reason, it is a city very targeted by pirates and corsairs, coming from all regions of the world, and due to this, eleven kilometers of wall were built between the seventeenth and eighteenth centuries.

In a tavern on Calle Estanco de Aguardiente, full of settlers, corsairs and pirates drinking rum and smoking cigars, there is no other topic of conversation than the attack of the English and the sinking of the San José which had happened the week before. The noise of loud conversation and laughter gets mixed with the smoke from tobacco cigars and glasses hitting tables, all by the half light of the oil lanterns hanging from the strong wooden beams supporting the ceiling.

At a dark rustic wooden table at the corner of the tavern, trying not to draw attention, Professor Perez's team is sitting, silently, some half-filled beer mugs illuminated by the table's candle stick. They're all now dressed as ordinary civilians. The women changed the sailor clothes for long dresses, with long sleeves and ruffles, typical of the Caribbean colonial era.

Paloma is the first to speak, running her finger on the edge of the mug:

- Four days…

- Four days of what? – asks Isabel

- That we've been here after the galleon's escape.

- Do you want to go away? – asks Thomas

She doesn't answer, still disappointed in the boy. Lorenzo speaks in a saddened tone:

- I feel like we failed the mission.

- We couldn't even stop the ship from sinking... – Isabel laments.

- But, after all, what was the mission's goal? – questions Soledad

- To find a supposed map made by Captain Sabogal that showed the exact location of the galleon's sinking – Paloma recites, word for word.

- But he's died in the disaster, hasn't he? – asks Diego

- We don't know, we escaped before we could check the survivors – Lorenzo informs

- But then how do we find him, if he's even alive? – asks Isabel – We'd better go back to our ship and return to Madrid.

Everyone is silent, evaluating what to do. With a knowingly look, Luna turns to Lorenzo and informs:

- He's alive.

Everyone looks at her surprised, she continues:

- ... and very active!

- How do you know? – asks Lorenzo.

- Through this.

She shows the tablet, the screen of which shows a map with a blue dotted line navigating through various parts of the screen, as a path. At the tip of the dashed line, a red dot blinks non-stop.

- What is this? – asks Thomas.

- It's Sabogal – Luna replies, satisfied.

- How?

- I put a tracker on him – she says cunningly.

No one believes it. She continues the explanation:

- Remember when we were inprisoned in the cell and he was near the grates, talking to you?

- Yes, I remember –Lorenzo answers

- And he felt a sting in his leg?

- He looked down, angry, and saw nothing – remembers Isabel.

- Yes, at that point I stuck a subcutaneous micro tracker on his calf!

- Wow! – cheers Thomas, happy – you're very smart!

The sound of English words catches the attention of some surrounding corsairs. They look at them suspiciously. Lorenzo says:

- Shush... keep your voice down, English are enemies around here!

- So? Have you been following in his footsteps? – asks Soledad.

- Yes, and a great number of steps that is! – comments Luna, swiping over the screen making the map move to other pages and showing a long dotted line.

- Where has he been? – asks Isabel.

Luna scrolls though the tablet's touch screen while explaining, all eyes are on the screen.

- From the history here, it appears that he was thrown away by the explosion, fell into the sea and was rescued by one of the French frigates fleeing to Cartagena. He stayed at the Fort Castle of San Felipe de Barajas. From there, he began to walk around the city, then went to several islands of the Rosario archipelago.

- Maybe he's making an oceanographic map – explains Paloma.

- Maybe – continues Luna – yesterday he was in Isla Grande.

- Where our ship is! – Isabel notes – Could he have found out?

- What about now? – Lorenzo asks – where does his sign come from?

Luna enlarges the image, which makes it less clear due to the nonexistence of signal-repeating antennas.

- He's at... He's at... it seems to be a building... of a church... San Pedro...

- San Pedro de Claver? – completes Isabel.

- That's right, that's it! – confirms Luna – it seems that he has been there for a few hours.

- How about we go over there and see what he's doing? – suggests Lorenzo.

- How far is it? – asks Soledad.

- About... seven hundred meters – Luna replies.

- Let's go, now! – shouts the excited Thomas, covering his own mouth soon after and looking sideways.

It's kind of late. The group of surly drunks from the next table gets up and comes to them. One of them, all dirty, with long black beard, long hair, sunburned skin, wearing an eye patch over the left eye, asks in grotesque Spanish:

- *¿El é un gringo?*

Paloma makes a lame excuse, in Spanish language

- No, sir, he is a Spanish who is learning English.

- *¡No se parece con un español!*

- He... does not come out on the sun much, that's why.

The group of four corsairs doesn't seem too convinced. They form a barrier at the exit and are about to draw their pistols when Diego, quickly, raises their own table pushing it to their side and knocking them down with it. The fight breaks. Lorenzo goes after the corsair leader, while Diego and Soledad face the other three. Punches, kicks, trips, and sword dodging going on everywhere. Thomas gets into the fight, but he's beaten rather more than does any beating.

In the fuss of the fight, they strike other tables, and confusion takes over the tavern where the customers, drunk, no longer know who hit whom. The owner of the bar is terrified by the damage to bottles, glasses, mugs, and other glass being broken mercilessly.

When they manage to knock out the four troublemakers who had started the fight, they leave the tavern amid a general havoc, passing through the door without attracting attention, but dodging bottles that burst onto the walls and windows.

As they leave, the young women notice the boys' wounds. They try to clean them with some bandages they carry on the backpacks, but Lorenzo is in a hurry:

- Let's go before Sabogal leaves.

He turns to Thomas and says:

- And you, for God's sake, keep your mouth shut!

- Yes, I will... – but he corrects himself when the others look pretty ugly at him – *Si, señor, así lo haré.*

- Come fast, he's moving inside the cathedral – warns Luna, checking the tablet.

It's 8:30 pm and the streets of the walled city are full of people walking around to enjoy the attenuated freshness of tropical winter nights. Ladies dressed dresses and tulle petticoats walk arm-in-arm with men also well-dressed in the period's social attire. As the streets were narrow, they had to share space with carriages and people riding horses, especially the city's night patrol.

The streets are well lit, with baroque-style cast iron light posts illuminated by long-lasting candles. Following the tablet's GPS, the seven crew members enter Calle de Santo Domingo, passing along several homes, barracks, shops, and flowered squares, turning left at Calle de la Inquisición. They pass in front of Palacio de La Inquisición and, when they arrive at Plaza de La Inquisición (now called Plaza del Bolívar), they are noticed by a beggar who is sitting on the ground, at the foot of a tree, among other beggars, with colorful blankets on their backs.

Sergeant Birdie, with great surprise, addresses her group:

- Hey, guys, look!

- What's it? – asks O'Connor.

She points out the Spanish crossing the park:

- That one over there. It's Thomas Dowell, our informant!

The group rouses immediately:

- Are you sure? – Laureen asks

- Yes, I am, we trained together for a few months in Port Down and we've seen each other several times in video messages, it's him alright.

They all get up, now dressed as ordinary Carthaginian citizens. Kendall asks:

- And who are the others?

- They must be the Spanish team that came from the future – Birdie deduces.

- That's lucky! – says Jack.

- We were already at a loss to what do next after so many days without news – agrees Laureen.

- Where are they going? – questions Emmett.

- Look, they turned right – Birdie points out.

- Let's follow them, folks, discreetly! – commands O'Connor.

The group gets up, leaves the blankets on the floor and begins to track the Spanish from a distance. They turn right, following Calle de las Iglesias towards the central part of the wall surrounding the city. They pass in front of the great house of the landlord Don Domingo de Miranda, the Marquis of Royal Prize, where a great party is being held.

They advance through Plaza de la Aduana, enter Calle de San Pedro de Claver until they reach the stone church dedicated to that saint, in front of Plaza de San Pedro de Claver. The clock on the walls' main door tower strikes ten o'clock at night. The large solid carved wood gate from the main entrance of the church, built in 1580 with stones brought from the Isla de Tierra Bomba, is closed.

- Is he still in there? – asks Isabel.

- The signal is still coming from inside, at a standstill for a long– Luna replies.

- How are we going to get in? – asks Thomas.

Lorenzo looks up, the facade is very high, with two side bell towers and a closed central triangle with the church clock. He concludes:

- We can't get up this way.

They walk further to the left of the facade, where the church building is attached to the convent of the Jesuits who live there. They find the first door of the convent, which is half open, as if someone had just gone in or out. They look to both sides. The square is a almost deserted, with few pedestrians and horses passing through it at that hour. Slowly, they push the door, which makes hinges noise and enter the Convent's hall.

The hall leads to a staircase that goes to the upper floor, where the dormitories are. There's no noise, the few lit candles provide little clarity to the environment. Moving forward a little further, the seven members go looking for a door that gives way to the main temple. They turn the flashlights they carry in their pockets on and try not to make noise or bump into modest furniture, they find the door, which is also half open.

Anxiety increases everyone's heartbeat. They are apprehensive, both knowing that they will meet Sabogal, and for sneaking into a sacred place.

Lorenzo asks Luna, in a low voice:

- So? Where's the signal coming from?

- From the front of the hall.

- Let's go, watch out!

As they advance, the flashing signal on the tablet gets stronger. They enter the main nave of the church. The brightness of full moon causes rays of light to filter through the stained-glass windows that border the top part of all the walls. Like every Catholic church of that time, it has a very high ceiling, with wooden pulpits embedded in the columns that form a corridor in the middle of the hall. The columns are joined to each other by arches at the top, from the entrance of the church to the altar, to the back. The wooden benches are parallel aligned, decreasing in width as they approach the front, which is called the sacristy.

The ceiling of the sacristy is domed, with round stained glass windows and curved beams that converge to a cross in the center which is its highest part. With their flashlights, they illuminate the large altar that is at the bottom of the sacristy, facing the central corridor between the benches, which is reached by a few steps.

The altar is completely made of marble, carved with sacred motifs, from floor to ceiling, with the image of San Pedro de Claver inside a shrine supported by marble columns and covered by a marble roof with motifs of saints. At the foot of the altar, inside a glass dome, the remains of that saint rest in peace.

The light beams of the flashlights cut the nave on all sides. Total silence. Luna leads the group as she is heading towards the spot where Sabogal's signal is. They climb the steps of the altar platform and come close the wall covered with the marble sculptures. The signal gets stronger, emitting circles that flash at the exact point where they are.

Luna looks down, crouches, and picks up something from the floor:

- Look. The transmitter!

- What? – asks Lorenzo, who is right behind her

He illuminates a small metallic object, that resemble a watch battery, with some red spots. Diego illuminates the ground, which shows a small trail of blood drops heading toward the back of the altar. Slowly, he circles the altar and goes behind the back, illuminating the floor and walls. Nobody. He goes back to the group and tells them:

- There's no one there.

- He must have discovered the transmitter on his skin, took it off and dropped it here – deduces Paloma.

- What now? How are we going to find him? – asks Thomas.

Nobody knows the answer. Luna has an idea:

- It looks like he's been here for a long time. Perhaps he hid the map around here?

- Let's do a quick search! – suggests Soledad.

- All right, be careful not to make any noise – Lorenzo commands –
you two go to the right side of the nave, up to the front; Paloma and
Thomas, check the left side; the three of us will check this front space
and behind the sacristy.

- What should we look for? – asks Soledad.

- I don't know, something like a parchment, or a box, a small chest,
I don't know which way he might have recorded it – Lorenzo replies.

- If he even recorded it... –Isabel warns

So they part and start searching every corner of the church: columns,
benches, small side shrines with figures and flowers, candles, in short,
every place where some different object might be hidden. They find
nothing, but they keep searching up to the front door of the hall.

Meanwhile, at the back of the sacristy, where the blood drops
disappear, Isabel, Luna and Lorenzo look for clues of hidden objects. A
little dust, ambulators, censers, golden crosses, monstrances, chalices
and other liturgical objects rest in cabinets and small tables. They open
the cabinets and look some chests that are scattered across the floor in
detail, but nothing catches their eye.

The hope of finding something there diminishes. Isabel asks:

- I wonder if he was really here.

- How do we know? – Lorenzo replies – he may have just passed
through here and gone somewhere else, until he made such a map, that
we don't know if really exists...

- But he stayed almost two hours around here – Luna remembers,
consulting the tablet – it must have been to do something special.

They go back to the front of the marble altar. Thinking out loud,
Isabel asks:

- Think with me... when you want to hide something so that no one
finds it, where do usually you hide it?

- In a place where no one would think it was hidden! – answers
Diego.

- And where there would little need for anyone to move or do maintenance – completes Luna.

- So... let's look around and see where we would never think to look and what doesn't need to be moved a lot – suggests Isabel.

Suddenly, as she turns around, her flashlight illuminates the dome of golden frames with the skeleton dressed as the Christian martyr. She looks at Lorenzo, who looks at Luna, who looks at her and asks:

- Could it be?

- He wouldn't commit such sacrilege! – condemns Isabel.

- There's only one way to find out – concludes Lorenzo.

He lights the interior of the sepulcher diagonally, so that the light reflection on the glass does not disturb the vision of what is inside. He takes the light down, from the skull of the skeleton to its trunk and arms, covered by a blue satin robe with golden Christian embroidery. He realizes that a part of the priest tunic looks a little messy at waist height.

He begins to illuminate the edges of gilded wood, richly carved, which seals the glass box, looking for signs of violation. There are none. He realizes that, in fact, the repository where the body rests is a glass coffin, surrounded by golden iron sculptures, with figures of angels holding tree leaves around him.

He signals the other ones to get closer and asks Diego:

- Help me out here!

- Do you have the guts to touch such a sacred thing? – asks Paloma.

- I didn't want to, but it seems that soulless man has already desecrated the rest of the holy man. Let's try not to take anything out of place.

He, Diego, Soledad and Thomas take the ends of the glass dome and, with all care, remove it from inside the place where it was embedded. The noise of the glass box surrounded by golden metal dragging on the floor breaks slightly the silence of that hall that, it being already near midnight, brings an almost funeral darkness. The group places the coffin on the floor of the altar platform and, very carefully, lifts its glass cover with the golden iron frame, each holding on one of the four corners. A not very pleasant smell comes up.

The figure of a skeleton in the midst of that darkness and width of the hall provokes some fear, it seemed that it would wake up at any moment. As Luna points the flashlight inwards, Lorenzo gently passes his hand though the inner side walls of the skiff, looking for something different. The young women project their flashlights' beams from time to time at the church and at the door through which they entered, to check that no one would appear.

At waist height, he stops and begins rummaging around something that appears to be under the hip bones. Very carefully, he sticks his hand and removes a small piece of parchment of about by eight six inches, rolled up and fastened to a golden key by a red ribbon with the insignia of imperial Spain.

Very carefully, he unties the ribbon and sees what it is a part of a larger map, but that mentioned only one place and one phrase.

More than quickly, Luna prepares the tablet (which, in fact, was a multi-tasking device) and takes one, two pictures of that piece of the open map. Happy, Lorenzo celebrates, in a slightly loud voice:

- We've found it! It's ours!

Then a male, unfamiliar voice comes from the back of the church:

- No, sir. It's ours!

Thinking that they were discovered by the Jesuits who had woken up, everyone looks at the door from which they had entered. O'Connor's group, him in the lead, is standing there, pointing firearms at them. Paloma asks:

- Who are you?

Thomas replies:

- They're the English group.

O'Connor and his comrades, weapons up, enter the hall and walk to them. He says in English:

- Give us the map and no one will get hurt.

- Captain – intercedes Thomas – let's negotiate, it's not like that...

O'Connor points his gun at him:

- Which side are you on?

- I've been with them so far; they have saved my life.

- But the mission is for our United Kingdom!

- This treasure belongs to Spain! – says Lorenzo, wielding the scroll.

- It belongs to England! Hand it over!

- We're the ones who accumulated this wealth.

- In fact, you have explored the poor colonies of America!

- They paid for the services rendered by the Crown! – justifies Lorenzo.

- Services? Do you call Philip V's luxury "services"? – questions Laureen.

- I do not believe – Isabel intervenes – that two groups from the future are debating the present?

- It is because we know very well that what your country will do with this money in the future will not be much different from what it would do in this century – Laureen argues.

- We're not going to give up what we've come to recover! – Diego rebuts.

The two groups are very close now. They hear a noise in the convent upstairs.

- Someone's up. Come on, hand it over at once! – orders O'Connor.

- No way, this has already cost us a life! – says Paloma, indignant.

- And one on our side too! – comments Kendall.

Sergeant Birdie, whose gun has a silencer, shoots the marble floor, causing the bullet to ricochet across the walls to the bottom of the church. It hits a vase and breaks it. This shows them they're not kidding.

- Life is made of choices – ironizes Emmett, reaching out her hand.

Lorenzo looks at Luna, who nods in agreement. Reluctantly, he hands over the piece of the map with the golden key to her hands, holding them a little while. She pulls it and puts it in her uniform's jacket pocket. Someone lights a candle at the top of the stars, whose dim light enters through the side door. O'Connor commands:

- Let's go!

Lorenzo still has time to say, with hate:

- We'll still see each other, Captain, here or in the future!

The English flee through the same side door, which leads to the convent and then the street. The Spanish, in desperation, are looking for a parallel exit before they are discovered, and someone calls the police. They run to the main gate, lift the heavy wooden lock and open the two-leaf gate, fleeing through Plaza de San Pedro de Claver toward the city wall. That's when Luna remembers:

- Not the wall, it's guarded at night!

- Let's go the other way – suggests Isabel.

They run along Calle San Juan de Dios, which ends in a large corner inn on the street of the east wing of the wall, which today would be the Charleston Hotel. They go in, ask for two rooms and go up, tired and defeated.

They fall into bed and sleep heavily.

The next morning, the first ones to wake up are the women. They go out and go to the other room and call the men. Thomas opens the door all unkempt, with a sleepy face. Paloma complains:

- How can you sleep so much with this whole situation?

He yawns and closes the door. They warn:

- We'll go down for breakfast, don't take too long!

They go down the wooden staircase, among other guests and cleaning staff. When they enter the crowded, noisy cafeteria, everyone stops talking to observe the three of them, especially Luna. They discreetly go to the fruit and other food counter to serve themselves. People retake their conversations.

Next to them, a mustached gentleman, who looks like a business traveler, is taking some food and talking to his traveling colleague, who is on the other side of the self-service counter.

- You can't hear about anything else in the city.

- Of course! What a crime!

- Who would have the courage to desecrate a holy place?

Paloma looks at Isabel, who, in silence, reciprocates her gaze. The companion of the man with the mustache answers, serving himself with Colombian coffee:

- Bandits, certainly looking for money.

- But what money would there be on the man's skeleton?

- Who knows? But the police is investigating all over the city. They will catch the fiends!

- I've heard they have a clue.

Paloma looks at Isabel again, increasingly worried.

- Indeed? What is it?It looks like they found a somewhat weird lamp.

- How so? – asks the man besides Paloma

- It looks like a tube that has a button. When you press a button on top, a strong light appears, stronger than a hundred lit candles.

Isabel drops her plate, drawing even more attention from those present. She crouches down to pick up the shards and the fallen food, along with Paloma who is by her side. She whispers:

- Eeech, we are screwed!

- I think we dropped a flashlight when we ran away – Paloma adds – we have to warn the boys and get out of here as soon as possible.

A cleaning helper comes to help clean. At this moment, the three boys appear at the door of the cafeteria and meet them near the food counter. Soledad warns:

- Grab all the food you can and let's go back room! Fast!

- Why is that? I'm starving! – protests Diego.

- We'll explain up there, let's go! – she orders

They take all the fruits, breads, cakes, and other breakfast foods they can carry. As they pass the reception desk to climb the stairs, the receptionist, a short, fat man with large brown chops, notices that group of strange people with their hands full of food. He calls Thomas, who is one of the last to pass:

- Hey, *muchacho!* Come here, please!

Thomas finds the call weird but goes back to stand in front of the fat man. The others go up the stairs, not realizing that he was left behind.

- Did you call me, sir?

- Your accent... I looks like you are not from here Cartagena, are you?

Thomas tries to speak in the best Spanish way possible:

- Well... no... I mean, more or less...

- Hum... Why are you bringing food to the rooms?

- It's just that... well... – he finds an excuse – the cafeteria is crowded and there is no place for us to sit together, that is why.

The man does not seem convinced:

- You are the ones who got here at the inn this morning around 1:00 a.m., were you not?

- Uh... I did not notice the time, sir...

The man takes the registration form and confirms it:

- Here you are! One thirty in the morning!

Thomas moves away to climb the stairs:

- Oh, yes, it could be... but what is problem? You are going to charge half a day, is that it?

He grimaces and go up the stairs in a hurry. The man follows him with a very suspicious look in his eyes. He calls the doorman and gives him some instruction. The doorman rushes out into the street.

Thomas enters the room, panting:

- Guys...

- What happened? – asks Lorenzo, eating.

- Don't say you got yourself into another trouble – comments Isabel.

He shortly recounts the receptionist's interview, which makes everyone even more worried.

- What now? – asks Luna.

- We have to get out of here as soon as poss...

Lorenzo can't finish the sentence. There is a strong knock on the door and an authority voice is heard from the outside:

- Open up! Police!

They stand up and squeeze themselves against one of the walls. Isabel asks:

- What are we going to do now?

- If we open, they will discover and arrest us – comments Paloma.

- We don't even have documents – completes Luna.

Lorenzo looks out the window and sees that it gives access to the roof of the restaurant. Then the street, the wall separates the city from the sea. He does not hesitate to order:

- This way! Quick!

The police starts breaking down the door:

- Open up!

- Quick!

The seven go out through the window and balance themselves along the roof. Lorenzo is the last one out of the room. Isabel, the first one out, jumps from the roof to the ground, drawing the attention of the citizens walking down the street and of some sentinels who make the rounds along the corridors at the top of the great stone wall.

They run through the street, a battalion of soldiers chase after them. Following through the street parallel to the wall, they bump into people walking down the street, knock down fruit wagons and are almost being reached by the soldiers when they find a carriage parked in front of a shop.

Diego and Soledad climb on it, knock down the coachman and whip the horses hard, while the others enter the cabin, completely breathless. The horses neigh, rear surprised by the whipping and run down the street. Soon horse-riding soldiers appear, and an intrepid chase begins through the city center.

Lorenzo puts his head out the window and shouts:

- Towards the sea!

Diego and Soledad drive the carriage at crazy speed, knocking everything in their path: store stalls, wagons, people crossing the path, bird cages, in total havoc. The riders run after them and start shooting to try to stop the coach.

Diego turns right, almost tipping over the coach, which tilts, balance on two wheels and falls back down rushing toward the city center. Other carriage crosses ttheir street and Diego, pulling the reins a little, slows down the coach, but they still hit the rear wheel of that carriage, knocking it down. The cavalry continues to chase them, shooting muskets, piercing the walls of the cabin, passing near Isabel and Paloma, who, frightened, duck and cling to what they can.

At one point, another carriage appears, this time guided by two soldiers and carrying others inside, all armed. A carriage race takes over the narrow streets of old Cartagena. Diego turns left, the soldiers' carriage turns right after, knocking and pulling out a light post. Diego turns right and enters a wider avenue, going the wrong way: a lot of other wagons and buggy come towards them. He has to swerve to the right and to the left, all at high speed. The other carriages swerve too, cursing the coachmen.

The police carriage at the other end of the avenue, facing the right way, which is favorable to them, can more easily reach theirs. As there is no sidewalk or partition between the street ways, the soldiers continue to fire and move to the left, until they touch each other's wheels, trying to throw them to the left.

The cavalry, chasing them from behind, stop shooting, afraid to hit their colleagues. Diego and Soledad have to sneak to the left, when they turns brutally to this side, and are forced to enter the arch corridor of the military barracks of Las Bóvedas, while the enemy carriage runs, in parallel, outside.

The group's carriage racing through the inner passage of the arches, tears away everything that lies ahead: flower shops, fruit stalls, dancers with typical costumes and other people who stood there to practice commercial activities. At the end of the arches, the carriage has to leave though the left and again it collides with that of the policemen who, shooting, hit Soledad's arm.

- Shit!

- Are you okay? – asks Diego, adrenaline coursing hard

- Run! – she says, while tying a piece of her own sleeve to her wound to stop the bleeding.

The two carriages border the wall until they reach the Clock Tower, which is on top of the main gate, and which gives access to the peninsula bathed by the Baía de las Ánimas, a small embankment that advances to the sea. Having been warned, the guards try to close the gates, but the carriages pass the gate in that crazy race.

When the tip of the sea appears, on the esplanade that gives access to the park, the two carriages are still running parallel to each other. Diego directs his horses to the left, pushing the other carriage toward the boundary between land and sea. The soldiers try to push the coach back to the right, but distracted, they don't see that there's a breakwater low wall ahead. They stumble over it and – horses, carriage, and riders – fall into the clear waters of the bay, splashing water on all pedestrians who, trying to avoid being run over, are running everywhere.

Diego and Soledad, injured, barely get to feel happy to have thrown off the persecutors when, still on the esplanade that gives access to the park, tripping over several plants and wooden benches, they find themselves being again chased by ten soldiers on horseback, firing muskets, bullets flying.

- Towards the port! – shouts Lorenzo.

- What are we going to do? – Isabel asks aloud, inside the cabin, through the loud noise of the chase

- There must be boats leaving for the islands – Luna informs, researching her multitask tablet.

- Hurry! – shouts Lorenzo.

He looks back and sees that the cavalry are very close. Even with the speed causing the carriage to shake a lot, he goes out the window and climbs up to the ceiling. From there, he begins to throw the suitcases that were tied there, causing several horses to trip and fall, diminishing the number of chasing soldiers. But the remaining ones keep shooting to try to stop the carriage.

- Go faster! – shouts Lorenzo.

They cross, like lightning, the stretch of land that goes from the Camellón de Los Mártires, pass along the Convent of San Francisco, and run towards the bridge that connects this peninsula to the Peninsula of Boca Grande, where the port is.

At this point, the whole town is already aware of the escape and the persecution. So, as they begin to cross the bridge, in front of the Fort of San Felipe de Barajas, the sentries begin firing cannon to intimidate them. The projectiles fall into the sea, around where they are passing, so close that a flood of water covers the bridge and showers the entire carriage. The soldiers in the back continue to ride and shoot. Another cannonball hits a part of the rock bridge, seconds after the carriage goes by.

The horses of the coach are already breathless and are slowing down, despite the whipping. They enter the port dock, filled with caravels, galleons, and medium-sized ships.

- What are we going to? – shouts Soledad, from above the coach

- See if there's a boat ready to set sail! – says Lorenzo, who had entered back into the cabin

- In this rush, how can we know?

- Look for the ones with the sails unfurled!

The carriage crosses the pedestrian-filled port dock, again knocking down everything that is ahead, but no one gets run over. Diego sees that, not far away, there is a small caravel with the sails well-stew by the wind. The boarding ramp is still lowered, and there's people entering along with suitcases. There are two sailors next to each entrance who begin to pull the ropes that tie the boat to the pier.

He whips the horses even harder, turning the reins towards that caravel:

- Come on! Just a little bit more!

Soledad shouts:

- Hold on tight!

Holding the reins firmly, she pulls them with full force, causing the horses to start a sudden braking, but with the weight, they get unbalanced and spin the carriage a hundred and eighty degrees, causing a sort of bootleg turn, tipping the cabin over and dragging it for a few meters. The guard riders, who were rushing right behind are unable to stop and some end up, in the confusion, hitting the carriage and falling, others getting thrown over the horses, others entering the shops that are at the edge of the port pier, total chaos, but that ends with the momentary incapacitation of the cavalry. People, flowers, goods, birds, horses, guns, everything flies everywhere.

In this mess, Lorenzo, Luna, Thomas, Isabel and Paloma manage to get out of the cabin without any injury. Along with Soledad, they run and climb the ramp which is being removed by the sailors, because the caravel is already moving away from the pier. Diego, the last one, jumps in the air and falls, holding on to the edge of the ramp board. With much sacrifice and helped by his colleagues, he climbs on it and manages to get on to the boat.

The soldiers stop at the edge of the pier, still shooting their pistols and shouting for the boat to stop. Lorenzo quickly takes out two large gold coins and gives the sailors who, satisfied, pretend not to hear the boarding order.

Dead tired, dirty, sweaty, panting, adrenaline rushing through them, after a few minutes to compose themselves, Isabel manages to ask the sailor:

- Where is this ship headed?

- For Havana, *señorita.*

After he walks away, Lorenzo remarks:

- It's going to pass by Isla Grande...

- ... where our ship is! – rejoices Paloma

- So, we're leaving? – asks Isabel

Lorenzo is saddened to recognize:

- We've failed... there's nothing left for us to do...

- Yes... – laments Thomas – we couldn't get the map... After all this work...

- I wouldn't say that – Luna says very assertively.

Everybody looks at her. Smiling, she shows, on the tablet screen, the photo she had taken at the church of the piece of map.

Half awake, half asleep, Jack is the first to be frightened by the noise and the walls shaking:

- Huh... what is... that noise?

O'Connor and the other English also wake up, gradually aware that they are sleeping on the floor, not really knowing where they are. Another loud noise sounds again and makes the walls shake. Then another, and another. They get scared. Kendall asks:

- Oh my god! What is this?

- Sounds like.... Cannon shots! – identifies Winston.

- Yes, they do – Birdie confirms – but... where are we? What's happening?

Alfie tries to explain:

- I don't know, I don't remember much about things, I just remember that we ran out of that church yesterday, late at night, it was very dark...

- ... we run a lot – Laureen amends – we entered what looked like a big shed and collapsed tired in a stone shelter.

Another cannon shot, even stronger, deafens them. Emmett, all messed up, walks towards a small window through which she can see the light of day to try to understand what's going on.

She sees a carriage rushing, with three people on top, chased by several other soldiers on horseback and cannonballs exploding into the water as they cross a bridge.

Not understanding what she was seeing, she looks down and sees that she's in a very high place, inside a wall of stones built on top of each other. A little further on, waves break into rocks, causing foam to jump everywhere.

She comes back and informs:

- We are close to sea cliffs, within a very large stone building.

Laureen thinks:

- Sea... wall... rocks... sea... cannon... – she looks at the room where they are and punches her fist onto the palm of the other hand – we must be in the Castle of San Felipe de Barajas!

Kendall seems to wake up:

- Where? In the Spanish fort?

Laureen runs her hands along the walls of rectangular stones, cut in an isonomic way, overlapped one to the other with a wide strip of clear mortar, she goes to the door of the room, with ovals sills, with heavy wooden door, looks out and sees corridors lighted by openings in the walls. There is no doubt:

- Exactly! The Castle of San Felipe, the largest fortress built by the Spaniards in the New World!

- Oh, boy!... we're fucked up! – exclaims Alfie.

- Why is that? – asks Jack.

- Because we're English people inside a Spanish headquarter, "just because of that"!

Another cannon shot makes the room vibrate again. Kendall collapses into a nervous breakdown, covering her ears with her hands:

- I can't take it anymore!

Laureen hugs her, while O'Connor tries to keep the rational:

- Let's stay calm. We have come this far. We got what we wanted.

- Let's go away then already! – speaks Emmett, already groping her time belt.

- Just a moment – says O'Connor – our mission was not to let the San José sink, we failed this.

Laureen takes the scroll out of her fanny pack:

- But we got the map.

- Let's see what it shows? – suggests Alfie.

She goes to a stone table that's in a corner of the room, and everyone surrounds her. She unrolls the piece of parchment and they begin to analyze it:

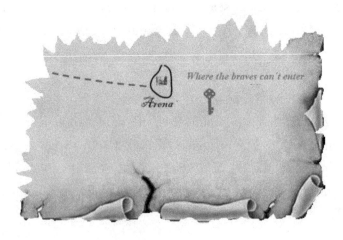

Laureen, using her cartography skills, begins to interpret it, sliding her finger over the piece of parchment as they chat.

- Isla Arena – completes O'Connor – where is it?

- South of Isla Grande, near Punta Barú, on the mainland, belonging to the Rosario archipelago – explains Alfie.

- What's that drawing there? – Birdie asks, approaching her face to take a closer look.

Winston takes a small magnifying glass out of his uniform and hands it to her:

- It seems to be... a kind of grotto ... or cavern...

- This is even stranger – points out Jack – what does this sentence next to it mean? "Where the brave cannot enter"

Laureen says:

- Whoever tore up this map intended for it make you interested on the other part, which must be in this place. They did this for anyone who wants to be smart to decipher it and...

Everyone looks at her suspense pause:

- ... want to risk their lives.

Evening is coming, with a beautiful sunset over the sea. They spot a little island about nearby. Lorenzo asks a passing sailor carrying two buckets of water somewhere:

- Sailor, what island is that?

- Isla Arena, *señor.*

- Will the boat go closer to it?

- No, sir, we are too close already. From here we will divert North.

- Why is that?

The sailor seems surprised by the question:

- Are you not from here, sir? You have never heard of Isla Arena?

The mystery sharpens their curiosity:

- No. Is there something wrong?

The boy is about to speak, but someone calls him. He moves away quickly. Lorenzo looks at the others and asks:

- Strange, but... What do you think? Shall we?

With some hesitation, Luna recalls:

- Our mission was to take the exact location of the galleon's sinking, right?

- Correct.

- Without the final map, we won't have accomplished our mission, right?

- Correct.

They all look at one another. Lorenzo extends his arm and everyone else puts their hands on top his, forming a human star.

- Together! – shouts Lorenzo.

- Together! – they all shout, raising their arms and letting go of their hands.

Lorenzo speaks:

- We're going to pay to take one of this ship's boats and we're going to paddle to Arena.

- "Where the brave can't enter" – recalls Isabel.

- There are no brave ones here, only calm people – translates Thomas

They walk towards the bow to talk to the vessel captain.

Suddenly, the door handle turns like someone's trying to get in. As the door is locked from the inside, a male voice shouts outside in Spanish, knocking on the door:

- Is anybody in there?

He force the doorknob and asks again:

- We heard some talk, who is in there?

O'Connor, coming to his senses, asks the others, in a low voice:

- Which one of you is good at Spanish to answer?

Sergeant Birdie raises her hand:

- *Yo, señor.*

- But you're a woman, a female voice doesn't belong inside a fort. So, of the men, who answers?

Alfie replies:

- I speak a little bit, but...

- But what?

- Wouldn't it be better if we keep quiet, pretending there's no one here?

The knocks on the door become stronger. The man shouts:

- I know there are people there! Iwilll call the guard if you don't open it!

O'Connor looks at him and indicates the door with his eyebrow. Alfie touches it and tries to answer:

- *¡Bue... buenos días, señor!*

- *¿Quién habla?*

- It's me, *yo, señor.*

- *¿Quien? ¿Cuál es su nombre?*

Alfie doesn't understand, he looks at Birdie, who whispers:

- He wants to know your name.

- *Es... es... Juan...*

- *Juan de que?*

He looks at Birdie, she explains:

He wants do know your surname.

He thinks, thinks, quickly and replies:

- *Juan... Juan Borracho!*

Outside, a second of silence, then:

- *Qué? ¿Estás borracho?*

- *¡Si, señor!*

- *¡No puedes beber em cuartel! ¡Abra la puerta!*

The man starts to shake the door harder, trying to get in. Alfie looks at Birdie:

- What did I do?

- You said you are drunk!

Alfie puts his hands on his head and speaks loudly to himself...

- *Ay, que burrito!*

... but the guard, on the other door side, thinks he was talking to him:

- *¿Me llamó de burrito?*

They hear more people gathering up outside. They start throwing themselves against the door to bring it down. O´Connor has no other option:

- Guys, prepare for combat! Don't shoot to kill, just to wound.

With each ever stronger strike, the thick wooden door gives way a little more. They all stand in a defensive position, wielding their weapons. O'Connor signals with his head for Birdie to position herself next to the door. When he realizes that the men outside will advance for another strike, he signals and she opens the lock, causing four soldiers, armed with swords, to advance into the room and fall to the ground.

Two more guards, who were standing, wield muskets and are ready to open fire, when O'Connor shouts:

- Fire!

The English crew begins to shoot the soldiers in their legs, they scream in pain and fall to the ground. This catches the attention of the entire quarter, which begins to mobilize towards the west wing. O´Connor commands:

- Go! Go!

Going over the wounded soldiers, they enter a massive stone corridor, with arch-shaped windows, the end of which leads to another corridor. Not knowing which side to flee to, the group encounters a small battalion of Spanish soldiers whose leader, in front of them, shouts:

- Stop or we'll shoot!

Alfie replies, in English:

- We just want to get out of here!

The boy in uniform is bewildered:

- What???? English here inside the fort? Fire!!

And the crossfire begins: the Spanish with muskets and swords, the crew with modern pistols, shooting them in the thighs just to take them out of combat. There are no more Spanish standing when O'Connor commands the group:

- Let's find a way out!

As she passes Alfie, Kendall says:

- How about you keep your mouth shut?

They go down a narrow stone staircase and reach a room full of noble wooden furniture. Another group of soldiers appears at the other exit of the room and new gunfire begins. The English knock down tables and cupboards to protect themselves, shooting to dispel the Spanish. Bullets ricochet off the walls. Gunpowder smoke from the old pistols fills the room and makes it difficult to see. A trumpet is heard outside, and Birdie warns:

- They're warning the whole platoon.

O'Connor signals them to stop shooting. Thinking that they had hurt everyone, the Spanish recklessly enter the room, still pointing their pistols. Taking advantage of the bait that's worked, O'Connor shouts:

- Fire!

The group stands up behind tables and cupboards and opens fire, injuring opponents but leaving everyone alive. Blood splatters fly everywhere but the group clears a way for them to go out and down another flight of stairs that goes into the basement.

At this moment, they reach the maze of secret passages built in the undergrounds of San Felipe de Barajas Fort. Panting, O'Connor asks Laureen:

- Where's this leads?

- To several places, it was built precisely to baffle any invaders.

Seeing several corridors leading to the right, to the left and forward, O'Connor makes a quick decision:

- The more people, the easier to get cornered. Let's split up – he turns to Winston – you, Laureen and Jack, go right – addressing Birdie – you, Emmett and Alfie, go left – Kendall and I will go forward. We meet... we meet...

- Where? – asks Winston

- ... at the closest point to the sea – he concludes, uncertainly – Turn on the ear radio communicators.

A shot scrapes his ear and hit the wall right behind him. He shouts:

- Go!

The group divides, each subgroup entering the indicated corridors. More shots are fired at O'Connor and Kendall and they flee, walking a little bent due to the low height of the tunnels. At one point, walking, Kendall says:

- I knew you'd want to be alone with me, honey.

- I just distributed our forces – he replies, wielding the gun at head level and looking at the end of the tunnel.

- You mean I'm the weakest part?

- Oh, please, this is no time to discuss the relationship.

She passes in front of him and insists:

- No, wait, I'm pretty good at all I do, ok?

- I didn't say you weren't.

- You, guys, think you're strong, macho, intelligent, and that we women have to be protected.

- But I only divided us so we wouldn't get stuck all together, that's all!

- Yes, but – she mimics his voice – "I divided to balance the forces". And you only put the men in charge!

He stops, look at her, who's furious. But he rationalizes:

- Oh, my God, we've got to get out of here, let's go on.

They reach a stone staircase that leads down. They're starting to descend it, keeping an attack position.

At this point, the entire battalion is aware that Englishmen had invaded the largest Spanish fortress built in the New World. Armed soldiers were running everywhere, the main courtyard has hoisted flags and gunners manning each cannon. Trumpets sound an alert.

Winston, Laureen and Jack go down a staircase and, upon hearing a noise just ahead, stop at the last step. Winston looks around the corner of the wall and sees a stone room filled with iron armor, swords, and spears. Three soldiers are watching through the stone window, distracted.

Winston nods for the two to follow. They appear at the entrance of the door, pointing the weapons at the soldiers who, surprised, stand still without reaction. But one of them takes a step forward, forcing Winston to trigger the gun. But that's when he realizes he's out of ammo. Laureen and Jack also try to shoot, but they're also out of ammo.

The guards take swords and advance on them, shouting. Winston, Laureen and Jack come out of the stairwell and advance into the middle of the room. Laureen takes a sword, Winston, a spear, and Jack is in a jiu-jitsu defense position. The three stand on one side and the three Spanish soldiers on the other, with mere seconds to decide on the attack.

Winston still has time to warn Laureen:

- You'd better stay behind, we'll defend you. Fighting with a sword is hard.

Looking at the soldier in front of her, she replies:

- Young man, don't be fooled by appearances!

The Spanish soldier in front of her advances and strikes a blow with his sword. Agile as a cat, the old lady turns back, runs towards the wall, climbs two steps on it to get impulse to do a backflip. She does a pirouette in the air, goes over the soldier and falls behind him, striking him with the sword in the butt making him jump and scream. Winston and Jack look at each other, surprised, but they don't have much time, as the fight begins. Winston tries to fend off the blows of the sword with the spear from all sides, while Jack dodges the other Spanish man's blows like a snake.

Laureen is fencing very efficiently, the opposing soldier advances his arm to pierce her, but she bends to the side, the noise of clinking metal increases in intensity, adrenaline is rushing. Jack fly kicks his soldier, knocking him to the ground, but he gets up and attacks back, causing Jack to use several jiu-jitsu defense blows quickly and masterfully. Winston advances with the spear, but his opposing soldier is also agile and dodges, advancing with sword blows at the height of his abdomen. Winston falls and the soldier jumps on top of him to struck him with the sword, but he dodges, and the soldier strucks the ground. Sparks come out of the fight between swords and spears.

Emmett, Birdie and Alfie, alert, walk down the narrow candle-lit stone corridor, pointing their guns forward. Alfie, the last in line, looks back from time to time to see if there's no one chasing them.

- Where will we end up? – asks Emmett.

- No idea, let's move on – Birdie replies.

A little further on there is an intersection with another corridor. They hear the noise of people approaching. They lean against the wall, even though this didn't hide them in anyway. In moments, a group of Spanish soldiers goes by from one side to the other, so quickly that they did not even look the sideways, otherwise they would have seen them. They disappear in the tunnel going to the right of where they are. They breathe a sigh of relief and are about to continue to walk when a straggler soldier, emerges from the same tunnel. He sees the invaders and shouts the alert:

- Here! They're here!

Birdie shoots the boy in the knee, and he falls screaming in pain. They quickly pass over him and run forward, keeping to the same corridor they were in. The group of soldiers, who had passed to the other side, comes back and chases them. And a great manhunt begins in the secret passages of San Felipe Fort. The three of them turn right and go down a staircase, the Spanish soldiers follow, firing shots that hit the walls. The three of them end up in a larger underground room filled with wine wood barrels, Birdie fires a machine gun vole at several of them, causing them to leak. They run through the left-side passage, but Alfie stops, joins his hands like a shell, collects in his hands some of the leaking wine and drinks it, closing his eyes in delight:

- Yum... Spanish wine... – he looks at the barrels leaking to the floor – what a waste!

He sees the soldiers arriving on the other side and flees. The soldiers run across the room but slip on the floor and fall tripping over one another. Some faint when their head hit the floor. But the ones that remain, even in wine soaked clothes, set out in search of them, increasingly furious.

Running through the narrow passages, Emmett has the idea of putting out of the candles on the way, making the tunnels dark, which makes it difficult for the soldiers to chase after them, being left ever farther behind.

They climb three flights of stairs and begin to see the light of day. Gasping a lot, breathless, they come to another room with several windows to the outside, also full of wooden barrels. Looking out of the window, they discover that they are high up in one of the castle's wide towers. The courtyard downstairs is teeming with soldiers running everywhere.

Alfie is very happy:

- Yay! Now I can drink!

- We don't have time for that, idiot - criticizes Emmett.

But as they approach the barrels, they find out that they're filled with not wine, but gunpowder.

After descending several stone stairs and passing through several rooms, O'Connor and Kendall hear sea sound coming from one of the passageways. They descend another flight of stairs and arrive at a kind of grotto, with a small sandy beach, where the sea invades with its strong and constant waves. A medium-sized boat is tied to a boarding pier.

Kendall cheers up:

- We found a way to escape! We have to warn the others!

O'Connor takes the small mobile-Bluetooth-looking intercom, puts it in his ear and says:

- Guys, attention, guys, are you there?

He waits a moment, but as no one responds, he repeats:

- Warning, attention. Do you copy?

He looks at Kendall, who explains:

- We're way below the castle, the signal's not reaching them.

- Let's go up then.

They climb two flights of stairs and reach a high-ceilinged circular room, with several entrance doors that lead there. The place is illuminated by torches on the walls. Kendall asks:

- Which door did we come from?

- I don't know, we should have left some signal during the passage.

- See if there's a signal now.

O'Connor sends the call again:

- Do you copy me? Are you listening?

Winston's voice sounds in the intercom:

- "Yes, I copy you!"

- Winston, we found a way out. You have to come here!

The answer takes a while, only crackles can be heard. O'Connor repeats:

- Winston, do you understand? You have to come here, follow the signal from my tracker! Answer!

Winston, lying on the ground, sweating hard, with blood scratches all over his face, is lying holding the spear as if it were a supine bar, with the Spanish soldier on top of him, trying to strangle him.

- We'll try, Captain. Over.

In a supreme effort, he manages to propel the soldier up and throw him away. He sticks the spear in his leg, and he screams in pain. Laureen still fights the other soldier on top of a rectangular table, she makes a 360 degree turn and, lowering herself, runs the blade though his legs, causing him to fall injured.

Jack slips-up receives a sword cut to his stomach, leaving a scratch-line that starts to bleed. The soldier bends his arm to give a fatal sword blow to cut off his head, but he, even though wounded, manages to lower himself and the blade passes close to his hair. He trips the soldier, causing him to fall. Jack looks around, takes the helmet of an iron armor that was nearby and sticks it on the head of the fallen soldier who stands up, but barely seeing, is hit hard by a high kick to the chest from Jack. He falls to the ground, unconscious.

Laureen comes to check Jack's bleeding wound, she picks up a flag that is on a pole and ties it tightly around his torso, trying to stop the bleeding.

- Shit! – he complains

Winston checks the signal on his wristwatch with O'Connor's location and speaks into the microphone:

- We're on our way, Captain!

They move out of the room towards the staircases leading to the lower tunnels.

O'Connor receives the answer:

- Great, quick!

He says to Kendall:

- Birdie has to answer.

He insists on the transmitter:

- Birdie! Sargent Birdie! Do you copy?

No answer, he calls louder:

- Emmett, Birdie, anyone hears me?

As he is looking down, focused on communication, Kendall shoves her elbow against him and points to one of the entrance doors. Someone, who's been crouching through the tunnel, starts coming in through it. When the man enters, he begins to unbend his trunk upwards,... revealing a 6'5" tall, very strong, muscular, hairy, bald, shirtless, and thug-looking giant. O'Connor bends his head up until he faces the man's huge-bearded frown.

- I thought the Spaniards were short.

- Maybe he's German – replies Kendall, also frightened.

- *Hasta la vista, baby* – says the giant man.

- He must be the eighteenth-century Schwarzenegger – concludes Kendall.

The man closes his fists, lets out a grunt and takes a few steps towards them. O'Connor points the gun at him, is about to shoot, but the giant man, with a slap, throws the gun away. He takes O'Connor by the neck and throws him against the wall. Kendall shoots him in the thigh, the bullet goes in, but he doesn't even feel it. He hits her gun and throw it away too.

O'Connor gets up, sort of stunned, and attacks the big soldier. He punches him in the stomach (which is at the height of his head), but nothing happens. He punches the giant in his balls, but still gets no reaction. The soldier responds with a huge punch at O' Connor, throwing him far again. It's a disproportionate fight. The giant walks towards him, but Kendall manages to jump on his back, climb up to his neck and fasten it with her legs. He struggles, pulls her legs with his hands and throws her far again. She falls and gets hurt, getting very dizzy for a few moments.

The big man goes after O'Connor, who's still lying down, and raises his thick leg to step on his chest, the sole of his boot full of nails. O'Connor has a second to dodge the blow, rolling to the side, he jumps and grabs the soldier from behind and chokes him in a headlock position. The man struggles to get rid of O'Connor, walks backwards and hits the wall behind him several times, until O'Connor, in pain, has to let go of his neck.

With the pain, the man gets even angrier and kicks O'Connor several times, who's already bloodied from so many blows. Kendall, desperate, takes the guns and sees they're broken, she can't use them. She looks around, looks up, and sees a rope hanging from the ceiling by an iron ring, with two ends hanging down. She has an idea, a single try. She takes one of the ends and ties it in a noose. As the giant is distracted kicking O'Connor, she comes from behind and jumps back on to his back, managing to fix her legs on his neck. He tries to get out of it, hitting her on the walls. During one of the blows, she manages to pick up a torch and burn his face, but he throws the torch away.

Still mounted on his shoulders, she manages to place rope knot around his neck and, like a cat, she jumps in the air and reaches the other end of the rope. With her weight, she manages to make the rope stretch, but not enough to lift the heavy giant, who stands on tiptoe, semi hanged, trying to remove the rope from his neck.

Meanwhile, O'Connor manages to recover a little bit, he stands up a little dizzy and sees the picture: Kendall, hanging on one end of the rope, trying to counterweight the soldier so he hangs. He runs and hangs himself on the rope next to her, with the weight of the two of them, the man comes out of the ground, hanging at the gallows. He struggles, and struggles, until he gets out of breath and faints.

Seeing that he was out of combat (but not dead), the two of them let go of the rope and the three of them fall to the ground, the man passed out and O'Connor and Kendall, broken.

Panting, wounded, with blood marks on their faces and arms, they look at each other and smile quickly. She says:

- Did you see I don't need balls?

- I saw... Thank you!

At this moment, still on the ground, he hears a voice through the intercom that is still in his right ear:

- Captain, captain! Do you copy me? Over!

- It's Birdie. Birdie, yes, I copy you, can you hear me now?

- Yes, sir. Over

- We found a way out, come quickly to the signal I sent on the tracker. Be quick, the tide is rising.

- "Where are you?"

- In the lower basement of the castle, follow the sign. But see if there's anything you can do to slow down the Spanish, they can't get to us, understand? Can you do anything?"

- Yes, I can, sir. Over.

Birdie looks at one of the entrances to the tower room they're in. Soldiers show up and point the pistols at them. She points to the ground, and everyone sees what she's showing: a powder trail goes from where she is, next to one of the windows, to the pile of barrels that are stored on the other side of the room.

They stop and take in what's about to happen. Alfie lights a match and ironically throws it at the beginning of the trail. It catches fire and, releasing a cloud of smoke typical of gunpowder, the fire begins to head toward the heave of stowed ammunition.

The terrified soldiers scream, drop their weapons and run down the stairs of the tower. Birdie, Alfie and Emmett look out of the window and see that the roof of the housing attached to the tower is about sixteen feet down. The powder fuse is approaching the vats. Birdie looks at Emmett and Alfie, who nod their heads.

They jump out of the window. The fire hits the huge stockpile of barrels and a large explosion blasts the entire tower of the San Felipe de Barajas Fort. As they fall on the roof, rolls of fire come out of the windows and down the tower staircase, causing it to collapse.

The fantastic explosion makes the whole fort tremble. The three of them fall onto the neighboring roof, they get a little hurt, but not enough to stop them from running to the nearest entrance to the secret passages below. They are not chased by the soldiers, who try to escape the flames and stones falling from the collapsing tower all around the fort.

They go down the stairs, following Birdie's wrist device signal, and on the way, they meet Laureen and Winston helping an injured Jack to run as well. The six descend until they reach the room where O'Connor and Kendall, also run over, are waiting.

O'Connor commands:

- Let's get out of here! Follow me!

They went down the two flights of stairs, but the tide had already risen enough to cover the small sandy beach. Nonetheless, without hesitation, everyone jumps in the water and goes swimming to where the boat is tied to the pier, they enter it, release the moorings, and leave the cave, paddling desperately.

They go out to the open sea, abandoning the scenery while the sun is setting amid the column of black smoke rising from the fort of San Felipe de Barajas. Only then Kendall notices Jack's wound and tries to fix the bandage.

- You've lost enough blood.

- I'm sorry... – says the weakened Asian.

- You're going to be fine, rest.

- Where are we going to? – Emmett asks.

O'Connor takes the map out of his pocket and points to the Isla Arena:

- Over here...

- ... "where the brave cannot enter" – completes Alfie.

In silence, exhausted, they continue paddling and moving away from the continent, under a beautiful twilight of the Caribbean sun.

INTERNATIONAL COURT OF JUSTICE - THE HAGUE, NETHERLANDS, YEAR 2021

The beautiful and imposing building of the Peace Palace shows a bustle beyond the normally seen in that courthouse. Several reporters are at the gates entrance, taking pictures of all the armored cars that pass through them.

Several black cars, with glasses so darkened that it is impossible see who is inside, enter through the main gate, go around the entrance garden and park at the main door of the castle, from where several authorities leave them with costumes typical of their countries.

In front of the entrance, among several others, a blonde reporter explains what is happening in front of a camera:

- Breaking News straight from the Netherlands. Today is the date of the trial on the rights of search and exploitation of the wreckage of Galleon San José, occurred in June 1708, whose cargo is valued at around twenty billion dollars. Since the beginning of their searches in the Caribbean Sea, several countries have claimed the ship's rescue rights, mostly the United States for having discovered probable traces of the shipwreck in 1986; Spain for claiming ownership over cargo and vessel; England for claiming rights of economic sharing over transportations at that time, and finally the Colombian government claims its rights over the marine waters in which the ship probably sank.

Behind her, men in suits surrounded by security guards, women in African saris, men in turbans and other people in costumes typical of their countries go by. The reporter continues:

- Our reporter Douglas Kent brings us news directly from inside the auditorium. Kent?

A man with blue eyes and a gray beard appears in front of the other camera, this time having as a background the stained-glass wall of the courtroom. He speaks in English with an Irish accent:

- Yes, Susy, good morning to our viewers. The trial is about to begin, and the expectations are high. There are two main currents among judges: one, which defends the exploratory right only for nations that entered the process more than twenty years ago and another current, which defends the freedom of exploitation for all nations, regardless of intercontinental treaties, on the grounds of historical humanity heritage. Let's wait for the session to start.

The meeting floor of the Dutch castle built in 1913 is huge and majestically decorated: from its 30-feet-high ceiling, with Renaissance paintings depicting Biblical scenes painted on wooden vaults, hanging crystal chandeliers with gilded fittings which hold fifty lamps each hang. There is a rectangular-shaped auditorium and, on the wall just behind the judges' tables, three large stained-glass windows let the natural and colorful lighting invade the plenary. Around the plenary, from the floor to halfway up the walls, brown wood paneling bring warmth and sobriety to the room, which is completed by the sky-blue carpet with mustard floral ornaments.

Within this environment of luxury and magnificence, the International Court of Justice has been functioning since 1945, aimed at judging cases directed by the United Nations Organization (UNO) that need impartiality. There are fifteen members in the jury, representing countries from all continents and mixing, on an equality basis, rich and poor countries: France, Somalia, Japan, Slovakia, Morocco, Brazil, Lebanon, China, United States, Germany, Uganda, India, Australia, Russia, and Jamaica. For that particular session, representatives from Spain, Colombia and England were also invited.

The bustle of the crowded auditorium gradually diminishes as the fifteen judges, wearing magistrates' togas, begin to enter through the doors that give entrance to the far end of the table and take their seats, identified with signs placed in front of the table's microphones.

The Ugandan representative, appointed as Chairman, opens the solemn session in the English official language and gives the floor to the Secretary, who is rapporteur for the case. After presenting the summary of the case, he opens the floor for debate among the participants.

The United States representative is the first to position himself:

- Given the facts, it is clear that the right of preference rests with those who first found the traces of the ship.

- It might be clear to those who have a capitalist vision, we need to see what other visions might bring – bombs, direct, the representative of Russia

- It is not a question of economic regime – the American defends his position – but of recognizing those who took initiative before the others.

- There had been no other initiative because we were in line with international marine property agreements – explains the Australian.

- Agreements that, due to the interests at stake – completes the German –seem to have been put on the back burner.

- We must not forget that the most important is the protection of the environment – the representative of Brazil positioned himself.

Everyone looks at him, half in awe. It turns red and continues:

- If we encourage a worldwide treasure hunt, we can say goodbye to the crystal-clear transparency of the Caribbean waters.

- You are right – the Chinese representative mocks – and you could start to set an example by taking care of your own waters...

The Brazilian gets a little redder, but also provokes:

- At least we haven't created and released any viruses up to this day...

The auditorium begins to murmur. The Chairman intervenes:

- Gentlemen, gentlemen, let's not lose focus. The theme is the deliberation on the rights to search for the shipwreck.

The representative of France speaks with the usual French diplomacy:

- Gentlemen, let's maintain order. Our country has always advocated freedom, equality and fraternity. Therefore, we are in favor of opening the research to all nations that are able to take up this exploitation, within the environmental rules and limits that this Court defines.

The Moroccan counter-argues:

- Forgive me, sir, but we are no longer in the Bastille times, where there was only one enemy in inferior conditions...

The Frenchman frowns, but the Moroccan continues:

- ... in the modern world, freedom is misunderstood for libertinism. Without rules and restrictions, we make piracy official.

The comment raises new murmuring among those present, a noise that increases because everyone wants to speak louder than the other.

The Chairman has to intervene again, hitting the gavel on the support in front of him:

- Silence in Court!

The American speaks again:

- The United States invested a fortune in 1986 to find the location for the first time. The Colombian government has not complied with the partition contract and since then we have been questioning this compliance in court.

The Russian cuts in again:

- Are you here to represent the interests of your country or to defend the impartiality this Court must have?

- That is correct – confirms the representative of India – this is a conflict of interest. He shouldn't vote.

- Wait, that's not what I'm talking about – the American defends himself – I'm presenting the principle of economic freedom, which rules the decisions of this Supreme Court.

- In the name of the "economic freedom" you mention – the Spanish provokes - Spain is the one who should receive back what was cowardly stolen from them by England.

The Colombian could not miss the cue:

- *Permiso, Señor, pero que* who was robbed were the Andean countries, especially Peru, from where Spain exploited, for centuries, the riches of the colonies. It's their wealth that's been hibernating at the bottom of the sea for all these centuries.

- Were they remunerated for services rendered – the Spanish says annoyed – and the military protection we gave? What about all the culture transferred? What about all the catechism, engineering and development of the Old World that we transferred?

To which the Colombian retorts:

- "Services"?!? How dare you call predatory colonization... "services"?

The conflict gets more intense by the minute, the members of the table talk amongst themselves, consulting with the nearest judge. Tumult takes over the hearing once more. The Ugandan chairman has to bang the gavel several times to recover silence:

- Your Honors! Should I ask you to recover your senses? Here no one defends anyone's cause! This Court is neutral! Be rational!

After a few minutes of fretting, the English representative presses the bell signaling he wishes to speak. The Chairman nods, allowing.

- Regardless of my nationality – ponders the polite English – and positioning above the individual interests on behalf of the collective ones, England declares that it is willing to cooperate in whatever it takes to rescue the San José.

The Indian representative whispers to the Jamaican, who is by his side:

- Empty words. We should know after centuries of their colonization…

- Be clearer, sir – asks the Jamaican, aloud.

- What I mean to say is that, respectfully, the British government can finance any initiative, public or private, of explorers who have the ability to rescue the remains of the galleon, dividing any profits equally.

- Do you present the proposal to split it half-and-half? – asks the Lebanese.

- Yes, sir.

- With any mercenary who might presents themselves?

- Well... let's call them specific purpose joint venture entrepreneurs.

- By Allah!! – exclaims the Lebanese aloud - he created a technical name for business pirates!!

There's general laughter. The situation is getting out of hand. The Chairman stands up and, in a threatening tone, shouts:

- Silence! Silence! I'm suspending the session!

He is about to press the button that triggers sound signaling the closing of the plenary, when the representative of Japan, an old man, who, until that moment, had heard everything with the typical silence of the Asians, asks for the floor. Everyone sits down again and the Ugandan signals for him to speak:

- Honorable judges – he begins, calmly and melodically – among our millennial wisdom, there are several proverbs spoken by wise thinkers throughout our history. One of these proverbs says, "Vision without action is a daydream. Action without vision is a nightmare." This means that without planning, no action will work. But without accomplishing what we have planned, we'll arrive nowhere. We're here to discuss who has the legitimate right to...to... – he does not remember the word in English and asks for help from the interpreter next to him – ... to hoist the remains of the Galleon San José, but thinking exclusively of each one's own benefit.

He stands up and continues his speech, holding everyone's attention. The cameras of all news channels around the world focus on his face marked by the wrinkles of time:

- No one here is thinking about how many in need there around the world this money could help – he looks at Somalis – how many children are skin and bones in their country? – he looks at the Indian and asks - how much need for basic sanitation? – he looks at the Jamaican – and how many farmers have nothing to eat, the fruit of their own crops? Gentlemen, the world is not made just where we can see. Our homes have air conditioning, sofa, high-tech kitchens. But we have brothers who have nowhere to sleep, where to sit, dying of cold or heat, lying on the streets. Our fridges are full, we throw food away. We leave the tap open while we do the dishes. But there are children who don't even have access water let alone food to store in refrigerators. We are here – he shows the room with his hands – in this wonderful, finely decorated place, while our fellow men die in wars, terrorist attacks and meaningless revolutions. Where's the charity? The perfect charity, preached by the Apostle Paul?

He pauses allowing the listeners to self-examine their conscience. He continues:

- If, instead of each country going out alone looking for this fortune – hypocritically disguised as a "rescue of human's history" – we joined our forces, our technologies, our experts, our financial resources, and created a multinational organization that kept half of the profit to be divided amongst the participants and donated the other half to UNICEF or another global welfare entity? Wouldn't we be more successful then? A single string can be easily broken, but intertwined with other strings, it forms a rope. "The sea is great because it does not despise the streams," says another Japanese proverb. Thank you.

He sits down and is given a standing ovation, both by the audience and by the other judges at the table. The Chairman announces the opening of the secret vote:

- Magistrates! We now have three solutions among which to choose on the matter of who will have the rights to exploit and enjoy the spoils of the Galleon San José, sunk in 1708. The first option is to give single and full right to one of the four countries that claim it. Those who vote for this option should indicate which country should be contemplated and why. The second option is to open the right of exploitation to all and allocate the spoils to those who first find their location and start their rescue. The third option is to authorize and regulate the creation of a multinational consortium that will hold all rights over the search and location of the shipwreck, and which shall receive half of what is found while the other half will be put towards humanitarian causes or organizations. The vote session is open.

The fifteen judges receive the form to vote in writing. Although the vote is secret, they have to write it in their own hands. After about thirty minutes, a collector employee, in the uniform of the Dutch navy, passes by with a wooden ballot box with golden adornments and the magistrates insert their forms, one by one. The auditorium is packed with people talking in low voices.

Kent, the reporter, appears again on the screens and announces:

- Ladies and gentlemen, the moment is of great expectation. Never in the history of this collegiate, so controversial a decision has been voted. All countries are waiting for an answer: who will claim the twenty billion dollars that are yet to be discovered by humans?

When the officer collects the last vote of those on the left end, he hands the closed box to the Chairman who, with much ceremony, opens the lid with a large golden key. He begins to take out the votes, one by one, and asks the Secretary to write them down on the official internal regulations' form. After counting every vote, the Secretary delivers the sheet to the representative of Uganda, who, very seriously, announces:

- Ladies and gentlemen, today this Court hands humanity one of its greatest challenges. Supreme result: all fifteen votes, unanimously, opt for the creation of an international collective cooperative consortium, which may be composed by public and private initiative. Said consortium will receive fifty percent of what is found, and the remaining fifty percent shall be donated to charities of international renown and reach. We will now appoint the management group that in charge of creating its regulation and structure. This session is closed. God Be Praised!

Everyone in the plenary celebrates, joyfully, the wise decision of the Court. Ministers greet the representative of Japan, who replies with humility.

- The more fuller a rice cob is, the more it leans.

CGHQ HEADQUARTERS - CHELTENHAM, UNITED KINGDOM - YEAR: 2021

General Walsh is watching the news broadcast direct from The Hague in his command room at CGHQ. Someone knocks on the door; he authorizes the entry:

- Ccome in!

A medium stature commandant, sporting medals on his uniform, enters with a report on his hand. He looks at the screen and comments:

- I see you've already heard the latest news.

- Yes, I have.

- So, what are the orders, sir?

Rolling the remote control between his fingers, holding it at eye height, he looks at the screen and answers:

- Tell Port Down to send the following message: come back quickly with the map in hands.

The officer salutes:

- Yes, sir!

He turns around and leaves, closing the door behind him. Walsh says to himself:

- Let's see which rice cob gets fuller first...

NATIONAL INTELLIGENCE CENTRE - MADRID, YEAR 2021

Breathless, Dr. Perez enters the room and finds Dr. Jimenez and Dr. Inez reading books. He holds a newspaper. Dr. Jimenez asks:

- What's it?

- Didn't you read the news today?

Dr. Inez looks over her glasses:

- Anything other than bad economics and fake politics?

Prof. Perez opens the newspaper and shows the front-page headline: "DISPUTE FOR THE SAN JOSÉ FINALLY COMES TO AN END". The two read the news quickly and look at Perez:

- What do we do?

Perez walks around the room, nervous:

- I don't know, I don't know... any sign of them?

- No – answers Dr. Jimenez – no sign. Communication can only be made from inside the capsule.

- It's been five days since they've been there – Dr. Inez adds – the hole will only remain open for another five.

- What happens if they run out of time, and they don't come back? – asks Perez.

- The time tunnel closes, and they will forever be trapped in the past – replies Dr. Inez.

- Or even worse – completes Dr. Jimenez – if the tunnel closes while they are crossing.

Prof. Perez walks from side to side, looks at them both and decides:

- Send a signal for them to return immediately!

- Even if they can't find the treasure map? – asks Dr. Jimenez

With his back to them, looking out the window, Prof. Perez replies:

- No treasure is worth more than their lives!

ISLA GRANDE, ROSÁRIO ARCHIPELAGO, COLOMBIA - YEAR: 1708

A red light begins to flash on the central control panel of the Columbus capsule, but no one is present to respond to it.

CHAPTER V
THE FOUR CHALLENGES

The ROSÁRIO ARCHIPELAGO, COLOMBIA - YEAR: 1708

The small sailboat sails quickly through the sea, driven by the Southeast wind. The last rays of sunlight still show on the horizon line. The young Spanish team are apprehensive about what lies ahead. Lorenzo is at the helm and Isabel goes over to meet him, taking care to walk in a way so as not to tip the boat over. She looks back and sees a small image of the caravel they've just left. She looks ahead and sees the tip of firm ground that begins to rise on the horizon. She asks Lorenzo:

- Have we made the best choice?
- I don't know. We're not going to know until this is all over.
- Will it be over?
- It will most surely be over'. I just don't know how it's going to end.
- Look! – says Luna, pointing to one side – whales!

They look and see the back of several whales surfacing to breathe, squirting water upwards. There are dozens, of all sizes, the babies accompanying their mothers. They pass right next to the boat, making it swing a lot, but they don't attack. They emit the characteristic noise of cetaceans, a mixture of whistle, with muffled locomotive whistle and short winches, that sound like hoooop, hoooop, hoooop, emitting sound waves that can be heard from a distance. One passes so close that Luna can stretch her arm and touch her body.

- Beautiful!

One of them jumps very close, lifting its ton-weighted-body and, when it falls, produces a wave that leaves everyone wet.

- Come on! – complains Thomas.

- Look – Paloma points out – there's a baby whale all wrapped in a fishing net!

- Indeed. This way it's going to die – confirms Thomas.

Without hesitation, Paloma jumps into the water and swims towards the cub, that is floating sideways, with a fin out of the water. Diego and Isabel jump over too. Getting close to it, they start cutting the ropes to get it out. Mom whale seems to understand that they are helping and does not attack them. In a few minutes, they release the cub from the net, and it jumps, happily, close to its mother. She sprays a jet of water up, as if thanking them.

They go back to the boat, which gradually moves away from them. Isabel, wet, feels cold and wraps her arms around herself. Lorenzo puts his arm over her shoulder, trying to warm her up. She says:

- I've been wondering why we're doing this.

- Me too...

- You know, at first, it was all new, challenging, an adventure...

- "To the service of the motherland," remember?

- I do... now I don't know if it's worth it

A tear falls down her face. Lorenzo drops the helm and, with his finger, catches her tear. The boat begins to go off course, which attracts the attention of the other. Lorenzo quickly holds the helm again:

- Either you stop crying or the boat will turn over.

She smiles and lays her head on his shoulder, feeling protected. He speaks softly:

- Do you remember our deal back at school?

- Which deal?

- When we have ten things in common you will let me kiss you?

She looks into his eyes and smiles:

- I remember you didn't even fill a hand.

- I did... plus one finger of the other hand.

He lets go of the helm again to show her five fingers. Once more the boat makes a slight turn. People look angrily back to see what's going on. He takes back the helm and sail on. Isabel says:

- You know what I admire about you?

- Yay! Am I going to listen to a compliment?

- Your persistence.

- That's it?

- Well... – she starts counting her right-hand fingers – ... persistence, courage, initiative, decision and a great heart!

- You see? It filled a hand!

She lifts a finger from her left hand and completes:

- And charm, lots of charm!

He takes his arm off from around her and starts counting on his fingers:

- Well... you are intelligent, curious – he lifts two fingers – very curious...

She laughs and lowers one of his fingers:

- They're not worth two fingers.

He continues:

- Supportive, creative and fun.

She's a little awkward. He closes all his fingers and opens his thumb to complete:

- And beautiful, you're so beautiful!

They look at each other seriously for a moment and approach to touch their lips. She closes her eyes, so does he, and they're almost kissing when Thomas, in front of the boat, yells:

- Land in sight!

It's already night, but the full moon illuminates the outline of Isla Arena on the horizon. They are approaching land and realize that there is a small fog around the island. Lorenzo comments:

- Fogs are not very common on tropical Caribbean islands, especially at this time of night.

They enter the fog and Thomas lights the flashlights they carry. They go around the rocky coastline of the island, avoiding getting too close so as not to break the boats hull on the rocks. They pass a small beach and make a right turn, sailing around the back portion of the island in relation to the mainland.

They are surprised and terrified by what they see: several shipwrecks are revealed, partially submerged. As if it were a graveyard of ships, there were sails torn just out of water, stuck broken hulls, ships of all sizes, a few large galleons among them, all sunk their wood blackened by time.

Along with the fog, this makes the place lugubrious. The team's boat sails among the wrecks, illuminated by the lanterns, trying not to hit any of them. Paloma leans over Thomas and asks:

- I wonder what happened to them.

- Whatever it was – he replies – I hope it doesn't happen to us.

- "Where the braves can't enter" ... would it be a warning?

After about ten minutes zigzagging among the wreckages, suddenly a stronger wind blows the sail of the boat, propelling it towards the island. Thomas illuminates the rocks and discovers that, among them, the sea enters through a large cave, with crystal clear water illuminated by the moonlight.

At the top of the entrance to the cave, a large bust of a beautiful woman, with long wavy hair covering her breasts, was carved in a stone of the island.

- Wow! Look at that!

The boat begins its entrance through the open cave between the cliffs. The moonlight lets them see the high walls, with stalactites everywhere on the ceiling, like melted stone cones, and stalagmites, on the floor, coming out of the water level, like melted candles. As they advance inward, the environment takes on various shades of blue, light, bright, navy, dark, in a mixture of magic and shivering. Several life-size sculptures of naked women, are carved on the stone walls. The flashlights hit them, and they reflect bright spots, like beautiful blue crystals. Soledad notices something moving underneath the boat and says:

- Guys, looks like there's something swimming under the boat.

- I didn't feel anything – replies Paloma.

- I think we'd better get out of here – warns Soledad.

The cave increases in height and width, as if they reached a kind of submerged lake. From the ceiling, mixed with even larger stalactites, hang algae and corals. Encrusted on the walls, close to the water, stone platforms resembled a pier where they could disembark and walk over. The cones of the stalagmites coming out of the water are even larger, making the scenery look like a large Gothic-style castle. Thomas has an idea:

- Shall we put out the flashlights?

The four turn off their flashlights and marvel at what they see: the entire ceiling of the cave lights up with the fluorescent algae and corals, in various bright blue, white and yellow tones. It looked like the cave ceiling was a very starry sky. Even the water is illuminated by the luminescence, as if it were a pool with lights in it.

- How is this possible?

- Plankton – explains Luna – they are fluorescent.

- It reminds me that, at this period in time, there is not as much pollution in the seas as in our time – Paloma laments.

In the middle of the lake, a large moonlight ray descends over a rock, which juts about six ½ feef out of the water, isolated, as if it were a small island. It is all covered by algae and corals, and shines brighter than the ceiling, producing an image of magic and amazement. They look all over, fascinated.

Lorenzo sees something different at the top of the rock, which shines under the moon's light. They approach and he screams, pointing at the spot:

- Look! A golden key!

- And it looks like there's something tied up to it – completes Thomas.

- Let's get closer.

They paddle towards the central rock, which looks even bigger from up close. When they get closer, Luna approaches her face to examine closely the shiny stones encrusted in the rock and fascinated, discovers:

- People! Topazes, tourmalines, and diamonds!

- Seriously? – asks Diego – he takes a knife and manages to take off a large blue topaz, looking closely at its intense glow.

- This one must be worth about 200,000 dollars.

Diego puts the stone in his pocket and readies himself to take another one, when Lorenzo warns:

- Guys, we're here for the key, so can we leave this for later?

- All right, captain!

Lorenzo approaches the boat as much as possible so that Diego can begin to climb the stone island. With great difficulty, due to the slippery algae, he climbs the rock, clinging to and propping on the precious stones embedded in it. When he is high enough, he stretches his arm and manages to take the key, tied to a piece of parchment with a red ribbon:

- Got it!

He throws the golden key and the paper tied into the boat and Luna picks it up from the ground. Everyone sits around her to see what it is, except Diego who's still on the rock waiting for orders.

She unties the key tie and opens its attached parchment:

- It's the other piece of the map! – deciphers Isabel.

As if by instinct, Luna pulls out her tablet and takes several pictures of that piece. Then, using the touch pad, she opens the photo of the previous piece and, sliding her finger on the screen, fits with them together:

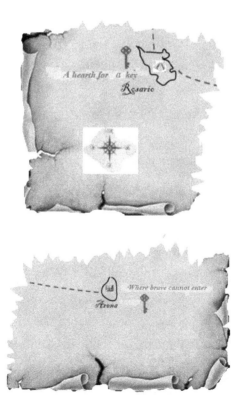

- Perfect fit! – comments Isabel.

- That's it, then – Lorenzo deciphers – Sabogal must have torn the map to pieces and left each piece in a different place...

- ... for us to follow as clues, one after each other – completes Luna.

- What island is this? – asks Paloma.

- It's Isla de Rosario– Luna replies.

- What's there? – asks Isabel.

- Rosario is the second largest island in the archipelago. It must be inhabited.

- "A heart for a key." What's that supposed to mean? – asks Thomas

- No idea – Luna replies – but there is a drawing of a... – Luna squeezes her eyes harder – ... Mayan pyramid?

- The Mayans? Did they still exist at this time?

Isabel, an archaeologist, explains:

- The final known classic period ended in the year 950. Then came the post-classical period, between 950 and 1539 and the period of contact with the Spanish colonizers, whose last news dates to 1697 according to some historians.

- Well, that's some hundred years ago – Paloma calculates, returning to the group.

- Which may indicate some remaining village, or at least remaining temples of the great Mayan cities that existed – completes Isabel.

- Anyway, we won't know unless we go there – defines Lorenzo.

Paloma asks:

- But... Are we going there?

At that moment, from they don't know where, they hear the singing of various female voices, as in choir. Without lyrics, only "aaaAAAaaaah" or "uuUUUuuuh", similar to Gregorian chants, the voices sing a melody so comforting and soft that, mixed with the sound of the waves of the sea, it makes them sleepy. The several voices perform, in tune, soprano and contralto solos, in a harmonious amazement of high and low registers, always in a cadence that resembled the sound of a very tuned orchestra.

Paloma lights up the flashlight and lights up the walls and ceiling to see where the music is coming from. She can see nothing. Soledad pokes her with her elbow and indicates to illuminate the water. Paloma throws the beam of light towards the banks of the cave and, completely stunned, sees several beautiful women, blondes, brunettes, redheads, eyes of all colors, one next to the other, singing around at the boat. Above the waist, beautiful and firm breasts, below the waistline, their body was shaped like a large fish, with silver-green scales up to the forked tail. They were mermaids.

- Oh my God! – she exclaims – Mermaids!

- So... they really exist? – asks Isabel, also illuminating the other side of the boat

- It seems so – confirms Soledad, distrustfully.

They swim around the boat, singing louder and louder. One of them, very beautiful, jumps out of the water and passes over the boat, like a dolphin's jump, sinking on the other side, forming an arc of water over everyone. The music is beautiful, however, due to the repetitive cadence and intersection of high and low tones it also becomes... hypnotic.

- So pretty! – exclaims Isabel and, still looking at her, asks Lorenzo: don't you think, Lorenzo?

Lorenzo's not answering. Isabel, still at his side, asks again:

- Which one do you think is the most beautiful?

He's silent again. Isabel then looks at him and sees that he is still, serious, his eyes glazed, looking at one of the mermaids with long black hair, green eyes, who begins to make gestures with her hands as if calling him smiling while singing. Isabel looks again at him, who is still serious, as if nothing else existed around him. Isabel shakes him by the shoulders:

- Hey, Lorenzo! Are you OK? Hey, look at me!

As he has no other reaction other than fixing his gaze on that mermaid, Isabel asks for the others to help. Only then she realizes that Diego and Thomas are also still, serious, enchanted by the mermaids' song, who swim around and start, all of them, calling them with their hands so that they jump into the water.

- Girls! Are you their state?

Paloma had already noticed and speaks, in a tone that already reflects a certain despair:

- Yes, they seem to be...

- ... hypnotized by their song – explains Luna.

- And why aren't we? – questions Soledad.

- Because we are women – Luna explains – and their spell enchants only men.

Isabel reflects a little and discovers:

- That's that, then! "Where the braves can't enter" means where men should not enter, because they will be captured and killed by them. Brave means men and not heroism in general!

- That's right – Luna agrees – that's why there are hundreds of shipwrecks out there, they usually lure sailors into the corner and make them crash into the rocks, sinking and killing everyone.

- Then they take the men to seabed, drowned – recalls Isabel.

- What are we going to do now? – asks Soledad, pulling out a dagger that she carries on a clip on her leg.

The circular swimming of the mermaids around the boat causes it to start spinning, like in a small whirlpool and making the boat gradually move away from the rock where Diego remains hanging and mesmerized.

The scenery is fantastic: the moonlight illuminating the center of the lagoon, with the rock reflecting the brightness of the precious stones encrusted in it; the whole dome of the cave shining like a constellation of blue, yellow and white stars, the stalactites like molten stone, also reflecting the brightness of the precious stones encrusted in them, the crystal blue and illuminated water, showing the mermaids' fins, who now begin to sing in an unknown dialect, but with strong trance-filled harmony.

The circular movement makes the women a little dizzy, almost entranced too. Paloma manages to clear her mind and sees that Thomas, serious, begins to move to jump into the water. She holds him:

- Thomas! No!

At the same time, Lorenzo takes a step towards the edge of the boat, but Isabel holds him:

- Lorenzo, don't!

She slaps him in the face, but to no avail. He pushes against her arms trying to jump.

- Girls, help me out here!

- I can't! – shouts Paloma behind her.

Isabel turns around and sees that she's trying to stop Thomas from jumping too. Paloma shouts:

- Hold tight, we have to stop the men!

- They're pushing too hard! - says Isabel.

That's when Soledad screams:

- Diego!! Don't jump!

Only then, they realize that they are a little distant from Diego, who, completely hypnotized, throws himself into the water. Immediately three mermaids surround him, caressing his face and hair, smiling and singing, but they suddenly grab him by the shoulder and legs and pull him to the bottom of the sea. Soledad shouts:

- Nooooooo!!!

She is about to jump to try and save her military companion when Luna holds her tightly:

- It's no use, he's already lost. If you jump, they'll tear you apart!

Soledad collapses in pain:

- No, this can't be!

- Luna, what are we going to do? – shouts Paloma, holding Thomas by the arms, on the left edge of the boat.

- Let's get out of here fast – cries Isabel, doing the same on the right side with Lorenzo.

- There's no one to row!

The mermaids increase the speed of their swimming, causing the boat's rotation to accelerate. They begin to lose their balance. Luna commands:

- We're going down if we stand up! Everybody lie down!

Paloma and Isabel concentrate the forces they can and knock Thomas and Lorenzo to the ground of the boat, both of whom still look like zombies. Luna also knocks down Soledad, who is still in tears. If they took a second more, they would all have been knocked over by the three mermaids who, getting momentum with their fins, jumped over the boat in an arc, falling on the other side, as a threatening warning to release the men.

Isabel takes over control:

- Soledad! Do you still have the flamethrower?

- No, it was lost in the carriage race.

- What weapon do you have?

- Just an automatic pistol.

- So, take a few shots to see if they're scattered away.

Soledad leans over the boat's wall and starts shooting, but they are faster and dodge the shots, which pierce the water without hitting anything. She runs out of ammo and a mermaid advances to pull her into the water. She manages to get rid of the blow but gets hit on her head by the tail and faints. Luna tries to wake her up.

The sound of the melancholy singing becomes more intense, causing Thomas and Lorenzo to struggle under the young women's bodies to get up and throw themselves into the sea.

In the body fight, Isabel remembers something:

- Ulysses! Do you know the story of Ulysses?

- This is no time to tell stories, Isabel – Paloma replies on top of Thomas.

- He also faced mermaids.

- So what? He's not here to help us!

- He covered his sailors' ears with wax so they wouldn't hear their singing!

- That's a good idea, but... we don't have any wax!

- Think of something!

- My shirt!

Paloma, kneeling on Thomas' chest, manages to rip off her own blouse and tries to tear it into pieces. The instability of the boat is at a critical level, the mermaids begin to swing it in an attempt to turn it over. Soledad wakes up and, with an oar, hits them on the head one by one, causing them to move away, but there is no stopping the ones underneath the boat. Luna has an idea and speaks to herself:

- You may be women, but you're fish too!

She holds the multitask tablet, look for something on the menu, all the while swinging like in an earthquake, waves crashing everywhere. She plunges it into the water almost entirely, leaning over the boat's wall.

Soledad sees this and asks:

- What are you doing?

- Calling someone who's part of the food chain...

Meanwhile, Paloma gets pieces of her blouse and begins to stop Thomas' ears with it. She throws it to Isabel, who does the same to Lorenzo. It works. Gradually, the spell breaks. Their eyes, gray before, go back to their original colors. The breathing, which had been very slow, begins to return to normal. Thomas is the first to wake up and sees Paloma, wearing only her bra, kneeling on top of his chest:

- Are we having sex?

- No time to explain! Hold on... we're sinking!

Lorenzo wakes up too. It takes him a few seconds to remember where they are, Isabel, happy, still on top of him, exclaims:

- You're back!

- What's happening?

- We're being attacked by mermaids!

But he can't hear:

- What?

He tries to take the cloths out of his ears, but Isabel screams, holding his hands:

- Don't do that!

He looks around and appraises the situation: they're still inside the cave, several mermaids are spinning around the boat, which is swinging with jerks coming from underneath, Soledad trying to push them away with the oar. He takes on the seriousness of the situation and, picking up an oar, tries to paddle them out of the lake. Thomas also picks up another one and helps him row. Luna continues with her arm in the water, holding the submerged tablet.

But the mermaids, seeing that they are losing their prey, get even more furious. They jump over the boat like dolphins, striking the boat with their back fins in order to break its wood. One of them manages to break the mast of the main sail.

Desperate, they row with all their might and manage to advance a few meters towards the exit of the cave. But the mermaids, in dozens, push the boat in the opposite direction, taking it back toward the rock that is in the middle of the lake. Soledad shouts:

- They want to break the boat against the rock!

- Hold tight! – shouts Paloma.

They're about thirty tree feet away from crashing against the rock. Thomas shouts:

- We're all going to die!

Luna looks at the entrance to the lake and gives a cynical smile:

- I don't think so!

From the middle of the lake, illuminated by the moonlight and the sparkles of stalactites, a large whale submerges with its mouth open right behind the four mermaids that are pushing the boat. In one mouthful, it swallows them all and sinks back downs, causing two giant waves that hit the sides of the cave.

The boat, without impulse, slows down and hits the rock lightly. Without believing that they are alive, the young people watch the surreal battle that presents itself before them: two whales, inside the cave, fight with the mermaids who, trapped, jump on them biting. The whale knocks them all down and hits the huge tail where they are, killing several of them. The other whale opens the mouth wide and swallows many others, sinking and emerging quickly. Mermaids fly everywhere, a few torn in half. A mermaid tail falls in the boat, Thomas catches it still moving like a fish out of water and throws it back into the sea. With each whale's tail strike, large wave rises, which hits the cave walls and makes the boat lift like in a storm.

With the stupendous waves and tail-thrashing of whales, the stalactites begin to fall, and the ceiling of the cave begins to crack. Lorenzo, trying to manage the boat to avoid the falling stones, shouts:

- The ceiling will cave-in!

- We've got to get out of here! – shouts Isabel.

The noise inside the cave is hellish, in addition to the numerous dangers that young people face: stones falling like arrows from the ceiling; mermaids still trying to attack them, giant waves making the boat go up and down, a deluge of deadly actions at the same time.

Defeated, the few remaining mermaids flee towards the exit of the cave, but are swallowed by the whale that was farther back. The crack on the ceiling extends through the side walls, in the shape of a cross and everything begins to tremble, with a very loud noise. One of the whales approaches the boat, sprays up a jet of water, sinks and gets under the boat, making it touch its back.

With care, it continues swimming towards the exit of the cave, while behind it, the entire stone ceiling and stalactites fall from the inside out. As soon as the whales exit with the boat on the back, the entrance to the cave is closed by a large collapse of the rocks from above.

The day is already dawning, and the fog is dissipated. The whale carries the precious cargo on its back through the wreckage of the shipwrecks, accompanied by the other whale. When they feel there is no more danger, they sink and let the boat float in calm waters. Soon after, it and its companion return to the surface further along with the baby whale they had freed from the net. Then they realize that one of the whales that saved them is its mother.

Lorenzo speaks, astonished:

- I can't believe what happened!

- Look! – Paloma points out – that is the mother of that baby!

- But... –Isabel is intrigued – ... how did they discover us inside the cave at night?

Luna shows off her tablet, still dripping water:

- I was able to simulate the sounds that whales use to communicate. Then I dived it underwater, hoping that the sound waves would be strong enough to get to where they were.

- Whales hear sounds more than 1,800 miles away – explains Lorenzo, the oceanographer.

- Thank God it worked! – says Luna, proud.

Thomas jokes to diminish her glory:

- Oh, this isn't your invention. You spoke whale, like Dory in "Finding Nemo."

As the adrenaline had passed, everyone was under great stress, and Thomas's joke provokes a nervous laugh. They realize that, sitting at the front end of the boat, Soledad has her head between her knees. Paloma comes to her and tries to comfort her:

- We're really sorry!

- Yes – Isabel completes – we didn't want to lose him.

Luna summarizes what happened to Lorenzo and Thomas, who had not witnessed the incident. They come to her, very constricted:

- He was a great soldier, he will never be forgotten – comments Lorenzo.

Soledad looks at them, eyes full of tears, and says:

- We've served for many years in many places and wars, we spent many dangers together, he saved my life several times, and I could do nothing. It was all my fault; I should have pulled him back to the boat!

Lorenzo, as leader of the expedition, tries to make her feel better:

- No way, it wasn't your fault, it was a fatality. No one would have imagined that we were in a danger like that. Don't torture yourself. If anyone here is responsible, it's me who didn't give the orders for him to come back from the rock as soon as he found the key.

Everyone feels the loss of their partner. After a few minutes in silence, Thomas asks:

- Speaking of the key... Where is it and that piece of the map?

Luna sticks her hand in her pocket and removes the golden key, which is an old model of bolt, just like the one in the priest's sarcophagus, along with that lower left corner of the map:

- By a miracle it didn't fall out of my pocket. So, are we going to Isla Rosario?

Paloma, who had managed to fashion a kind of top to cover the bra with the remains of her shirt, says:

- What other dangers await us?

At this minute, they hear the sound of a gunshot and a bullet sticks itself to bow of the boat. They look back, frightened, and discover that they were so distracted consoling Soledad that they did not notice the approach of another boat, about the same size as theirs: that of the English team.

Standing at the tip of it, Emmett, still pointing the gun at them, shouts:

- I believe no introductions are needed!

Thomas says:

- Oh, not again!

Their boat approaches and Lorenzo asks:

- You guys again?

- We can't live without you – mocks O'Connor.

Lorenzo says with a poker face:

- What do you want from us here at high sea? That we catch lobsters for your dinner?

- Very funny, commander. Hand over what you found back in the island! Now!

Emmett shoots again, this time passing near Isabel, causing her to duck and almost lose her balance and fall into the water. Emmett, cold, warns:

- I'm not going to waste the next shot, darling!

Lorenzo, with no other way out, looks at Luna, who nods. She hands the piece of parchment and the key to Laureen, who has her arm outstretched. Isabel, disgusted, protests:

- You have no idea what we've been through to get hold of this! It cost a life!

- Not mine, though. This is your problem! – answers Emmett, insensitive.

- Your time will come! – curses Isabel.

- We'll see!

With a sarcastic smile on her lips, Emmett, still pointing the gun, moves away along with the English boat, where some are rowing, and others hoisting the sails so that the wind would take them farther and farther away. While they can still be seen as a point on the horizon, Thomas collapses:

- Shit! I feel the same way I did when we arrived at the hotel after the church thing!

- Now what are we going to do? – asks Paloma.

After a few minutes, Lorenzo replies:

- "Those who know when to fight and when to wait triumph"

- Sun Tzu? – asks Luna.

Lorenzo confirms with his head. And completes, looking at that dot on the horizon:

- Let's do as them: we follow them and take the opportunity to attack.

Lorenzo hoists what is left of the sail on the main mast and, with the help of the oars, they follow the same path as the English, trying to keep the necessary distance not to be seen.

Laureen, surrounded by her team workers except Winston who is manning the helm and Kendall, who is next to Jack, still badly injured, lying in front, puts together the two pieces of map and holds up the two identical golden keys:

- The Spanish were mad angry again.

Emmett, rude as ever, replies:

- They just need to kill some bulls, in that horrible bullfighting, that their rage will abate.

O'Connor focuses on the map:

- So, Laureen, what does this all mean?

- It was as I imagined – she says, putting the magnifying glass over the drawing of the island of the second map piece – someone left another clue to be harvested as resolution to previous one ...

- ... as a hide-and-seek game – completes Alfie.

- Yes, but much more deadly and dangerous – Laureen corrects.

Birdie points to the triangle drawn in the middle of the island and observes:

- What is this? It looks like a...

- ... pyramid – completes Laureen – a pyramid in the style of the ancient Mayan civilization.

- Or Inca, or Aztec – completes Alfie.

Laureen explains:

- Incas and Aztecs did not build pyramids, only the Mayans, who used them as religious temples. The most famous ones are those of Kukulcán, Tikal and Uxmal, in Mexico and Guatemala. I don't remember there being records of pyramids here on the coast of Colombia, but the Mayans used to dwell in isolated city-states, different from the other two pre-Columbian civilizations.

- "A heart for a key" – reads O'Connor – what does it mean?

Laureen shows the two golden keys, twins, which she has on her hands:

- The key should be a third, which goes together with these.

- What about the heart?

- I don't know, it's not part of the archaeological history of this region.

Birdie makes her interpretation:

- It connotes some sort of exchange

- That Captain Sabogal was very mysterious and liked riddles.

- Bullshit! - comments Emmett – The key can be exchanged by anything. Let's go to see!

The wind blows harder and propels the boat faster towards Rosario Island. Jack groans; Kendall squeezes a little more the bloody flag cloth that is still around him. He laments:

- I think I'm going to die.

- Yes, one day. And so am I.

- I'm dying now, sooner than you, you'll be free.

- We're together in this journey, where one goes, everyone goes too.

She is quiet for a while and asks:

- Do you want to enable your belt and go back to the future?

- But there's the rule... it's only going to work if everyone comes back together, remember?

- You only need to convince the others.

- "Only"? You think that's easy?

- I'll talk to O'Connor, he'll agree. There's no gold in the world that's worth more than a life.

- No, leave it at that... – he says, weakened – I'll hold on as long as I can. My father came from a very old Eastern family, and we had a motto.

- And what was it?

- Dignity is above our very existence.

- Nice.

- My family was very rich, but lost everything in the Hiroshima explosion. Only me and my younger sister, by a miracle, managed to survive, we were raised by a relative on the other side of Japan and, when older, we were granted geological sciences' scholarships in England and that's how, always alone and struggling, we managed to get here.

He takes off a thin gold pendant that he carries around his neck and opens a small picture holder that is hanging on it. There is a black and white photo of a boy in sailor clothes and a smaller girl holding his hand. He puts the pendant in Kendall's hand and says:

- Give this to my sister, please, and tell her I did everything I could to protect her. And that I love her so much!

Kendall does her best to hold back the tears, returns the pendant to him and says:

- You're going to give it to her yourself.

At this point, Winston, who was watching the surroundings at the helm of the boat, shouts:

- Look! The island!

Everyone looks ahead and sees the outline of an island with many trees, shaped like an irregular five-pointed star that begins to appear on the sea line. It's already a little over noon and they're very anxious. They quickly get closer to it and stay alert to any dangers that might be around. When they arrive near the beach sand, with several high waves, Winston and Birdie jump into the crystal-clear water and push the boat to ground it on the limestone white sand.

O'Connor helps Jack, Kendall and Laureen off the boat and, looking to the sides, they reach the first tropical coconut trees that, by the thousands, make a wall between the inner jungle and the sand of the beach. They sit down and get some rest.

O'Connor gives the first instructions:

- A few minutes to eat.

They open a part of their belt and take some concentrated food pills. Alfie, sitting next to Winston, looks out to sea and daydreams:

- Oh, a coal-roasted fish would be very nice right now!

- Do you want me to catch one?

- I doubt it!

Winston lifts his big body, walks to the sea and peeks into the water for a few moments. After a minutes, with a quick movement, he sticks both hands in and brings them clinging a large fish. He goes back and throws the fish, still struggling, into Alfie's lap, who cries out:

- You're kidding! How do you do it?

- War training.

- You're the man! Now what do we do?

- You eat.

- But... raw? Where's the fire?

- In war we eat the way we can.

Alfie looks at O'Connor, who makes an affirmative sign. He looks at the fish, looks at them, takes a knife, opens the fish, takes out the entrails and eats a piece of fish filet. He bites on one side, bites on the other... but ends up swallowing it.

- Sashimi!

They both laugh, take a piece of the fish and eat too. They pass it to the others and Emmett is the only one not to eat it, nauseated. After these minutes of relaxation, Birdie asks O'Connor:

- What now, Captain?

- Guns check?

- We still have three firearms operating, sir.

- Ammo check?

- About three hundred bullets, sir.

- Communication check?

- Radio transmitters in order, although the solar battery may fail, sir.

He stands up and says to everyone:

- We don't know what awaits us. We were trained in an urban city, although some here have wilderness experience. We follow our mission, motivated by acquiring the map and its possible use for the progress of our country in our time. But we can't let our guards down, we have to stick together. We'll follow in Indian line, at military step. Winston goes ahead with a gun, another in the middle with me and another in the rear with Birdie.

He looks at Jack, increasingly weakened.

- You stay here and wait for us.

Kendall comes to his defense:

- We can't leave him here alone!

- We have no choice.

- We can make a stretcher and carry him

- Too much work in an enemy area we don't know.

- Then I'll stay with him!

- We'll need a doctor with us.

She stares at him, but he doesn't even blink. She looks at the others, who, unfortunately, have to agree with their commander. Overruled, she turns to Jack, who nods in agreement. He takes off the pendant and gives it to her again, without saying anything. She understands, takes it and puts it in her pocket, sad.

Everyone gets up, forms the line, and begins to enter the dense tropical forest. Birdie, the last to enter, looks at Jack one last time, he raises his canteen in a toast sign and says to her, smiling:

- See you later!

When Birdie disappears in the middle of the foliage, Jack sighs, looks at the sea, opens the canteen and is about to take a sip of water when some shadows appear above his body.

The forest of the island is dense, full of large foliage, such as ferns, split-leaf philodendrons, coconut trees and hanging vines, amid stones covered with green moss. With the gun in one hand and a machete in the other, Winston is picking his way through the jungle. The others, apprehensive, follow slowly, aware in case of any danger or surprise. Typical closed jungle noises, such as exotic birds and indecipherable animals, echo from all sides

A paradise birds flock takes off near Winston, frightened by the movement of his arms. Moving forward a little, they reach a narrow path, open in the woods, whose end cannot be seen, neither to the right nor to the left.

When O'Connor arrives on this path, Winston asks:

- So, Captain?

- I don't know where to go.

Emmett approaches and asks:

- Worse than where it's going, I was wondering who made this path?

O'Connor asks Laureen:

- Was the island inhabited at this time?

- Based on the official records, it doesn't. But it could be some native or runaway slave from Cartagena or from another place near the mainland.

- Whoever it is... says Birdie, making a sign with her head to indicate where she is looking ahead – ... was not very friendly.

They look at a small clearing that is at the end of the path left direction and are terrified by the sight: on top, human skeletons are tied to stakes stuck in the ground, forming a macabre circle. Some of them still in a state of decomposition, with flies flying around them.

Kendall is shocked:

- Oh my God!

- What is that?!? – speaks Alfie

Laureen explains:

- It's a warning to enemies not to approach.

- What enemies? – asks Kendall

- I don't know… some native tribe, maybe...

Laureen approaches one of the skeletons, observes it well, then addresses another, until she reaches that semi-decomposed, covering her nose with a handkerchief. She calls Kendall to confirm a finding:

- Look, all of them had cut their chest bone off.

- That's right – confirms Kendall

- And... see this... – she shows the latest corpse – note if anything is missing?

Kendall, covering her nose with her hand, looks up from the bottom and exclaims, perplexed:

- Jesus!

- What's up? – asks Alfie from behind

Kendall and Laureen turned to the other. Laureen explains:

- They all had their hearts ripped out... Alive!

Everyone's face mixes surprise, fear, pain and survival instinct spark the alert within each one. Birdie is the first to return to the rational mode:

- Wasn't this part of a ritual?

- Yes – Laureen replies – one ritual of the ancient Mayans. They ripped out the hearts of men, women, and even children to offer them to the sun god in exchange for protection and victory over their enemies.

- Wasn't that a legend? – asks Alfie

- There have always been doubts, but several Mayan civilization's drawings with scenes of human sacrifices were found by archaeologists

Emmett remembers something:

- Wait. What is written on that map again?

O'Connor takes both pieces and reads:

- "A heart for a key"

Everyone looks each other, even more scared of what starts making sense. Suddenly, they listen to several drums sound not far from there. They look for where the drum sound comes from and they think it comes from behind a small mound covered by low vegetation a little further on, to the left direction of the path.

O'Connor commands:

- Let's go! Be aware all danger!

The three of them advance along the open path in the jungle wielding their guns and they climb the small mound. When they reach the top, lying on the sloping ground, they are dazzled by the view that is presented in front of them: surrounded by closed vegetation, a large Mayan city, with streets bustling by people heading towards the main central avenue. Light gray stone houses lined in symmetrical blocks show the advanced engineering for that century. Squared two-floors houses mingled with watchtowers in some corners of the city. A large stone pyramid is sitting at the center of the city, which stairs in the middle of its four sides climb geometrically equal and end in a upper stone temple with an open door. They city should have more than a thousand inhabitants.

- Incredible! – exclaims Alfie

- A Mayan city-state! – confirms Laureen

- Look at the people walking – notes Emmett

- But... – notes Birdie – ... it looks like something special is going on.

In fact, lots of sunburned brunette skin men and woman, with straight black hair, indigenous type, dressed in colorful tunics, stone necklaces and ornaments on their hair, like feathers of birds of various colors, walk to the pyramid frontal staircase to meet a group of soldiers banging on large bamboo and leather drums, as if giving a sign of some important event.

A human corridor begins to be formed on the left side of the forest up to the drums band's place, with the Mayans making small leaps, wielding their hands up and shouting words in their native language. Within minutes, a procession of Mayan warriors comes out forest, with their naked torso painted in various colored bands, enter wielding spears. Soon after two warriors leave the bush and walk-through human corridor, four guards appear carrying a stretcher in their hands. Lying and tied to it, Jack scares himself in great despair.

Kendall says loudly:

- They've got Jack!

On impulse, she gets up and threatens to run downhill, butWinston holds her:

- They'll capture you too if you show up.

She starts crying nervously:

- I told you we should not leave him alone!

- What can we do? – asks Winston

O'Connor thinks and replies:

- We can't stand up to so many people, we don't have guns enough, either bullets...

Kendall crouches next to him and stares:

- So? You're going to let him die?

He looks away, embarrassed:

- I don't know what to do.

- This mission is beyond bearable!

- There's no turning back right now.

- We have to do something, think, please!

The warriors arrive with the stretcher at the foot of the pyramid and stop. The drum players stop too, a suffocating silence starts. After a few minutes, a great man appears, from the temple on top of the pyramid, ornated with multicolored bird-feathers headdresses, necklaces on his naked torso, and orange linen sari with figures of monsters frowns.

- He must be the great priest – explains Laureen

The drums beats are replayed at a different pace and the man begins to descend the stairs, followed by four other strong warriors, all masked and painted bodies, as if starting a ritual. The city dwellers crowds around the warriors with Jack, who continues to struggle.

When the priest comes near them, he looks forward. He begins to tremble, like going into a trance and babbling words interspersed by spasms. He picks up a type of handmade sprinkler from an auxiliary's hands and starts throwing a liquid at Jack, who is completely scared.

The gang screams around, going into a trance too, as collective catharsis. The priest makes a sign, and the warriors begin to carry Jack's stretcher upstairs toward the temple at the top of the pyramid.

Alfie asks Laureen:

- How were these rituals done?

- They worship the god Itzmana, the chief creator of men. They offer human sacrifices to pay for all the effort the gods made to turn the first animals on Earth into men. Due to the gods bled to men to be born, they reciprocate with the same sacrifice. There are special stone made chambers inside that temple, reachable through internal staircases and secret passages. In one of these chambers, a red stone altar of medium stature is used as a sacrificial table, where they tied the victims and removed their hearts out, still alive.

Nervousness increases as the group of warriors climbs the ninety-one steps of the ladder. Kendall presses again:

- Are we just stay here, watching?

O'Connor asks:

- Is there a specific hour to make the sacrifices?

- Usually at sunset time – Laureen replies

They look behind the pyramid and see that the sun is about to hide on the horizon line. The funeral procession reaches the temple door. The priest turns to the crowd and wields a large machete, adorned with precious stones and bird feathers. The crowd, below, shouts in cheers for the sacrifice. The group enters and disappears into the darkness of the temple.

O'Connor speaks to Birdie and Winston:

- Both of you, come with me. The other ones, wait here.

- I'll go! – orders Kendall

- No, you don't, you don't have the same military training as us.

- You said the same thing when you stood up to that big guy at the fort, do you remember?

- Now it's more serious situation, it's life or death, I don't want anything to happen to you.

Laureen advices:

- Look, the people are dispersing. If you have to do anything, this is the time.

- Let's go! – orders O'Connor – and all of you stay here.

He, Birdie, and Winston begin to descend the hill toward the city; Emmett, Kendall and Laureen keep up with them, distressed. The early evening soft darkness makes it easier for them not to be noticed, although torches of fire begin to be lit in some parts of the streets.

The three of them arrive at one of the houses on the outskirts, near the woods, and they lurk who is nearby. They advance ahead, closed to a house wall. O'Connor makes a signal and the three install silencers on the ends of their weapons and set up triggers. Still leaning on the wall, in a police raid position, move forward and spot three crouched men eating something near a fire pit. No one else around, the darkness is almost total.

They bounce in front of the three men and shoot them, killing them noiselessly. O´Connor commands:

- Let's put their clothes on.

After a few minutes, the three of them are completely disguised as Mayans, with colorful tunics on top of their uniforms, animal tooth necklaces and feather head on their heads. They hide their weapons under the tunics. and begin to walk the streets without being noticed by the inhabitants, who, full of smoking narcotics, are doped and fallen on all sides.

Some men and women walk on the streets, partially illuminated, and the three of them get to reach the foot of the back pyramid staircase unnoticed. They begin to climb through it, being fortunate that it was not guarded by Mayan soldiers, as on the main staircase.

The group of priests carry the stretcher with Jack thru a torched-lit staircase, descending two flights, until they reach a stone low ceiling room. It has a semi-closed wall, letting see another smaller hall, illuminated by torches, and the floor all stained red.

In the center of this second room, a lion-shaped sculpture, with the loin straight as a table, was the altar of sacrifices. The frown of the lion has ivory teeth and green jade eyes, terrifying. Jack starts screaming and kicking even harder, but he's weak from so much blood he's already lost.

- Help! Get me out of here!

The four warriors put the stretcher on the ground and lift Jack by his shoulders and legs. They begin to drag him toward the altar, but he struggles, trying to hinder his drag. He tries to make a jiu-jitsu strike position, but weakness causes him to fall to the ground. The guards lift him up again, hold him by their arms, and drag him to the sacrifice altar.

They lay Jack on his back and headed with the lion statue head, tying his waist and legs. They rip off his shirt, leaving his chest bare. Torches illuminate the gloomy and macabre scenery. A cruel and painful death approaches and Jack can do nothing.

The chief priest approaches him and begins to say his pagan thanksgiving pray for the offering. The other escorts start to go into a trance as well.

Jack begins to have blurred vision due to weakness, barely breathes, he is dying from deep anemia. He looks around to see if he finds anything that could save him at last chance. Look at the frown just above his head and a glow coming out of the lion's figure's mouth catches his eye. He raises his arm and takes the object that was hidden there and, with great surprise, despite the suffering, he sees that it is a golden key tied on a piece of parchment. The priest turns around and begins to lift the mortal knife to pierce Jack's chest.

Birdie, Winston and O'Connor arrive at the house back on top of the pyramid. They're turning it around cautiously until they reach its only front door, guarded by two great Mayan guards. O'Connor comes in from the right, while Birdie and Winston, on the left. They arrive at the same time and make the two guards look to each side of them. They try to scream and point out their spears, but the muted shot guns kill them immediately. Their bodies will roll down stairs, but they are hold by them, so that they are not noticed for those who were still at the pyramid footage.

They turn the pistols laser sight on and enter through the front door. They hear the noises of the songs and strange words coming from downstairs. They descend carefully, aiming everywhere, the stone walls darkened by mosses mix with snakes coming out of its cracks. A small water strand flows from one of the walls, increasing the claustrophobic and suffocating environmental.

When they arrive at the sacrificial room, they see two guards leaning against the wall. O'Connor and Winston approach from behind them and give a twisting blow to their necks, breaking and killing them on the spot. They approach the main room and see the priest turned on his back, raising the knife for the deadly outcome.

O'Connor takes aim and shoots the back of the man, who does not fall immediately. He turns around and gets another shot, this time from Birdie. The other two priests appear behind the walls, and receive gunshot wounds to the head, falling dead.

This distracted them for seconds, long enough for the main priest, large and strong, to turn around and gives the fatal blow into Jack's heart, seriously injuring him.

Birdie screams:

- Nooooo!

The three unload their pistols, stooling the giant, who falls dead on top of Jack. They run and take the body off him, but it's late. Jack, with a strand of blood dripping from his mouth, panting a lot, manages to speak with difficulty:

- End of journey, Captain...

O'Connor leans over him, while Birdie and Winston stand at the door, safe in case any more soldiers show up.

- No, stay strong, Jack, let's get you out of here!

- Don't waste time, Captain, you... have to leave... hence... it's already over....

With O' Connor crying, desperate, on top of him, Jack gathers his last strength and opens his right hand, showing the key and piece of parchment he is holding. He can say, smiling lightly:

- Mission.... done.... my... heart... for the... key...

And turn his face, dead.

- Jack!! No!!! Jack!!!

Desperate, O'Connor is pulled by the two companions, also very sad, but still driven by the survival sense:

- Captain, come on, we've got to get out of here! Fast!

O'Connor takes the little package from Jack's hands without thinking and they climb the stairs towards the temple exit.

But the pyramid footage guardians are missing the priest's delay in going out and showing the heart of sacrifice on his hands as he was used to do. While they climb up the main staircase, the three of them go down the back stairwell. When they reach the ground, the guards find the dead priests inside the room and return, sounding alarm at screams from the top of the pyramid.

The city goes on full alert. Warriors appear everywhere, looking for an enemy who doesn't quite know whom. The three of them, still dressed as Mayans, manage to leave the outskirts of the city, and climb the hill where the remaining three of the team are still.

Some warriors identify them on the hill and lead dozens of them to pursuit them, holding torches and spears.

Kendall still has time to ask:

- And Jack?

O'Connor grabs her by her clothes and makes her run, wildly. They merge in the forest and come through the same path they came, being chased by the Mayan who, screaming, run after them. They pass through that hanging-bodies open area, the Mayans, a few seconds later. O'Connor and Winston stop, see and shoot, killing the Mayans are closest and run again. They pass through the closed forest, even harder by the night darkness. The Mayans begin to fling spears through the air, which fall very close to where they are passing.

They manage to reach the beach with great difficulty and breathlessly, so they run through the sand to the dinghy that left them stranded nearby. The warriors also come out of the woods and throw more spears at them.

Alfie shouts:

- Let's go! Strength! Push!

They join the most force as possible; Birdie still manages to turn around and shoot some warriors who are approaching them, knocking them down sand. The other warriors are afraid because they have never seen a firearm.

- To the water! – commands Emmett

Still with warriors throwing arrows and spears through the air, they get on board and, paddling, move away from the beach, leaving the tribe screaming behind them.

Lorenzo, Soledad and Luna also come out of the woods about three hundred feet further. They also run towards the sea where their boat is anchored with Isabel, Paloma and Thomas who were on watch, push the boat into the water and sneak out of the sea, to distance themselves before anyone noticed their presence.

They had followed the English group and witnessed part of their hostile adventure.

The boat sails aimlessly, with little wind hitting the sail, with no oars being moved. The silence is general, just broken by the noise of the waves crashing against the hull. Everyone looks away, without the courage to say a word. Pain and sadness dominate the crew's hearts, except for one of them.

Emmett gets up from the end of the boat, balances through its middle, reaches the other end, where O'Connor is, and asks:

- I want to see the map.

He hands over the third golden key without looking to her, with the new piece of parchment is tied to it. She unfolds it and sees that it is the torn map upper left part with similar information than the previous: two drawings and a mysterious phare under the dotted line ...

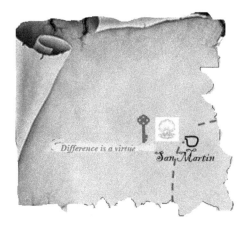

... that amends to the two other pieces:

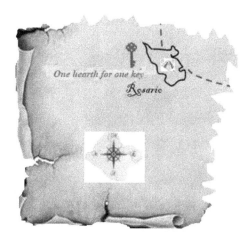

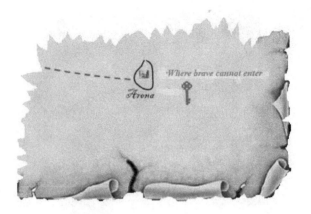

She comments in loud voice

- Look, it's another piece of the map.

She analyzes a little and asks:

- Where's Isla San Martin?

Nobody answers. She asks again:

- "Difference is a virtue," what does it mean?

Everyone keeps looking at the sea. She talks alone:

- And this drawing here... it looks like an... oyster...

She comes and shows it to Kendall to insist:

- What do you think?

Kendall looks at her and responds, resentmently:

- How can you be worried about that when we lost one of our friends yesterday?

Emmett responds with her usual indifference:

- He wasn't my friend, he was one of team members, that's all.

- What do you mean - "that's all"?

- We all got into the game, darling, assuming the risks..

The other ones begin to follow the discussion. Kendall, increasingly nervous, retorts:

- "Game"? You call loss of life like... "game"?

- Life is a game, darling.

- And don't call me "darling"!

- If you don't want to go on anymore, fasten your belt and come back... darling.

- I'm the one who should squeeze yours... bitch!

Aggression increases between them:

- I'll not leave without my money!

- Our life is worth more than this!

- Everyone here has military life, they've been trained for survival, for the fight! I'm the one who's least prepared, and I'm not giving up!

- You call blind ambition "preparation"?

Emmett takes the key with the piece of parchment, puts them in a transparent plastic box that she carried in the uniform, closes the airtight cap and shows it close to Kendall's face:

- Call it what you want, darling.., but this will never get out of my hands!

Kendall, in anger, slaps Emmet's hand so hard that she makes the little box flies and falls far into the sea. It floats for seconds and sinks.

Emmett is possessed:

- What you did, you idiot!

She pushes Kendall so hard that, losing balance, she falls overboard. Immediately, Emmett jumps in the sea and dives in search of the box. Kendall, taken by surprise, sinks dropping air bubbles. In this, Alfie sees a shark fin tip out of the water coming towards the boat. He points and screams:

- Shark! Shark!

Everyone despairs. Laureen shouts:

- Back!

- Swim back fast!

Emmett sees the fin coming towards her, turns around and gives the fastest strokes she can. Kendall returns to the surface, seeking new breath of air. She's close to the boat, but she's not aware of the surrounded danger. O'Connor yells at her:

\- Kendall! Get over here, quick!

\- What?

The shark is very close to Emmett, who swims anxiety. She's closer to the boat. Kendall takes a few strokes, gets to the edge and is hoisted by O'Connor and Winston. Emmett's still swimming, about five strokes to the boat. The shark appears on the surface and opens its yawn to do the first bite.

\- It's a white! – identifies Alfie

\- Come on, it's not long! – shouts Laureen

Emmett enforces to get to the boat edge and tries to put one of her legs in. The shark is a few feet away from her. Winston and O'Connor take her under her arms to start pushing her in. The boat swings a lot, almost turning. The shark will take the fatal bite when a gunshot is heard. It dives and passes under the boat, moving away from the other side and leaving a thin blood trail.

Emmett is finally pulled in, falls lying on the boat ground, all soaked, gasping a lot, spitting water through drowning. Everyone looks at the tip of the boat and sees Kendall, standing, with her arm raised wielding the gun.

Emmett sits, hugging her knees and still panting. She looks at Kendall, who, still dripping with water, reciprocates with a cold glance. Emmett puts her head between her knees, panting and embarrassed.

Lorenzo watches everything through the digital binocular embedded in Luna's thousand-and-one-utilities super tablet, standing up his small ship.

He lowers his binoculars, turns around and sees that the other ones are waiting for what he saw in the English's boat. Thomas asks:

\- Hey, what's up?

\- Looks like the team's in crisis.

\- Crisis? – asks Paloma

- They discussed hardly, as far as I understand it, and the key was lost in the sea.

- What???

- Did they lose the key? – asks Luna

- I don't know, but it looked like it was in a package...

- And why didn't they pick it up? – asks Isabel

- Due to the shark – explains Lorenzo

- Shark? – Soledad wants to confirm

- Shark? – asks Thomas

- Yes – Lorenzo replies

- Did it eat anyone? – Thomas asks again

- What a question, Thomas! – Paloma censors

- No, but it was close... – Lorenzo explains

- So? What are we going to do now? – asks Luna

- I don't know... – Lorenzo scratches his head – I think it's time for us to take off...

He does not finish the sentence, because a small glow coming from a part of the sea nearby catches his attention.

- Hey! Did you see that?

He points to where the sun reflection comes from. Thomas and Soledad begin paddling toward the point. When they arrive, they realize it's a floating plastic box, with the key inside.

Thomas is going to jump on impulse but he is hold by Paloma. She joins her hands palms behind her nape making a sign of a shark fin. Lorenzo leads the boat to where the box is and, stretching his arm, rescues it from the water.

Everyone's around him. Lorenzo opens the box, removes the key and opens the piece of parchment, a little wet but legible. Lorenzo explains, touching around the small drawing:

- The map refers to Isla de San Martin. San Martin is one of the smallest islands that cluster to the Northwest of the archipelago, along with the Isla Los Pajalares, El Peñón, Maria del Mar and other.

- The key drawing appears to be next to a... – Isabel approaches her face from the map – ... open oyster shell?

Luna passes her magnifying glass over the drawing and confirms:

- That's right, a shell with a pearl inside.

- This region has been distinguised on the planet due to its marine pearls production– confirms Lorenzo – It is easy to reach the bottom of corals and find oysters in clean waters.

- This is another predatory practices on the planet. They kill oysters unnecessarily – Paloma, the environmentalist, says.

- "The difference is a virtue" – Lorenzo reads

- What's that supposed to mean? – Thomas asks

- One more Sabogal' s riddle – Lorenzo answers

- As he said he liked riddles – Isabel confirms

- Another mortal danger to face – prophesies Soledad

Everyone remains quiet for minutes, wondering if acing another danger would be worth. Lorenzo looks one by one, asking for their opinion. Thomas is the first:

- Well, I don't know about you guys, but I'm still in the mood to keep going.

- What motivates me in all this – Isabel explains – is the chance to help so many need people with the money that is there.

- For me, moreover – Luna explains – is the contribution this will make to the world history.

- And for the environment, stopping these exploratory searches that only leave dirt in the sea – complete Paloma

- A military mission must be accomplished – Soledad says

Lorenzo's opinion is missing which, after a few minutes, closes:

- Despite the dangers, I believe that the benefit to humanity is far greater than the problems we have faced. So far, we've done well, thank God, and we're going to do everything we can to close the mission. I still believe in Spain, I still believe in the people who govern it and that if we take this map successfully, everyone will benefit. I think about how many hospitals could be built up, how many schools to educate children, how much food could be bought to feed them. Well, anyway, let's move on!

- But taking all kinds of care – Soledad reminds
- Absolutely.
- What's San Martin direction? – asks Isabel

Luna opens a kind of digital compass on the tablet screen:

- Northwest of where we are.
- Hoist sails! – Lorenzo commands

They sail for about two hours, aided by the surrounding sea currents. Gradually, the silhouette of an island aligns on the horizon. As they approach, the beautiful rocks around the island become clearer, surrounded by the beaches white sand. Another Caribbean paradise.

Luna consults the parchment piece:

- By the appointment, we should stop here.

They're about 150 yards from beach. The transparent water lets them see a non-ending beautiful and colorful corals structure in the seabed. It must be about 32 feet deep.

Paloma states in a question mood:

- I guess we must dive to hunt oysters.
- Did he hide a key inside an oyster? – doubts Isabel
- Sabogal was very daring, almost crazy, it is likely that yes – confirms Luna
- But... – Thomas asks – we don't have a diving device.
- It's going to have to be in the same breath – concludes Lorenzo, who starts taking his shirt off.
- Like Indonesian pearl divers?
- Like a diver who hunts all over the place.
- Is everyone going? – asks Isabel
- No – Lorenzo replies – you stay here to take care of the boat.

- Why me?

He tries to find an excuse to spare his favorite:

- Because... You don't know how to swim very well and...

Isabel takes off her blouse, wearing a pink baby bra, dives into the water and returns to the surface:

- Well, who told you that?

Soledad asks:

- What's to be done?

Lorenzo replies:

- Take a good breath, dive, swim around the corals. If you find an oyster, try opening it to see what's inside.

- OK – Soledad replies, jumping with all her clothes.

Luna takes diving pool goggles from the backpack she still carries and distributes to everyone. Thomas throws the little anchor, takes off his shirt, inspirates three times to stuff his chest and jumps into the water, followed by Lorenzo and Luna. A short distance from each other, they beat their legs towards down the sea. Amazed, as in a pool, they see multicolored fish sailing among the beautiful corals, algae swinging with the sea current, as well as other marine plants with tips, stars, in short, all the marine fauna dazzled with its beauty. But no oyster shells.

They return to the surface, take air and dive again. They go to another part of the coral wall and keep looking. A giant turtle swims so close Paloma touches its belly. After unsuccessful tentative, down an up, Lorenzo suggests:

- Let's try a little further, turn the coral tips and move to its other side.

- All right – Thomas confirms

They dive again and, swimming a little faster, follow in parallel to a high coral wall. They get to its end and swim to its left. That's when Thomas finds an oyster shell in the coral's footer. He thinks he has found the only one shell, he makes a positive signal to the other, but

Paloma indicates a point ahead:, thousands of all sizes, colors and shapes matching shelves are encrusted along the coral walls. Among them, dozens of tridactnas, the giant oysters, some open and other closed.

Lorenzo signals to rise to the surface. They get there almost drowned, gasping a lot. Tapping arms and legs to float on the surface, Isabel asks:

- And... now? How... Let's find... an oyster .... in the midst of thousands?

- I... don´t ... know... – Lorenzo pants

- Never... Let's... get... – Paloma completes

- It... that there's... information... – says Luna, who is a good swimmer– I'm going to get my tablet.

- For what? – Lorenzo asks

She swims to the boat, picks up the tablet, touches some touchscreen keys, swims back with it and explains:

- It´s a metal detector.

- All right, let's dive again –Lorenzo agrees.

They dive to the the seabed again, this time with Luna scanning the sand with the tablet to see if it picks up any signal. But to no avail Due to no signal their lungs already bursting, all come back to the surface again.

Thomas regrets:

- It's no use! No way! They all look the same!

This awakens Isabel:

- Yes, of course. The tip on the map!

- "Difference is a virtue" – Soledad reminds

- Let's go back and try to find some "different" oyster – Lorenzo says

- Oysters are all the same! – Thomas claims

They wear their goggles on, bite small knives, breathe, hold as much air as they can, and then dive back together. Lorenzo, Isabel, and Luna go to one end of the submerged wall and Paloma, Thomas, and Soledad, to another. Thomas sinks as deep as he can, opens a shell with a knife and sees he has nothing. Opens the closest second, also empty. Open the third, about the size of his hand and find an egg-sized white pearl. He submerges holding the shell on his hand and gasping a lot. He swims to the boat and keeps the shell in it. The others return to the surface, after finding nothing.

- I found! – shouts Thomas.

Lorenzo, half away, shouts:

- The key?

- No, a pearl!

- We didn't come here to find pearls!

- But I can get rich if I find more!

- Focus on!

They dive again once, twice, three, four, five times, open some shells they judge different from the others, but finding nothing, just a few more pearls. Productivity is very low, because they can spend little time at the bottom of the sea, opening one or two shells among the thousands that exist, in an endless work.

They go up again very exhausted. The afternoon is almost over. Isabel comments her frustration:

- We'll never find it, it's a possibility among millions.

- It's like finding a grain in the sand – Luna agrees

- How did the man get to do this? – Paloma asks

- If he has succeeded – says Lorenzo – we will do too.

- Is it really inside a shell?

- The design suggests a shell... so... big... – Lorenzo reminds

Saying that, he comes up with an idea:

- Tridacna!

- What?

Lorenzo dives his torso down and sees, half in the distance, dozens of tridacnas lined up in the sand, as a sea-bottom mattress. He says hopefully

- This must be it! There are fewer tridacnas than normal shells.

- What's a tridacna? – asks Paloma

- They're giant oysters, almost the human size. Come check it out.

He dives again and everyone follows him to the bottom. They approach a large sand-stucked shell vertically, with its two open sides. In the middle of it, a tube-shaped gland opens and closes, as if breathing. This one has cobalt blue edges. When he goes to touch it, it starts closing it shells.

They return to the surface. Soledad questions:

- They look dangerous.

- More or less. They close when they fell are threated, but it's not a very fast move – Lorenzo explains

- Pearl must be the football size, huh? – Thomas covets

- Tridacnas do not produce pearls – explains Lorenzo

- Would the key is inside? – Isabel wonders

- Well, if it were me, I'd keep it in a shell that's easier to identify if I had to come back later, because there are fewer than the other ones – Lorenzo reasons

- There's a logic... let's try a little more – suggests Thomas

- We go in pairs, never go solo –Lorenzo organizes – looking for a different tridacna, you come up and try to see what's inside.

The group takes breath once more and dive into pairs, going in different directions. Now they have to go straight to the bottom of the sea, because the tridacnas are stuck in the sand, vertically, with their entrance facing upwards. But all of them look a lot like each other, all with cobalt-blue or red edges, beautiful scenery to see. As they approach them, they close slowly on protective instinct.

Luna and Soledad distance themselves a little from the rest, going to the tip of the coral wall and find the same tridacnas in the same formats. Luna goes past the metal sensor near their openings, but no signal. Both will rise to the surface when Soledad sees, at a distance of about sixty feet, a yellow-edged tridacna. The only one in the midst of hundreds of blue and red big oysters.

Instead of following Luna up, still with air in her lungs, she decides to swim herself to it. Luna doesn't realize she hadn't come with her. Tapping her legs and giving wide strokes, she does not take long to get close to the big oyster with yellow edges.

The water clarity is becoming small penumbra due to the end of the day. She turns her flashlight on and lights up inside the oyster, which remains motionless, only with its inner tube dropping bubbles. Illuminated by the light beam, enchanted, she sees the reflection of a golden key in the mantle that covers the interior of the animal.

The air begins to miss, and it causes her to rise, but, afraid of no longer finding the location of the tridacna, sticks her arm to try to reach the object, which is also tied to something. Her arm does not reach the bottom, so large that it is the shell. She looks sideways and sees no one to ask for help. She then decides to enter the shell to get the key. Almost her entire body fits inside it, with minnows sailing and seaweed encrusted.

With great difficulty and illuminating the bottom, Soledad manages to pick up the key tied to piece of parchment wrapped in a waterproof packaging, turns to leave but... her foot passes near that transparent tube in the middle of it and it sucks it in.

The shell begins to close. Soledad, desperate, begins to struggle. Stick the shell with her knife, but this only causes the monster to speed up its closure. Soledad releases her remaining air bubbles when she screams:

- Help!

The feeling of drowning is desperate. She tries to pull the air, but water enters her nostrils, invading her trachea, which closes in reaction to this. Hence begins the suffocation process, agonizing and endless. Soledad's mind begins to lose its meaning, darkening the sights until it completely goes out. A drowned, even unconscious, has up to five minutes before he has cardiac arrest.

Luna returns and notices the flashlight beam coming out between the ends of the almost completely closed yellow shell. She swims as fast as she can and sees Soledad's hand out only, holding the key in her hand. Luna tries to pull Soledad's hand, standing on the tridacna edges, but because in reason of the suction force inside it, plus the lack of support point, brings great difficulty to her. She blows the shell, but with no reaction. The last air bubbles coming out of it, indicating Soledad was already dead. But Luna keeps insisting, pulling by her hand, but the wrench with the wrapper is the only thing that slips from her hand to Luna's.

The penumbra begins to turn into darkness and Luna feeling her hold air on her lungs is come to the end, has to abandon the poor woman to her own destiny. She appears on the surface panting a lot and swims towards the boat, where the other are already sheltered. Her heart is sadness broken.

Paloma helps her climb on it and she is the first to ask:

- And Soledad?

Luna's not answering. She only opens her hand and shows the golden key with the isolated parchment, sadly.

- You've done it! –Thomas rejoices

Isabel looks to the water to see if Soledad appears swimming to meet them, but nothing beyond the moonlight reflected on the clear but increasingly deadly waters. Isabel looks at Luna and after she confirms her understanding, tears begin to fall from her eyes, in silence. They hug. Paloma also joins them.

Lorenzo and Thomas just looks, with nothing to say also devastated. Pain is shared by all of them. Luna tries to get back on her and tells how the tragedy happened. She looks at the key in her hand and throws it to the boat ground, as contempt for another life-costly trophy.

They lie down along the boat and wait for a new day to come. And who knows, renew their hopes.

ENGLISH PARLIAMENT - LONDON, UNITED KINGDOM - YEAR: 2021

General Walsh walks through the gothic corridors of the Palace of Westminster, accompanied by three uniformed guards and three men in well-lined suits and a woman in a tailleur, all carrying briefcases in their arms. They cross several other officers, executives and parliamentarians in the richly decorated Elizabethan environment.

After folding left and right in several corridors, they stop at a solid wooded-door room.. The woman knocks and an officer in uniform opens from it. They enter in a rectangular high standing courthouse-shaped room, illuminated by several crystal chandeliers. Its semicircular counter faces other tables in half-moon format, where several people is sitting there. They sit on chairs arranged in front of the central counter. There is a small hanging gallery in back, filled with reporters and cameras.

The conversation buzz diminishes as a door opens and a seven blue-sea togas and white wigs lords procession enters and sits at the semicircular central table. All of them look over sixty years old and no smile or sympathy is emblazoned on their faces.

The lord at the center opens the solemn session:

- This Special Inquiry Committee's session is open!

Everybody be quiet and get up. The recorded U.K. national anthem begins playing through the speakers installed on the walls. Everyone sits down again when it finishes. The Chairman opens one of the books, reads it briefly and, address a question to General Walsh

- Dear General Winston Walsh. You are one of the greatest soldiers in the Great Britain history, with many pages of your career of dedication and heroism in various wars, a brave servant to His Majesty.

- Your servant, Sir.

- This dossier was made about a research project led by you about an old sunken Spanish ship, called... – he looks for its name in the file.

- San José – the general helps – Galleon San José.

- That's right, thank you. Going straight to the point, as far as we read, the reports point to several non-conformities regarding Anglo-Saxon national security standards, over expenditures and even the involvement of civilians in military missions. Could you please confirm that such irregularities proceed?

Walsh takes a minute in silence to think about the answer. Look at the girl in the suit next to him, who nods. He faces the magistrate and replies, naturally firm:

- No, Sir, they're not irregularities. We followed all security protocols within the DSTL budget, and all team members were properly trained.

- What is this project... – he reads again in the book – ... TRON exactly?

- Due to secrecy for national security, Sir, I can say nothing.

- But you are in front of a parliamentary court, everything here is also confidential.

The general turns around and sees the bunch of reporters working back there. He turns around and says to the magistrate:

- You have please to advice the press back there.

- I give the floor to the rapporteur of this case.

Another tall, toga-and-white-wig-dressing mustached black man raises picks one of the books up and begins his interrogation:

- General Walsh, this report states your managed department has formed a research team with the purpose of "exploring the Spanish ship disappearance in the 18th century", is that correct?

- Yes, milord.

- Why is the interest in this shipwreck?

- There are several, milord, but I would say the main thing is the enrichment of scientific knowledge for Great Britain History.

Walsh's cold look clashes directly with the rapporteur's ironic gaze. This insinuates with the same irony:

- Would it be their own enrichment, General?

Walsh remains impassive:

- I believe the Royal Crown too, milord.

- What do you mean, General?

He looks at the tailleur girl again, who makes a "beware-what-you-going-to-say" look. Walsh, always in a calm mode, replies:

- The supposed galleon was rich full of various seasons and natures: shipbuilding, logistics, adventure, customs, navigation history, medieval battles, among others.

- Like gold, silver, precious stones and other riches, valued at twenty billion dollars?

- That's an unqualified detail, milord.

A conversational noise begins to break the silence. The rapporteur flips through a few more pages of the brochure, trying to control himself:

- This ship legacy was recently judged by the International Court of The Hague, which ruled that it would be shared fifty percent to a multinational exploration consortium and the remaining fifty percent to one or more humanitarian child aid organizations.

- Equitable decision.

- Then why hasn't the general aborted the project yet?

- Because... we still can't communicate with our team.

The rapporteur opens a cynical, forced smile and addresses to the audience:

- How can we not get to communicate each other thru today's technology?

- You misunderstood what I said, milord.

- You're irresponsible!

The tailleur girl protests:

- Protest, my lord! Personal hostilities are not acceptable!

The Court Chairman annuls:

- The objection is accepted. Mr. Rapporteur, just be on the facts, please.

The rapporteur tries to recompose his instigation:

- Why can't you communicate with your team?

The general doesn't answer. The rapporteur insists:

- General, I asked you a question, please. Where is the team so that it cannot receive contacts?

The general continues to think about the answer, begins to increase his internal pressure. The rapporteur asks for the third time, animosity:

- General! One more time! Why can't you talk to them handling so many messaging ways on these days?

Walsh loses his self-control and, rising, lets slip:

- Because they're not on these days, you stupid lord!

The amazed widespread general conversation noise resounds throughout the plenary. Flashes start from the back gallery. Walsh looks at the girl and other lawyers, who reciprocate with the "you-fucked-it-up" look.

The Chairman hits the wooden hammer on the table:

- Silence! Silence at court!

Gradually the noise decreases, until the rapporteur, recomposed, asks again:

- I will relieve the offense to my person, General, to ask you to explain what you meant by "they're not in the present"?

Walsh looks at the lawyers for helping him. Seeing that he could no longer bear this responsibility alone, he has to confess:

- No. They returned to the year of 1708.

It´s not possible to describe the confusion such revelation provokes in plenary. Parliamentarians stand up, gesticulate at each other; the press gallery almost collapses from so many questions and photos. Even the lawyers are blown away.

The chief lord hammers the table several times vainlessly. The security guards at the courthouse are scattered and try to maintain order. Gradually, the noise decreases.

The rapporteur tries to get himself back again:

- What did you say, Sir?

- I told you the team travelled to the past thru a time machine

- Explain what's going on.

Walsh summarizes the history of the project, the time machine, the research, the team, the mission, in short, everything that has happened up to that date. It felt like he was telling a science-fiction movie. He had to stop several times, due to the plenary uproar. After two hours testimony, he ends:

- Did you understand why we have not communicated with the team?

The entire Court merges is stupefactive. All lords discuss with the nearest seat colleague, mixed with the audience's loudness. The rapporteur is able to argue

- How far is this project known and authorized by the British Government, Mr. General?

- The entire high-ranking British Armed Forces and Secret Service are aware of it and they authorized this project.

- And what's left to bring the team back?

- I don't know, I think as soon as they find the map...

- Are you still waiting for them to find a map you're not even sure if it exists?

- Yes. Indeed, there's no way to rescue them, due to they have to trigger their teleportation device themselves when they're on at least five crew members.

- Isn't that nine crew members?

Walsh pauses a minute, looks again at the girl, and replies:

- We've lost the signal of two.

The turmoil increases. Noise, controversy, positions for or against of the mission's end polarize those present. The rapporteur shouts:

- You must bring the survivors back immediately!

- There was no accident to say "survivors", milord.

- You can call it as you want, but they have to return!

- It's not up to you!

- This is a Supreme Court!

- That it's just starting a pointless inquiry, as there was no breach of order, law, or any other kind of ordinance of the United Kingdom!

- But there was breach of the ethics! – shouts the rapporteur, at top of his nervousness.

Walsh goes dumb. Red. Everyone looks to see if he's going to shoot the rapporteur or have a heart attack. He looks seriously and coldly at the opponent, and, taking his self-control, responds:

- What's my first name, Sir?

The rapporteur does not understand.

- Pardon?

- I asked what my first name is.

- Winston... General Winston Walsh, isn't?

- Exact. And do you know why?

The rapporteur looks at the Chairman, who shakes his shoulders without understanding either. Walsh continues:

- My father was a great World War II soldier. He fought for years against Germany on several battlefields. When I was born, a little after he went to reserve by the loss of both legs, he baptized me with the same name as Sir Churchill, the great prime minister. One of my favorite phrases of him, is "The whole history of the world is summed up in the fact that when nations are strong they are not always just, and when they wish to be just, they are often no longer strong." What is justice? What's it be strong? What is ethics? There is no way to apply the same values in a war as in peaceful times. In a war, the survival instinct makes us forget education, respect, morality, kindness... makes us emerge our inner badness.. Churchill also said that "a war prisoner is a man who tried to kill you, failed and now begs you not to kill him." We're not at armed war, of course, but this shows ife ambiguity, its ups and downturn, the giant wheel spins. And life is a constant battle. Ethics? Unfortunately, it's a useless word nowadays ... I don't see ethics in politics, I don't see it in business, in human relations, nor between nations... each of us thinks first of our own benefit, like to take advantage of everything, regardless of the others' rights and feelings. Where's the ethics in monopolies? Where is the ethics in company contracts with governments? Where is the family structure moral and values we passed on to our children, the understanding that we have to share with our neighbors?

He pauses, total silence in the room, and continues:

- I saw in San Jose the opportunity to change this. To bring British pride back, as a victory over an unresolved past. By finding that sunken ship, the object of dispute and greed of so many selfish nations, we would show the world, "see what the United Kingdom is capable of"! We have always had the best navy in human history, but it has always been used more for war and destruction than for development. And now, we have the opportunity to conquer what is ours and show the world our greatness and generosity! "It's better to die in combat than to see our nation outraged," said the greatest statesman we've had.

Excited by his speech, Walsh stands up, turns to the plenary, and ends:

- That's why I don't call back the brave team who are there in the past, trying to show England's supremacy. And I summon all of you to join us in this cheer for success, progress and ethics in conquering what was once denied to our beloved Queen! It's no longer a matter of a simple sunken boat. It is British pride that needs to be re-erected! "Never was so much owed by so many to so few."

He gets applauded by everyone standing up Everybody stands up and applauds his, enthusiastically. Parliamentarians, reporters and even the inquiry committee members, ignited by his nationalist discourse, cheer him for several minutes. The rapporteur is the only one serious, looking at the plenary.

The next day, all the newspapers, social networks, and electronic media, printed the headline on the front page: "ENGLAND BACK TO THE PAST TO REVISIT ITS LOST TREASURE", with the photo of General Walsh next to old painting of the Galleon San José.

Immediately this vainglory spreads throughout the country and the world. England folk give support to the general thoughts, taking to the streets in marches in solidarity with his cause. Some marches stop in front of the Spanish General Consulate in London, shouting words of order and threats.

The conflict between the two countries, centuries later, begin to be reborn.

ISLA SAN MARTÍN, ROSARIO ARCHIPELAGO - YEAR: 1708

The boat sails at random, near the coast of Isla de San Martín. Small waves swing it, and the sea current begins to drive it away from the beach aimlessly. The sails are lowered, but the wind is not strong. The temperature about 104 F°. is unbearable. Sea air, laziness, sweat, slowness, unwillingness.

Alfie takes his water bottle and turns it just above his mouth, which few drops fall from. He looks around and sees that every water bottles are almost empty. He calls Kendall, who is lying on one of the boat woods seats:

- Kendall, can I borrow your water?
- Lend it for what? Shal you pay me back?

- If it is God's will, along with a bottle of the best Scottish whisky.

She passes her bottle, with a bit of water in the bottom. He drinks everything like a big barrel. He speaks to O'Connor, also thrown near the helm:

- Captain?

- Huh...?

- Captain, the water is over.

- I know...

- What are we going to do about it?

- I don't know... Do you have any ideas?

- Go to the nearest island, maybe...

O'Connor raises his head barely and sees the far-away small island horizon. It's even more discouraged.

- It seems too far away...

Kendall gathers strength to speak:

- I have another idea!

- Oh, is it? – asks Alfie – What?

She gets up, half slowly, shows off her tele transporter belt and says:

- It's time for us to come back.

Everyone looks at her, who continues:

- We've come to the end. No map, no keys, no water, no food... not knowing what the next step is. I'm done.

- I don't agree – Emmett counters – we're not done.

- Your disagreement makes sense – ironizes Kendall

- People are used to see the empty half of the beer glass – continues Emmett

- Beer? Did I hear beer? – Alfie asks, half delusional

- We have three keys – continues Emmett – and three parts of the map. We know the next island is San Martin. It's not just because we lost a fourth part that we're have to give up. Let's go all the way.

- And what's this ending? – Laureen challenges – San Martin

would indicate the next stage. Is it the last one or how many more will come?

- Let's go there to search, there must be something right in sight, like the pyramid...

Everyone looks at her ugly, censuring her insensitiveness to what had just happened. Birdie asks:

- O'Connor, you're the commander. What do you think?

He's in doubt:

- Shall we vote? Most win. Who does choose to go back to our time?

Kendall, Alfie and Birdie raise their hands. Everybody gets a little surprised.

- And who's in the mood to try go further?

Laureen, Winston and Emmett raise their hands. Kendall, asks Laureen, surprised:

- You? Why do you feel good for staying in this madness?

Laureen looks away, sighs, and explains:

- I spent forty-five years of my life in archeological research, ancient civilizations, stories, legends, travels, great achievements of the discoverers. I visited classic well-known places such as Egypt, Mexico, Brazil, China, African continent... where there were civilization's traces, there I was, excited about the discovery of the Human being's... I have always sought answers, especially to the following question: why is man ambitious?

Her story begins to wake the people up. She goes on, like those storytellers who delight children:

- Why has they always fought for wealth and power, rather than fighting for their own kind development? Why was they the only animal that didn't kill to feed? I haven't found the full answer yet. The more I researched, the more I pursued human history, the more I was unhappy to see few noble, selfless acts, almost erased amid so many acts of self-deputes.

- Self... what? – asks Alfie

Laureen simplifies the term patiently and continues:

- Selfishness, my son, think only of yourself. Nero, Hitler, Ramses, among other examples of genocide in the name of a personal ideology that borders on madness. The San José explosion has not been explained up to date, but one of the theories was that the commander had blown his own ship up, crew and passengers. I didn't want to believe that anyone could be so selfish at this point. So, I assembled a great postdoctoral thesis at Cambridge to prove that this is not what happened. But, for more arguments, documents, and facts I gathered, I could not prove it – she begins to remember – and on the day of the dissertation, I was humiliated, despised, and threatened to lose my professor job at that institution if I would not base my thesis on something substantial. Then I heard about this special search mission from a great military friend of mine. – she looks out to sea – so, I don't want to go back, once again, to be ashamed of what I believe so much: even human selfishness has limits.

She stops and changes her gaze from the horizon into the boat: they are all sitting around her, enchanted by her narrative. Kendall turns to Winston, who had also voted in favor of staying, and asks:

- Well, and about you, Winston, why don't you want to come back now?

Half awkward, the big, strong black man, whose beard had grown, looks down and begins to explain:

- My skin shows I didn't have an easy life. Ever since I was a kid, I was discriminated against at school, nobody sat next to me except the boys of my color. The bullying had accompanied me for my entire adolescence. There are many people who says they aren't racist, but, heartly, they think black people goes with black, white with white. I enrolled as a Marine precisely to prove to myself that I was able to do everything better than a white: I always had the best student grades, best performance in the gym, best shot, best in endurance... – his eyes begin to fill with tears – ... but I never managed to be the best son for my father. He always ignored me, always praised my brothers, nothing I did had merit for him.

He looks at Birdie, who encourages him to put out, which he continues:

- On my graduation party, he showed up with my mother – who always gave support to me – and when I approached to show my diploma, he told me, "This is just a piece of paper, everyone has too. Do something extraordinary that will impress me." It devastated me and since then I've tried to exceed every challenge that comes up, to show him that I am capable, much better than himself. Due to this, I did not want to come back as a loser, to show him and to myself, that I am able to win the most extraordinary adventure that anyone has ever lived.

Kendall wipes some tears coming down her face away. At the end, she turns to O'Connor and throws:

- Well, we're even. You have Minerva's vote. Are we leaving right now or staying?

Everyone looks at him, who, of course, is in a difficult situation. Also bearded, he thinks, ponders, looks one by one. He is going to speak his vote out when Birdie points to something on the sea and shouts:

- See! A ship!

Everyone looks at where she's pointing. A large dark wood frigate, with three sail masts, navigates along where they are, at rapid speed. Alfie shouts:

- Water! They must have food and water!

And he starts jumping and waving his arms, screams,

- Hey!! Here!! Help!

- Alfie... – alerts O'Connor – ... Careful, we don't know who they are...

- Help!!! Hey!!! Here!!!

It seems that someone on the ship notices the alert, because it leaves the route it was on and turns toward where they are. As it gets much closer, O'Connor sees the flag that is hoisted on the stern: black, with a skull on top of two crossbones in X. He holds Alfie and speaks:

- Pirates! They're pirates!

He picks up the oars and tries to start the escape, but it's too late. The large ship maneuvers and stands in parallel to the boat, ramming it. They unbalance and are about to fall into the water when a large net is thrown over them, wraps everyone like in a bag and starts to take them off as fish struggling to get rid of. The boat they were in, with the shock, sparts in half and sinks. When they reach the ship's wall, they are pulled, one by one, by strong, bearded, and smelly men.

As soon as they are on deck, untangled from the net, the seven Englishmen form a semicircle in a defensive position, having the ship's wall behind them, surrounded by sunburned, sweaty, dirty men, some with hats, others without teeth, all with swords in hand, forming a circle around them.

They don't know if they wait for being attacked or they'd have to attack, the weather is pretty tense. When, behind the pirates wall, a familiar voice is heard, in well-spoken British English:

- Well, well, well... Did I not tell you we would still meet each other in the future... Captain O'Connor?

The pirates make way for a high-awarded-officer-overcoated mid-thirties, tall, rugged, blond, blue-eyed man, and a parrot on his shoulder, approaches and faces O'Connor very close.

After few seconds researching in his memories, O'Connor recognizes him:

- Captain... Henry Every?

Henry takes his three-pointed-black hat out with his right hand and bows in kindness gesture showing the ship with his extended left arm. The parrot screams and walks on his back:

- Welcome to the Fancy!

Thomas rows quietly and sweaty. He looks at the rest of them, who are still screwed in deep sleep. The sun is already showing its first raising rays over the ocean, in theits every morning beautiful spectacle watched by few people.

He looks forward and sees the beach is just a few yards away. He descends to the water carefully to avoid swinging the boat too much and wake up the other sleepers. With water up to his chest, he pushes the boat hardly alone until it runs aground in the sand. He grabs a water bottle, some food pills and a small package that's wrapped around Lorenzo's feet. Finally, he picks up the tablet that is next to Luna, who sleeps like a baby.

Again, without making any fuss, As quiet as he can, he lands, walks on the sand, and disappears through the tropical vegetation that is very close. Before entering in it, he still looks back, sadly, at one last thought whether to do that or not. He finds a large Y-shaped tree after a couple of yards ahead. He sits in its shadow, unwraps the package to release two keys and two torn parchment pieces.

Looking sideways to see if there was anyone, he analyses the new piece of parchment that emerged in the sad accident with Soledad. It appeared to be a middle piece of the top side of the entire scroll, between its left and right corners, which could be the last. He leans over the parchment left corner and sees that it's really the track sequence:

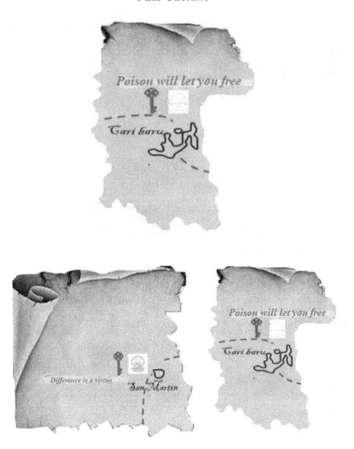

He gets the tablet, touches the Virtual Attendant button in accordance to what he learned from Luna and asks:

- Am I in Isla of Caribarú?

He increases the robotic voice sound coming out of the device slightly, always looking sideways to make sure he's really alone. He does not realize there is someone watching him at distance, hidden by the foliage......

- "Yes. Isla de Cari Barú. Rosario Archipelago. Coast of the Colombian continent. It has the format of the letter N seen from above. It is located to the left of Isla Grande, almost forming a channel between them. It is the second largest island of the archipelago, it has a lot of native vegetation, climbable hills and very rugged topography".

Thomas approaches the tablet again and asks:

- Is it inhabited?

- "Yes, there are many five-star hotels and resorts. Do you want to book a reservation?"

The tablet opens a series of windows, with typical tropical hotels and inns photos, with chalets suspended on the water connected by wooden walkways.

- Stupid tablet...

- "Idiot: person who says nonsense, things without nonsense. Synonym: donkey"

He twists his lips to avoid saying anything else. He open the piece of parchment and reads the enigmatic phrase to himself:

- "Poison will set you free"

- "Meaningless phrase. Please repeat"

It covers the device sound pickup. He looks at the drawing that seems to be an indigenous hut.

- It's here... looks like an indigenous house...

It uncovers the voice capture sensor and asks, without seeing that the foliage he is, begins to move near where he is sitting:

- Colombia, year 1708. Were there indigenous at that time?

The screen shows the internal computer is searching. It takes a few seconds and returns:

- "Affirmative. There were many natives of indigenous origin in Colombia, as well as in Brazil and throughout South America..."

Thomas, distracted, does not see that a bow, with the rope resonated and armed with an arrow, comes out of the foliage, held by two arms, pointing to his direction

- "... one of the most famous tribes was the Miranhas."

- Famous for being in large numbers?

- "No... famous because they were cannibals."

The released arrow is flies few inches from Thomas' nose, causing him to release the tablet in fright. He looks back to understand what happened and sees the arrow stuck in a large poisonous snake in the Y tree trunk just behind him which would attack him treacherously.

Frightened, he looks at where the shot came out and sees a beautiful young Indian come out through the foliage, still holding the bow. She is of short stature, long straight black hair, black eyes, tanned skin, turned thighs and not too fat or slim body. She appears to be 18. She wears a various-colored-birds-feather skirt, but her breasts are partially covered by her hair and colorful beads necklaces.

She slowly approaches Thomas staring him with a mixed curiosity and caution, half bent over and still wielding and pointing another armed arrow in the bow to him., who remains seated, very surprised. He makes to go up, but she points the arrow at him even more, as telling him not to move.

He raises his hands to show that they are free and says, in Spanish:

- See. I don't have any guns.

She seems to understand, but still very suspicious, she doesn't lower the bow. He continues:

- You saved my life! Thank you!

She doesn't understand. He shows the stuck snake on the tree trunk behind him and repeats, smiling:

- Thank you!

The boy's white teeth seem to catch her attention. She gets even closer, loses her distrust, crouches next to him. She touches his blond hair, passes her hand by his face, as if examining how different the boy is in relation to the people she knows.

He's a little awkward:

- You... like... me?

He raises his hand to pet her. She gets scared at first, but seeing that he doesn't want to hurt her, lets him grabs her hair. When he touches her face, she closes her eyes in cuddling sign. He tries to communicate by showing himself:

- Me... Thomas... you...?

She doesn't understand. He shows himself again and points to her:

- Me... Thomas... you... name?

- Indira.

- Indira?

She nods and smiles, shyly.

- Nice name.

She repeats Thomas' action, touching herself with her right hand and then touching Thomas' chest:

- Indira... Thomas...

- Good! Now that we've met, where do you come from?

She doesn't understand. He's got an idea. He takes the golden key and shows her:

- Key... know... where... I... can... find... key?

But it's like he had shown another snake to her. She gets up, scared, very scared, walks away, talking loudly and showing the beach to him:

- *Kuimba'e anã... kuimba'e anã...*

- What?

- *Kimba'e anã... mombyri...*

He gets up too, keeps the key in his pocket and starts walking to meet her.

- Calm down, easy, ready, I've kept it, don't worry...

He's very close to her when, from the same foliage she came out, someone screams:

- Indira!

She turns when three average stature natives come out foliage, one of them taller and stronger, who pulls Indira by her arm to his side. They wear only one type of skin-colored swimwear, some necklaces, and feathers on the head. The three of them point arrows at Thomas who, frightened, begins to walk backwards:

- Hellooooo... I didn't do anything to her...

But a fourth Indian appears behind him and hits him with an animal bone on his head, causing him to faint.

Well... at least it looked like a bone of an animal...

O'Connor is still concatenating the ideas:

- I can't believe this. Last time...

- ... we toast to the future, remember? – says pirate Henry

He looks at Kendall and seems to recognize her:

- And you... were not ... that doctor?

Kendall makes that thick voice again:

- Yes, he was me.

- So – he says, approaching and picking up her hair – you are a woman... very attractive...

She takes his hand off and stares him seriously. He gives an ironic smile and turns to O'Connor:

- You were Wager's sweetie hero.

The parrot imitates: "Sweetie Wager"

- And how is he doing?

Henry makes a disgusted look:

- He must be flattering and being flattered at court... *ostentatious*!

- But you were the number two in charge.

- That is why I left, my dear. I no longer agreed to sustain the Stuarts ′luxuries and whims – he spins on himself, showing the ship around – now I own my wealth, my freedom and work on my own business.

Birdie lets slip her restrained anger:

- Piracy is a crime; it is not a work.

He stops spinning and looks at her with explicit contempt:

- Who cheats a cheat and robs a thief, earns a dispensation of a hundred years. I just make the rich share what they stole from other people whit me. Taxes, spills, luxury, social inequality. I call it income distribution. All ships passing through the Caribbean carry what they have explored from the colonies. They leave only what doesn't matter.

Birdie answers:

- You've killed a lot of people in this... "income redistribution"

- This is kerfuffle.

The parrot repeats: "kerfuffle". The pirate continues:

- They exaggerate what they say, but I do not care. If they did not resist, they would not have to be killed. But... – he begins to pay more attention on her – ... are you also a... woman?

- Full of pride!

- My men have been at sea for a long time... Maybe you can help.

Winston sets himself in with a step forward:

- Don't you even dare!

All the pirates crowd on the deck around them as soon they were aware of being women on board. Seeing that the situation is taking a very bad turn, O'Connor asks:

- Captain don't do this, please. You were once a nobleman.

- And I did not get anything out of it.

He raises his arm and signals to attack. The pirates advance on O'Connor, Winston and Alfie, while Kendall, Birdie, Laureen and Emmett run to other ship side. Two fights at two poles begin. The three Englishmen throw punches, kicks, scoffs, but they also get a lot of punches. It doesn't take long to they get dominated by the pirates.

The four women stand with their backs to each other, forming cross-defense circle. The dirty, sweaty, ragamuffin, bearded, violent pirates surround them. They held hands in defense. Laureen gets a sword. The pirates advance on them at the same time from all four sides. Emmett throws punches, kicks, elbows on each approached man. Laureen strikes her sword, scaring away those who try to attack her. Birdie strikes karate and jiu-jitsu, just like Kendall. The men attack, but some of them fall unconscious, others take punches in their face, kicks and drop down.

But the number of men is much greater than the women can defend themselves. One of them disarms Laureen with his sword. Three others brut pirates hold Emmett by her arms, another holds her neck behind. Six other men manage to hold and take down Birdie and Kendall. The situation is out of control. Connor, Winston and Alfie struggle, trying to get rid of one of the mast they were roped. The pirates, in angry mob, take down the four women on deck, shouting profanities and threats.

When all seems lost main mast basket vigilant shouts:

- Ship to port!

Everyone looks and identifies a Spanish flag frigate approaching not far away.

Henry shouts:

- Men! To combat!

They set the women free and prepare for another pirate attack.

Lorenzo is the first to wake up. Still a little sleepy, he opens his water canteen, drinks a few sips, and throws a little over his head, dripping through the well-grown beard. He looks around and sees that they are stranded on a beach. He wakes the other ones up:

- Paloma, Isabel, Luna... wake!

The three ladies wake up with their bodies sore from the discomfort of the boat. Isabel asks, also half sleepy:

- What's up?

- Look, we're on a beach.

- How did we get here? – asks Paloma

- Where's Thomas? – asks Isabel

Instinctively, Lorenzo searches for the key package that were at his side. He finds nothing.

- I'm afraid of what I'm thinking.

Luna also misses her tablet:

- Where's my tablet?

The four of them look at each other, understanding what had happened. They get off the boat quickly and walk towards the woods, following the Thomas' sand trail. They reach the small clearing where he was and find the tablet lying at the foot of the Y-shaped tree. Isabel finds the small wrapping with the two pieces of parchment and only one golden key.

- Guys, I found something.

- I wonder why he left this behind. – asks Paloma

- If he was trying to follow the lead, he should have taken this too – concludes Lorenzo

- Listen to this – warns Luna, who was messing with the tablet –he was researching something about the island.

She downloads Thomas-tablet recorded conversations and all of them listen up to the phrase "... famous because they were cannibals." They stares each other in a mixture of fear and anxiety. Paloma looks at the tree and sees the dead snake, skewered by the arrow:

- Look!

Isabel is going to scream due to so terrible presumed expectation when Lorenzo covers her mouth with his hand. He asks to Luna, trying to stay as rational as possible:

- Research on anthropophagy.

She slides her finger on the screens until she finds the articles and explains:

- There are, in general, two groups of cannibals: those who kill for their god's grateful ritual and those who simply think that human flesh is a type of food just like the other animals. This local tribe, the Miranhas, belong to the second group, but they follow the same procedure. The prisoner is locked in a tent and he is fed with best food in the village. He gets a woman to serve him. Sacrifices are made at sunset, with parties, dances and drinking. After being well fed, the prisoner is killed with blows to the head, his body is cut into...

Isabel shouts:

- Enough! I don't want to hear it anymore!

- We have to save him! – Paloma moans

Lorenzo has no doubt:

- You stay here, I'll go alone.

- No way, let's go with you – says Paloma

- No, it's too dangerous.

- Let's go all together! – Luna reinforces

- Listen to me... the more people exposed, harder and risky the situation will be...

He walks towards the foliage which leaves seems to be crumpled by the Indians previously.. He turns around and says:

- If I'm not back in an hour, get back on the boat, escape to the pod and get out of this hellhole.

- Promise you'll come back? – asks Isabel.

- I do!

He disappears into the woods, trying to follow the trail signs. Luna marks on the tablet the time: four o'clock p.m. She looks at the horizon and sees that the sun is already low.

The Fancy ship looks like hell. Several cannonballs' gusts destroy everything at the same time. Dead or armless men, shrapnel, falling sails, screaming. The armed pirates assemble the forty-six cannons with bullets rapidly and begin to shoot at the Spanish frigate, very close. They stand side by side and only a gunpowder smokescreen sits between the two ships.

But Henry doesn't look scared. He screams at all his lungs:

- Gunsmiths, fire! Helmsman, on the port! Let's board it on! Kill all of them!

Planks begin to appear on the walls of the Spanish ship among the smoke fog. Suddenly, hundreds of pirates begin to emerge, running over them. Others appear in the air, hanging from ropes like monkeys in vines, docking the cargo ship. Spanish soldiers also jump on to the pirate boat. A bloody hand-to-hand fights begin, pirates against soldiers, with swords, knives, arquebuses and what else serves as a weapon.

O'Connor shouts:

- Let's get out of here!

Amid all the confusion of gunfire, screams, swords and men popping up everywhere, O'Connor leads his people to a lifeboat that lies at the stern. It's about 22 yards that look like miles to advance. They have to dodge blows, push bodies that fall on them, lower themselves to escape gunfire. They have to crawl on the floor to escape the aerial firefight when they get close to the lifeboat.

O'Connor reaches the rope-tied boat first and helps one by one. But when Alfie, the last one, is going to jump in it, a lost bullet goes through his back. He falls near the wall; a blood stain begins to grow on his shirt.

O'Connor puts his head on his thigh and tries to help:

- Alfie! Strength! Take a deep breath!

- It's my turn, Captain...

- We're going to get you out of here!

Alfie holds O'Connor's hand tightly and says:

- When you get back to London... gives a kiss in my mother... tell her I love her very much...

- You'll do it yourself! – O'Connor tries to raise him up

- I've boarded on this mission... thinking about making some money... I was a drug addict; I caused lots of my mother's heartbreaks... but I managed to clean myself and ... had the desire to give her all the best... I thought I was going to get a good reward. if we could find the treasure... but... did not give ... Goodbye, Captain!

Alfie dies. Winston screams from inside boat, not seeing what had happened:

- Captain! Let's go! Everything is going off!

O'Connor closed Alfie's eyelids and is forced to abandon his companion with his heart on pain. He jumps on the boat, Winston lowers its ropes to get down, and when they're near the water, he cuts them off to fall faster. They leave paddling with full force, abandoning the well-damaged pirate ship, next to the Spanish frigate.

- Where's Alfie? – Laureen asks

O'Connor responds with red eyes full of held tears only.

Gradually, a little clarity is appearing. The blurred vision brings colorful images, some striped, some in black. A blurred face's image shines. The luminosity increases, the image of the face becoming sharper, the colors taking shape of objects, a dry straw ceiling.

Thomas opens his eyes and sees Indira's face in front of him, with a pity face. He feels his limbs movements are coming back and realizes he is lying on a round-enclosure floor, bamboo built with thatched ceiling. A pain behind his head reminds him of what had happened.

He lifts his trunk and sits on the floor next to the Indira who gently wets a rag in water in a clay bowl and passes on his forehead.

- Ouch... Ui... my head...

- *Anavarã che rupápe.*

- I don't understand your language, but I think you like me.

He gets up and goes to the hollow entrance, closed by beads-seeds cords curtain. He opens it a little with one hand to spy on what's going on out there. The sun is starting to set, but he can see there's a lot of excitement around. Many native men, women and children walk hastily from side to side, carrying stuffs, such as in preparations for a big party. Several hollows are lined up in a circle, and in the center, like a square, men are lighting a firewood that is under a large iron grate, suspended by four stakes, like a bed. He looks further and sees semi naked indigenous dance in a circle, smoking something that leaves them in a trance, to the sound of drums played by other natives, totally covered by animal skins and colorful birds feathers.

In a panic, Thomas understands they're preparing a barbecue. Of him. He Ggoes back inside and, desperately, looks for some gap between the walls to get away, but they are made with bamboo intertwined by strong strips, without leaving any hole. He looks for some object that can cut the strips or pierce the ceiling, but there are clay bowls or braided straws only.

The curtain opens and some girls come in to leave pots with water, bowls with lots of fruit and a piece of roasted monkey meat. One of them looks at Indira as giving a signal. All of them come out soon, not without first casting a pleased look at Thomas.

Indira takes a piece of meat and offers it to Thomas.

- *Mba'erepa nde nderekarui yva ha ka'avo.*

- Thank you, I'm not hungry... I want to get out of here.

The outside drums sound begins to get faster, increasing his distress inside. Their hollow curtain opens again suddenly, and four very ugly natives enter. Two of them bodyguard's of a taller, bigger and stronger Indian, headed with large feather headdress and painted-whole body. He has several animal-and-human-teeth necklaces hanging from his neck. He calls Indira to come to him and she obeys on the spot, frightened. Thomas understands he's the chief of the tribe and her father.

The fourth oldest, thinner and wrinkled Indian wears a black & white gray feathered robe. He holds a long, black stick, on whose tip is stuck a rubies-eyed small human skull. He's the sorcerer.

He approaches Thomas and pushes his shoulders down, causing him to kneel. He rips the poor boy's shirt off and begins to surround him, doing macabre dances around, as if offering him to the spirits. Thomas gets up and tries to escape, but the chief and his big and strong bodyguards prevent him. Struggling against them, Thomas notices one of the chief′s collars has a pendant with the golden key tied by a piece of parchment mixed among the others feathered and teeth ones.

Thomas manages to bust the necklace without the chief's noticing during their fight to free himself, despite he is desperate to get away with. He quickly hides it in his pants pocket and starts crying and calling out:

- Somebody help me! I want to get out of here!

The chief, the sorcerer and the two other Indians leave the hollow, letting him alone with Indira again. As if she was his last salvation, he holds her by her shoulders and begs:

- I don't want to die this horrible way!

Staring at her, he feels she's in love with him. Even in that panic and fearful environment, a quick romantic mood forms among them. Slowly, Thomas approaches, holds the back of the girl's neck and gives a long and sweet kiss on Indira's lips.

When he turns his face away from her, he sees that her eyes are still closed, enchanted. The drums sound ceases, and a very strong voice begins to say something outside. It's an indication that the sacrifice moment is closer.

Indira runs to one of the clay pots the girls had brought. She sticks her hand in and grabs a handful of small branches with green leaves and small tentacles-shaped white flowers. She removes the leaves and flowers from the branches, throws them in a clay bowl, fills it with a few of water and, with a stone, begins to smash them, until it forms a dark green paste.

She run to Thomas and, with her hand, take a handful of that leafcase and offers him to eat. He asks:

- What is this?

- *Curare.*

- What's "curare"?

- *Karu, karu curare.*

He doesn't understand, but trusting the girl, he takes a large handful of the paste and starts eating. It tastes bitter like Chile boldo. He swallows it. She gives him some more and, with some sacrifice, he eats another big portion. His mouth turns green mustached.

She walks away and two very strong cannibals enter, each holding a five-and-a-half-meter-long stick, which is the club or axe they use to blow their victims' head.. They approach menacingly Thomas walk backwards, terrified.

One of them lifts his bloody-stained-ended club, and will give the first blow, when Thomas feels a strong pain in his stomach.

- Uuuuggghhh...

They stop. The pain comes back with more intensity, causing him to twist his torso down and put his hands on his belly.

- Uuugggghh... ... what pain... uuggghhhh…. Help…

The natives look and perceive the boy's green mouth. They look around and see the pot with the rest of the crumpled leaves. They smell the pot and, frightened, point at the boy and shout together:

- *Curare!*

They hurry out hollow. The pain increases further, and Thomas begins to feel back pain and burning in the throat. The poison is starting to make its tragic reaction.

Indira kneels to comfort him. The chief and the sorcerer return to the hollow, very frowning. The old man approaches Thomas who is lying down, writhing. The sorcerer smells his body closely, raises his arms and speaks a few words to the chief such as "we can't eat him."

Thomas begins to feel stronger breath shortness. His vision gets blurred, his throat closes, it looks like his diaphragm is stopping working. His lips are purplish. He throws a greenish paste up. The pain in his stomach is unbearable. The chief and the sorcerer go out, then three Indians enter, take Thomas by his legs and arms, take him out of the hollow, carry him into the middle of the bush and throw him into a ditch full of human skeletons, so that no one from the tribe would be contaminated.

The poison had freed him, indeed. Lorenzo arrives hidden by the dark night. He finds his inert friend, thrown into the bones ditch. He comes down to him, tries to revive him, desperate but noiselessly. He soon understands that, by the signs, Thomas has been poisoned. He gets his friend out of the ditch with great difficulty and drag him into a large chard nearby.

He puts his friend's head on his legs and, also desperate, doesn't know what to do. Thomas is having his terminal spasms as a reaction to the muscles paralysis. Purple and puffy face. He's going to die by asphyxias, because his diaphragm doesn't really work as his entire body organs. Lorenzo cries. Indira appears from the middle of the bush, holding a clay jug.

She says to the surprised and devasted Lorenzo:

- *Curare.*

- Curare? Oh my God! He needs prostigmine!

He looks around, looking for any recognizable plant. That's when Indira opens Thomas's mouth and drops a light green tea-like liquid, which she brought in the jar, looking back and sideways not to get her tribe's attention.

Part of the liquid flows down the corners of his mouth, but part of it can be swallowed. Thomas' heart stop beating. Lorenzo initiates cardiac massage and mouth-to-mouth breathing.

- Come on, brother, react... Let's go... one... two... three... Reacts.... one... two... three...please, man!

Indira gives him more tea to drink. Lorenzo, tired, stop doing emergency care. Thomas gives no sign of life. Lorenzo collapses:

- No.....

Suddenly, Thomas raises his torso and vomits, vomits so much that he chokes. Lorenzo's and Indira's joy are indescribable. They lift their friend up and, holding him by the shoulders, begin to carry him away from there.

When they arrive at the beach, in the light of the full moon, Isabel, Paloma and Luna come to meet them. Thomas is still very weak.

- What happened? – asks Paloma, helping to carry the boy.

- I'll tell you later – says Lorenzo – quick, let's get out of here!

Thomas manages to babble a few words, looking for something:

- T... ta...ble... ta...blet...

- Quiet, man – says Lorenzo, beginning to take him to the sand.

But he insists:

- Ta...blet... tablet...

Luna understands:

- I think he wants my tablet...

She delivers it. No one understands why. Thomas firms his eyes and slides his finger on the screens with some difficulty. He finds the language translator, chooses from English for indigenous language. He look at Indira tenderly and speaks into the microphone:

- Thank you from my heart!

The translator speaks on speakerphone:

- *Aguyjé !*

The young Indian understands and reciprocates with a beautiful smile and passionate look. But they have to run away before the tribe realizes the farce. The four of them rush to the boat, supporting the Englishman who still feels breath shortage. Indira stays among the foliage, sad that she cannot accompany her beloved, but happy to have saved his life.

Thomas is placed inside the boat, which, rowed by colleagues, moves away from the beach. He fixes a gratitude gaze to the young woman, while her image goes diminishing, diminishing, until she disappears among the foliage, forever.

CHAPTER VI
THE LAST JOURNEY

PALACE OF CORTES, NATIONAL CONGRESS - MADRID, YEAR 2021

The semicircle room of Salón de Plenos is crowded of uniformed officers, suit-dressed parliamentarians and white apron scientists, sitting over where under very high conversation. The issue is unique: the last British's affronts to the Spanish country. The present at the plenary lower their voices when two black-and-golden uniformed security soldiers hit their flagged sticks on the floor three times, in silence request.

The side door is opened to let enter twenty members of the executive staff of that Special Plenary Session, led by the President of Spain. Professor Perez, Dr. Jimenez, and Dr. Inez enter among several medal awarded officers, priests and other society's representatives.

Television cameramen focus on the head tribune to initiate the TV national transmission. The President sits on the central chair, picks the microphone up and announces the agenda:

- Dear Ministers, Gentlemen, dear doctors, scientists, officers of the Armed Forces; representatives of Spanish society. Our nation faces one of its greatest international and political crises of the modern era. Our British neighbors – which we respect so much in the today's civilized worldwide diplomacy – inflamed by far-right ultranationalist movements, accuses us of a crime we have not made in the hole History. Our past has immeasurable events always done towards the country crown's protection and the human rights defense. For this reason, it is no longer a simple dispute over a sunken ship, but rather the principle of rights equality and pride in Spain!

He's applauded for a few minutes. He asks for silence and continues:

- I call the award-winning Professor Iago Perez, head of the Scientific Research Department of the National Intelligence Center of the Ministry of Defense.

Applauses are heard again, Dr. Perez stands up and goes at the main pulpit. His clumsy mood demonstrates not having much practice in lectures:

- Ladies and gentlemen, good afternoon, all right?

As no one answers, he tries to make fun:

- I think sleepless people here is now going to find a solution...

As all of the entire audience stays staring him seriously, he looks at Dr. Inez who makes signs with her hand to behead him.. He clears his throat and continues:

- Going to the point. The Government of Spain commissioned us a study about the disappearance of Galleon San José, a project that, after researching over ten years, made us to assemble...

He looks to the President in order to see if he could move on. This one nods, as knowing the matter. Perez continues:

- ... a time machine!

A general "hoo-hah" spreads over the audience, mixed with conversation. He continues:

- We connected several physical and quantum theories and, briefly speaking, we built a capsule that guided eight crew members into the 18th century to look for a supposed map of the shipwreck exact location. It's has taken eight days already they left, - in our time counting – and we have not heard from them due to the lack of real-time communication.

He takes about one hour and a half to summarize the project and everything that was going on up there. He reaches the end of his narrative in front of an attentive and amazed audience

- It's been eight days since they left, and even without communication, I believe they are firm in their mission purposes. Even though they were young and civil, they believed in a better future and they could help all needy people with the recovered treasure. They risked their own lives for a greater ideal. Therefore, we count on your admiration and support for this cause, so that, once again, the science of our country will have another unimaginable Modern Age success!

All the present give him a standing ovation. He thanks, sits again and the President returns to talk on the microphone, rhetorically increasing his speech tone:

- We decided to publicize this project to demystify unfounded accusations and hostile manifestations to our people. We need the entire Spanish people's support to our team wins this mission, focused solely on the world wellness. We have to defend peace, but we also have to defend our flag, our values, our King! History will reveal who is right and who is wrong. If we find the ship remains – which ownership, by the way, belongs to the Spanish crown – the benefit will be passed on to our folk. In accordance to the Hague Court's agreement, the Spanish Ministry of Economy announces and officializes...

He does a strategic break to bring more suspense to what he will announce:

- ... the granting of the 2,000 euros per month to all of Spanish citizen for a period of twenty years with our heritage treasure share! It is called "galleon aid"!

The crowd of people watching outside the parliament building on a big screen, screams, vibrates, rings horns and national flags flutter on all sides.

- Therefore, people of our beloved homeland, let us unite and be prepared against an enemy who wants to take our rights away. United, we will never be defeated!

The plenary comes down with so many palms of those present. Everyone comes to greet the three scientists who, astonished, cannot overcome shyness. At one point, Dr. Jimenez's cell phone rings and he answers, departing from the greetings:

- What?..... I didn't understand .... Are you sure? Wait, we're going straight there!

He "swims" among the people are around Perez and Inez and speaks in their ears:

- Urgent, let's go to the NIC! Now!

They get the plenary out, where people keep hugging each other. This feeling of unity and confrontation spreads rapidly throughout the country. The crowd begins to march in protest procession.

International political news warm up. On television, newspapers and digital media on the planet, there is nothing else to talk besides the race – past and present – for those who find the map of the sunken galleon first. International provocation messages pop up on social media. Protesters invade the streets of Madrid and make a riot in front of the British embassy. In Cádiz, a large rally, with music show, is held in front of the University in honor of the young students who left for the great time travel adventure.

Clashes between Spanish working-class people and British police leave several injured in Gibraltar borders with a British territory.

The British Navy launches an aircraft carrier with some destroyers from Portsmouth towards the Galician region, north of the Iberian Peninsula, in order to conduct "military exercises".

At the same time, the Spanish Navy sends a submarine and some cruisers to that same region to conduct same "military trainings".

NATIONAL INTELLIGENCE CENTER - MADRID, YEAR 2021

Perez, Inez, and Jimenez arrive in the Tempor Experimental Center hurriedly. The control room is very busy, where its operational control panels staff pulls several buttons, analyze lighted graphics screens and data arrays.

The cyclic particle tubular accelerator reactors´ panels lights are diminishing gradually. The doctors look up and realize the wormhole orange spiral is getting weaker, leaving some rings no longer to be seen.

Zara, a red-short-haired and flecked-face assistant, in apron with NIC comes to meet them dressed on NIC symbolled apron:

- Gentlemen, the situation is getting out of our control.

- What's going on, Zara? – Dr. Inez asks

She conduces them to the large center control panel screen. Some frequency waves pass through thick wires, but they get thinner as they walk on the screen. They become thick again, they get thin later, in the sine wave. Zara explains:

- It's been three days longer than scheduled by the project. Reactor fuel's running low.

- And there's no way to refuel it? – asks Perez

- Our silica reserves are exhausted unfortunately.

- Why don't you buy more?

- Because the large reserves are in countries with trade agreements with the United Kingdom.

They understand. Dr. Inez completes:

- And they adhered to the embargo.

- Yes, Doctor.

- And how much time do we have, then?

She queries the screen and replies:

- Two more hours, forty-three minutes and fourteen seconds, ma'am.

- That's it?

- But that equates to almost twenty-four hours in the past, Doctor.

They look at each other. Dr. Jimenez asks:

- And what's going to happen?

- If they don't come back in this period, doctor, the tunnel will close, and they're stuck in the past... forever.

- We can't let this happen at all! – Perez's bravery

- What are the solution alternatives? – asks Dr. Jimenez

- We've analyzed all of them, Doctor, but none of them are complete.

- Still, what are they? – asks Perez

- There're the legal ones and the... say... not-too-legal... Which do you want to know first? – asks the girl with an ingenious loo

- Whatever is the fastest, young lady – replies Perez

ISLA GRANDE, BARÚ ARCHIPELAGO - YEAR: 1708

Recovered Thomas opens the piece of parchment he kept in his pants pocket during the mess along with the fifth golden key. It is the map upper right corner, showing the drawing of another larger island with a key, a treasure chest, over the word "Hell" and, leaving the island, a dotted line that indicated a cross next to the Galleon San Jose drawing.

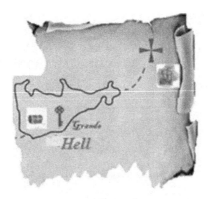

He approaches this corner of the other two he holds and finally sees that ends the entire map upper half:

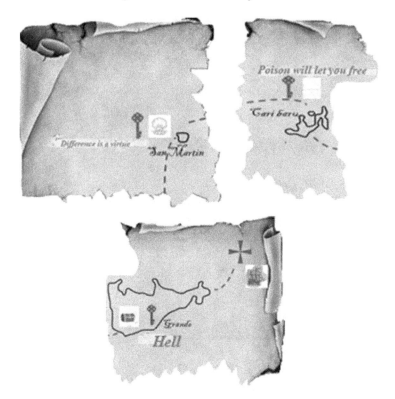

He calls his colleagues. Lorenzo, Paloma, Isabel and Luna approach. They are all still inside the boat, but close to the Isla Grande coast, whose steamy volcano mountain can be seen from afar.

Thomas shows the conquered three pieces and speaks:

- Well, it looks like it's the last part...

Isabel comments:

- It'd be nice if we had the whole map, wouldn't it?

Luna pulls her tablet out and speaks:

- I have the bottom pictures, let me try to assemble them...

She takes pictures of the top three pieces, takes a few minutes dragging the files to the corners and satisfied, she reports out:

- I think it's.

She shows the complete map, assembled with five scratched pieces:

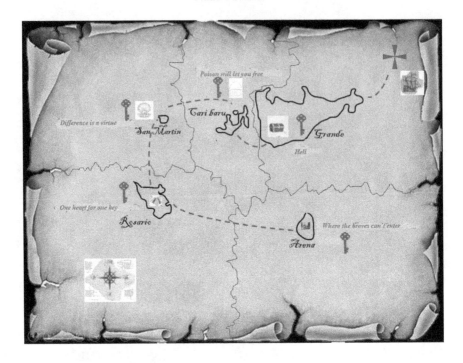

Lorenzo comments:

- Everything begins to make sense now... they were partial clues that connect to each other.

- Like a children's play – says Isabel

- Yes – Paloma agrees – but more dangerous and deadly...

After a few minutes to reflect, Luna asks:

- Well... let's try this last game phase?

Isabel looks at the parchment pierce and concludes:

- Isla Grande, with the figure of a chest...

- ... where it might keep the exact shipwreck location – Lorenzo completes

- Or a real treasure, who knows? – comments Thomas

- And where is our ship – Paloma remembers longingly

- Yes... it's time to go home – agrees Lorenzo

He turns the rudder toward the island. Despite almost costing his life, Thomas is still motivated to find the sink real map. He suggests:

- On the way back, we can pass this location and try to find the chest.

- Are you serious? – asks Paloma

- Since we´ve gone this far, so close, it doesn't hurt to try the last move.

- But we don't have all the keys – Isabel reminds

- We have two – shows Thomas – and the English team, three: the one who stole us from the priest´s tomb; the second they robbed us (again) on mermaid island and the third they took on the island of the Mayans themselves...

Isabel looks again at the map and replies:

- Here shows five keys, being the fifty obtained in Isla Grande. Would we need all of them?

- For what? – questions Paloma

- We will only know if we go there – defines Lorenzo

- But there... where? – asks Isabel

- Here it says "Hell" – Luna reminds

The boat reaches the beach of Isla Grande, whose range is much wider than the previous islands. All of them land and pulls the boat until it runs the sand aground. Isabel looks to both very beautiful and calm beach sides, with very white sand, coconut trees and transparent water up to the waist.

Isabel asks:

- But where can there be a hell in this paradise?

She has just asked, the several miles far volcano erupts violently, squeaking the entire island. It releases a large block of chimney-shaped smoke, ash flies everywhere and some lava rivers begin to flow down its slopes.

Everybody looks at each other. Lorenzo remembers and warns aloud:

- Our ship! It's at that volcano foot!

- Truth! – confirms Paloma

Led by Lorenzo, they all run and disappear through the tropical forest, while the blue sky turns to gray by the volcano's expelled cloud.

The young men and girls cross trails, forests, small streams, climb and descend stones, getting closer and closer to the mountain foot, which continues snoring as a bad-humor-woken giant up.

Lorenzo asks Luna, guiding herself through the tablet again:

- Where's the Columbus?

- Based on the compass indicator, on the other mountain side.

- How can we get there?

- We have to dodge the rolling stones and the lava if they show up. Let's go this way – says Luna.

Paloma explains during the tortuous path between the mountain slopes using her geology acknowledgement:

- This is a large, conical-shaped magma-made stratovolcano and it must be on top of the destructive boundary of a tectonic plate. There may exist some ventilation channels or cracks besides the main crater. I don't know how long it's been on eruptive work, but after this first explosion, the second and following will come with much more intensity and destructive power.

- We've to get out of here fastly! – says Isabel

When they turn one of the volcano's middle-height slope folds they find, with surprise a kind of cave entrance in front of stone platform, surprisely. A reddish glow signalizes that there is something inside the cave.

- It must be one of the fissures I talked about – explains Paloma

- Let's continue on our path straight ahead – indicates Luna

Lorenzo, Luna, Isabel and Paloma pass. When the latter Thomas goes across the platform, he looks at its ground and sees, surprised, some fallen golden coins. He looks closely and notices there are more all-sized coins dropped as in a line that enters in the cave. As his other companions went forward, they did not realize that he had been left behind.

He collects a coin from the ground and identifies himself as a large Spanish doubloon. He bites it and confirms pure gold. He looks into the cave, looks at the path through which his colleagues went away and, once again driven a little by curiosity and a little by ambition, he enters the cave following the trail of coins lined up on the ground.

Some yards ahead, Paloma looks back and doesn't see Thomas anymore. She awarms:

- Hey, guys, where Thomas is?

They stop and turn to her. Isabel asks:

- Wasn't he after you?

- Yes, he was, but I went straight and thought he was following me...

The volcano unleashes another intrepid explosion, dropping sparks and burning rocks everywhere. Some of them go rolling around where they are. Lorenzo shouts:

- Care! Let's take shelter in that cave!

Between earthquakes, ashes and flaming rocks rolling downhill, they succeed to return to the platform and enter in the cave. They find, of course, Thomas picking coins from the ground.

- Thomas! – Lorenzo criticizes – what the hell are you doing?

He shows the golden coins trail on the ground:

- I got distracted a little, sorry...

- "Sorry"?!? We're inside a bomb and you think about coins?

But they continue to walk in the cave tunnel, which gets as brighter as they advance. And warmer too.

- We'd better get back – advises Isabel

- I think we aren't far from finding something out – Thomas guesses

They walk a small slope down in the magma cave, they turn left and stop, perplexed by the scenery they glimpse ahead: the tunnel ends up a large vertical, wide and cylindrical channel. They look up and see the half-bluish-half-gray sky about fifty feet high. They look down and see an incandescent red-orange lava lake, dropping releasing sulfuric gases about three hundred feet deep. A one-meter-wide rough stone beam makes an aerial passageway between their tunnel exit with the other channel side, as a very impressive land-carved bridge.. Another tunnel comes from inside the mountain to the opposite gorge side, at the same height as where they are.

Paloma alerts:

- We're inside the volcano chimney!

- What a hellish heat! – Isabel moans

- Look! – Thomas shouts, pointing to something further ahead.

A capped large cast iron chest is on the middle of the suspended walkway, whose width is slight larger and where the gold coins trail ends. It is locked by five large iron locks that hold an iron belt-shaped latch around the chest.

Fascinated, Thomas starts walking forward the narrow passage, but the lava lake, which is about one thousand feet below, begins to shake and bursts large molten lava bubbles along loud noise. The heat increases. Thomas unbalances and is going to fall when Paloma grabs him from behind and pulls him back to their tunnel entrance:

- You're crazy!

The pressure inside the chimney increases. More bubbles begin to boil from the lava tank, foreshadowing that the large eruption is near. They have to speak out loud due to the noise. Lorenzo shouts:

- Let's get out of here now!

But to what Thomas answers:

- No! We've just to walk over there and open the locks!

A male voice is heard from somewhere:

- But you'll need the five keys!

- Who said that? – asks Isabel

O'Connor, Laureen, Kendall, Winston, Emmett and Birdie come out the opposite side tunnel. Birdie points the only one weapon left. They stop on top of the small magma platform that is glued to the chimney wall.

Paloma speaks out:

- Why are you so predictable?

- Hell and heaven are very close – Emmett ironizes

- All of us is going to die if we don't get out of here now – warns Lorenzo

- You just pass your keys, and you can leave – says O'Connor

- Why don't you guys pass on yours? – asks Lorenzo

The moods of tension and conflict fires again. The heat increases even more, all sweaty pressure, between life and death. Suddenly they hear Isabel's scream and they look to where she is. For everyone's astonishment, Alejandro César de Sabogal, dressed in the Spanish navy uniform and red velvet hat, with his left side of his face disfigured by burns, holds Isabel from behind with a long-barreled pistol against her ear. Five privateers appear behind him, with pistols and swords pointed at the Spanish group. Other group of corsairs appear behind the English at the other side of the tunnel, also armed, closing the siege.

Luna doesn't believe:

- You????

- Yes, horrible creature. Who else could it be?

Lorenzo gets very nervous and goes toward them:

- Let her go! Now!

Sabogal triggers the pistol. Isabel looks panicked at Lorenzo. The English team are also perplexed and they do not know what to do.

Paloma speaks:

- You monster! Aren't the deaths you've caused with those damn leads enough?

Sabogal laughs sarcastically and explains:

- My sweet, innocent child! I'm not the one who made that map.

- How... Like this? So... Who did it?

- Alcázar, that bastard!

Laureen listens and speaks from the other walkway side:

- Don Juan Santín de Alcázar, the second admiral of San Joaquín?

- Himself... I wish his soul is burning in hell!

As Sabogal begins to tell what had happened, everyone there begins to imagine the scenes, as if watching a movie in flashback:

"CARIBBEAN SEA, NEAR TREASURE ISLAND, JUNE 1708.

Battle between Galleon San Jose and the Expedition. Cannon fires, falling masts, shattered soldiers, fire, despair. Sabogal, alone, goes lifeboat ropes down at the ship's rear.

When he is on the sea, oaring the boat so far, he looks backward when San Jose explodes in fire.

"When I saw San Jose would be taken over by the English, I... well... saved the one I love the most... he, he, he"

CARTAGENA DE INDIAS, COLOMBIA, JUNE 1708.

Sabogal and Alcázar chat in a noisy tavern full of drunk sailors, corsairs and dancing prostitutes. Sabogal picks up one of the candles that illuminate the table and, with its flame, begins to write on a small round tree trunk piece is hanging on the wall, near his head.

"Although that bastard abandoned me in combat, when Wager came to attack, I trusted him once more and wrote, on a piece of tree trunk that was nearby, the exact coordinates, longitude, and latitude, of the place where San José had sunk, by the explosion that, up today, I do not understand why..."

Alcázar wets rum on Sabogal's hat and throws the candle over it. While his head burns severely, Alcázar takes the wood and runs the tavern away.

"But the scoundrel betrayed me once again. It set me on fire, I fainted. When I woke up, he was gone, and my memory never worked again. I had forgotten the numbers."

Sabogal, staggering like a drunk, searches for the traitor on the Cartagena streets during the night. He finds him near the Clock Tower, at the main door of the city wall.

"I found him few days later. I smashed him on the city wall and forced him to tell me what he had done, as I was hateful for his second betrayal. as the more he told me, the more I couldn't believe how anyone could have made such madness..."

INACTIVE VOLCANO IN ISLA GRANDE – DAY

Alcázar and four very strong privateers carry the iron chest, place it in the center of the inactive volcano chimney walkway. He begins to lock it with five golden keys.

"Are you seeing this iron chest out front? He kept that wood with my sea coordinates I had written that night in the tavern. Then, he brought the trunk here when the volcano was inactive because he did not expect it would wake up so soon. He locked the safe so that it could be opened with the turning of the five keys at the same time only."

PIRATE TAVERN, CARTAGENA – NIGHT

Alcázar handles a feather to draw a map on a large parchment sitting at a candlestick lighted wood table, with drawings of islands, keys, symbols and, after drinking a glass of black beer in on shot, he rips the parchment into five parts. He burps.

"That bastard liked riddles. And he would do anything to make it harder for anyone who wanted to find such great treasure. So, he invented a catch-up game, where a challenged step had to be solved to indicate the next challenge. He drew a map, tore it into five pieces and tied each piece to one of the keys that would open the chest"…"

ISLA ARENA, ROSARIO ARCHIPELA–O - DAY

Alcázar, ahead in a dinghy rowed by the same corsairs, enters the mermaids' cave, put caps on their ears and row toward the lake central big rock., placing a key on top of it. Mermaids sing and swim around them, but nothing happens.

"The damn knew about the mermaids.... then he and his gang covered theirs ears with wax, entered in the mermaids' cave and left the second part of the map with the second key..."

CARTAGENA, EXTREMELY POOR HOUSE – NIGHT

Alcázar talks to a thin, poor, sick-looking man. The sad man lowers his head and nods. Later, Alcázar gives money to the man's wife, who is with her two young hungry daughters crying, by the light of a few candles in a very poor room, almost no furniture.

"There was a poor guy with terminal illness who, so weak, could no longer work to support his family. Taking advantage of this, Alcázar promised to protect and support his family, but he must surrender himself to the Mayans to be sacrificed..."

ROSÁRIO ISLAND, ROSARIO ARCHIPELAGO - NIGHT

The poor very weak old man, almost dead, lies on the red marble altar. With his trembling hand, he places the third key with the parchment piece in the mouth of the lion frown that heads the human sacrifice table In front of him, the priest raises his knife to deliver the mortal blow.

"The poor man, seconds before his heart was ripped out, placed the third key with the third piece of parchment in the mouth of the frown of that disgusting people's sacrificial table..."

SAN MARTIN ISLAND – AFTERNOON

A pearl fisherman swims to the bottom of the crystalline sea, inserts the wax-wrapped-isolated fourth key with the fourth piece of parchment, inside the yellow-edged tridacna. He swims to the surface up, dropping air bubbles on the way.

"Alcázar was insane. He thought of the impossible to be found. He hired the best pearl-hunting diver to merge to the bottom of the sea and keep the key inside a giant oyster unlike the others. But when he emerged back..."

Alcázar, inside a boat, points an archebuses toward the swimmer, who is still floating in the water, and shoots.

ISLA DE CARIBARÚ, ROSARIO ARCHIPELAGO – DAY

The arching second admiral, always surrounded by his four comrades, talks to the Miranha tribe's chief, sitting on a circle next to a campfire. They smoke and pass cigarettes of hallucinogenic grass one to the other. Large amount of gold bars, mirrors, and precious stones are placed beside them. Indira approaches to serve something in basins and she is slyly looked by the admiral. She, afraid, walks away and goes to her hollow.

"In fact, Alcázar was not insane, he was a monster. But he had a great relationship with the chief of the worst cannibal tribe in these seas. He offered gold, jewelry, smoked with them, he was the white man friend of an Indian. He became interested in the chief's daughter, a beautiful young woman who had not yet met anyone..."

Drugged Alcázar enters in the hollow, rips his shirt off, slaps Indira's face. He goes over her, she tries to defend herself, but he is stronger. Suddenly, he collapses, asleep.

"He gave the fifth key as a gift to the chief and asked him to exchange his own daughter to his worldly desires, which he could not fulfill because he was very drugged..."

It reminds Thomas the scene of Indira's terror feelings when he showed the golden key to her. He tries to jump over Sabogal, but he is hold by one of the pirates:

- You son of a bitch!

Sabogal continues his narrative, still with his gun to Isabel's head:

CARTAGENA, WALL CLOCK TOWER - NIGHT

Sabogal argues with Alcázar after he tells him what he had done with the keys. In the end, he shoots Alcazar's head.

"After so much barbarism, I threatened him to retrieve my wooden trunk, but he laughed in my face, saying he wouldn't do anything about it and that I would never find it back... He told me how he hid the other keys... so I shot him three times in the middle of his eyes and killed him... with the same pistol I'm using right now... it opens a hole the size of a coconut... he, he, he..."

Sabogal searches Alcazar's outfit looking for some clue. He finds the first golden key, wrapped in a piece of parchment. Then he pushes Alcazar's corpse into the dark sea, which floats away.

"Before I throw that fetid rat into the sea, I searched his clothes and found the first golden key, with the first piece of the map"

CARTAGENA DE INDIAS, OLD INN - LATE

Sabogal is lying in a warm water fully bathtub, only with his head and feet out of it. He holds a bottle of wine, which he drinks in sips once in a while. Suddenly, something catches his eye on his foot, and he passes his hand on his right ankle.

"I had already given up trying to recover all that ruse, when, one afternoon, I noticed something strange on my right foot... I passed my hand and felt, under my skin, a small round, flattened metal. I took a knife to take whatever it was, when I remembered...

GALLEON SAN JOSE, CARIBBEAN SEA - AFTERNOON

Luna, from inside the basement jail of Galleon San Jose Galleon, inserts a tracking chip into Captain Sabogal' s right ankle. He feels a sting in his leg, which makes him jump back. He looks down but sees nothing besides Luna looking across the cell next to the railing.

"... of a sting in my leg that this hideous creature made me in the ship"

CARTAGENA DE INDIAS, OLD INN - LATE

Sabogal, in the bathtub, realizes he has something in his leg, smiles as having an idea.

"I believed that you really came from the future and had put something in me... and I left it by purpose..."

CARTAGENA DE INDIAS, CITY CENTER - NIGHT

Sabogal walks Cartagena's city center streets, being followed by the youth Spanish team. He pretends he does not notice them, but he looks back occasionally.

"So, I let you follow me, pretending I wasn't realizing it, until I got into church...

SAN PEDRO DE CLAVER CHURCH – EARLY MORNING

Sabogal hides the first key in the tomb with the remains of San Pedro de Claver, grabs a small knife and removes the tracker chip from his heel and throws it close.

"I knew I couldn't face all those challenges, so I threw the bait... and you bit it right"

He finishes the retrospective, still pointing the pistol at Isabel's head, who, although distressed, is very angry. Lorenzo, even more so:
- *¡Su grande perro!* So, you used us in this infamous way!
Laureen also does not contain herself:
- It cost our friends' lives!
But Sabogal shakes his shoulders in a insignificance signal:

- It doesn't matter to me...

The volcano begins to tremble again. Everyone holds themselves to the walls to avoid falling. The lava from the bottom of the well explodes upwards, almost reaching the bridge where they are. The noise is too loud, everything is about to explode.

Sabogal, still taking Isabel hostage, threatens:

- Either you open this chest, or you're all going to die! First the beautiful young lady here, of course!

Seeing that there is no other way, Lorenzo takes his two keys, looks at O'Connor who nods at the opposite tunnel exit and takes his three keys as well. Sabogal shouts:

- The five keys have to be rotated at the same time. Otherwise, the secret will lock the iron chest forever!

Lorenzo stares Isabel upset, who makes a sign with her head not to obey. But he gives one key to Thomas and another to Paloma. O'Connor gives another for Winston. The five of them begin to walk along the narrow stone bridge, the three Spanish from one side and two English from the other, toward the bridge larger center.. The heat is intense. Height brings dizziness and insecurity. But the five of them succeed to reach the widest middle platform, kneel next to each other. They stick their key in the interconnected locks.

O'Connor suggests:

- On three. One... two... three!

The five of them turn the keys to left simultaneously. Nothing happens. Everyone looks at each other, as thinking they have done something wrong. But after a few seconds, the first left padlock turns on and opens itself alone. Then, the second. Then the third, the fourth, until the fifth also opens on its own.

Lorenzo and Winston lift the heavy iron belt slowly that surrounded the chest and throw it down. The belt falls into the lava and melts in a few seconds. O'Connor and Lorenzo lift the heavy chest lid and get to open it. Several gold coins fall out of it, gnaw the floor of the stone platform.

The chest is fully packed with pure gold doubloons and ducats, necklaces of pearls, emeralds, rubies, and an untold number of diamonds of all sizes and carats. Hundreds of every kind of coins, minted with Peruvian viceroyalty seals roll the chest out.

Lorenzo searches for the piece of wood said by Sabogal, but he finds nothing:

- There's no wood trunk in here!

- Move in the background, assholes!

Lorenzo and O'Connor stick their arms in and start rummaging through the coins. Suddenly, Lorenzo feels to touch in something and removes a slice of half dark and greasy cut tree trunk, with the drawing of islands and some scorched numbers written next to it:

Everyone looks that wood slice as a trophy, finally held after they chase it for so long time, dangers, lives costly. Lorenzo feels contradictory emotions mix: rejoicing, anger; satisfaction, frustration; victory, defeat. He thinks, "Is this what's worth 20 billion dollars?"

He turns to O' Connor and says something in a low voice. O'Connor looks at the wood. Impatient Sabogal shouts, from afar:

- Show me what you've gotten!

Lorenzo raises the piece of wood log and shows it to Sabogal, who recognizes t it was what he had done in the tavern. He smiles letting see his bad teeth:

- That's right, sailor! Bring it to me, carefully!

Lorenzo hesitates a little, but sees that Isabel is still a hostage. He speaks to O'Connor:

- Let's give this to him together.

The two of them get up slowly, each holding the edges. They walk towards the platform near the chimney wall. Paloma and Thomas follow them, while Winston returns to the other side, still escorted by the privateers.

Lorenzo asks Paloma in low tone:

- How often do eruption happen?

- Every 15 minutes, more or less.

- And how long ago did the last one happen?

- I think about ten minutes ago, I'm not sure.

When they arrive in front of Sabogal, Lorenzo tries to say something, O'Connor takes the lead:

- Let the girl go first.

Lorenzo looks at him, astonished. But Sabogal replies:

- How do you dare, as Englishman, to talk to me like that?

- I'm asking you, please.

- None of this would have happened if you had not attacked us.

- Loose... her... now – Lorenzo warns

He stretches his arm to offer the wood to Sabogal. This one makes a sign for one of his pirates to pick the piece up. In this second, the volcano shakes again, making a very loud snoring and releasing a burst of smoke and ash that rises through the chimney up toward be expelled several feet high from the crater

This causes everyone to lose their balance and go blind, coughing heavily. Sabogal is obliged to set Isabel free. Lorenzo pulls her to the side. Sabogal fires a shot, with the intention of injuring the boy, but the bullet goes through the tunnel and, on the other side, hits Birdie's full chest. She falls, badly injured. Laureen, who is closer, tries to help her, but it's too late. She dies holding the lady's hand.

A fierce struggle between the bandits and the two teams start. Punches, kicks, jumps, flying. O'Connor disarms one of the pirates and elbows his neck to put him out of combat. Thomas runs over the bridge, and jumps over the chest, chased by one corsair. The pirate tries to do the same, but he loses his balance and plummets to his death. Isabel and Paloma, together, hold Sabogal from behind, trying to hang him, but he throws them both over his back and they fall to the ground, getting hurt. O'Connor comes to defend them, calling Sabogal to fight him. On the other side, Winston is secured by two corsairs, one on his legs and the other by his neck. The pirate takes a knife and goes to slit his throat, but Laureen, picking a fallen sword up, gives a fatal blow to the dead-falling pirate's back. Winston manages to get rid of the other and, with several punches, knocks him out also. Kendall throws her body over her opponent and gives him her famous neck-blow, trapping her legs around his face. Suffocated, he falls, inert. Lorenzo gives boxing blows to one of the mercenaries, who also beats him back, but with a punch-hook, the boy knocks the brute down, unconscious. Only Emmett does not fight, trying to dodge the others, because she is aiming at the piece of wood that is forgotten near the edge of the platform on the other side. She begins to cross the bridge, intending to catch it.

Sabogal draws his sword and threatens O'Connor. Smiling sarcastically, he makes a Z in the air and advances on him. The Englishman strays, Sabogal strikes horizontally, O'Connor crouches down and the blade goes over him.

- You fight well for an Englishman! – mocks the old Spanish captain

Struggling, they approach the platform edge where starts the stone bridge from. They're close to where the wooden piece is dumped.

Emmett comes from behind to pick it up. Sabogal notices and, with his foot, throws the slice of wood to the other corner. The piece stops at the edge of the cliff. Sabogal refocuses on O'Connor. Emmett arrives at the platform and picks up the piece of wood, but another privateer comes and pushes her, almost making her falls into the lava pit. The pirate takes the piece of wood, perhaps not knowing well the value it has and, like a disc, throws it to the other side of the chimney toward the hands of one free corsair. But it hits the open lid of the chest and falls back into it. Due to the beat, the lid falls and closes the safe again.

Sabogal, seeing that, yells at the pirate and crosses the sword into his belly, killing him:

- You idiot!

Another corsair begins to fight Emmett, who defends herself with jiu-jitsu moves. Thomas manages to cross the bridge, takes the Birdie's gun and starts shooting. He kills one, two privateers, but the ammo runs out. Emmett and a pirate and Sabogal with O'Connor are the only ones now in fight.

The volcano begins to signal that it will erupt again. This time, stronger. In a moment of the pirate's distraction, Emmett kicks the chest's man and makes him fall into the lava pit. O'Connor, walking backwards, stumbles on a rock and falls on his belly upwards, almost also falling into the abyss. Sabogal comes over and prepares the sword to strike the fatal blow at the fallen captain. That's when he feels a blow to the back of the head. He turns around, is bleeding heavily, and he sees hatred Paloma and Isabel, both holding a large stone.

Sabogal still speaks before losing his balance:

- Damn... women!

He falls into the lava lake. His body sinks slowly he ignites, while he slows down and melts completely, screaming hideously. All of the corsairs are defeated, or unconscious, or dead. That's when a big tremor starts inside the chimney and big lava bubbles starts popping up at the bottom of it. The lava level begins to rise. Magma plates begin to loosen from the chimney walls, indicating that a tremendous eruption is close.

Paloma shouts:

- We've to get out of here!

Lorenzo yells at Thomas, Laureen, Kendall and Winston, who are still on the other side of the bridge:

- Quick, come this way!

The three English walk across the suspended bridge with great difficulty to balance themselves, among falling stones and lava drops. They pass through the center where the chest remains closed and walk towards the other side. Due to the trepidation, Kendall loses her balance and falls, but she hangs on the edge of the passage.

- Help!

- Hang in there! – says Thomas

He, who was coming after her, crouches down and helps Kendall get back to the bridge. The lava is increasing in volume, rising through the chimney channel, like a milk when it boils in the milkmaid.

The three of them arrive to the other side and start escaping through the tunnel. Isabel, Thomas, Paloma, Laureen, Winston, Lorenzo, Luna, Kendall, and O'Connor come out. Emmett stands on the platform, looking at the chest that will be lost forever. O'Connor realizes that she has stayed behind and, turning, screams:

- Emmett! Come! Run away!

But she's in doubt. All her investment is there, just a few steps away. Her bank will go bankrupt if she doesn't bring the map she comes to get. Without hesitation, she begins to run across the stone bridge towards the central platform.

O'Connor shouts:

- No! Your life is worth a lot more than this!

But she doesn't listen him, ambitiously blind. Between falling magma stones, She walks among falling magma stones on a very warm temperature. She reaches the chest, picks up the lid to lift it, but it is very hot. The lava level is coming up. She tries again to lid the hot lid when the bridge begins to crack. She gathers all her last strength and, burning her palms, lifts the lid of the safe, but that's when the last support of the stone bridge falls and Emmett falls to her death, along with the chest, with the map and with her ambition.

O'Connor, still at the tunnel entrance, sees her falling, but he can do nothing besides feeling sorry for her. At this time, the raising lava hits the tunnel where he stays and begins to drain toward it. Terrified and suffocated by the heat and the smell of sulfur, he begins to run towards the opposite -side tunnel exit, chased by the fast river of incandescent lava. The tunnel begins to collapse, several small stones fall in the path in front and behind him. After climbing that little slope, he reaches the exit of the tunnel, he takes the last steps to escape, but a stone falls and presses his foot. the lava river is coming behind him, closer.

When he thinks everything is lost, Lorenzo appears, who came back looking for his missed O'Connor. Lorenzo, more than quickly, helps remove the stone, frees O'Connor, and helps him get away of there, just as the lava river begins to come out through the crack opening and drains mountain surface down.

The whole island looks like it's going to explode. The volcano detonates a large cloud of ash. Flamed magma stones rain everywhere as meteors. Lava rivers drain through the crater and side tunnels, causing a real infernal scenario. The remaining nine passengers run down the mountain, towards the Spanish capsule, which, very crumpled, is right in the path of a river of lava not far away.

It's already at night, but the volcano fire lights up enough for them to reach the site. The wormhole spiral, though weak, is still spinning over Columbus. While Luna, Lorenzo, Thomas, Isabel and Paloma try to open the ship's door, the English tighten the belt and the full uniform comes out as inflated from inside the belt. They put on their clothes and put on their helmets, staying the same way they arrived on the time travel. The volcanic snore increases, signaling that it will make its last, most violent, and most destructive gases explosion.

O'Connor waves goodbye to the Spaniards, and together him, Kendall, Winston and Laureen trigger the buttons on their uniform's arms to active the time travel devices.

O'Connor counts down:

- Five... four... three... two... one...

They close their eyes to start the journey. But nothing happens. They open their eyes, confused. O'Connor reprograms his computer arm-in-arm, requesting to the rest of them to do the same. New countdown begins:

- Five... four... three... two... one... Trigger!

Again, they don't disappear, no wormhole spiral comes. They are out of order again up to Winston remembers one of the conditions:

- Captain, I think I know what's going on.

- Say, fast!

- The time-teleportation system only works with at least five belts activated.

O'Connor hits his forehead:

- Indeed! It was to avoid individual deserters...

- And now? – asks Kendall, very distressed.

An incandescent rock falls right next to her. She falls on the ground, scorched. Winston helps her up.

- Think... think... – says O'Connor to himself... – we would have to get one more belt.

- Impossible! – Winston says, sadly, looking at the volcano, where, he had to leave Birdie behind.

They hear Lorenzo's voice:

- Come with us.

They look and discover that he had heard everything along with the three Spanish. Once enemies, now they offered salvation. Kendall asks:

- But... can more people fit in there?

- In Spain we have a popular saying that says "*donde cabe uno, se cabe todos*"

- In addition – remember, sadly, Thomas – we have three empty seats...

- But we are four – O'Connor reminds

- I'm staying

Everybody's looking at who said that. Laureen completes:

- I've lived all my life, you're young and you've got your whole life ahead of you

Lorenzo takes her hand and says:

- There's no way we depart without you. Who also has a whole life ahead of you. There's an extra seat on the ship to transport the wounded.

- Yes, you're coming with us! – confirms Thomas

She looks at everyone who agrees. The continuous earthquake rushes their decision. Kendall's the first to accept.

- So let's go!

Everyone enters Columbus is working, despite the damage to its structure. Lights flash on the panels, many red signs on the screens appear, warning them to leave as soon as possible.

They're sitting on their chairs, buckle their seat belts and are wearing their helmets when the upper wormhole spiral disappears, and all the ship's power goes out.

A tragedy is about to happen.

NATIONAL INTELLIGENCE CENTRE - MADRID, YEAR 2021

Professor Perez, Dr. Inez, Dr. Jimenez and Zara are in front of the cyclic particle accelerator control room panels, anxious, when the energy drops completely. The buzz that the gigantic equipment was making intermittently, stops being heard. The emergency lights come on, leaving only a few panels with lights on due to the extra energy generator.

Zara explains:

- Power reserve is over, Professor.

- Come on, go tot plan B we agreed on, quickly, please!

- I don't know if it's going to work, Professor.

- Daughter, in experimental science, there's only one way to know if things are going to work out: experimenting them.

Zara still tries to justify:

- It's the simplest alternative of all...

Dr. Jimenez intervenes:

- The biggest science discoveries came from the simplest measures.

- What if they don't want to cooperate?

- Our king has already talked to their queen... it's all arranged. Let's go!

She didn't think it would work even, Zara goes to one of the panels and presses some numbers. All of the technicians and scientists' staff in the room stay watching. The figure of a handsome 30's white-coated-red-hair half tousled man appears on the unique big screen that remained powered by the emergency generator. Several blue-and-white-lighted panels are flashing behind him. They look like they're in a television broadcast room. He responds with a strong Scottish accent:

- Yes?

She starts speaking in English:

- This is Zara Cortez, from Spain's National Intelligence Center

He seems to like the girl. He smiles and speaks:

- Hugh Walter, from DSTL, Port Down. Are you OK?

Perez, Jimenez and Inez realize the boy liked Zara's look. But she tries to disguise that she reciprocates the felling. She answers seriously:

- More or less.

- What can I do for you?

- We have to active the Step Help Plan, please.

He gestures a lot as he speaks:

- Yes, we're aware. It came top-down hardly here. You're powerful, huh?

Dr. Inez smiles at her, who closes her face:

- Do you want the coordinates?

- Yes, please pass.

She picks her notebook up and reads as he touches a three-dimensional screen that floats beside him:

- Isla Grande, Rosario Bay, Cartagena de Indias, Colombia. Latitude 10°17'71.4 N - longitude: 75°71'00.7W

- Date?

She gets insecure, looks at Dr. Jimenez and says:

- It's not a precise date.

- Pass the best you have.

She says to Hugh:

- Based on our accounts, it would be June 20, 1708

- Load?

- Twenty tons.

- Power source?

- You know very well what it is...

- What do you mean, "you know"?

- Well, you spied on us to find out.

The boy's awkward. Prof. Perez advices Zara:

- This is no time to talk about it, give it to him!

Half sour, she informs:

- Silica purity 100%

- Wait a minute while I set up the equipment.

- Any more questions?

- Do you have a boyfriend?

There's no one who's not surprised. Zara is very awkward, but she does not disguise that liked the flirt.

- This data is not necessary for transportation, Mr. Walter.

- Ready... we've already set up TRON. In a few minutes he must send a signal to the destination and, if there is a reaction, it'll enter phase two which is the removal of the ship.

- What reaction?

- Our linear particle accelerator has enough energy to create a second wormhole, because we must keep the main one for the English team that is still there. Therefore, it will open a parallel time tunnel only, but your ship must have its own power to make the propulsion.

Prof. Perez is concerned:

- How do you know if there's such reaction?

- A receptive signal comes back in fractions of seconds. This is phase one. If it doesn't come back, it's an indication that it didn't work out, or, there is none in there. If we bring him in without enough propulsion power, the ship could disintegrate on the way.

Dr. Inez intervenes:

- If you increase the molecular mass in the Lorentz formula does not solve it?

- No, doctor, our accelerator only works with a space mass limit.

- Or, what about increasing the R variable in the Einstein Field Equation?

- We can try, but it's not guaranteed.

- We must minimize losses, Mr. Walter – supports Dr. Jimenez

- I will do my best, sir.

Hugh receives green signs on his control panels:

- We're ready to send the search signal.

- Let's ask God it works.

- Oh, just one more detail.

- What? – asks Zara

- We don't know where the ship will arrive.

- What do you mean, you don't know?

- Our systems are not fully compatible with yours. Start-up and arrival settings are specific to linear acceleration and cyclic acceleration models. We were able to schedule them to arrive today, December 15, 2021, but anywhere on the planet.

Zara looks to Prof. Perez, Dr. Jimenez and Dr. Inez to share the responsibility of that operation:

- It doesn't seem that "simple".

Prof. Perez repeats an old Spanish saying:

- *A falta de pan, buenas son tortas.*

- May I proceed with the first phase? – asks Hugh

- Please – confirms the girl

He winks one eye at her and touches a blue virtual circle that is on his hologram-style keyboard. Everyone gets apprehensive. The circle changes to green after few seconds.

- All right, gentlemen, the reaction was positive. We've located the ship.

Everyone in the room celebrates. Hugh opens another circle, still, yellow, on the screen and asks:

- May I start the second phase? We will open the time tunnel, and if they have enough propulsion energy to take off, they will be transported to our time in few seconds. Ready?

Dr. Inez holds Zara's hand to encourage her to say:

- Ready.

The boy touches the yellow circle, which begins to pulsate. The gigantic linear accelerator is triggered twice, and projects a second wormhole into space.

ISLA GRANDE, BARÚ ARCHIPELAGO - YEAR: 1708

A blue-laser-cylindered beams, rotating in a spiral, comes from the sky like a comet and falls over Columbus. Its internal lights come on and all equipment starts working again.

People celebrate. Luna speaks:

- Something triggered the teleporter!

Lorenzo, the team commander, speaks:

- Everyone in their positions, fasten your seat belts! Thomas, quick, set the clock for Madrid, it'll calculate the date.

Thomas programs the timer, but nothing appears on the panel suspended on the roof of the ship. The earthquakes increase, the volcano is about to unleash its last devastating explosion. A wide river of lava approaches the ship. They can feel its intense heat.

- It's not working – warns Thomas

- Why is that? – asks Lorenzo

- I think it was damaged by the stones – Thomas tries to explain

- Luna, fire the power thrusters!

Luna presses several buttons and several switches, but when she presses the main one that connects the ship's propulsion jets, these don't work.

- We're out of power, Captain! – warns Luna

- That's not possible! – despairs Isabel

- We've got to get out of here! – says Lorenzo

- What can be done? – asks O'Connor

- I don't know, we don't have a power reserve tank – Lorenzo replies

- Where's the reservoir? – Laureen asks

- In a cube, at the bottom of the right corner of the ship – explains Lorenzo

- We need a charge of silica energy – Luna adds

The heat from the ship begins to rise. Rocks hit the body shop, making bumps into the capsule. If one more stone cross the metal, everything will be lost.

Winston remembers something and wishes to confirm:

- Silica? Did you say silica?

- Yes – confirms Lorenzo while pressing several buttons to see if he can get any additional functional information.

- There is a single and final attempt – says the black officer

- Which? – asks Paloma, stressed

Winston signalsout of the ship's window with his head:

- Lava. It's made of pure silica. Silicon with oxygen.

- Are you sure? – asks, admired, O'Connor

- Yes, true – Luna confirms, happy – lava is made of silicon and oxygen!

- But are we going to have to let the lava hit us? – Thomas wants to confirm

- What's the lava temperature? – asks Lorenzo

- It reaches up to 2.190 Fahrenheit degrees – Paloma informs

- And what's Columbus's structure resistance? – asks Lorenzo

Luna quickly searches the commands and brings the information:

- It resists up to 2,370 F°. degrees.

- But we can't resist more than 100! – recalls Isabel

- What is the internal cooling capacity? – asks Lorenzo

- Up to minus 1,470 Fahrenheit degrees – Luna replies

Lorenzo does a quick math and decides:

- If we stay for no longer than five seconds, we shall survive!

- It's our only way out! – confirms Winston

- We'll trigger our belts together, maybe it'll help – offers O'Connor

- Absolutely! – confirms Lorenzo

The lava hits the capsule, which begins to swing like a boat in the water. The walls start to get red; the heat begins to rise. In reaction, the cooling system is triggered, but the agony and pressure are very damaging.

Lorenzo shouts for Luna:

- Power the thrusters!

- Trigger your seat belts – shouts O'Connor

A silver laser light beam begins to rotate in the center of the ship in the form of a centrifuge. Circular rings that rise around the throttle's ray ducts increase their speed to the point of turning into a single orange, red, and blue light. The vibration increases and the noise too.

The internal thermometer shows 115 F° degrees. The lava is carrying the ship mountain down. Fire flames begin to come out of the sides.

Isabel shouts:

- It's unbearable!

- We're going to make it, my love! – shouts Lorenzo, holding her hand

The lightning beam widens, reaching the capsule walls and the passengers who are sitting there. They feel the rising pressure in their heads, bringing a lot of discomfort and breath shortness. The internal temperature rises to 118 degrees F°.

The volcano explodes and releases energy equivalent to an atomic bomb. The cloud of soot, ash and stones rises in a deadly mushroom shape. Lava golfs splash everywhere. It seems to be the end of the World.

The rollers of destructive smoke go down all sides of the mountain. They're coming close to the spaceship. It looks like a big coal ember.

The lava silica is working, however. Suddenly, the silver-ray tube goes up over itself, overtaking the cap of the capsule. Everything spins, like a crazy centrifuge.

The control system shows 2,220 degrees F° outdoors.

The destructive volcano could hit the spaceship, making it disappear.

CANTABRIAN SEA, NORTHERN SPAIN - YEAR: 2021

The gigantic aircraft carrier HMS Queen Elizabeth is anchored in the dark blue sea that bathes from the Northern coast of Spain to Western France. Their airplanes and helicopters are ready to take off.

The well-known figure of General Walsh, is in charge of the military operation in the cockpit of one of the three English destroyers are escorting the aircraft.

He looks through the binoculars and sees, not far away, three Spanish-flagged large cruisers not far away. But he doesn't see Isaac Per S-81, the powerful Spanish-made submarine is sailing submerged next to them.

A naval officer climbs up the command tower, salutes and asks Walsh:

- General! The entire fleet is ready, awaiting your orders.

- Throw a warning shot into the water.

- Yes, sir!

The officer retreats. Looking up at the horizon, Walsh remembers of a scene from his past in his mind, as if it were a movie: "he is walking with his wife and two children, a twelve-year-old boy and a seven-year-old girl in Bilbao, a populous city of the Province of Biscay, Basque Country, Spain. It was the year 1997. They enter in a cafeteria in an old and traditional city building. They sit at the only empty table in the crowded environment and the waiter begins to serve them. Walsh goes out to smoke on the sidewalk, staying a little by the door. Suddenly, a terrorist attack explodes a great powered bomb, making fireballs, broken glass, pieces of furniture, pieces of people, be thrown on the sidewalk. Walsh is thrown away and, on the ground, stunned, has severe cut on his forehead. He just remembers his family who was inside, dead. Later, he knew it was an ETA attack."

- Damn Spanish... – he speaks in a low voice to himself.

The destroyer points one of its long-range cannons and fires a projectile. It falls near one of the Spanish cruisers who also has its cannons armed with ammunition.

Walsh calls for the same naval officer. This reappears, beats salute, and asks:

- Did you send for a call, General?

- Yes. The next shot should be in the middle of that cruiser.

- Yes, sir!

The naval officer retreats, Walsh looks at the enemy ship expressing pain, anger, and resentment.

The Spanish S-81 submarine does not interpret the shot as a warning only and its commander orders to arm all torpedoes in its compartments. He hoists the telescope out of water and targets the center of the casco of the Walsh's destroyer. The submarine shot operator wait for his signal to push the trigger button. The commander raises his arm to give the signal, while he adjusts the telescope's crosshairs center.

On destroyers side, British Marines aim their cannons at Spanish cruisers. The whole world follows this movement through reporters who, by helicopter, film everything, despite the cloudy day.

The same 18th century naval battle is raised again.

When the English destroyer captain is going to shout "Fire" at the same time the Spanish submarine commander is going to lower his arm, a flash in the sky catches everyone's attention. One more flash, everyone thinks it's lightning. Suddenly, a circle opens with red and orange edges in the clouds, like a portal, and the Columbus capsule emerges from inside it, spinning and leaving a helical trail behind it.

It falls into the sea, right between the destroyers and cruisers, sinks and then submerges, floating. The commander, who saw everything through his telescope, collects his arm and gives no signal for firing. The destroyer's captain shouts, "Abort shots!". Walsh also sees through the cockpit window.

The image of the floating spaceship is shown in every television and public LED building screens across the planet.

The technicians the National Intelligence Center control room, who were monitoring the naval conflict through the broadcast cameras, all surprised, celebrate.

Dr. Jimenez hugs Dr. Inez, who hugs Professor Perez.

Scientists at the Port Down Defense, Science and Technology Laboratory in front of the TRON accelerator room also celebrate the success of their transfer.

Hugh looks at Zara appearing on his communication screen. He blinks an eye. She reciprocates with a smile and he, with his hand, make mimic gestures to ask for her cell phone number.

Columbus's crumpled door opens from the inside. A yellow inflatable dinghy begins to fill with air and floats, close to its door. The first to leave, wearing a life jacket, is Lorenzo. He gives his hand to help Isabel get out. They both get in the inflatable boat. Lorenzo helps the others who is going to get the spaceship off.

O'Connor is the second to leave, surprising the both countries scientists. He gives his hand and helps Laureen get out and then Kendall. The three of them board on the boat, wearing life jackets..

Next out is Thomas, half-dizzy, life jacket in hand. He boards, with O'Connor's help, in the inflatable boat, but returns to the ship's door and hands it to Paloma, who comes out so happy that she cries.. Soon after, Luna appears alone at the door. She raises one of her arms as a sign of victory.

The last one out is Winston. He stops at the door and the cameras zoom in on him.

At home, Winston's father, along with his mother and siblings, watch the capsule rescue. His father smiles proudful.

All seated, Thomas unties the inflatable boat moorings and it floats into the middle of the sea. They're all black-looking with dirt and soot. Thomas speaks:

- I don't want to ride a boat anytime soon.

Isabel lays her head on Lorenzo's shoulder, which passes her arm over her shoulders. Kendall looks at heavy-bearded O'Connor by her side, dubious. But he does the same, hugging her by the shoulders. He feels something in his pocket, sticks his hand in and, surprised, gets the gold watch given by Sir Wager off. He looks at it and smiles.

A Spanish rescue boat is coming to meet them. General Walsh looks at everything, with a disgusted face.

The adventure is finally over. But none of them come back the same ones they left.

UNITED NATIONS HEADQUARTERS, NEW YORK - YEAR: 2021

It's 31 December of the year of two thousand twenty-one's night. Among the snowed hills surrounding the flashy 39-story glass building of the UN headquarters on the East River banks, several official cars and limousines stop in front of its main entrance, from which ministers, State heads, military officials and various authorities from all member countries get off. Dozens of reporters, restrained by aluminum fences and security guards, take photos of celebrities who disembark and enter the building on Manhattan's east side.

A reporter announces to the microphone in front of the LIVE broadcast camera:

- This is an important moment for our History. Today, the team of time travelers will be honored for their achievements. And they, too, will finally highlight the real location of Galleon San José shipwreck.

The planetary hall of the General Assembly is crowded. The world globe map coat of arms, surrounded by peaceful tree olive branches, brings more grandeur to the central tribune when are illuminated by yellow spots. A big Christmas tree is illumined closer it. Guests from all countries sit in their respective places, watched by a strong security scheme. The interpreters are already in their simultaneous translation room.

O'Connor, Winston, Kendall, Laureen, Paloma, Thomas, Isabel, Luna and Lorenzo are sitting in the front row. O'Connor and Winston are dressed in British navy gala uniform. Thomas and Lorenzo in tuxedos and the women in beautiful long party dresses. The UNO Secretary-General makes the solemn session opening. He makes a brief speech, summarizing the story and greatly praising the bravery and courage of the nine heroes. He ends up congratulating them. Everybody applauds.

The Secretary then calls the high-level admirals of the navies of Spain and of the United Kingdom for the distinction of their respective crew. The nine members get up, climb the two-step small stage and stand aligned in front of the audience. The admirals of the respective navies come, one from the left and the other from the right side, nailing medals on the lad of men or placing medals with satin necklaces around the women's necks, greeting one-by-one. The secretary descends from the tribune and greets one by one too, bowing diplomatically. The boys and girls return to their seats under applauses.

Then the master of ceremonies announces:

- And now, we call who will announce the Galleon San José's location. As stablished by the General Assembly of this House, from this moment on. when such information will become public the determination made by the noble Justice International Court is valid: half of the rescue – if any – will go to a consortium of nations affiliated to this secretariat and half will be given to UNICEF and other philanthropic organizations – he pauses and, looking at where the young people are sitting, he calls – well, who will come to speak?

previously, Lorenzo looks at O 'Connor, signals with his head and the two get up at the same time, walk to the tribune and stand behind the microphone, surprising those present, who are not knowing what will happen. Both of them had combined nothing to talk previously.

Full of medals-tuxedoed, Lorenzo is the first to speak, in Spanish, with simultaneous translation to all present. He looks to Isabel to take courage; she, beautiful, reciprocates with a smile of confidence:

- Ladies and gentlemen, good evening. I don't have much ability to give speeches, but I promise not to let anyone sleep on New Year's Eve – laughter from the audience – I speak on behalf of the Team of Spain that was chosen for this great mission. Although I had participated in military experiences, I was a young man who lived around myself, without projects, without much ambition and, like all my age, addicted to mobile phones. This mission made me take so many risks that I learned, among many things, the importance of life. Valuing my family. Seeing that there are such important things, that they are close to us, and we do not care. I learned not to waste food, because I felt hungry, like the countries of Africa. I learned not to throw water away because I felt thirsty, as in the Middle East. I learned to love... – he looks at Isabel, who is shy – ... I learned to fight for my life and for my companions, and, due to this, I learned once again that war brings no benefit to anyone.

He has to stop due to the huge audience's applauses. After they subside, he continues, thrilledly:

- And speaking of comrades, I ask for a minute's silence in honor of our colleagues who lost their lives on this mission.

Two high-definition screens, which are on each side of the central coat of arms, project, on one side, the photos of Birdie, Emmett, River and Jack under the United Kingdom flag and, on the other side, the photos of Pablo, Diego, and Soledad, under the flag of Spain.

The emotion takes the entire plenary over, some weep during the minute's silence. After this, O'Connor goes to the microphone, speaking in his native language:

- Ladies and Gentlemen, good evening! I'm not also good speaker, but in this same Lorenzo's sense, I also want to say what I learned in this adventure, in addition to what my companion here said. I also learned to respect different cultures from our own because I had to face foreign peoples; I learned to value the environment, because I traveled through clear beaches, but they are polluted by irresponsible tourists nowadays; I learned mainly that when you have the same goal, there are no enemies. Joining forces is much better and more effective than competing to see who else owns it. We lost some crew members for not having this vision. Personal desire cannot be superior to the collective one. So, today, I've learned to share and not want instead of taking advantage just for myself.

He takes Wager's pocket watches off and shows, hanging it by its golden thread. He continues emotionally:

- I won this watch from a noble captain. I learned good deeds generate gratitude with him, we always receive a reward, even if we are not waiting for it. This planet is big and has room for everyone. Wars begins for stupid reasons inside a selfish dictator's head, who thinks only him has reasonable thoughts and rights. They are impassioned by an irreal and sordid idea that "only by force we get to block the progress of enemies' ideologies". But both of sides are crazy: the bigger nation for felling more belic powerful, as bad the lower because they resist even knowing they do not have win chances. Their soldiers, their population, their men, women and children pay the bill, as running away or dying are the only action they can do.

He makes a break and, very emotionally, he finishes:

- Tomorrow is International Day of Peace. May there be peace among all peoples and nations!

He gets a standing ovation. Except for Walsh, who's in the middle of the audience, quiet. Lorenzo returns to the microphone after subsiding the applauses:

- Well, I think everyone here is waiting for the biggest moment, the revelation of the ship's sinking site. I need to tell you that its map was written on a piece of wooden trunk, which we found in the core of a volcano about to explode.

A murmur takes the audience over. Reporters get even more attentive. Lorenzo continues:

- When the two of us – he indicates O'Connor beside him - opened the lid of the chest and found that simple piece of carved wood, I thought, "is this what's worth twenty billion dollars?" So, it was something else I learned: that the most valuable things are stored within the simplest. Like our heart. Unfortunately, however, the wooden trunk burned in the lava of the volcano and it's gone.

Another murmuring wave crosses the plenary, this time of disappointment.

"ISLA GRANDE - INTERIOR OF THE ERUPTING VOLCANO

Lorenzo turns to O'Connor and says something in a low voice:
- Let's memorize these numbers... me, the top, you, the bottom one.
O'Connor looks at the wood. Sabogal, afar, impatient, shouts:

- Show me what you've gotten!"

Everyone gets frustrated, until Lorenzo, after a few minutes, completes:

- I memorized the latitude: 10°18'47.9 North...

O'Connor stretches his neck and completes to the microphone:

- ... and, me, the longitude: 75°71'97.2 West.

The plenary collapses. Mix of palms, whistles, expressions of surprise, flashes of reporters and lots, lots of joy. Even the members of both teams, who knew nothing about this and thought everyone had lost the mission.

The audience stands up to cheer the two of them, who come down and join the others. Soon the master of ceremonies announces:

- Ladies and gentlemen, this last UN General Assembly is closed. They are all invited to the cocktail party already being served in the next lounge. Happy New Year to all!

Everyone gets up and goes to the party lobby, grab champagne to celebrate New Year's Eve. Luna is surrounded by reporters, who want to know all about her adventure. Laureen is surrounded by academic doctors, who invite her to a worldwide lecture schedule. Winston is heavily embraced by his father, his mother, wife and picks up his little boy in his lap. Paloma and Thomas go to the back balcony overlooking the river and stare at all-lit Manhattan.

Pretty Paloma holds a champagne crystal glass and says, looking to the river,:

- She messed up with you, didn't she?

- Who?

- That Indian.

Thomas thinks a little and responds, also holding the glass and looking forward:

- No, I don't think so. We just shared very intense moment...

- I saw the mood you left staring at her.

- It was just an opportunity I couldn't take advantage of.

- Sometimes the biggest opportunities are in front of us all the time and we don't see...

He turns to her and, with his usual difficulty, he does not understand her tip:

- What're you talking about?

She turns around and stares at him. Her eyes sparkle in the city lights:

- How I'd like you to look at me like that...

He finally understands. They get close to each other, he holds the back of her neck, closes his eyes and exchanges a sweet, long kiss. When they move away, they're in love. Thomas speaks:

- I always realized that you were by my side at all...

- That's the way: the one you love, you protect.

The boy, handsome in the tuxedo with medals, remembers one thing:

- Ops! I forgot to tell you something.

- What?

He touches his jack's pocket and pulls that chicken-egg-sized pearl out he's caught at the bottom of the sea. He gives it her to hold, which is fascinated:

- I can't believe it!

- Saw? I'm not that silly. we will sell and share the bonus with all our friends.

She hugs her boyfriend; glad he has a good heart. They kiss again. O'Connor and Kendall arrive at the same wall and exchange a few words:

- Happy 2022, captain!

- For you too, Doctor!

- How about making a wish at the night turn? Throw the champagne over your shoulders, close your eyes and make a wish. They say it works.

- I don't believe in these things, but, okay, you first – he asks

She closes her eyes, gives a beautiful smile and throws the contents of her glass over her shoulders.

- Now it's your turn

O'Connor does the same. He closes his eyes and throws the contents of the cup over his shoulder on the river. Then he opens his eyes to question:

- You know what I wished for?

- No...

He takes a little box out of his pocket, opens it, and shows a loner ring with a diamond. She smiles and replies:

- I asked you to accept my marriage proposal...

She looks at the ring, very surprised. She stares him and tear in her eye, says:

- But we don't even live together yet! How do you know we're going to work out?

He holds her by her waist and says, looking into her eyes:

- Everything we've lived in these days has given me the certainty that you're the woman of my life. So, will you take it?

- Of course, I do! That's what I just wished for. See how it works?

She interweaves her arms around his neck and they exchange a long, passionate kiss. It's at midnight. Fireworks begin to burst on New York skyline.

Isabel, holding hands with Lorenzo, also outside, observes the two couples. Isabel speaks:

- Looks like we're going to have two happy couples.

He pulls her to himself and says:

- I'm sure it's going to be three couples.

She pretends not to understand:

- But you still owe me two common points between us... just said eight so far.

He shows his fingers, lowers one and says:

- Courage and...

- And...

- God... I can't find...

- So how about meeting it together?

- That's a great idea.

They approach and exchange a passionate kiss. They hear someone clearing his throat behind them. They turn and see, surprised, tuxedo-dressed Professor Perez, holding a champagne glass and, smiling:

- I'm proud of you!

Lorenzo replies:

- We couldn't have done it without you, Professor!

- Yes, true, perhaps don't..., but all of you showed not only how to unravel the past, but mainly how to learn lessons from it to improve the future. Congratulations!

He turns around and takes a few steps to leave. Lorenzo and Isabel, finally alone, are approaching again to kiss under the fireworks.

But Perez stops, turns around and asks:

- Have you ever heard about Genghis Khan's Lost Tomb?

They look at him very curious.

- o – o – THE END – o – o –

BIBLIOGRAPHY

ATUESTA, Francisco Hernando Muñoz. História del Señor Galeón San José, parte I, II e III – vídeo YouTube
https://www.youtube.com/watch?v=-WWGVi_iZu0

LOOS, Pedro Emilio Niebr. Ciência Todo Dia, vídeo sobre Burado de Minhoca
https://www.youtube.com/watch?v=yv-MFM2BJQI

PHILLIPS, Carla Rahn, The Treasury of San José: Death at Sea in the War of Spanish Succession, Amazon, 2007

WIKIPEDIA

Printed in the USA
CPSIA information can be obtained
at www.ICGtesting.com
LVHW091620140724
785463LV00025B/160

9 781665 562355